Book Cover by Duy Phan

Blurb by Emma Roussel

Illustrations by Irul (@mwkhoirul) and Michael Dovigi

First printing edition 2025

ISBN: 978-0646720807

For
Megan and Michael

0

<blockquote>

The other day, I went for a walk with several of the other *inhabitants* to help survey and map out the area. It's a beautiful place, almost idyllic. Someone once called it an Eden. The word felt familiar to all of us for reasons we couldn't explain. Even the person who said it couldn't explain why he said it. But the name stuck. It spread in a way none of us had control over, as if our old, forgotten lives had made the decision for us. Welcome to Eden. Our prison.

—THE FIRST PEOPLE OF EDEN

Journal of Morgan #38

Day 6

</blockquote>

Only four people stood in attendance.

It wasn't a funeral in the traditional sense, but the atmosphere carried the same weight of finality. The air was thick with an unsettling stillness broken up only by the faint whisper of Eden's breeze stirring the grass and leaves. It felt as if the world held its collective breath, waiting for an inevitable, earth-shattering moment.

The first was a tall, inconsequential man from the Eden administration, tasked with maintaining records. He was there to check a box. Nothing more. It was all a foregone conclusion in his eyes. He might have hoped to find some unknown details, but he had no real expectation. He was there to do his job. What he was about to witness would be unpleasant, but in this day and age, it was a rare opportunity. Events like this weren't expected to happen—not in the year 436. Only three times this century had it occurred. It wasn't something he wanted to see, so he lowered his gaze and waited.

The second individual present was a young man named Edgar. He didn't know the combatants well. But, in a close-knit community like Eden, where everyone lived within a thirty-minute walk of each other, being at least somewhat acquainted with your neighbors was inevitable. At nineteen, eleven years younger than them, Edgar was there to mourn not only for them but also for himself, knowing he would face a similar fate when he reached the age of thirty.

He fixed his eyes on the door ahead, and every breath reminded him that his own time was running out. Each inhale felt like the ticking of a clock, counting down with no way to stop it. His hands trembled at the thought of his life ending before it truly began. But the real reason he was present was for the third person's sake. He glanced to his left and reached out to take their hand. They recoiled, crossing their arms, their body trembling. He hesitated, then moved his arm to lightly rest on their back, settling for the smallest gesture of comfort.

That person was Leah, also nineteen. The two brave souls had taken her into their home as a young teenager. She considered them her parents as much as her biological ones, whom she barely knew. Already fighting back tears, Leah could not bear to watch. She'd said her goodbyes minutes ago, pleading with them to reconsider. They refused to consider the alternative. It was still death, but a more painless, peaceful one. In either case, her pillars of support disappeared today, never to return. Why she stayed and watched, she wasn't sure.

Was it obligation? Maybe.

Hope that they would somehow survive? No.

The truth was simple: She wanted to see them one more time, even if only for a fleeting moment. To be there for them during their darkest hour, as they had been there for her in every one of hers. It was the least she could do, making sure they weren't alone at the end.

Lastly, there was Cole, the only biological child of the combatants. Hidden away and perched on a tree branch, he watched with trepidation. What he was about to witness was too much for a ten-year-old. For that reason, Leah had warned him to stay away.

The four stood small and insignificant before dark metallic walls that stretched so high they bled into and then vanished into the sky. Three doors built into the walls, each a different color, sat side by side. Each measuring two meters wide and two meters tall. A large digital display hung high above them, stretching the length of the doors. It listed over four hundred numbers, all four digits long, divided into several rows, with a countdown beside every one. Each number marked a life. In the top left, someone had only a month remaining. In the bottom right, the newest soul had just under thirty years. Everyone else sat somewhere in between.

Finally, it began. The four onlookers snapped to attention as a screen above the crimson door flickered to life. The display showed the two who had entered moments earlier: a man holding a spear and a woman clutching a short blade. They stood hand in hand, their free arms bearing the weapons, their stance defiant.

The camera pointed downward, capturing only a few feet on either side of the pair. They faced an unseen threat, hidden beyond the screen's frame. Those watching knew well what lay before them, an enemy pieced together through years of fragmented descriptions.

It was a thing of nightmares.

They had two doors they could have chosen from: one midnight blue, the other crimson red. There was a third door, green, but it remained locked, unable to be opened by anyone, leaving only two choices. Once a door was entered, there was no coming out. Both led to the same end. It was only a matter of which monster they would die at the hands of. The door they entered brought them face to face with the creature they feared most. They called it the Wolf, though it was no actual wolf. Its immense size defied description: a nightmarish, chimeric entity.

The creature stood out of the camera's view. Its presence was enough to break the will of even the bravest soul. Countless battle records documented people fleeing in terror, crying, and begging for help. Some had even taken their own lives before it could touch them. In the face of such despair and dread, dignity and self-respect ceased to matter. Confronting one's mortality in such a harsh way was too much to bear. Those few who found the courage to fight never lasted more than a few seconds. Not a single recorded encounter noted a successful blow against the creature. It was hopeless, a death sentence masquerading as a choice.

The two souls turned to face each other, stealing a final moment together. They embraced and kissed. Then the man looked up at the screen and waved. The woman kissed her hand and raised it to their loved ones. Impossibly bright smiles graced their faces, masking the grim reality of their situation.

In that moment, Cole felt the last remnants of his courage shatter. Unchecked tears streamed down his face. He watched as the two ran forward, charging at the monstrosity. The brief moments that followed would forever haunt him. He'd thought he could handle it, that he could be strong for them. He believed they could live, that they would return, and this wouldn't be the last time he saw the parents he had only known for a few fleeting weeks. He wanted more time with them, but this would never come to pass. His mind struggled to protect him from a truth he couldn't and wouldn't accept. But reality didn't wait.

It was over in an instant.

A giant claw flashed through the picture, and a cascade of blood followed.

The screen was awash with red.

The last thing Cole saw was the monstrosity's sharp, glowing eyes—bright blue, filled with malice. The screen froze on them for a moment before it went black. The two green lights above the door, signifying the presence of people inside, flickered off and turned red.

Cole let out a scream that echoed throughout half of Eden. He jumped down from the tree, landing awkwardly and twisting his ankle, but without a whimper, he charged forward, limping. Tears streamed down his face as he ran toward the door.

Leah stood numb with shock at the horror she'd witnessed, but the sight of Cole running past jolted her into action. She'd made one promise to Rose and Rory, and she wasn't going to break it for anything. Not for any amount of pain, grief, or suffering.

Before he could reach the door, she grabbed him from behind, wrapping her arms around his torso as Cole flailed wildly. "Cole! Stop it! Stop! Please . . ." she begged as she attempted to tighten her grip.

He struggled against her, desperate to break free. His elbow connected with her face, causing her to recoil. But she refused to let go as blood flowed from her nose, clinging to him as if her life depended on it.

Finally, Cole collapsed, turning to sob into her lap while her own tears flowed freely. Edgar stood nearby, silent and powerless, unsure how to offer any support. This was what she'd tried to keep Cole from, the trauma she had hoped to spare him.

She held him close, determined never to let go.

Ever.

LAND DIVISION FOR YEAR ENDING 445

1. RESIDENTIAL
2. COMMUNITY TOWN CENTER
3. FOOD PRODUCTION
4. PARK
5. NOTHERN WOODS
6. ORPHANAGE
7. DOORS / PEACEFUL PASSAGE

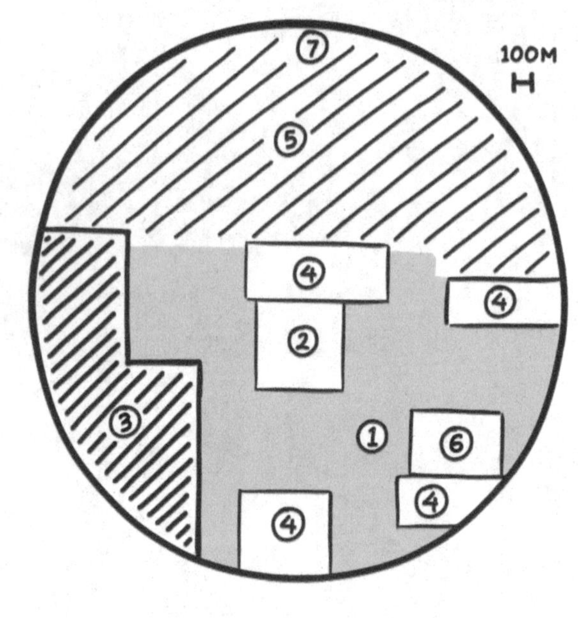

Eden Annual Report for Year Ending 445

Reporter: Alex #8732 [Date 02.01.446]

Population: 426 (-6 from last year)

Mayor: Owen #8640
Deputy: (Vacant)

Sheriff: Ian #8648
Deputy: Sophia #8664
Arrests: 12
Time penalties: 1
[see page 5 for full sheriff's report]

DEATHS AND BIRTHS
Expiry deaths: 15
Non-expiry deaths: 7
Due to expire in the coming year: 18
Births: 16
[see page 12 for full details]

AGE DEMOGRAPHIC
[see page 20 for full details]

JOBS
Required jobs vacant: 6 (+3 from previous year)
Unemployment: 25 (-3 from previous year)
[see page 20 for full details]

INFRASTRUCTURE
Homes built: 3
Homes due for rebuilding: 5
[see page 25 for full details]

FOOD PRODUCTION
Food production stockpiles: Overcapacity
[see page 32 for full details]

ORPHANAGE
Children: 72
[see page 35 for full details]

HIGHLIGHTS
- Orphanage upgrades
- Food Production surplus

CHALLENGES
- Dispenser schedule

SUE: Due to a recent incident, we're having an excursion. A tour of Eden. We usually do this next year, when you turn ten. But it's best you learn everything about Eden now. So there are no more avoidable incidents.

REN: Is this because of Tom? What happened to him?

SUE: He interfered with a Ghost, and . . . he—

COLE: He's dead, Ren.

SUE: Cole! But, yes. He is dead. Ghosts are not to be stopped from doing their duties.

REN: Ghosts? You mean those things with the white heads and four arms?

IVY: What are they?

SUE: They're machines. They come and go to remove problems like trash, and dead trees . . . things of that nature. If you don't bother them, they won't bother you. Just act like they're invisible.

IVY: But the Ghost didn't touch Tom. How did he die?

SUE: As you know, we all have implants in our ankles. They were put there by the beings keeping us in Eden. If we do anything that displeases them, the implants activate and hurt us. We know most of the things to avoid doing so we will not be harmed. Interfering with Ghosts in any way is one of them. Who can name another?

ALEX: Don't touch or try to remove our implants.

SUE: Correct. You all have locked ankle braces over your implants so you won't accidentally touch them. When you turn ten, those safeguards will be removed.

IVY: Why?

SUE: Because by then, we trust you'll know better. Before that, it's for your protection.

COLE: The older kids touch theirs all the time. And they're fine.

SUE: Stupidity. They're not fine. They're in pain. Not a good pain. You won't die just from touching it, but you'll regret it. I promise. All right, who can name another thing not to do?

ALEX: Don't dig too far down. Or try to dig under the walls.

SUE: Good. Any action that might look like escape. They . . . will . . . kill you. It doesn't matter how old you are or what your intention was. I can't stress that enough.

PENELOPE: Miss, I'm scared.

SUE: I'm sorry, Penelope. I don't mean to frighten you. You are safe. As long as you follow the rules. They don't care if it's an accident. They don't care if you didn't mean it. They'll punish you all the same.

COLE: Have people tried to escape before?

SUE: Many times and they all . . .

COLE: Died?

SUE: Yes, Cole. I need you all to pay close attention today. You're going to learn the most important lessons of life in Eden. Don't be afraid to ask questions. All right. Let's begin. Our first stop is the memorial.

*****

SUE: Class. This wall holds the names and numbers of everyone who has ever lived in Eden.

IVY: Oh, that's me. How do they know my number? 8756?

SUE: The ankle bracers also cover your numbers.

IVY: Oh.

COLE: What came before Eden?

SUE: Nobody knows what came before our 435 years here. There are many theories, but no answers.

COLE: Are we from Earth?

SUE: That's what most people believe. Our library is filled with Earth books. So it's fair to assume we came from there. But we can't know for sure.

OLIVER: Who put us here? My dad says it's aliens.

SUE: Maybe. We don't know. We have no evidence.

MAX: One of the older kids said the mayor is keeping us trapped here.

SUE: Don't listen to that. He's trying to trick you. No one person in Eden is keeping us here. We're all in the same situation. The mayor and the central administration do their best to make life better for all of us. One of you may be mayor one day.

IVY: Why are they doing this to us? When will they let us leave?

REN: Ivy, she just said she doesn't know.

SUE: It's unfortunate, but this is our life. We cannot leave Eden. And trying to escape is too dangerous.

COLE: What about the doors?

SUE: Yes . . . The doors. Actually, that's our next stop. Come along.

*****

REN: Vella, you should touch the glowing thing next to the red door.

SUE: Ren! Apologize. Now.

REN: Sorry . . .

SUE: Never say that to anyone. Ever.

REN: Yes, Miss.

SUE: If you put your hand on the scanner beside a door, it opens. And once it does, you have to go in. You don't want to. Believe me . . . These doors are the only way out of Eden. The green one stays locked, but the red and blue—

OLIVER: The monsters! Can we see them?

SUE: Hope you never see them, Oliver. Behind the blue door lives the monster we call the Bear . . . and the red one holds the Wolf.

ALEX: Miss, what happens if you touch the scanner and don't go in?

SUE: Well . . . your implant will trigger and keep inflicting pain until you do. And if you still don't, they'll kill you.

ALEX: Can anyone go in?

SUE: Yes. But you shouldn't.

COLE: Why?

SUE: You won't be able to come out. You'll die.

COLE: But what if we kill them?

SUE: No one can kill them. See that oak tree behind us? They say the monsters are twice that size.

COLE: Oh . . . But what if we all went in together? It can't get all of us.

SUE: See the two lights above each door? They mean only two people can enter at once. If anyone else tries, their implants will trigger.

COLE: I'll still kill them.

IVY: Shut up, Cole.

PENELOPE: Can they get out and get us?

SUE: No. You're safe in Eden. There's no evidence they can enter. They exist only to stop us from leaving.

REN: Miss, what are all the numbers up there?

SUE: This is the hard part. So I need you to listen carefully. Those numbers on the board show everyone alive today, and how long they have left to live.

VELLA: The one at the top right doesn't have long.

SUE: That's right. They only have a week left.

VELLA: What happens to them?

SUE: They have two options. They go through the doors. Or they go to that small building over there—the Peaceful Passage.

VELLA: What happens in there?

SUE: They are given a painless, peaceful death.

VELLA: Oh.

SUE: I know it's hard to talk about death. But it's necessary. You need all the information.

COLE: What if they don't choose either? Can they run and hide?

SUE: No. There is no running. No hiding. The implants trigger an extremely painful death.

IVY: Like Tom?

SUE: Like Tom.

REN: How long do we have left?

SUE: Most of you—twenty-one years.

ALEX: What about you, Miss?

SUE: Three months.

ALEX: That's not fair.

SUE: It's the same for all of us. So it is fair. Is it right? No. It isn't.

ALEX: Why do we only get that many years?

SUE: No one knows. There are theories. But no proof.

OLIVER: My dad said humans on Earth are able to live up to a hundred.

SUE: That's true. But we are not them. We don't get to choose.

OLIVER: How do the people of Earth die if no one makes them die?

SUE: They grow old, and their body stops working. They call it dying of natural causes.

PENELOPE: What would you do, Miss, if you could live to a hundred?

SUE: I try not to think about it, Penelope. We live with what we have. And that's what we focus on here in Eden.

COLE: Are you going to fight?

SUE: I'd like to, Cole. But sometimes . . . there's nothing we can do. We're going back to class now. If you have any questions, speak up. All the information I've given—and more—is available in the library. Nothing is hidden from you. We tell you everything at a young age for a reason. Confusion causes panic. Panic leads to recklessness. And recklessness gets people hurt.

1

We know the names of things we come across, like objects and animals. I can say the word *sheep* and close my eyes, and the only image that appears is the one I saw in the field yesterday. Nothing from before this place. Some things come naturally, like writing and motor skills. But names? Memories of others? Gone. I couldn't tell you my own name. I could reel off hundreds of names people use, but they have no association with a face. We have been wiped clean. No memories. Nothing. Fragments of other things linger. I kept wondering, "Where are the power outlets?" I didn't even know what they were, just that the homes should have them. I only found out from a book just today. I hate this. The answers feel just out of reach, locked away in some part of my brain I can't access. Inaccessible. Trapped.

—THE FIRST PEOPLE OF EDEN
Journal of Morgan #38
Day 4

Cole squinted up at the artificial sun, its steady glow quartering the sky. He felt its warmth press against his skin, gentle and comforting. But he couldn't help wondering: What did the actual sun feel like? Was it hotter? Colder? Brighter? Dimmer? He wished he knew. It made no difference to them. The artificial sun did the same job as the real one. But in those rare moments when he remembered it was only a fabrication, a chill crept across his skin, as if his body were rejecting its warmth.

Eden's climate was perfect. Too perfect, he knew. Even though he'd experienced nothing outside Eden, he felt deep down that the never-too-hot, never-too-cold weather, day in and day out, was unnatural.

He let out a weary sigh, unsure whether to be grateful that the workday was almost over. At twenty, his body still possessed the boundless energy of youth, but the exhaustion he felt came from the relentless anxiety of what today marked.

He grabbed a nearby bucket and tipped out the water inside. It was still fresh from the early morning rain that had fallen before sunrise. Like clockwork, it happened at the same time every day, lasting exactly thirty minutes, keeping the land fertile. Every day was the same: a soft drizzle, warm sunshine, and a sky painted with just the right shade of blue, dotted with clouds that had no real purpose.

Three hundred and sixty-five identical days a year of perfect, predictable weather. The crops flourished, and the air was always fresh, but the sameness ate at him. He wanted something, anything, to come along and break the monotony.

He walked through a tomato patch, picking out the less desirable ones and tossing them in the bucket. Then it was on to the carrots, and after that, he continued to pass mindlessly through a few other patches of crops. Before leaving the area, he paused by a cabbage, then gave it a swift kick. It hit the perimeter wall. He stared at the wall for a moment before picking up the cabbage and adding it to the bucket.

As Cole made his way to the pigpens, he couldn't help but think about a book he'd recently read about Earth. What had captured his attention most was Earth's unpredictable weather— rainstorms, snow, and the exhilarating and terrifying idea of bolts of lightning falling from the sky. He smiled at the thought of experiencing something so thrilling. Excitement turned to lament, the realization settling in: he would never experience such things in Eden. Here, they were little more than legend, like the changing seasons or the taste and smell of real, imperfect air.

Entering the pen, he could hear the pigs grunting in anticipation. "Calm yourselves. I'm coming. You'll all get your turn," he said, smiling in amusement at seeing them press against the fence.

There were a dozen pigs in total, grouped two or three to a pen. Each shared a spacious area, separated by light wooden fencing. He went around feeding them one by one. When he reached the final stall, a pang of guilt hit him.

Gus, the oldest and plumpest pig, looked up with a curious snout.

"Sorry, Gus," Cole murmured, setting down the last of the crops. "I heard them say your time's almost up."

The thought made his stomach turn. He knelt by the pen, rubbing the pig's bristly head. "Don't worry, I could never eat you."

Working with the animals, Cole couldn't help but feel guilty every time he fed them. Over time, the thought of eating them became unbearable. He hadn't touched meat in years. But he knew it wouldn't change Gus's fate. The pigs lived well in Eden, but they were still a food source. It was the same with everything here: perfectly controlled, perfectly predictable, and utterly inescapable.

"If they got to know you, they wouldn't eat you," he said. "We aren't so different, you and I. We're both fated to be food for monsters. Just know I won't stop trying for the both of us. How does that sound?"

Gus snorted.

"Appreciate the support, bud."

The town bell echoed twice through the fields, a low, familiar toll that signaled the end of the workday. Cole straightened up, brushing dirt from his knees. He didn't need to look at a clock. The bells were as precise as the clockwork sun. There were three other bells that rang each day: one in the morning, one at midday for lunch, and another two hours later to signal the end of the break. At least the people of Eden controlled this.

He glanced beyond the pens, where towering metallic walls loomed in the distance, imposing, spotless, and matte as they absorbed rather than reflected the light. They curved ever so slightly, fading at about a hundred meters into the picturesque artificial sky overhead. From the center of Eden, it resembled a low wall of cloud spreading out along the horizon in all directions.

Cole knew there was a ceiling up there, a top, unseen but always felt.

No matter where you stood in Eden, the walls were never more than a short walk away and served as a constant reminder of how small their world truly was. For all its lush, green beauty, Eden was still a cage—one they would never be free of—and it was, as if by intention, designed to make sure no one ever forgot that.

The longer he stared at the walls, the sharper and faster his breathing became. He could see it: the doors, the screen. The blood. The blue eyes.

Then Gus snorted, snapping him back. He glanced down, catching his breath. When he looked up again, there were no doors, no screen—just the walls. He shook his head and left the pen.

As he walked home, he couldn't shake the feeling of being trapped. His chest tightened. The walls were too high, too thick, too difficult to surmount, and the reality too harsh to deny. But it never stopped him from thinking about trying to make it to the other side. There was a fire burning within that he couldn't ignore, making him want to reach for more. He wasn't sure if it had always been there or if he'd just forgotten its origin. He didn't know and didn't care. Now it only intensified as today marked a bleak milestone for one he cared for dearly.

"Twenty-nine," he muttered.

The walk back was short, with only a few houses to pass by along the way. He lived on the town's outskirts, by the woods. He disliked the busy town center. So, he chose to work in food production, where it was remote and there was limited human contact.

At the inception of Eden, there were 150 homes prepared for the first people near its center. They dubbed them Permahomes. They were made of a carbon-fiber-like material. The number of homes was nowhere near enough for everyone, so they built more. The first iterations had been crude, but they'd gotten better over time. These wooden-and-brick homes were hand-built by the construction division of Eden. They called these Crafthomes. They knocked down and rebuilt the homes once they reached around seventy years old.

It was all a matter of preference which one people chose to live in. Once sixteen, anyone could become a homeowner at no cost, so long as there was supply, and with a shrinking population, there always was.

The home Cole and Leah shared was a weathered three-bedroom Crafthome, built around sixty years ago. Leah had taken him in when he was thirteen. She wasn't family, not by blood, but she might as well be. The bedrooms were small and practical. The unpainted wood had become weathered over the years, its surface worn and beginning to warp, with vines and grasses weaving through the gaps. Above, the tin roof offered a soft, pleasant tune during the morning drizzle. The house took up a quarter of the property. This left space for Leah's garden in the spacious backyard. The front was less curated, dotted with wildflowers. A well-worn dirt path, marked by years of footsteps, led to the front door.

Leah greeted him, standing over the sink by the back window, peeling potatoes. The evening light shone through, casting a warm glow on the worn wooden counters, which smelled faintly of herbs and freshly cut vegetables.

"You're not making dinner on your birthday," Cole declared.

She gave him a wry smile.

"Sit down," he commanded. He approached her and carefully pried the peeler from her hand.

She relented and sat down at the dining room table, which felt too large for just the two of them. The kitchen and living room merged into a single open space, also a little too large for the two of them. Off to the side, a single door led down a hallway to the bedrooms and the lone bathroom.

"How was your day?" she asked.

"Same as always. Dig, plant, harvest, feed, clean. Riveting stuff . . . yours?"

"Ugh, so annoying . . . I was almost done with a dress for Ellie, but we ran out of material. It was meant to be our turn to get a bulk order of fabrics from the dispenser, but due to some *missing spades from food production*, our order got pushed back to next week."

"Don't look at me. I didn't take them."

"Well, regardless, the metals order got pushed ahead, so now we have to wait. The wait time after the metals orders is so damn long," she groaned.

Cole had only glimpsed the dispenser once as a kid. Eden's administration fenced off and guarded the area to prevent misuse. Nestled against the southeast perimeter wall was a small digital display. Next to it was a metallic floor section. It was designed to open and allow requested items to come up from the hidden lower level.

With a single press of a button, nearly anything could be summoned from a catalog of a thousand items—raw materials like wood, metal, and clay; essentials like medical supplies and seeds; or more specialized goods like fabrics, bricks, pipes, nails, and rare manufactured products like typewriters and shineballs. A superstore in a tiny panel.

But there was a catch: Each order triggered a system lockout, with a cool-down period that grew longer depending on the value and quantity of the item.

The dispenser served as more than a convenience; it functioned as a carefully regulated resource, controlled by Eden's central administration, with each request planned and scheduled in detail. They never wanted for anything thanks to the dispenser. The one thing it didn't provide was food or water. The exception was that farm animals could be requested but it cost a lot of lockout time, so they made sure to breed them instead. Food was taken care of by the food production division, while water was readily available from a dozen pumps scattered throughout Eden.

Leah let out a weary sigh. "What a day . . ."

"Oh, please . . . cut it out. How was your day, *really*?" Cole pressed.

A smile spread across her face. "It was wonderful. I got so many thoughtful presents," she said, pointing to a bag on the seat next to her. "Kate made this amazing lemon cheesecake. I was going to save you some, but it didn't last long."

"I'll live," he said, setting aside a freshly peeled potato.

"There are some cookies you'll love that I managed to save." She paused to exhale. "I never thought I would say this, but all that attention has exhausted me."

Cole laughed. "*Oh, you poor thing.* How did you manage?"

She snorted a laugh. "Shut up."

"And tonight? Are you going to be fine dealing with all that *dreaded attention*?"

"Very funny. Speaking of which . . ." She hesitated. "Are you coming . . . to . . . tonight's party?" she asked.

Cole turned around to say something but stopped himself. He breathed out softly and turned back to his task. She knew it took all his power not to blurt out, "Hell no."

"I know it sucks, but come, please. The whole town will be there," she said.

"That's exactly why I don't want to go."

"It'll be good for you."

He glanced over his shoulder, eyebrow raised. "Good for me? You say that like I'm some freak."

"Don't twist my words." She leaned forward, resting her chin on her hand.

"Why is it good for me, then?"

"Not today, Cole," she sighed, exasperation creeping into her voice.

He bit his tongue and let it go, focusing on the potatoes in front of him.

"You can bring Vella," Leah suggested.

Cole snorted in amusement. "Good one."

"I'm serious."

"Then you understand why, one, she would never come, and two, I would never want her to," he said, his tone even but firm.

"Who knows? She might enjoy it."

"If you think that, you don't know Vella." A touch of irritation edged into his voice.

Leah sighed, picking at leftover cake. "Remember when you said you didn't like avocados because of how they looked? But then you finally tried them after I made them with toast, and now you love them?"

Cole turned to face her, incredulous. "How in the hell are you relating the two things?"

"I'm just saying you never know until you try," she insisted.

"I know already," he muttered, turning back to his task.

"There is very little you actually know, my dear boy."

Cole shook his head and continued peeling.

"It's actually really fun," Leah continued, her tone earnest. "You should learn to have fun every now and then."

Leah recoiled as soon as the words left her mouth. *Here it comes*, she thought.

"Fun?" he snapped.

Leah buried her head in her hands.

"Oh, let's just forget everything and have fun. All is well, all is good. What a wonderful life." The sarcasm came across more aggressively than he intended. "Let's pretend you won't be dead in a year, and we all don't die at thirty. Or that everyone has given up as we rot in this place. But let's have fun as everyone around us dies while we pretend everything is normal."

"No one's pretending," she said quietly.

"Their whole lives are a lie."

"They're doing what they can. Making the most of what they have. What would you have them do?" she countered, frustration bubbling to the surface.

"Try!"

She slammed a fist on the table, startling him. "Cole. No more today, please."

He stopped peeling, noticing fresh cuts on his hands. He grabbed a nearby towel, wrapping it around his hand, and resumed peeling with a more controlled motion. "Sorry," he muttered.

They sat in strained silence, waiting for the air to cool between them.

"Twenty . . . nine . . ."

Cole's bitter words left his lips quietly, but they seemed to echo through the house, growing louder as they traveled.

Leah closed her eyes and took a deep breath. When she opened them, she turned to Cole. "You know, Alex might be there tonight," she ventured.

"Is that the best you've got?" he said with a dry chuckle. "I was hoping I wouldn't have to see him."

"Just try to talk to him."

Cole said nothing.

"I didn't want it to come to this, but . . . I'm invoking the 'I'll be dead soon' card."

Cole dropped his shoulders, slumped into the sink, and let out a soft groan.

"It would mean the world to me if you came," she continued. "You know I don't ask for much, but—"

His groaning grew louder until it stopped Leah midsentence. "Enough! All right, I'll come," he conceded.

"Thank you," she said, a small, relieved smile breaking through. "I didn't want it to have to come to that."

"I was always going to come . . . for you," he said, "and to see Amy."

Leah hesitated when he said her name, wanting to say more but holding back.

"I'll ask Vella to come, but don't get your hopes up," Cole added.

"That's all I wanted. And also—" She closed her eyes and braced herself. "Please be nice."

"I'm always nice," he replied with a hint of indignation.

Leah couldn't help but scoff.

"Fine. I'll try extra hard," he said. "For you."

2

Some still haven't given up on escape, even after all the death they've witnessed. I've seen people killed for setting fires, building a structure too high, attacking a Ghost, trying to dismantle a shineball, or digging too deep, to name just a few. And some have died for even less. Ninety-three people so far. We are hopelessly outmatched. What keeps them going? Stupidity? Rage? Delusion? Hope? Anything to keep them going because they cannot accept being trapped here. Others keep going for different reasons; they have people to fight for. Irrational, ignorant. But I get it. To give up feels like giving up on them.

—THE FIRST PEOPLE OF EDEN
Journal of Morgan #38
Day 121

After dinner, Cole headed for the front door.

Leah called out, "Off to see Vella? Be back around seven. I want to leave shortly after."

Without electricity, precise timekeeping in Eden was difficult. After several generations, they built the first working wind-up clock. Now, four hundred years later, every home had one. Household clocks lasted a day before needing to be wound again, while the main clock in central Eden ran for a full week.

Each morning, a bell rang out at eight o'clock, giving people a reference point to set their clocks to. Beyond that, sunrise at six and sunset at seven were the only consistent markers. Midnight was judged by the moon at its zenith.

There was another method they could rely on for accurate timekeeping, but it was rarely employed because it reminded them of something they preferred not to think about.

"Sure. Not a problem," Cole said.

The thought of the party made his stomach clench and twist, but if Vella were there, it might be bearable. Her aversion to social situations was much stronger than his. So, it was a tough ask. Against his better judgment, he thought it was worth trying to convince her.

Cole went to see Vella after dinner every afternoon almost without exception. Leah liked to tease him about these visits, referring to them as their "daily make-out sessions." Any time she wanted to get under Cole's skin, she'd break it out. Today was an exception; she wanted to keep him in a good mood to ensure he would come out.

"Tell her I have something nice for her to wear tonight," Leah said.

Cole chuckled, imagining Vella in a dress. The image was so improbable it was almost comical. There was a higher likelihood of them being graciously freed from Eden.

He grabbed a long wooden object wrapped in cloth and headed out the door.

One of their favorite meeting spots was a secluded clearing near the doors, far from prying eyes. People rarely ventured near the doors if they could help it; they evoked too much existential dread. As a result, the northern parts of Eden remained largely untouched, filled with dense woodland.

Wandering through the woods, he admired the variety of trees and flowers surrounding him. He'd recently read about the first ecological survey, conducted forty years in, and how it had identified around two hundred unique plant species. Not including the seeds that were available from the dispenser, which would have added to that total over the centuries. Certain areas in the forest had developed a dense canopy. It prevented the more colorful flowers from blooming there. This was not one of those areas.

A wash of blue greeted him everywhere he turned, the color bleeding from a field of bluebells, with trees dotted in between. A loud buzzing from a beehive above startled him, and he quickened his pace until he was out of the vicinity.

As the flowers thinned out and the trees grew denser, he knew he was fast approaching the clearing.

Moving quietly, he tensed, scanning his surroundings and listening for any movement. He watched where he placed his feet, careful to avoid making any unnecessary noise. The scent of damp earth and pine filled his nostrils, his senses on high alert.

He unwrapped the hand-carved wooden sword, the familiar weight comforting in his hands.

Through a break in the trees, he saw the clearing. A wide field of grass stretched before him. He caught no glimpse of Vella, forcing him to remain on high alert.

A stick cracked behind him. He whirled, sword raised, just as something hard hit him squarely on the shoulder.

"Got you! That's two points," Vella announced, grinning.

He grabbed his shoulder, grimacing. "I need to stop falling for that."

He faced Vella, who was twenty, the same age as him. She tied her shoulder-length black hair back in a ponytail. This accentuated her sharp nose and a droopy left eyelid that covered half her eye. Her bangs hung to the left, attempting to hide her insecurity. Her features, marked by the asymmetry of her eyelid and the angularity of her face, didn't match the conventional standards of beauty admired by boys her age. Growing up in the orphanage, she faced many difficulties because of her perceived physical imperfections, her droopy eyelid being the main source of torment. There were days when it worsened, partially obstructing her vision, making her an easy target for cruel children. The relentless bullying had made her life a nightmare, with few willing to stand up for her.

Cole had been one of those few, if not the only one, often getting into trouble defending her. The bond they'd forged had become a lifeline for Vella. Especially after a particularly traumatic incident when she was thirteen. She'd left the orphanage, and Cole, refusing to abandon her, had found her a place to stay on the outskirts of Eden, hiding her away from harm. He himself had chosen not to return, seeking refuge with Leah.

Now, seven years later, it was still the two of them against the world.

They faced off, slipping into familiar stances. Poised and focused. Vella broke the silence. "First to twenty, let's go. Two, zero. My advantage."

"That hit doesn't count to your score!"

"It did for you yesterday."

"Fine."

The game had no name; it needed none, its rules simple: one point for arm and leg hits, two for the torso. Head hits had been outlawed early on after some *incidents*.

They assessed each other, seeking vulnerabilities in each other's defense. Tension mounted in their muscles with each passing moment. Cole could always count on Vella to make the first move, and today was no exception. A counter was available, and he took the bait. Anticipating his move, she initiated with a feint, then attacked the opening on his left side. He had just enough time to parry the shot.

The initial tension of their contest faded into a rhythmic exchange that echoed throughout the clearing. Their surroundings blurred.

They sparred with great intensity; with every swing, hit, and parry, the world faded further away as they moved in sync, lost in their own rhythm. For those moments, nothing else existed. The past and future faded. It was just the two of them in a dance of unspoken understanding.

Vella won the match, grinning in triumph. "Again," she insisted.

"Not today." He paused to catch his breath. "It's Leah's birthday. I'm going to the party and . . . I want you to come."

Visible loathing marked her expression. "Hell no," she spat.

He'd expected as much. With a quiet sigh, he sat down and leaned back against a tree. "Leah's turning twenty-nine."

Vella joined him on the ground. "One more year . . ."

Cole cursed under his breath. "I can't lose her too," he whispered, barely audible. *Why thirty? Why can't it be forty, fifty, or sixty?* Even after 446 years, the people of Eden still had no answers.

Vella's jaw clenched, but her confidence didn't waver. "We should take down the Wolf and Bear. We can do it."

Cole smiled faintly at her boldness. "I wish."

"Why not try next year?"

"We only get one shot."

"Now's just as good as when we're thirty. What are we staying here for?"

"Each other," he said under his breath.

"What?"

"Nothing. We need to be ready. We don't know what it's like in there, with those monsters."

"We just need to train harder," she insisted. "Then we can leave this place for good."

Cole nodded, his gaze drifting to the ground. "It would mean a lot to Leah if you came," he said, maneuvering the conversation back.

Vella hesitated, thinking on the unspoken debt she owed Leah. Most of her clothes and bedding had come from her. But the guilt wasn't quite enough to move her.

"I don't know . . ."

"It would mean a lot to me."

Cole noticed a faint blush creeping up her cheeks. "It's going to suck," she said.

"I know it will. But I don't want to be alone around them. Having you there will make it suck a lot less," he admitted, smiling.

She turned her head away. Being needed by someone was an alien feeling to her.

He added, "I want to make it a special night for Leah. All she has ever wanted is for us to come out with her. It would mean a lot if we did."

"What about them . . . ?"

"You won't have to see anyone but Leah and her friends," he said. "Just until Leah gets her present and then we can go. If it gets too much at any point, tell me, and we'll leave."

She sat staring at the ground in silence for a moment, her mouth twitching from side to side. Then she glanced up at his pleading eyes and sighed, finally giving in to her major weakness.

"Fine . . . but you better not leave me alone around them."

"Really? Thank you so much. I won't let anything happen. I promise," he said. "You're the best."

She smiled, the blush still warm on her cheeks as she glanced away. "I wouldn't mind finally hearing the band up close."

"Yeah, that wouldn't be too bad; Leah always raves about them." He got up and brushed himself off. "Ah, also, Leah said she has something you can wear," he added with a grin.

"Don't push it."

3

How do you keep people working together under such oppressive conditions? It comes down to building trust and fostering a sense of community. Easier said than done. How do you keep people united? Can shared suffering be enough to bind us together? I don't know. All I know is that we're in this together. And having a common enemy makes it easier to stay on the same side. The books from Earth help. We have learned from their examples what to do and what not to do. It's going to be a long, grueling process, but it has to start somewhere. We have already begun organizing community events and services to promote the benefits of cooperation. We can't let people splinter off and form their own little factions. We need to be one. We've started planning with a community council with all of this in mind. All this effort just to stop us from destroying each other. It makes no sense. It shouldn't be this hard. But it will get easier. That's what I tell myself. I just hope we're not here long enough for any of it to matter.

—THE FIRST PEOPLE OF EDEN
Journal of Morgan #38
Day 71

Leah had tried, and failed, to coax Vella into something more formal but she refused to budge. Vella had shown up in her usual shorts and a T-shirt. Her clothes, like everyone else's, were made in Eden, cut and stitched from linen, cotton, and wool produced by the dispenser. The soft earth tones of her slightly oversized cotton garments had long since faded.

Cole watched with great amusement. It was the clash of the immovable object and the unstoppable force.

After a long standoff, Leah managed to negotiate her way into a compromise: clean pants and a shirt. It wasn't much, but Leah was content with her small victory.

They were about to leave when Leah stopped, eyeing them warily. "Oh my goodness . . . look at you two. You're way too uptight," she said, shaking her head. "I feel like if I touch either of you, you'll launch into the ceiling."

She went to the kitchen, rummaging through the cupboards. "What you two need is . . . ah . . . here it is." Leah pulled out a bottle filled with clear liquid. She grabbed three cups and set them on the table, pouring a little into each. "As I was saying, what you two need is a little *help*. To get you relaxed and get you out of your heads. Get you in the mood."

"Mood?" Cole asked.

"Yes, mood, not whatever *this* is," she said, motioning at them. "You need to learn to just *be*, go with the flow, and this will help. Get you in that mood."

Cole and Vella exchanged cautious glances as Leah handed each of them a cup.

"Drink," she insisted.

Vella swirled and studied the liquid. "What is it?"

"The good stuff," Leah replied with a grin.

Cole glanced at the cup, shrugged, and downed it in one go. He coughed immediately, his eyes watering.

"Ah, Leah," he said, his throat still burning. "I don't think Vella has ever had a drink before. This might be a little much for a first."

"Nonsense. You underestimate her."

Vella looked at Cole again. He shrugged and gave her a look that said *You might as well try it.*

She tilted her head back and downed the drink. Almost immediately, she started coughing and wheezing.

"Attagirl," Leah said and then downed her own.

When the coughing subsided, Vella said, "What the hell? People drink that?"

"They usually mix it with other stuff," Cole said with a light chuckle.

Leah stood back, watching them as quiet excitement swelled within her.

"You good?" Cole asked, eyeing Vella.

"Yeah. I feel . . . warm," she said, her voice lighter.

"All right! Now look at you two. Much better," Leah said, satisfied. "This is the best birthday present I could've hoped for. It's going to be a good night; I can feel it. Let's go."

The fresh night air carried a crisp lightness as they strolled the gravel streets toward the party. It was just a fifteen-minute walk. Everything in Eden was just a small hike away. It was estimated you could walk from one wall to the opposite one in thirty minutes. The terrain was flat from end to end, with the only unevenness in the forest area where trees and roots had shifted the earth around them.

Cole and Vella trailed a few steps behind Leah, who waved and greeted people along the way. Vella avoided eye contact with those around them. She fixed her gaze on the front yards of the homes they passed. Rows of Crafthomes flanked them on either side. They followed a similar template, with the age of the homes being the main differentiator. Brick was mainly used for support, while wood made up most of the structure. They all had tin roofs and chimneys, but the chimneys weren't used for fireplaces—it never got cold enough at night to need one. Instead, they were used for wood-fired kitchen stoves and shower water heating systems. A small water tank sat at the back of the roof, feeding a simple gravity-based water system. Rain from the early morning shower collected in the gutters and fed the tank. Each had a generous wooden porch. Many had large, lavish front gardens, some with fruit trees and all with colorful flowers. Some were neatly organized, while others had been left to grow wild, spilling past the bounds of what most would call tidy.

"You all right?" Cole whispered.

She turned, forced a smile, and nodded.

He gestured to a nearby garden bed. "The white roses look nice. We should take a few for your garden."

"I was thinking of the—" She froze, noticing the mass of people at the entrance of the party at the end of the street. Huddles of people stood in small groups, some caught in conversation, others simply waiting for those who hadn't yet arrived.

Cole followed her eyes, and his breathing halted for a moment. He swallowed and turned to her.

"You sure?"

"I'm okay. Come on."

He cursed himself. Her courage was hanging on by a thread, and he reminded himself that he had to put on a braver face.

Cole slid his arm around her and tapped her. She turned her head, glancing around to see what had touched her. He looked up and away as she looked around, confused. She caught on and slapped him on the arm with the back of her hand. He gave her a wry smile. She returned one, this time lighter and more natural than before.

It wasn't much, but it was enough to ease some of the anxiety they shared as they continued down the street.

Eden held a party every Friday night for those who had birthdays during the week. Even if there were no birthdays, the event still took place. Leah would attend most of them; Cole avoided them like his life depended on it. He'd been to a couple, dragged along by Leah, but always left as soon as he could. Vella had never been. She'd only ever caught glimpses from the outskirts.

They held the party in a public park in the southernmost part of Eden. Rows of wooden benches spread across the vast open area. Each one could seat a dozen people. A stage for the band occupied the front, with an open area below serving as a dance floor. Snacks and desserts filled a buffet table. Beside it was an alcohol dispensary that offered beers, ciders, and an array of spirits mixed with fruit juices.

At the entrance, guests over eighteen were given three drink tokens, though the age limit didn't stop younger attendees from getting a drink or two, and most people ended up with more than three anyway.

Leah led the way as they neared the entrance, the sounds of the crowd growing louder with each step. The crowd surged on all sides, voices overlapping in a growing hum.

Others had clearly dressed for the occasion—clean shirts, woven vests, or modest dresses stitched with care. Cole's outfit was functional but plain; Vella looked especially out of place, still in her stiff compromise of clean pants and a borrowed shirt.

She glanced nervously at the organized chaos around her, her eyes darting from face to face, hoping not to recognize anyone. Even the unfamiliar faces seemed to carry a weight of judgment. She gripped her arm, her nails digging into her skin as she stayed close behind Cole and Leah. When someone brushed past her, she flinched, bumping into Cole.

There's only so much a shot of shine can do, he thought.

Noticing her growing agitation, Cole felt his chest tighten. *Should I have even asked her to come? This must be torture for her. I can't let anything happen*, he thought, repeating the last part to himself.

Leah accepted their drink tokens, her face lighting up as familiar voices called out to her. She passed tokens to Cole and Vella, then waved them ahead so she could stop and greet several well-wishers.

The two of them entered the park, moving through the crowd, bumping into several people. They were caught in a river of people; Cole moved them out of the way of the commotion. At the sideways glances from people he knew, he felt his unease build. He pointed to a table in the back corner, and Vella followed. Before they could go anywhere, Leah grabbed Cole's arm.

"No, you don't," she said, ushering them toward a table near the stage where her coworkers sat. Cole knew a few of them from brief encounters.

"Leah!" a woman shouted, waving. As they approached, everyone got up to greet Leah, exchanging hugs. Cole and Vella stood back, hoping to avoid the same treatment.

"Everyone, this is Cole—as you may know—and *this* is his friend, Vella," Leah said.

"Cole! I wasn't sure when we would see you again. And you brought a surprise," said the woman closest to Cole, nudging him. He forced a smile.

"Cole, you should know everyone. Vella, this is Edward, Maria, Daniel, Frieda, and Siona—the best coworkers and friends a woman could ask for," Leah said, pointing out each one as she said their names. In Eden, work groups served a dual purpose: they were as much social groups as they were professional teams. Leah and her coworkers handled everything related to making and altering clothes, but they also helped in other related areas.

They worked with the few fabrics available—mostly linen, wool, and cotton—to produce clothing that was simple, functional, and long-lasting. Patterns were rare, colors plain. What little variety existed came down to stitching and trim, making tailoring a quiet art in Eden. Clothing needed to be practical, nothing more. Heavier winter wear wasn't necessary in Eden's mild climate, which made Leah's job a little easier and gave her more time for what little creativity the restrictions allowed.

Edward, Daniel, and Siona waved. Frieda and Maria gave Cole and Vella a warm hug. Vella instinctively jumped back as Frieda approached, but Frieda would not be denied and hugged her anyway. Vella looked at Cole, silently pleading for help. He just smiled and shrugged.

They squeezed into the table, with Vella between Cole and Leah. The excitement enveloped them, words flying from every direction. Vella froze, overwhelmed by the noise. Cole adjusted slightly better. Over time, they both relaxed, caught up in the contagious energy.

Cole did his best to respond to Leah's colleagues, answering for both himself and Vella. Though Vella remained closed off, she found herself wanting to answer some questions, but the words stuck in her throat.

Cole found himself caught in an increasingly personal conversation with Maria next to him.

"So, Cole . . . is this your girlfriend?" she asked.

Vella blushed and stiffened. Cole, flustered, managed to say, "We're friends."

Maria laughed. "Just friends? You two? Really?" she said, eyebrows raised.

To Cole's relief, Leah interrupted. "Cole, get a drink for Vella and me."

"Sure. What do you want?" Cole asked, eager to escape the questions and catch his breath.

"Get her the Leah special," one of her colleagues, Frieda, shouted, which elicited a good laugh from the table.

"What's that?" Cole asked.

"One half shine, one half cider," Siona said, sparking more laughter.

"Hey! Don't make them think I'm some kind of alcoholic. Don't listen to her; I have never done that," Leah laughed, playfully slapping Frieda. "Cider. Same for Vella," she said, turning back to Cole.

"Got it," he replied, turning to Vella. She nodded, indifferent.

He felt bad leaving her but knew she was safer with Leah and her friends. As he made his way through the crowd, his uneasiness rose. He found his way to the back of the drink line, hoping he would avoid anyone he knew. One of those people—Alex—was across the park. Cole spotted him and let out a sigh of relief.

The air buzzed with restless bodies and constant chatter. It surrounded him, closing in, fueling his growing disdain. How could they be so oblivious? Acting like everything was okay. *What is wrong with them?* he thought.

Looking back at the table, he could faintly see Vella in the distance. She was peering around Leah at the five-piece band as they played some light music. It made him smile. She appeared like she belonged in the sea of people enjoying themselves. Time passed quickly as he watched her, and before long, he found himself near the front of the line.

He snapped back to his immediate surroundings when he heard a couple of girls whispering behind him.

"Isn't that Cole?" one said.

"Is it?" the other inquired.

"Looks like it. What's he doing here?"

Their laughter grated on his ears like nails on a chalkboard. Cole clenched his fists and gritted his teeth. He knew the voices. Of all the people to run into, it had to be these two.

For Leah, he repeated in his head.

"I think I saw that one-eyed freak here too," one said, giggling.

Hearing the words made something inside him snap. Cole whirled around, his eyes alight with rage. "Oh, Ren and Ivy! Speaking of freaks, I hardly recognized you two. You've aged poorly; I know cows more attractive than you two. Next time they slaughter the pigs, you two should stay away. You know, just in case. They might get confused."

The girls' faces dropped as they fell into stunned silence. Cole turned back, his heart racing, a different kind of fury lining his face. The exchange hadn't gone down well with those nearby. A woman behind him turned to say something but caught Cole's expression and thought better of it.

The silence around him was deafening as time slowed to an agonizing crawl. He squeezed his eyes shut, wishing he had never come. *For Leah indeed. Idiot . . .*

On his way back, he still fumed, angry at the girls and himself for losing his composure. Sitting back down, he ignored everyone else and stared at his drink.

"What's up?" Vella asked, nudging him.

"Sorry I made you come," he whispered.

"Why? Did something happen?"

He unclenched his fists and sat up, trying to hide his anger. "No, no. I just hope this isn't too much."

She smiled. "It's fine. Leah's friends aren't so bad."

Vella's tone was light and effortless, and seeing her more at ease helped Cole relax. He allowed himself to exhale, realizing being here wasn't so bad after all.

She took a cautious sip, still wary from the earlier shot of shine. "It's pretty good," she said, smacking her lips. "Tasty."

Cole smiled, taking a sip himself. "Right you are," he said, looking at her with a quiet sense of wonder. "Thanks for coming."

She tried to keep her smile faint. Her mouth opened for a moment as if to say something, but instead, she nodded and moved her attention to the conversation happening around them.

The next few hours were filled with laughter. They shared embarrassing stories about Leah, and even Cole contributed a few. His face ached from laughing, a feeling he hadn't known was possible.

Vella no longer sat closed off; she leaned forward, her hands resting on the seat. The alcohol was doing its job. Cole continued to get the drinks, not wanting to risk Vella encountering the girls.

Late in the evening, a man approached the band. He whispered something to them. The band stopped playing, and the crowd quieted.

The man stepped onto the stage. As he approached the center, the noise reduced to a low murmur.

"Hello, everyone!" he projected.

Cole recognized him from the orphanage; his name was Owen. He was a former teacher and now the mayor, the highest authority in Eden aside from their captors. He was twenty-seven and would likely see out his remaining time as mayor. He was well liked and respected in the community, so he won the annual election with little trouble.

It bothered Cole how nice he was. Cole knew the cold and brutal nature of people, which was why he trusted the nicest ones the least. What monsters were they hiding inside? Where were the bodies they left in their wake?

Owen stood there, smiling and waving, waiting for complete silence. A loud shout and whistle erupted from one of the center tables. Owen pointed toward the source. "If anyone's looking for Lachlan tomorrow morning, you'll find him in lockup at this rate!" The comment drew laughter from the crowd.

Soon it grew quiet, and Owen began, "Welcome. Thank you for coming. I'm glad to see you all here tonight. Before we go on, I'd like to pay respect to the brothers and sisters we lost this week. Three people were taken from us, but they will forever remain in our hearts: Lucy, Nathan, and Ryan. Many of their family and friends are here tonight. We have three people who will speak on their behalf and share a story or two about what made them special to us. But first, please join me in a moment of silence."

A hush fell over the crowd, silencing even the faintest

whisper. This was a moment to remember all the lost souls, not just the three being honored. Everyone here carried at least one person in their heart whom they mourned.

After the moment of silence, they gave the pseudo-eulogies. The tradition was to tell entertaining and light-hearted stories about the deceased. Yet people still cried, as they always did.

When they finished, Owen returned to center stage. He thanked them and added a final tribute of his own, finishing with, "They're gone but never forgotten."

It was a difficult thing to move on from, but Owen masterfully guided the transition.

As this was going on, Cole watched as Leah scanned the crowd, as though she were looking for someone. After a minute, she stopped, and her face flashed disappointment. *Is she looking for Alex? No. She knows he's around.* There was only one other possibility he could think of: *Edgar? But why?*

Owen continued, "Next, we have three special guests tonight. We also want to celebrate those still with us. We must appreciate and value them while we can. We have three special birthday guests. Birthdays are a time of celebration and remembrance of life's fragility and preciousness. Let's honor them. Where are they?"

He scanned the crowd. "There's one, Sam, and another, John, and where is—" He turned his head down and noticed Leah. It was hard not to, with her coworkers pointing and shouting at her. "Ah, there you are. Hello, Leah."

Leah ducked in her seat, half-feigning embarrassment. Owen continued, "Let's begin with Leah. It's her twenty-ninth birthday. She doesn't look a day over twenty, if you ask me."

The crowd clapped and cheered. Leah's cheeks were redder than Cole had ever seen.

"Let's get the birthday girl up here," Owen announced.

It dawned on Cole what was about to happen. A sinking feeling settled in his stomach as Leah scrambled off the bench and straightened her blouse. Now he understood why she was looking for Edgar. She walked to the stage, smiling and waving at the audience. Leah glanced at Cole; he flashed a smile for her.

He wanted to be happy for her, but he couldn't shake the feeling that this would be more torturous than truly joyful.

Owen embraced and congratulated her before turning back to the crowd. With a smile, he said, "We have a present organized for Leah, and here to deliver it is a special young girl."

Cole's anxiety grew as he dropped his gaze away from Leah. The crowd fell silent, understanding the moment's significance.

"Sasha, can you bring Amy forward?" Owen said, turning to his right.

Cole couldn't bear to look up; his fingers tapped on his leg in a nervous rhythm. Without warning, Vella grabbed his hand and gave it a firm squeeze, motioning toward Leah. Cole froze, surprised by the rare act of physical affection. He couldn't think of a time when she had initiated physical contact of any kind.

She's definitely drunk, he thought. The thought made him laugh internally, which, along with the feeling of warmth from her gentle hands, eased some of his tension. Cole nodded and looked up at Leah as Vella continued to squeeze his hand.

A girl of around five, holding a bouquet of flowers, stood with a woman from the orphanage. The woman brought her to the edge of the stage and pointed Amy toward Leah. The little girl dawdled across the stage, her features unmistakably Leah's.

Leah fought back tears, bending down to accept the flowers. She set them aside and embraced her daughter. Cole shared her joy, as did the crowd. They emitted a collective "aww" at the heartwarming scene.

In Eden, the central administration organized birthday presents, and often a relative or coworker delivered them. Those with children received gifts from them. It was one of the few times when parents who had left their children at the orphanage saw them. Only if requested; some didn't even afford themselves that.

Some viewed the practice of giving up their children while they were still alive as a kindness, believing it was in the children's best interests. Others because they wanted to rid themselves of a burden either they couldn't or didn't want to handle.

Most raised their children until their time was up, only then giving them to the orphanage or to someone they knew. A large network of families in Eden operated on mutual trust, agreeing to care for one another's children. Those who had once been taken in gave back by taking in someone else's children, much like Leah had taken in Cole when he was thirteen after being taken in by Cole's parents at a similar age.

At first, most of Eden had participated; however, breaks in trust (some refusing to take in children or mistreating them, among other reasons) caused the network to shrink over time. Even so, though the numbers fluctuated over the decades, the orphanage always housed at least half of Eden's children. The majority were over the age of ten. They remained there until they turned sixteen, at which point they were considered full members of society, able to work and own a home.

Children in the orphanage fell into two main categories: those born to unprepared parents who struggled to raise a child, and those whose parents had died or were nearing death, leaving them without anyone to take them in. Regardless of the circumstances, it was a difficult decision for parents in Eden. Those forced to give their children to the orphanage had confidence they would be looked after by Eden just as they themselves had been.

Leah had given up Amy when she was one. She had her reasons, like many others.

Some in attendance saw this moment from their own viewpoint. They'd once been that child unknowingly meeting their parents. Few were lucky enough to remember the moment. Others were reminded of their own children they'd had to part with. Whatever it was that connected them to the moment, those were the ones Cole saw unable to hold back tears.

Leah savored the moment, holding Amy for as long as she could bear.

Before it got too much, she let it end, kissing Amy on the cheek and whispering, "I love you, baby."

"Thank you, Amy. Everyone a round of applause," Owen declared.

Leah watched her go, unable to look away. Cole felt the weight of her anguish with every step the little girl took.

A tear landed on his hand as Vella let it go to wipe her eyes.

4

Today was the last day for Fred. He was the first person to have his timer run out. Just as we all expected, it wasn't freedom that awaited him. Instead, he was met with the same excruciating pain that others experienced when they transgressed against our captors. The pain was unbearable, yet he retained some mobility. When he moved toward the doors, the pain subsided, allowing him to walk with some freedom. But the moment he stopped or hesitated, it returned with full force. When he finally reached the doors, he didn't want to go in. Fred begged us to kill him instead. We didn't know what to do. None of us could bring ourselves to do it. But neither could he enter. Now that I think about it, I should have helped him. Ending it for him would have been kinder. He chose the pain. It only grew worse until they thought he'd suffered enough. Then they ended it. Twelve hundred and eight people remain. I know, down to the second, when every single one of them will die. Something deep down tells me people aren't supposed to know that kind of thing about themselves.

—THE FIRST PEOPLE OF EDEN

Journal of Morgan #38

Day 168

After the birthday presentation part of the night concluded, the festivities ramped up. The band played their more upbeat, dance-inducing set of songs. As the space in front of the band filled with people, Maria grabbed Leah and a few others from the table to go dance.

By then, Cole and Vella were drunk enough to consider following her. Leah waved them over, her eyes brimming with excitement. Vella's eyes darted up and down at the mass of people, mouth thin and tight. Despite the barrier holding her back, he could feel her eagerness in the way she tapped along to the beat, occasionally swaying and bobbing.

Cole's eyes moved from Leah to Vella as she looked longingly at the people enjoying themselves. He raised a hand to Leah, shaking his head. She frowned slightly, nodded, and returned to her friends.

He watched with growing sadness as Vella sank into the seat, her feet still tapping along to the music. His eyes darted around, searching for something he could do. His eyes lit up as he shifted his gaze away from the lights and the people.

In a sudden burst of energy, he pulled himself up and held out his hand to her.

"Come on," he urged.

Vella hesitated, looking from his hand to the crowd. "No, I—"

"Not up there," he said. "I want to show you something."

She glanced at him, still unsure. But she trusted him. So, she put her hand in his. He pulled her up from the seat, guiding her away from the crowd to a quiet spot behind the stage, where they could be alone.

"This better? Just you, me, and the music," Cole said with a playful smile. "Come on, dance with me."

He didn't know how to dance, not at all, but he didn't care. Cole swayed and moved his feet with abandon. He tried to make her more comfortable, mimicking what he'd seen and making up the rest as he went.

Vella stood still, watching him. Her lips formed a small smile as her eyes flickered between amusement and uncertainty.

"Come on," he implored, this time with more energy. He took her hand and tried to get her to move.

Slowly, she allowed herself to be pulled into his rhythm. The music began to take hold. Her movements were stiff at first, but as her muscles relaxed, she moved with more confidence, finding the rhythm of the music as it guided her.

Just as Vella was warming up, the song ended and the band launched into a new tune, one that immediately roused the crowd. The energy was contagious, sinking into them both, making their bodies move almost instinctively. They danced like they sparred, in silent understanding, their movements in sync with one another and the music as the world faded around them.

This had a different air to their sparring, though. Lighter. Freer. There was nothing to prove. No anxiety. Just the sheer joy of the moment. They even sang along with the crowd, their voices joining in the catchy chorus. For once, Vella completely let go, her usual guardedness replaced by a carefree joy that in turn made Cole feel freer than he ever had. It was just them, lost in the music and each other.

Cole and Vella danced through a few more songs. Then, breathless and laughing, they retired to the bench.

Leah returned not long after. Noticing how light their expressions were and how comfortable they looked, she remained silent, glancing at Cole with a smile.

They lingered a while longer, but the energy that had fueled their dancing faded, leaving Vella and Cole exhausted. Cole felt Vella's body leaning on him. He turned to see her yawning, struggling to keep her eyes open, a sure sign the night was reaching its end.

Meanwhile, Leah and her friends were still full of energy, their vivacious chatter filling the night air.

Leah glanced over at Cole and mouthed, "Take her home." Cole placed a hand on Vella's shoulder to bring her back to awareness.

They said their goodbyes. Met with hearty hugs from the partygoers, too tired to resist, they accepted them.

The walk home was quiet. The soft crunch of gravel was their only company. A deep physical exhaustion settled over them, heavier than anything they'd felt after sparring. But they also felt a carefree ease from the social chaos and alcohol. The silence was occasionally broken up by Vella humming the melody of the song they'd lost themselves to.

Without a word, they walked past Cole's place. A quiet smile formed on Vella's lips at the knowledge that he hadn't left her side. Cole knew he didn't have to walk her all the way home, but it felt like the right thing to do.

Vella turned her head and gave Cole a knowing smile.

He furrowed his eyebrows. "What is it?"

She raised her hand, revealing an object draped in cloth. Cole was surprised that he hadn't noticed her carrying something. She pulled away the cloth to reveal a mug. "One last drink?" she ventured.

Cole smiled and clapped. "Of course."

Vella handed it to him. He took a sip and passed it back.

The nights in Eden were always beautiful and serene. An artificial full moon and a scattering of fake stars lit up the night sky, casting light for those still awake.

Cole was staring up as he walked, lost in thought. *What would the real night sky look like right about now?*

The moon and stars were recreations of those on Earth. The first people of Eden confirmed this from books. The moon floated across the sky, mirroring the sun's path during the day. The positions of the stars never changed. As static as their existence. There were too many to be counted, thousands upon thousands, with many more not bright enough to stand out on their own. These blurred together to form what they knew to be the Milky Way.

Vella couldn't help but look up as well. "Do you think the stars look better out there?" she asked, reading his mind.

"That's what we're going to find out someday."

Before long, their relaxed stroll led them to one of the furthest points from the town center, where a dense barrier of trees and bushes greeted them. They ducked and weaved through the shrubbery until a small pocket of space opened up and Vella's home came into view. It was a repurposed wooden tool shed with a patched-up, rusty tin roof. It sat against the cold metal wall, abandoned centuries ago.

Cole felt a wave of nostalgia, as if seeing it for the first time, remembering the moment he'd discovered the secret as a child. The location offered several advantages when it came to privacy. It had once been used for agriculture, but as the population shrank and food demand declined, much of the farmland was scaled back. The food production department quietly abandoned the area, allowing the forest to claim it. Remnants like the shed and the secluded patch where it stood were left behind. It was also located in the north, near the doors, a place most people avoided. Lastly, the pocket of space sat on a slight decline, with plant life obstructing any view from afar.

Cole had brought her here to give her a place to hide.

A refuge from the orphanage. Over time, that refuge had become her home.

He'd helped her make repairs to make it livable. It was quite the project for two thirteen-year-olds, but one they'd relished. Plants still overgrew the shed even after their repairs. Vella said she liked it that way. They installed a makeshift shower and toilet on the right side and her own private garden on the left. Inside was basic: a propped-up mattress in the back corner, a sink and countertop in the other, rows of shelves on either side, and a small table and two chairs in the middle.

With some consultation from Leah's partner at the time, Edgar—who worked in construction—they put together a basic gravity-fed water system for the sink and shower, and even managed to set up a septic tank for the outhouse.

She grew some of her own food, and each week, Cole brought her excess produce from his job. As a result of her setup, she rarely needed to leave for anything.

Leah constantly pressured Cole to get her to move in with them, but while he'd tried many times to convince her, she always refused. He didn't blame her.

She was safe here. That was enough for him.

With the drink unfinished, they sat against an oak tree, side by side, passing the mug between them. Cole glanced around, occasionally looking at the sky. Vella, however, stared straight ahead.

"Who do you think they are?" Vella asked, pointing to the perimeter wall.

"Our *masters?*"

"I like to refer to them as . . ."

Vella then effortlessly reeled off every insult she could think of. She only stopped when Cole laughed at how elaborate they had become. Losing her train of thought, she joined in the laughter. Cole added a few insulting epithets of his own, sparking more laughter.

When they calmed down, she asked, "Well . . . what's your theory? Everyone had one growing up. Is yours the same, or has it changed?"

"You remember mine?" Cole sat up, looking at her with a raised eyebrow.

"Of course."

"I don't even remember having one."

She laughed, recalling the memory. "Yours was so funny; that's why I remember it. You were *so* serious. You said, 'It was the Earth spiders that got us!' You were scared to death of them when we looked at the picture books of Earth animals."

"Ah, now I remember." He paused, chuckling to himself. "Earth spiders are terrifying. All those eyes and legs."

"I don't think spiders, one one-hundredth the size of a chicken, could do all this," she countered.

They both had a long laugh at his expense. "You can't exactly tell the size of something from a picture. I thought they were a lot bigger than they actually are, and I was *seven years old*," he argued.

The only animals they had ever seen were sheep, pigs, chickens, and cows. Eden had smaller creatures too, such as insects, small birds, and essential pollinators like bees, all contributing to a healthy ecosystem. But most other animal species, like fish or any water-dwelling creatures, were nothing but things of fantasy, only seen in picture books.

"I can't believe you remembered that . . ." he said, laughter fading. Vella grew unnaturally quiet. Sensing her discomfort, he cut in. "Well, what was yours?"

She cleared her throat. "The dinosaurs got their revenge."

"On us? Despite humans never having existed at the same time? And what are they getting revenge for? What did we do to them?"

She shrugged. "Earth humans used their bones as a fuel source." They looked at each other and burst into laughter again.

After a moment, they calmed down, a wash of reality coming over them.

Vella adopted a serious tone. "Now that we're older and have had time to think about it, what's your final theory?"

"Hmm . . . I've gone over it a million times in my mind . . ." Cole shook his head. "I want to hear yours first."

Vella took a sip and looked down at the drink. "I think we did this. Humans. It feels like something humans would do. Only humans could do. Cruelty is in our nature. It's the only thing that makes sense to me."

"I can see that, but why?"

"Entertainment."

"Like they're watching us?"

"Yeah."

"That's bleak," he said, before adding, "It's pretty boring entertainment."

She laughed. "It is," she conceded.

"Eden is kind of like that ant farm we had in class."

"The one you cracked the glass on?"

"That was an accident! But yes, that one."

"I actually liked watching them. Seeing all the tunnels they built and how they worked together."

"Reminded me of tonight. Ants running around, busying themselves . . . going nowhere."

She pressed her mouth into a tight line as she passed him the mug. "Your turn. What's your theory?"

"The founders thought it was aliens that abducted them, right?" Cole asked.

"No, I read the reports. The only thing they—"

"You read the reports?" Cole interrupted.

"I was curious, so I went to the library one day many years ago. I read some accounts and journals. Anyway, the only thing they remembered before waking up here is a bright green light. Nothing else. They just guessed aliens," she explained.

Cole finished the last of his drink. "Logically, it's most likely—"

"I don't care what's most logical. What do you think?"

He paused. "There's a lot to consider. Just think about what it takes to keep this place running. It's not like an ant farm. It's more than glass and dirt. The scale, the technology . . . it's hard to fathom. So who could have built something like this? And for what reason?" He let out a slow breath. "My head says some advanced alien race, but gut tells me it's humans. But according to the books, the people of Earth never had the means to build a place this advanced. But I get the feeling we were never told the whole truth. Or the full story. Accounts of Earth cut off at the year two thousand but what if a lot more time has passed since then." He glanced at the ground. "Then there's the question of why . . . Why would they do this to us? Maybe our ancestors did something awful to deserve it . . . I don't know. My guess? Because they could. And sometimes, that's all the reason people need."

Cole hurled the empty mug. It hit the wall with a dull thud, the sound echoing into the darkness. "Over four hundred years and no contact, nothing. Every time I try to make sense of it, I'm less sure than I was before."

"I know what you mean," Vella said. "What if we're already dead and this is some sort of waiting room for the afterlife?"

"That's a new one. I hate it," he said, poking fun. "What if we're literally just food for the monsters? Like that's it. They can only eat human meat."

"That makes no sense. How about . . . they need our excrement. Like this is a human shit farm."

Cole shook his head, smiling, trying not to laugh. "And they eat it because it's all they can consume."

"Exactly," she said, laughing.

The air settled, and their smiles faded away.

Cole looked up at the sky. "We could drone on for hours and hours about who and why, and we'd still be in the same place. Aliens, humans, machines, gods, or anything else. What does it matter? Maybe it doesn't and never will. All that matters is we'll get out of here. Anywhere has to be better than here."

It felt good for him to say it without reservation, the alcohol dulling reason and doubt.

"We'll make them pay. Whoever they are," she said, adding louder, "Whoever you are!"

"Just think, we'll be free to choose to go anywhere we want among the stars."

"That would be nice."

Yes, it would be, he thought.

Their breathing was light and easy as they shared glances. Neither of them said anything for a while, letting the peace of the night envelop them.

Vella's hand drifted to her eyelid, trying to shift it up with the back of her index finger. Her mouth contorted in her attempt to hide her agitation. She'd never told him, but he'd learned through experience that when she was tired, it bothered her more and, in turn, made her more irritable. He didn't want to make her uncomfortable by asking about her eye, so he let her be, quietly taking his leave whenever he saw the signs.

He thought about going but felt heavy, so he gave himself a minute before getting up.

She stopped touching her eyelid and slumped down against the tree, defeated. She stared to the side, shaking her head.

After a moment, she broke the silence. "I remember when I was six, meeting my mother like Amy did."

"I never did. What was it like?" Cole asked.

"S-she said something to me." Vella cleared her throat. "She said . . . I was beautiful." She trailed off, shaking her head again.

His response was delayed. It was only two seconds, but it was two seconds too long when Cole said, "She was r—"

Before he could finish, Vella got up and declared, "I'm going to bed."

She rushed to open the door. "Night, Cole," she snapped, not looking back before slamming the door behind her. And just like that, he was sitting alone.

Cole punched the ground beside him, cursing himself.

Why did I have to hesitate . . .

5

Laura told me she's pregnant. It's wonderful news. Really. But bringing a child into this godforsaken place. It doesn't sit right with me. And with less than five years left. How can we have a child, knowing they will have to grow up without us? That's the least of my concerns for them. It doesn't seem fair. Are we terrible people? Maybe. But I do believe in the people of this place. I have to. There's nowhere else to put my faith.

—THE FIRST PEOPLE OF EDEN

Journal of Morgan #38

Day 563

Cole waited around in front of Vella's place a little too long, pacing back and forth.

Going home would be admitting defeat, and that wasn't a feeling he wanted to leave with. But there was no fixing it tonight. He chose a petty compromise and walked the perimeter.

As he ambled along, his mind wandered. The echoes of light conversation and laughter still rang in his ears.

Everyone there tonight was able to enjoy themselves so effortlessly . . . why can't we? Are we broken? That could've been our lives . . . I don't deserve it, but she deserves to have that life. Maybe she still can.

Cole pictured all the people and how they looked at each other, smiling and enjoying each other's company. He clenched his fists as the hate inside boiled over. At the people who made her life a living hell, stopping her from having a life surrounded by others. But he directed most of that hate at himself.

It's all your fault. You could've done more. Should've done more. What—

His pace slowed as he realized where he was. A towering door stood to his left, its crimson red looming over him, halting his breath. He felt the cold, blue hue of the display screen above him. It showed 426 numbers, each with a countdown ticking down in unison. He kept his eyes fixed forward.

He resisted looking up at the board. For years, he'd watched as Leah's number—8591—had been creeping closer to the top left-hand corner of the board. She was already in the leftmost column, and he didn't want to know if she had climbed up any further.

In the distance, the dim light of a shineball illuminated a small brick building. They'd dubbed it the Peaceful Passage, a name too kind for what it actually was: the place where people went when they reached that dreaded top left-hand corner on the board. It was their solution to avoid worse deaths. Cole's breathing returned sharp and quick, and he took an abrupt right turn, heading for home.

He hadn't realized how fast he'd been walking until he made it through the woods to the end of his street. He took a deep breath and slowed, continuing at a controlled pace. Nearing his house, he noticed a man hanging around the front.

Cole approached. "Can I help you?" he snapped.

A few steps closer, and he recognized the man. "Leah's still at the party, Edgar."

Edgar was Leah's former partner. They'd been together since they were teenagers but split up not long after giving up Amy. Since then, they hadn't had much contact. Cole didn't have much of a relationship with him. They had lived under the same roof for several years, but Cole had chosen to ignore his existence. Not out of hatred. They had little in common. And he spent most of his time with Vella anyway.

I don't remember seeing him at the party, Cole mused. *I'd have thought he might've wanted to see Amy at the very least.*

"I know Leah's at the party. I came to see you," Edgar said.

Before Cole could respond, Edgar put a hand up to stop him. "I've already heard what I need to. It's all yours now. Here. Catch." Edgar threw a small round object at Cole. "I don't want to see it again . . ."

Cole caught it in the middle of his chest. Before he could react, Edgar ambled off, his steps wavering and uneven.

Glancing down, Cole felt the cold metal of the dark object. "What is this?" he called out after him. "Hey!"

Edgar stopped and turned. "See for yourself. Just . . . be careful." He continued on his way, pausing once to glance back before disappearing.

"Whatever, damn drunk," Cole muttered to himself, pocketing the object and heading inside. His mind was still fixed on Vella, eating him up inside.

He poured himself some water, drank half, and sank into a chair at the dining room table, resting his head in his hands. After some time of self-torment, he heard the front door creak open.

"Why are you still up?" Leah asked.

Cole shifted his head to look at her, still resting on the table. He studied the soft, fading euphoria in her relaxed expression. "Are you okay?" he asked.

After pouring a cup of water of her own, Leah came over and sat beside him. "Why would I not be? Tonight was all I could have hoped for."

"I miss Amy. I can't imagine how it felt for you."

Leah leaned back in her chair. "Yes, it hurt. I miss her every day, but seeing her safe and healthy made me feel like it was all worth it," she said. "That's all that matters to me."

Cole buried his head in his arms. "I don't know how you do it."

"I got you."

He raised his head and sat up. "Seems like a poor substitute."

"I don't know, you're just as cute."

He shook his head and smiled. "Seriously, though."

"I am serious. I got you and your parents had me."

"They had a better deal."

"Not sure about that. I was a bit of a monster as a teenager. I used to argue with them more than you ever did with me."

Cole's eyes widened, and a smile spread across his face. "Really? You?"

"Believe it or not," she said with a chuckle. "Point is, I wouldn't have it any other way."

"Why? I don't get it."

"Your mom used to say if you don't wish for anything different, you will never have a bad day. Things are as they are. Change what you can and don't worry about the rest," she said as if she was reciting the words from memory.

"Is that what you believe?"

She hesitated, taking a sip of water. "I try to. Don't get me wrong, I'm not any different. I have my doubts about giving her up as early as I did. Then I remember the kids who came into the orphanage at a later age. They always had a worse life growing up. You could see them at school before and after their parents left them. It was night and day. They shut themselves off and took a long time to accept their new lives without them. Even when they did, they weren't the same as the kids who grew up in the orphanage. You could always pick them, even as teenagers. You could see they were missing something important. The kids who grew up there weren't missing anything because they didn't know any better. Sure, we knew there was a piece missing inside, and I would be lying if I didn't say I was a little jealous, but some of those who came later . . . they never recovered. Sometimes ignorance is the best mercy you can give. But then those kids had something you can't replace, even if it was hard for them to deal with losing." She shook her head. "I don't know. How do you ever know if you're doing the right thing?"

"You did the right thing," he assured her.

"I never intended to have children. But sometimes, things happen that you can't control, and you're left to deal with them the best you can."

"I'm sorry, I can't imagine how tough it would've been. Truly, you're the strongest person I know."

"You don't know enough people . . . Your parents were the strongest people I knew."

"Growing up, I'd always assumed they were dead . . . I never got to ask them . . . Why didn't they want me?" Cole asked. "Why did they give me up?"

"It wasn't you, if that's what you're thinking. I promise. They weren't the selfish type, the kind to get rid of a child because it was annoying or so they could have more free time. I know those types. That wasn't them. As for your parents, I can't say. If I had to guess, I think they believed it was in your best interest not to know them. For what reason? I don't know. Some people . . . feel like they are unfit to raise children. I can't say really. They were an enigma—the only two people to enter the doors in two decades—and they never struck me as fighting types. I feel like I never truly knew them. Whatever the case, they must've thought it best you not know them. They wanted to protect you. Think of it like that. I trust they had a good reason. They cared about you, a lot, and had your best interests at heart."

"Is that why I never saw them until I found them? Not even for their birthdays?"

"That took real strength," she said. "Still, they wanted to know everything about you. That's why I ended up spying on you for them."

"You weren't subtle about seeking me out . . ." he said with a grin. "Was that the only reason you volunteered at the orphanage?"

"Pretty much. It wasn't hard to pick out their son. You had your dad's hair, your mom's eyes, and her nose," she said, smiling as she studied his face.

"Was that their idea?"

"It was all me. I felt indebted to them. They didn't like to talk about you with me around, but I overheard them a few times, wondering how you were doing." She shook her head. "I couldn't help myself."

"Do you regret it? Knowing I found them because of you?"

He saw something twist inside her; a flash of a grimace came and went.

"Sometimes . . ." she said. Then, looking up at him, she forced a smile. "But seeing how happy they were with you . . . in those last days . . . I feel like I gave them something they'd been missing. So . . . no, I don't think I do."

Cole formed a melancholic smile and then turned serious. "If they wanted to protect me and keep me away, why didn't they turn me away when I came to their doorstep?"

"That's easy. Think of it like this: Your favorite food is the brownies I make, right?"

"Yeah."

"Say you were trying to quit eating brownies, for some unknown reason. It would be pretty easy to stop eating them if you never saw them again. But if I were to place freshly baked brownies in front of you? What would you do? You wouldn't be able to help yourself. You would eat them, right?"

"Yeah, I guess."

"They were human, like the rest of us. There was a limit to their willpower."

"So, I'm their brownies," Cole said with a chuckle.

"Their weakness," Leah said. "With only a few weeks left, I'm guessing they thought they could disappear without you noticing. We both know now, with how you are, that it was never going to work."

Cole paused to meet her gaze. "I hope you don't blame yourself for that day."

She looked away and swallowed. He filled the silence, sensing her guilt. "It's like you said. It happened because of how I am. It was my fault. Not yours."

"Cole," she said, flat and serious.

"What?"

"Enough."

"Sorry, I didn't mean to . . ."

Leah's earlier lingering euphoria had well and truly faded now. "It's okay."

"I wish I had never found them," he muttered, "for your sake. I just . . . ruin everything. Even now."

"Stop that," she said, giving him a light push. "Can we change any of it? What purpose does it serve to think like that?"

He tried to answer but came up short. "None," she said, answering for him.

Leah got up, put both their cups in the sink, and moved to go to bed.

"Do you wish they'd chosen the other path?" he asked.

She stopped short of the hallway door. "Even if I did," she said without turning, "I couldn't stop them." Leah took a deep breath. "Night, Cole."

"I don't think I've ever thanked you for taking me in and

looking after me."

She turned and smiled. "Don't need to. I promised them I would be there for you. Like I know you'll be there for Amy." She slumped as her eyes faded. "Cole . . . in this life, we get what we're given, not always what we want. That's the way it is. Make the most of what you've been given, all right?"

He nodded, his eyes cast down.

She took a deep, steady breath, her lips forming a soft smile. "I knew it was going to be a good night," she said. "And I was right. This was by far the best birthday I've ever had. Thank you."

He closed his eyes and heard her bedroom door close.

Cole slumped forward, dropping his forehead onto the table. He let out a soft groan, realizing he might have inadvertently ruined the one day she didn't need reminders like that. The one day that was supposed to be hers and hers alone.

He went to his room, and luckily for him, the alcohol made sleep come easier than it normally would have.

6

Creating the Peaceful Passage aims to alleviate the fear of death by offering a serene and "painless" transition. Some pain may still occur, but with ongoing refinement, we will make the process as gentle as possible. This initiative seeks to reduce the anxiety surrounding life's inevitable end, providing a humane and carefully guided process that allows individuals to approach their final moments with dignity and peace of mind. While we can't control when we die, we can control how we face death. Action is unavoidable, forced upon us by circumstances beyond our control. Incident after incident has scarred much of our population, and we must act now. For the well-being of our society, this solution is the most logical and humane path forward. As we have observed, the alternatives are at best cruel and at worst socially destructive.

—THE PEACEFUL PASSAGE PROPOSAL

Dated Year 1, Day 200

Cole arose in a haze, his mouth dry and his forehead pulsing. Dehydration and lack of sleep had taken their toll on him. Leah was making breakfast when he stumbled into the kitchen. The crackle of the wood-fired stove and the smell of fried eggs and buttered toast hit him, making his mouth water even as his stomach churned at the thought of eating anything.

"Morning, sunshine," she chirped, not looking up.

"Are you even human?" he grumbled, rubbing his eyes.

Leah just smiled and motioned to a small, enclosed fireplace built into the wall above the stove. "Having a shower? You want me to light the fire for the water heater?"

"That would be amazing. Thanks."

Leah grabbed a handful of wood from the bucket at her feet and began stacking it into the pit.

"You two seemed to enjoy yourselves last night. I told you that you would like it if you gave it a try."

"It was all right, I suppose," he conceded.

She turned, leaning on the counter. "How was she after you left? Did she enjoy it?"

Rather than tell the whole truth, he said, "She had a good time."

That reminded him to go check on her after breakfast. The entirety of the night's events was still reemerging in his mind.

"Happy to hear. She really opened up," Leah said with glee, handing him a glass of water.

"Alcohol will do that," he said. "By the way, Edgar stopped by last night."

"Oh? I only saw him from afar on the way back home. What did he want?"

"He didn't even mention you. Said he wanted to see me."

She stopped what she was doing. "You? Why?"

"Don't know. He gave me a ball and left without saying anything."

"A ball? Why a ball?"

Cole shrugged. "What's his deal?"

She placed a plate of eggs and toast in front of him, chewing on her lower lip. "Someone told me he hasn't been going into work much lately. I've been meaning to check in on him. I should . . ."

"You don't hate him?"

"Why would I hate him?"

"I don't know. I thought since . . ." He trailed off.

No emotion filled her voice. "It's no one's fault."

Cole left it at that. They ate breakfast in silence. Leah stared out the front window, her mind elsewhere. He regretted bringing up Edgar. The last thing he wanted was to remind her of that painful time in her life.

"What are you up to today?" she asked, turning to him.

He knew this to be a ploy to divert her attention elsewhere, and he obliged.

After breakfast, Cole showered and dressed. As he tossed aside his clothes from the night before, he heard a clunk. Puzzled, he sifted through the pile and found something hard in the pocket of his pants. He pulled out a black orb, the object Edgar had given him last night. In the dark of night, he hadn't gotten a good look at it.

Now, in the light of day, he could see it clearly and realized he had never seen anything like it before. It fit snugly in his palm. As he turned it over in his hands, he felt hypnotized by its reflective exterior. The longer he inspected it, the more he felt this. The blackness of the sphere was so deep it seemed to swallow the light around it; Cole feared he might get lost in its depths if he stared into it long enough.

Running his fingers over the surface, he couldn't believe how smooth it was, and it was impossibly clean. He tried rubbing his fingers on it, but he was unable to leave even a small smudge.

Creepy.

He couldn't identify what kind of metal it was made of. He hefted it up and down in his palm to get a feel for it; the mass of the sphere was distributed more toward the center, making it seem light and heavy at the same time.

After staring at it, he did a double take, thinking he must be seeing things.

Wait, it's moving! No . . . it's rotating.

He found a midline running around the orb, separating two hemispheres, almost invisible because it was so minute. The midline appeared to be shifting. Then he saw them. Two indentations running vertically from the midline. Both seemed to be crawling toward each other, about to converge. It wasn't just the top or bottom hemisphere that appeared to be moving—it was both, turning in unison.

With bated breath, he watched them come together, forming a single line for a split second. A sharp clicking sound came from the object. Then nothing.

He sat down on his bed, confused. *What's the point of this thing? Is it a child's toy? No. This is . . . something else.*

Studying it further, he tried to see if it held any more secrets. There was one more. On top of one of the hemispheres, there was a faint outline of a small circle.

He used a finger to feel the outline, then moved his finger to the center and pressed down.

A sudden jolt hit him. It sent a sharp shockwave through his brain, and a flash of black filled his vision for an instant. Instinctively, he put a hand to his forehead; as he did, he turned his head down.

He blinked. The floor felt further away, and he realized he was no longer sitting—he was standing. *I was sitting. I was sitting,* he repeated to himself. *What is going on . . . ? I must be more hungover than I thought.*

With a shake of his head, he pressed the button again. The same jolt, the same black flash, but nothing changed. He was still standing in the same spot.

Is this some kind of practical joke? he thought. *Edgar . . . what an idiot.*

"Leah!" he called out.

"What?"

Cole moved toward the door, pausing as a sparrow landed in his open window. He gave it a quick scare, waving his hand to keep it out, and it flew off. Shaking his head, he headed to the kitchen, where Leah was busy.

"Check out this thing Edgar gave me," he said, holding the orb out for her to see.

She gave it a quick glance, frowning. "Never seen anything like that before. What is it?"

"No idea, but if you press this button, it gives you a nice brain shock."

To show her, he pressed the button again. The wave of electricity hit his brain like before, and the next thing he knew, he was back in his room.

"What the . . . ?"

He looked around in confusion. After a few seconds, a familiar sparrow landed in the open window. He stared at it, not liking the implications.

What the hell . . . ? I think I might be losing it . . .

For his sanity, he pressed the button again. The window was empty. But a few seconds later, the sparrow landed exactly as before.

Maybe it's a different sparrow? So, he marked a defining feature on it. *The small white mark on the side of its right eye.*

He reset and not long after, there it was—the sparrow with the white mark.

No way!

"Leah!" he shouted. "Did I show you a black orb?"

"Orb? What are you talking about?" she called back.

Cole sat down and rubbed his eyes. *Okay, think.*

He turned the orb over in his hand again, more cautious now. The shifting hemispheres and the indentations weren't just decorative. He couldn't be sure, but they appeared to be slowly moving. They had to mean something.

Do they mark . . . time? A countdown?

He watched as they separated further apart and then crept toward one another again, ready to meet up on the other side of the orb. He felt like they had lined up earlier, right before he'd ended up standing. When he heard the click, he wondered, *Could that be the trigger? But what does it actually do? Take me back? But how far?*

He waited. Minutes dragged on. When the lines finally met again, a soft click followed. Hesitating, he waited a few seconds then pressed the button. The jolt hit him. He was standing again. But in a different position.

This is insane.

He checked the orb. The lines had just met again and were now drifting apart. Slowly.

Okay. Maybe it sends you back to the exact moment the lines converge. Maybe. But why? Why not just a fixed time? Ten seconds? A minute?

It didn't make sense. And he wasn't ready to assume anything.

Edgar . . . what did you give me?

He pocketed the orb and took a few hurried steps, pausing to watch for the sparrow to land on the window. It never came. That time had come and gone.

An ant crawled along the upper window's glass. He reset, curious to see if it would return. It did, tracing the exact same path.

Shaking his head with a faint smile, he ran out of the house, stopping a few paces from the door. Unsure what to do, he decided to see Vella, hoping she could help him make sense of the orb. More importantly, he needed to check on her after the way they'd left things last night.

Lost in thought, Cole wandered down the street, not registering the faint sound of footsteps passing by. A muffled thud jolted him back to reality. He turned in time to see Penny, a neighbor he'd rarely spoken to, hit the ground hard. The wicker basket she'd been clutching slipped from her grasp, scattering fruit across the gravel. Unable to brace her fall, she scraped her face against the rough path. A sharp cry pierced the quiet.

Cole rushed to help her up. As he did, some of the blood from her cuts dripped onto his arm. He could feel her body trembling from the shock of the fall as he steadied her. He cringed when he saw the severity of some of the wounds up close, especially the ones on her cheek. Several people in the vicinity hurried over to lend a hand. He let go and stepped back as others took over. He stood there watching, in shock at how something so small and incidental had turned so horrific. He stared down at the blood smeared on his forearm, then back at her.

Even when it heals, it'll still leave scars, he thought. *It doesn't seem fair. If only I could've done something . . . maybe I could've caught her if I was just a second slower . . .*

Wait . . .

His eyes snapped to where she'd fallen. A jagged rock jutted up just enough to catch an unaware foot.

No way this actually works. Right?

But he was already pulling the orb from his pocket.

"Okay," he murmured. "Let's test this."

He pressed the button.

Another shock, and sure enough, he was back in his room. He paused for a second to see the ant moving across the window.

Cole burst out the front door. He saw Penny emerge from her house and hurried to the spot where he'd seen her trip. He looked down and saw the rock protruding from the ground—the same one she would trip on. With his foot, he dug it out of the ground and brushed it off the footpath.

Cole waited with nervous anticipation as she approached. He pleaded for it to work as she stepped onto the same patch of ground. To his relief, she walked past without incident. He let out a breath he hadn't realized he was holding, a giddy laugh escaping in the same breath. The woman turned around, confused.

He smiled, trying to suppress his laughter, and said, "Lovely day, isn't it?" She frowned, eyed him, and kept walking.

Cole stared at the now-empty path, the implications of what he'd done sinking in. He'd changed it. He'd fixed it.

His smile widened, and his hands trembled with excitement as he thought about the possibilities the orb held. Still, he had so many questions and no answers. But the most pressing question was *What did Edgar expect me to do with this?*

In his eagerness, he almost turned around and went straight to see Edgar, but at that moment, the priority was Vella. Answers would have to wait.

As he walked, he ran through what he knew so far:

One: When I—or rather, when anyone holding it—press the button, it seems to take us back to the last moment the lines converged. The click might be the signal and confirmation.

But I don't know for sure. Could be a fixed interval. Could be based on time of day. Some other unknown factor. More testing required.

Two: Let's assume that's correct. The lines converge, the click happens, and a new reset point in time is created, one that returns the user to where they were at that moment. A fixed state in time to go back to. A reset point (I'll use that term for now).

But does creating a new reset point invalidate the old one? Can you go back further?

He looked at the orb. The lines had converged not long ago. He pressed the button and found himself still in the woods, but now a good hundred meters back from where he'd been. He pressed the button repeatedly, but nothing changed. He was stuck in the same spot.

It can't take you back further than the last reset point. No matter how many times you press the button. Maybe there is a way? From inspecting the orb there doesn't seem to be any other way to interact with it?

He tried twisting the two hemispheres, attempting to manipulate the position of the indentations. It didn't budge. It continued its slow, steady rotation.

How is it this tough? This thing isn't natural.

Alright, there is probably no way to go further back than the latest reset point.

Three: Only the user remembers what happened after the reset point if the button was pressed, erasing all other events. This is shown by Leah and Penny having no recollection of previous events.

Four: How long do these reset points last before a new one makes the old one invalid? No idea. Could be up to ten minutes. I'll need to test that later and check how long it takes for a full rotation.

Five: How does it work? How does it make time travel possible? Not important at the moment.

Six: Where did it come from? I doubt Edgar was capable of making something like this. He must've found it. But where? Was it given to him? No one else in Eden would have the technology to create such a thing.

His summary ended there as he pondered its possible uses.

Time travel, he mused. *Limited, but still time travel!*

He broke from his thoughts as he approached Vella's secluded corner of Eden, weaving and ducking through several trees and bushes to find her. Vella sat with her knees tucked under a towering oak. It was the same tree they had sat under the night before. A well-worn book was in her hands. The morning light filtered through the canopy above, flickering across her like the ebb and flow of the ocean tide.

The library was the only place Vella visited in town. It was a safe retreat with countless doors to other worlds. She made sure to go when the fewest people would be around, either early in the morning or late in the evening. The only other thing she needed from town was some shopping, and Cole took care of that, bringing her a box of food once a week.

She was reading a book she'd read over a dozen times: *The Knights of Acidalia.* It was about noble knights fighting to protect their kingdom against evil behemoths.

Fictional books hadn't been included in the initial collection of books provided at Eden's inception. Only nonfiction, focused on instructive texts. They all seemed to originate from a place called Earth. All the books had identical paper sizes, bland titles, and uniform bindings, making it almost impossible to tell them apart without the titles on the spines. The people of Eden were able to discern Earth's history from these books, up to the year two thousand, where all accounts completely cut off.

Over the years, the people of Eden had created their own works of fiction, from children's books to dense fantasy novels and everything in between. There weren't enough of them to assign to specific genres, so they chose to place them all under an Eden Fiction section in the library, separated only into children's and adult categories. Despite their lives being confined to a space no larger than a small town, the human imagination remained boundless. The book Vella was reading was by an anonymous author, written some twenty years ago. Though typewriters were available, this person had chosen to use their own handwriting. It was beautifully clean and a pleasure to look at, as Vella described it to Cole.

"Vel," Cole called out.

She didn't respond or lift her head.

He sat down next to her. "How're you feeling? I woke up feeling a little out of it," he said with a laugh.

"Fine," she replied, sharp and flat, keeping her gaze firmly down at the book.

In one word, he knew what was happening. This was a state he was familiar with. One or two days a week, she would grow cold and unresponsive even to him. But he got the feeling this was more. His indecisiveness from last night stabbed him.

Rather than stop like his instincts told him, he asked, "Did you have fun last night?"

She said nothing; her eyes remained fixed on the page. Her hair fell forward, hiding her face.

After a moment of sitting in anxious silence, he uttered the word, "Time?"

This was the system Cole had devised, a way for them to communicate how they were really feeling without the need for words.

One day, when she was feeling down and completely unresponsive, he couldn't bring himself to leave her alone. So he'd told her, "I have an idea. I'll say the word *time*. You respond by holding up your fingers. One means *stay*. Two means *leave*. Three means you don't care either way, and it's up to me to decide." He paused, thinking, then added, "Also, if you hold up your thumb along with your fingers, it's an explicit order. Something neither of us can ignore. *Ever.* All right?" She'd nodded her agreement.

That day she'd held up one: *Stay.* Telling him she didn't want to talk, but she didn't want to be alone either. He was hoping for the same response today.

Her eyelid fluttered, and she jerked her head to the side, showing a slight scowl. She tapped two fingers to her shoulder: *Leave.*

The urge to show her the orb tempted him. It could give them something to talk about, something to distract her. But he stopped himself, swallowing the lump in his throat. He knew better than to ignore her wishes.

He felt for the orb in his pocket, found the button, and pressed it.

Now he could no longer see her. A wall of shrubbery stood between them, and from afar, she read in peace. He turned and left.

7

The doors keep bothering me. What is the point of them? One won't open, and the other two lead to certain death. Are we here to kill the beasts, or are we here to feed them? The latter makes no sense, and the former feels impossible. Even if we could kill them, why? What purpose would that serve the ones keeping us here? I'm left at a loss. Still, I press on. Let's discuss the green door: two red lights above it, flanked by two doors on either side. It feels like we're supposed to do something in the blue and red doors to change those lights. Kill the monsters? But why make it so difficult? Why not help us accomplish the task? If anything, we're discouraged from trying. It seems designed to make us feel hopeless, and the fact that everyone has given up only seems to confirm that. And then there's the time limit: thirty years. Why kill us off at thirty? It feels like a countdown, a message telling us, "You have thirty years to prepare to enter a door and fight for your life." But no one wants to. Suicide seems preferable. That's why we built the euthanasia facility, to give people a painless way out. They don't stop us from ending things ourselves. So again, what is the point of the doors? Of any of this? There's something we're not seeing, and we may never see it. I'm tired of trying to rationalize things that are clearly beyond our understanding. I'm done. I will no longer waste my precious time on this madness. We're here because we're here. That's the only conclusion I have left.

—THE FIRST PEOPLE OF EDEN

Journal of Morgan #38

Day 302

Cole wandered through the town center. He couldn't quite remember where Edgar lived; he knew it was on one of two streets. He stopped everyone he passed, hoping they knew. In a place as small as Eden, he figured he wouldn't have to ask many people, and he was right. He ran into one of Edgar's coworkers, who pointed him in the right direction.

He found the place without much trouble, despite it being one of Eden's replica Permahomes. He was able to distinguish Edgar's house by the number on the front, but the biggest giveaway was the state of the front yard, making it seem like no one had lived there in months. The white exterior blended into the rows of identical houses. They were only one-story homes, but tall enough to be mistaken for two-story houses, adding to their uncanny appearance. Their pale, sterile design clashed with Eden's vibrant and colorful aesthetic.

The homes were impossibly strong, showing no signs of wear even after four hundred years. The people of Eden had no clear reference for what the material was, so they made guesses based on the books they had. But none described any material this advanced.

No one could break the windows. They were as strong as the structure's carbon-fiber-like material. To Cole, these homes felt soulless, as if designed to remind you they weren't yours and never would be. The idea of living in something made by their captors repulsed him.

A prison within a prison.

Cole stepped through the tall grass to the front door.

He knocked and waited. Thirty seconds passed. No answer. He tried again. Nothing. Even calling out yielded no response.

Frustrated, Cole circled the house, trying to peer in through the windows, but the blinds were all drawn, and it was too dark to see through any of the gaps he found.

After another knock, he began pacing. Losing patience, he tried the front door. To his surprise, it opened.

Cole stepped in with caution. "Edgar," he called out, his voice echoing through the eerie stillness of the house.

The place was a mess, with trash and random objects strewn across the floor. Cole was careful to step through the clutter, like he had with the overgrown grass in the front yard. The air inside was suffocating, stale and thick with the lack of air circulation. On the wall to his right, the clock sat unwound, a thin layer of dust coating its surface, as if it hadn't been touched in weeks.

Passing through the kitchen and coming into the living room, he found Edgar lying on the couch, wrapped in a blanket. He was wide awake, his eyes glazed over and ringed with heavy, dark circles. Empty bottles littered the floor at the foot of the couch.

As he crept forward, his voice dropped into a soft murmur. "Edgar?"

Edgar tightened his grip on the blanket, his gaze distant and unfocused.

Cole dragged a chair from the dining room and placed it in front of the couch, sitting down to face Edgar. "Are you all right?"

Edgar didn't bother to respond; his gaze drifted away from Cole.

Dumb question, Cole thought.

He tried a more direct approach, pulling out the orb and holding it in front of Edgar's eyes. "Where did you get it?"

At the sight of the orb, Edgar buried his head under the covers. "Leave," he groaned.

Cole tried a different tack. "I can use this as much as I like to get the answers I need. Make it easy for the both of us. Please."

Edgar remained silent.

Cole blew out a long breath. "I need an explanation. You don't get to just hand me this *thing*—whatever it is—and say nothing. That's not how this works."

"Get it away from me," Edgar grumbled.

"What exactly happened last night?"

"I should have died," he whispered.

"What do you mean?" Cole leaned in. Edgar mumbled something unintelligible and turned to face away from him.

Cole sighed. "I'll come back later. Get your shit together by then."

Caught between Vella and Edgar, Cole felt at a loss for what to do. He got up, picked up an empty bottle, and brought it to his nostrils and was hit with the strong smell of moonshine. He took it to the kitchen, filled it with water, and then placed it next to the couch. He took one last look at Edgar, shook his head, and left.

It was midday, and the streets of Eden swarmed with people going about their weekend. Cole made his way through the heart of town, hoping to save time. A huge mistake, he realized. He shuffled through the buzzing, crowded streets, bumping into people as he navigated past Eden's busiest quarter. It wasn't as bad as he had expected. After last night, crowds were something he felt a little more used to. Still, their smiles and carefree chatter grated on him.

To his right, a group was setting up for a soccer game in the park. Multiple organized matches took place over the weekend, which always attracted a crowd. On the fringes of the park, people had laid out blankets and set up tables, displaying food, arts, and crafts to exchange for goods and services.

In Eden, there was no real currency. Instead, they used a universal credit system. Everyone got a basic amount of credits for the central Eden store. These credits couldn't be exchanged between people but could be spent on food and household items or saved for larger household purchases. To prevent hoarding, unused credits expired after six months. Not that it was an issue.

Even those who chose not to work were still given a basic amount of credits. Throughout Eden's history, a mix of attitudes toward work had always existed. Some people dedicated themselves, giving their all to the community, while others showed little interest and avoided work altogether. Most people fell somewhere in the middle, recognizing the importance of contributing to the community but also valuing time to enjoy their lives.

Eden's system offered flexibility. No one imposed penalties for not working, and no one cut off food or water. Nothing harsh. Just an occasional visit from the administration to see if someone could help fill short-staffed roles or suggest activities the person might enjoy to help them contribute, even in small ways. These visits also aimed to keep people socially engaged and highlight the importance of community and doing one's part. On the opposite end, Eden rewarded people for going above and beyond in their jobs with perks like personal dispenser orders or extra store credits.

Since they had no money and couldn't exchange credits, people relied on bartering. Many residents grew produce in their backyards, crafted items, traded possessions, or offered services to trade.

Cole noticed some signs advertising services. The one that caught his eye was a teen offering lawn cutting in exchange for whatever people could trade. He felt tempted to enlist his services for Edgar, but he had nothing on his person to exchange, so he moved on.

On his left stood the town hall, where people filtered in and out, partaking in similar exchanges. The area inside the building buzzed with activity: some were setting up more stalls, while others gathered to play board games like chess and checkers. People took chess almost as seriously as soccer, and players coveted the title of Eden's best player. They held at least one tournament every month. Even Cole and Vella were competitive when it came to chess, thinking themselves capable of beating anyone in Eden, though they'd yet to test this idle boast, for obvious reasons.

As Cole continued through the crowd, he passed his neighbor Penny, who had set up a table with someone else, displaying a colorful array of fruits. He waved, but Penny only stared back, still wary after their last encounter. Cole cast his eyes down and kept walking.

Out of the mass of people, he heard someone call his name. He winced, immediately recognizing the voice.

I should use the orb and take the long way home. Not too late, he pondered.

For some unknown reason, he resisted the urge and turned to see Alex approaching.

Cole and Alex had grown up together in the orphanage. Alex, nearly a year older, had been like a brother to him. They'd done everything together, always sharing the same bunk bed for as long as Cole could remember—until his abrupt departure. As they'd grown older, they'd grown apart. No one incident was to blame. The similarities they'd shared as children had simply dissolved when they were young teenagers.

As Alex became more social and outgoing, Cole withdrew. Alex's natural good looks and upbeat personality made him magnetic to the other youth around them. Cole despised the added attention surrounding them, making him want to be around Alex less.

At the same time, Vella's life got harder as the years pressed on, while Alex's seemed to get easier. This only deepened Cole's resentment toward people like Alex. They seemed to coast through life on natural gifts.

Presently, it was how Alex looked at him that annoyed him. Not as equals. Was it pity? Almost. Condescension? Not quite. He couldn't pin it down, but either way, Cole couldn't help but feel irritated.

"How are you?" Alex asked, smiling. "I saw you at the party last night. Sorry I didn't say hi. I got caught up with other responsibilities."

Sure you did, Cole thought.

"Good. You?" he said, the lack of enthusiasm not lost on either of them.

"Can't complain. I saw Vella was there last night. How is she?"

Cole could already feel his patience wearing thin. "Getting by."

"Are you two, you know . . . ?"

"Friends. Yes," Cole said, giving him nothing.

Alex nodded, looking away. Cole narrowed his eyes, thinking he saw disappointment.

What does he care? Cole wondered.

As they stood close together, Alex's height—several inches taller—irked Cole. Alex had always been taller, and now that they were young adults, the difference had only become more pronounced. Everything about him rubbed Cole the wrong way. Always superior.

"How's work? How is it being a hard-working man of the fields?"

"It's fine."

"If you ever want a job more central—"

"I like my job." And before Alex could respond, Cole added, "Look, I'm in a bit of a rush."

"Oh, sorry, of course. Well, we should catch up soon. I would love to have you, Leah, and Vella over for dinner sometime."

Cole gathered all his willpower to stop himself from rolling his eyes. Instead, he did his best to feign a smile and said, "Sounds good." Before Alex could say anything else, he turned to leave. "See you around."

"Sure . . . see you around. Good to see you're well!" Alex called after him, waving.

Good to see you're well, Cole mocked to himself, bitterness pressing in his throat. *Screw you.*

By the time he got home, his encounter with Alex lingered, stewing in his mind and leaving him in a foul mood.

He approached the front door in a trance, only to be jolted back to awareness by a scream from inside. It wasn't a cry for help or attention. He knew that sound too well by now. He'd heard it many times over the past couple of years, and it had only become more frequent. Usually it came late at night, unlike this one.

It was Leah.

Screams torn from somewhere deep, full of pain, frustration, and anguish. The kind that needed release. He'd learned to recognize the signs build over days—how she grew tense and quiet—and he knew it was only a matter of time before it all spilled out.

He stood frozen at the front door, helpless, waiting for the storm to pass. There was nothing he could do. This was something he was powerless to fix.

More sounds. Something thrown against the wall, muffled shouts, the dull thud of something heavy hitting the floor. Then, finally, a door slammed shut.

Only then did he move.

He opened the door quietly and tiptoed inside. A chair lay knocked over. A cup and spoon, on the floor on the other side of the table. A book crumpled on the other side of the room. He picked them up in silence, setting them back in place. He moved to the hallway and his eyes stopped on Leah's closed door. He paused there. Sometimes, he would hear sobs through the door.

But not this time. That didn't mean they weren't happening, though.

He slunk off to his room and curled up on his bed, staring at the wall. Sadness welled up inside him, mingled with sharp surges of frustration.

What am I supposed to do . . . ? Edgar . . . Vella . . . Leah . . .

Eden is killing them. And I can't do anything about it.

He shifted, and something jabbed his leg.

The orb.

He pulled it out, holding it up to his face. Its subtle movements enthralled him, the deep, dark surface almost hypnotic, as though it was drawing him into a void.

Could this . . . ?

The soft click of the orb broke his reverie.

He set it aside and mused. *How long does a reset point last? It creates a new reset point every time the points converge. How long is that window? A few minutes?*

On the way to and from Edgar's, he'd heard the faint clicking coming from his pocket every now and then. It had startled him a few times. He thought it was a few minutes, then other times he thought it was longer, around ten minutes. He couldn't quite tell.

He pulled the orb close to his face again and watched it rotate, counting in his head. But he lost track after a few minutes. There was another way to measure the time accurately—one he didn't particularly like.

Above his ankle, Cole wore a bit of cloth tied around his calf. He hesitated before rolling up his right pant leg to reveal the strip of fabric. No one liked doing this; most had it covered for a reason.

He let out a deep breath and pulled up the cloth to reveal a number that looked tattooed on his skin: 8745. Below it, a series of numbers read: 09:234:12:47:53. And counting. Down.

It went in order: years, days, hours, minutes, and seconds, a grim reminder of death that no one cared for. The numbers appeared tattooed onto the skin, but they shifted, counting down, giving them a surreal and unnatural quality as if the skin itself morphed to form the numbers.

Between the numbers, a small protrusion rose from his skin. It was the device implanted at birth that caused the numbers to appear. But that wasn't the full extent of its capabilities. It was a tool for controlling them, much like a shock collar on a dog. With it, any resistance or attempt to escape Eden could be easily quelled.

Cole watched the timer on his ankle, waiting for the next click. It came at 09:234:12:46:43. The next one followed at 09:234:12:41:20. He did the math. It came to five minutes and twenty-three seconds.

He tested again to confirm it was consistent. Sure enough, it was the same: five minutes and twenty-three seconds. He covered the numbers back up and rolled down his pant leg.

Around five minutes of leeway . . . he thought. *It should be long enough.*

Cole stared at the orb and his smile widened. He'd been sitting on a thought, but now he seriously entertained the idea. He could feel this was it, what he'd waited his whole life for.

But as he explored the idea and its implications, he froze up, his breathing stalling. Dread mixed with excitement, creating an almost manic anxiety.

Is that why he gave it to me? What was he thinking?

8

Death and chaos still run rampant. I keep hearing, "There has to be a way out." But there isn't. Every path ends in death. At any moment, they could kill us by triggering these implants inside us. I can see the small dimple on my left ankle. I tried to touch it and—HOLY HELL—the pain. It was only in my arm for a small time, but I've never experienced anything like it before. Someone died attempting to cut out another person's implant. They didn't even get close enough with the knife to touch the skin. The pain in my arm is what they felt in their entire body. After making him suffer for such a long time, it killed him. There must be something in the implant, like poison, that finishes us off, or the severe pain triggers something like heart failure. We may never know. Not that it matters. We are completely at their mercy. They could discard us tomorrow without a second thought.

—THE FIRST PEOPLE OF EDEN
Journal of Morgan #38
Day 15

Vella was tending to her garden when Cole arrived, her figure flashing in and out of his view as he made his way through the dense border that guarded the space. Inside, the garden and surrounding area was vivid and full of life. The garden brimmed with dozens of flowers spanning the entire spectrum of color, which she added to year after year.

She kept her head down as Cole approached. Kneeling in the dirt, she pressed her gloved hands into the soil to form a shallow hole for her latest addition.

Without a word, he crouched beside her and inspected the flowers waiting to be planted.

"I like the lilies; where did you find them?" he asked.

"Where've you been?" she asked, irritation slipping through in her tone.

Cole hesitated, his eyes wandering. He was unsure how to approach her after their tense morning. Deciding that distraction might be the best course of action, he puffed his cheeks and blew out a long breath.

"I got something to show you," he said with a sly grin.

He hesitated, uncertain about showing her the orb, but there was no point in hiding anything from her. So, against his better judgment, he decided it was time to bring her up to speed. He pulled out the orb, holding it out for her to take.

Vella glanced up, her eyes narrowing as she studied the object. She removed a glove and reached out to take it from him.

"What is it?" she asked.

"I can't quite explain it," Cole replied, standing up. "I'll have to show you."

"I really don't care, Cole."

"Oh, you will."

He had her stand in one spot, and then he walked back five steps. Running through the process, he told her to wait until the two lines converged and she heard a click. He then asked her to take three steps and press the button on the top.

"Where is it?" She fumbled for a moment. "Got it. It's hard to see. Wait . . . they're about to touch," she added.

"Remember, just do as I said. Nothing more," he cautioned.

The lines converged with a familiar click. Cole didn't see her move, but the look on her face changed. Her eyes widened, and face lit up as she observed the space around her.

"This is insane. You said Edgar gave it to you?"

Cole blinked, confused. He hadn't mentioned Edgar. Realization dawned, and he asked, "How many times have you tried it?"

"Five," she admitted with a sheepish smile.

"All right, hand it back." He darted forward, hoping to avoid a sixth. She hesitated, holding it out of his reach.

"One more," she said, holding it away from him.

"Later. Not now. Please."

She reluctantly relented and handed it back. "So, no one else remembers anything?" she asked, a mischievous grin spreading across her face.

"No, only you." He shot her a startled glare. "You didn't do anything to me, did you?"

She clicked her tongue, disappointed. "Didn't think of that," she said.

He pocketed the orb and asked, "How much did I tell you?"

"The night Edgar gave it to you, how long until it creates a new reset point, blah, blah, blah. So, where did he get it?"

"I don't know. When I went to speak to him, he was . . . out of it. I'm gonna go check on him again."

"Why would he give it to you?"

"I don't know. That's what I want to find out." Cole drew out the words in annoyance at the redundant question.

"All right, all right. No need to be an ass," she said. "Let's go see him. Come on."

"I don't know . . . he looked in a bad way. I should go alone."

"Screw that. I want to come."

"Not a chance."

"Well . . . say if I were to walk in the same general direction as you."

Cole, already tense and anxious, wasn't in the mood to play games.

"Fine. Come. But stay back and let me talk to him," he snapped.

"You're the boss man," she said with a grin.

They took the scenic route, unmarked by any path. Cole knew the way by heart and was able to avoid the town altogether. The canopy overhead dappled the ground with sunlight, softly brushing their skin as they walked. The rustling leaves beneath their feet, combined with the soft buzz of bees and distant chirps of small birds, created a quiet, comfortable backdrop.

As they walked, the silence was broken up by the crunch of Vella darting around, stepping on dried leaves. It unnerved him, sensing the all-too-familiar feeling of Vella's mind racing.

Should I have even told her about it? he wondered.

He knew where all of this led, and it was nowhere he wanted to take her.

Still, her mood had lightened considerably, and that brought him a sliver of joy.

She glanced at him, snapping out her thoughts. "You think we could use it to get out of this place? Kill the Wolf and Bear? Think about it—unlimited attempts."

There it is . . .

He squeezed his eyes shut, wincing at the words finally spoken out loud. This was what he'd been considering nonstop since learning what the orb could do.

"I don't think it's that simple," he said.

"Why not?"

"You can still die. It doesn't make you invincible. And if you die with it, it's stuck in there. No do-overs."

"Still, it gives us a chance," she said with a hopeful smile.

He couldn't help but shake his head in amusement. "It might." Her optimism eased some of the anxiety that had been gnawing at him.

Still, he stewed on the question: *Do we even stand a chance?*

Cole stopped abruptly. "Just a second, I want to test something."

"What's that?" she asked.

"I was wondering, can the orb work with multiple people? That is, can it send us both back in time if we both hold it?"

He took the orb out of his pocket and laid it out on the palm of his hand.

Her relaxed, playful demeanor retreated as her expression hardened. "W-what do you want me to do?"

"Hold the top and press the button. I'll hold the bottom half."

He cupped the bottom half and held it out to her.

"Uh, right . . ." She stared at his hand, then at the orb, before looking up at him; her hesitation was palpable.

"What's wrong?" he asked.

She shook her head, swallowed, and inched her hand toward the orb, cupping her hand to bring down the top half. Her hand hovered above his, trembling. Cole watched her face tighten and her eyes dart around. When she got close to touching his hand, she flinched and withdrew.

"Can I just press the button? Do I need to hold it?" she

asked.

Catching on to her discomfort a little too late, he nodded and gave her a reassuring smile. "Yeah, not a problem. Just press the button."

She looked away, her back heel jittering.

"Don't worry," he said. "It's no problem."

She exhaled, eyes fixed on the orb, and pressed the button without touching his hand.

Nothing happened.

"Feel any zap?" he asked.

She shook her head.

He glanced around, checking if anything had changed. "No good," Cole said. "Damn."

He looked back to her for her reaction, but Vella had already turned her back to him.

"It was worth a try," he said. "Let's go."

He wanted to apologize for pushing her too far, but he knew it would only make her feel worse by acknowledging it.

They kept walking, now in tense silence. *I should've known better*, he thought.

Last night, she'd held his hand without issue, and he'd foolishly assumed it had changed things. He realized the alcohol and circumstances had made physical touch bearable for her. In the cold light of day, her anxiety about being touched remained. Also, she had been the one to initiate it.

It has to be on her terms, he reminded himself.

She'd learned early on that being touched never meant anything good. The only contact she'd known growing up at the orphanage was being hit, shoved, or pushed. There were no comforting hands, only cruel ones.

Cole wanted to change that, but how could he? How could he show her there was more when her conditioning to touch was so deeply ingrained? He could feel helplessness passing through him, manifesting into frustration and sorrow.

He snapped out of his thoughts at the sound of movement behind them. Turning his head to the left, he caught a glimpse of a Ghost out of the corner of his eye.

That was one of many names they'd given to the robot drones. They were humanoid in appearance, with two multijointed legs that made them far more agile than any human. Each had four arms, extending gracefully from their sleek white torsos, ending in hands equipped with six dexterous fingers. Their heads were featureless, pure white spheres, giving them an eerie, enigmatic presence. These robots did their captors' bidding when required.

One of their functions was serving as midwives. The death timers and identifying numbers on each person's ankle came from the device implanted at birth by them.

The robots seemed to know when an expectant mother was about to go into labor. All mothers reported the same thing. The robots would appear and follow them just as their water was about to break. They administered sedatives and performed C-sections if necessary. Thanks to them, no deaths during childbirth had ever been recorded. They were a blessing sent to deliver a curse.

Besides assisting with childbirth, the robots roamed around tending to ecological issues and removing waste. They'd learned the hard way what it meant to try and mess with the Ghosts, so they were left alone and treated like background noise—hence their name. People called them by various names—Implanters, Shadows, Spiders—but Ghosts had become the most common.

They came and went from hidden doors in the walls. When people inspected them after they left through these "doors," they could find no trace of a gap. If anyone got too close as they were passing through one of these hidden doors, they would be stunned into painful immobilization until it closed.

Seeing one now, Cole felt his stomach drop. He snapped his head forward after catching a glimpse of it. The flash of white was enough to make his muscles tense up. He cast a worried glance at Vella, who was a step ahead of him. His heart raced as he positioned himself between her and the Ghost. It wasn't normal fear he was experiencing but something deeper, more visceral.

She froze as she turned to speak to Cole. "What do—"

He put a hand on her back, nudging her forward. "It's okay."

She flinched at his touch but turned her head and kept walking in dead silence, as if he held a knife to her back.

Dammit!

Everyone had their own reaction to seeing the Ghosts. Most barely raised an eyebrow. For others, it was a painful reminder of their captivity and impending death.

But for Cole and Vella, it was different. A single memory lingered, leaving a lasting scar.

His breathing quickened, and he felt his hands tremble. Cole decided to take an even longer scenic route. Not for Vella's sake.

"L-let's play eleven q-questions," he suggested, voice quivering.

Vella remained silent, walking further ahead.

"I'll s-start. I-I have something in mind."

She still said nothing.

Curse this place.

He caught up beside her, wishing he could put an arm around her, hug her, anything to help her feel safe. In the past, his attempts at comfort through physical contact had been met with violent rejection. He didn't want to risk it, so he walked as close as he could, occasionally "accidentally" brushing against her to help her feel less alone.

So he could feel less alone.

9

In the early days, faced with overwhelming adversity, unity became essential for survival. The founders of Eden's society were forced to make swift, difficult decisions. Failing to do so would have been catastrophic. Fortunately, strong leaders emerged, rising to the occasion. As recorded in early transcripts, their message was clear: "Loyalty to each other is all we have left. We live together or die apart."

—A PEOPLE THAT SHOULD HAVE NEVER BEEN

The History of Eden

by Luke #4342

The amber glow of the setting sun filled the sky. It bled into a deep scarlet as Cole and Vella approached Edgar's house.

"It hurts my eyes to look at these places. Too white," Vella said.

"I know, right?" Cole said.

"I've never been in one before."

"You're not missing out. It feels like they were made to suck the life out of you."

She rubbed her eyes. "I feel tired already . . ."

Cole stopped at the door, turning to Vella. "Hang back. Let me do the talking."

She rolled her eyes and motioned him to hurry up.

Cole didn't bother knocking; he pushed the door open and stepped inside. He expected to find Edgar still catatonic on the couch. To his surprise, when they closed the door, Edgar was sitting at the dining room table, staring at them.

A bottle of moonshine sat in front of him, a quarter gone, with no glass in sight. The table was bare, in stark contrast to the cluttered sink and counters behind him.

Edgar didn't react to Cole's intrusion, though he did wince at the sight of Vella. He shook his head and motioned for them to sit.

They obliged, taking a seat across from him. Cole noted he was looking a little better; exhaustion didn't plague his eyes.

Perhaps the alcohol had returned some semblance of normalcy to him. But the glassy stare remained.

"I was hoping you would be sober," Cole said.

"I've hoped for many things, Cole. But that's not the way life works," Edgar replied.

An uneasy silence settled over the room as Edgar scrutinized them with his eyes. Vella's posture tensed each time his gaze fell on her. He took a swig of the shine and breathed out.

"Well?" he said, leaving an opening for them to speak.

Momentarily thrown off by Edgar's intensity, Cole glanced at Vella. She rested her eyes on Edgar as she relaxed, her brow furrowed as if he were a riddle to solve.

Turning back to Edgar, Cole cleared his throat. "Where did you get it?" he asked, placing the orb on the table.

Edgar eyed the orb bitterly, its swirling darkness pulling him in. He drew his eyes away and finally spoke. "Doubt you'd believe me."

Vella, who had been surveying the room, turned her attention back to Edgar. Without hesitation, she asked, "Which door was it?"

Edgar cringed before a smile broke through.

Cole glared sideways at her; he had been thinking the same thing but hadn't dared to say it out loud. It sounded too crazy. But they both knew there was nowhere inside Eden he could have found something like this.

"The red one," he said with a bitter chuckle.

They sat there, stunned, waiting for him to say he was joking, but he didn't. They hadn't actually expected him to confirm such an absurd thing.

For Cole, the mere mention of what lay beyond the red door brought everything from that day surging back, like he was reliving it in real time. The blood, those bright blue eyes, flashed to the forefront of his mind as numbness enveloped him.

"The . . . red . . ." Cole managed.

Edgar nodded regretfully, knowing the look in Cole's eyes.

"Why?" Vella asked.

Ignoring her question, he said, "Took you one day, and you

already roped her in. You two can't do anything apart, can you?" He glanced sharply at Cole, who looked away.

"What was it like?" Vella asked, her voice filled with genuine fascination.

Her directness pulled Cole back to the moment. "Vel," he warned.

"It's fine," Edgar cut in. "It was—" He broke off, cringing as pain flashed across his face. He took a breath, composed himself, and continued, "It was . . . somehow more horrifying than I'd ever imagined."

Cole's breathing faltered. He was reminded again of the monster that had killed his parents, yet here was Edgar, who had faced it and somehow survived. The only person to go inside a door and live.

"And you got out using it?" Vella asked.

He nodded. "One moment I was . . ." He took a breath and cleared his throat. "In there . . . then the next I was back in Eden, and it was like it had never happened and that thing was in my hands."

"Is it as big as the records say?" Vella asked.

"Bigger," Edgar replied, eyeing the bottle. "Can we not talk about it?" He took another quick drink. "Look, I found the orb by accident. I thought I was about to die, but thanks to that, or despite that"—he gestured to the orb—"I'm alive."

"Yeah, but why give it to Cole?" Vella asked.

"That thing is a curse. I wanted to be rid of it. Why Cole? I don't know. Maybe it's because he was the first person I saw."

"Bullshit," Cole said. "Why give it to anyone? Why not hide it or bury it? You want me to use it."

Edgar leaned in, his eyes narrowing. "For what?"

"You know my history. You know I want revenge and to leave this godforsaken place. And you know I'm the only one crazy enough to think about fighting those monsters." Cole put his hands on the table and leaned forward, meeting Edgar's gaze. "You want us to save Leah. And Amy. That's why you gave it to me."

Edgar roared with laughter. "Is that so?"

"We know it is, so let's stop pretending," Cole said.

Edgar's amusement faded. He looked away, sweeping his hand across the table.

"Why not use it yourself?" Vella asked.

"Look at me," Edgar scoffed. "What am I going to do?"

"So, make us do the dirty work?" Cole pressed.

Edgar shook his head. "I wasn't thinking straight. As you might imagine, flirting with death can mess with a person." Edgar eyed them both and sighed. "I didn't think it through. I was stupid and didn't want to see that *thing* anymore."

He stood up and pulled back the curtain to let the last of the day's light in. He slumped over the countertop, caught in contemplation and regret. He raised his hand as if to strike the counter, then stopped halfway.

"Leah would kill me if she knew I gave that to you. You're right; I can't let you do it for me. I'll take it back."

"No way," Vella protested. "We'll do it. Won't we, Cole?"

Cole hesitated, staring past Edgar. *I can finally get revenge. Kill it! Save them all.*

Then suddenly his thoughts turned, and he felt a paralyzing dread grip him. He swallowed hard, trying to steady himself. *This is it; I can't give in. No more fear . . .*

He gritted his teeth, feeling the fire burn within.

For Leah. For Amy. For Vella.

"I'll do it. You were right to give it to me," Cole affirmed. "I didn't come here to tell you off or make you feel guilty. I just wanted to know more about it. I wasn't about to let this opportunity slip away." The intensity in Cole's eyes forced Edgar to look away.

"I knew you would say some dumb shit like that," Edgar muttered, sitting back down and taking his largest swig yet. "I wish I would've died in there . . . I should have."

"Hey!" Vella's voice came over sharp and chiding.

Cole looked at her and saw the hard lines of anger forming around her eyes.

"Why would you say that?"

"I . . ."

"Don't say that. Did you think of the people who would miss you? Did you think of Leah? Amy?"

Edgar's mouth hung open. Cole glanced at her, wide-eyed and just as stunned.

Her eyes softened. "We're glad you're alive."

Cole, still staring at her, thought, *She doesn't know Edgar, and she's glad he's alive?*

Edgar shook his head, managing a faint smile. Turning to Cole, he cleared his throat and said, "You're lucky to have her."

Cole and Vella stiffened, turning away at almost the same moment as their eyes darted around the room.

"You two are something else." Edgar sighed. "But I can't let you keep it."

"Seems like you already gave it to Cole, so now it's ours, not yours," Vella said.

"You have no idea what it means. Facing those things . . . I don't know how anyone could, even with that. It's not worth throwing your lives away."

"It is possible, though," Cole added.

"In theory, but . . ."

A sudden fierceness filled Cole's eyes. "As long as it's possible, that's good enough for me. You're not going to stop me."

"Us," Vella corrected.

"I could just take it back by force."

"In your state? I'd like to see you try," Vella said.

Edgar sighed and slumped back in his chair, defeated. "Dammit . . . if you're set on doing this, I can't let you do it alone."

"We can handle it ourselves," Vella insisted.

"Maybe, but I can't live with that. Especially if you get killed. For Leah's sake, I can't."

"Actually . . . we could use your help," Cole said. "You know more about this than we do."

"Cole," Vella warned.

He looked at her and smiled. "Trust me."

"Stupid," she muttered, shaking her head.

Then he faced Edgar, his tone firm. "If you're going to help us, I have one condition: stop drinking."

Edgar eyed the bottle, then glanced back at them. "Tomorrow," he said. He grabbed the neck of the bottle and took another swig.

Cole had one more pressing question: Why had Edgar gone through the door in the first place? But, looking at the broken man sitting across from him, he knew he didn't need to ask. His eyes held no fire, not even a spark.

Seeing this, Cole knew he was right in his decision.

We don't need him, but he could use us.

10

These are the words of my predecessor, found in the journal she passed to me before she died: "Their eyes. Always their eyes. Silent. Pleading. They all try so hard to be brave, to keep their heads high as the end draws near. But no matter who it is, they always break. I've learned not to tell them when it will happen, when they will lose consciousness. So, I keep them talking, distracted. It is the only fair thing I can offer. While I prepare the procedure and make them comfortable in their final moments, I ask about their favorite childhood memory. Afterward, I write them all down to preserve their stories, so a part of them can live on. Why childhood memories? Why not just their favorite memory? Easy. Childhood is simple, pure, and full of the best moments you will ever have with the best friends you will ever know. There are no ifs or buts in childhood. No future. No past. No complexity. Only the moment. It comforts them. And maybe it comforts me too. These are their stories."

—"RILEY'S FOREWORD"
CHILDREN OF THE PEACEFUL PASSAGE
by Aleister #8990

Cole had suggested they meet tomorrow to figure out a plan. For now, he returned home alone for dinner.

Leah had prepared a variety of roasted vegetables on skewers and a side of split pea soup with bread.

The light from two shineballs, positioned in different corners of the room, cast long shadows that shifted with every movement.

He got up and went to another shineball. This one was turned off. He held a finger against its cloudy surface for a few seconds until it emitted a dim light. He tapped it rapidly, trying to make it brighter. He recoiled from the blinding light as he tapped on it five times instead of three like he wanted. Squinting, he quickly tapped again, cycling the shineball back to its lowest setting. This time, he was careful to tap only three times, adjusting it to the level of light he wanted.

"Is this a new one?" Cole asked.

Leah grunted in response, her mouth full.

"What happened to the old one?"

She swallowed before answering. "It died. It was about ten years beyond its intended lifespan. Think it was over sixty years old."

"So, you had to waste your store credit. Dammit. Should've let me know and I would've gotten it."

"Don't worry. You need yours for Vella."

"Mine are useless. I always take the excess food we have from work for her and us."

"Then I thank you in advance for the new pots and pans."

"I wish we got more things from the dispenser, like shineballs, that were worth spending credits on."

"We're lucky to have those. Be thankful. Imagine the amount of wood and candles we'd waste without them."

"Is anyone going to figure out how these damn things are powered?"

"Without being killed trying to crack it open? Not happening."

Cole sighed. "I'll get your pots and pans . . ."

As he sat back down, Leah asked, "Vella didn't want to come over for dinner?"

He shook his head.

"You did ask, right?"

"I did," Cole lied.

He hadn't asked in several months.

"Shame," she said, her expression softening. "I thought after last night she might be more open to it."

He glanced past her at the kitchen counter, where another serving sat cooling.

"Bad dream last night?" Leah asked.

"Last night?"

"I heard you shouting."

"No . . . not that I remember. Sorry if I woke you."

"Are you—"

"I'm fine."

"Right . . ."

After a few minutes of eating in quiet, Leah decided to break the deafening silence.

"I ran into Alex today," she said.

"Oh, nice," Cole said, voice flat. "Me too."

"You did? What did you talk about?"

"Nothing. We said hello, and I left," he said, not bothering to look up.

"Cole." Her tone was sharp, like she was scolding a child. "Why don't you talk to him?"

"What's the point?"

"Maybe to have friends?"

"Friends?" He let out a soft, amused breath. "He decided to stop being my friend when I was no longer useful," Cole said, making no effort to hide his disdain.

"He still cares. Meet him halfway," she pleaded.

"What did you talk to him about?" he asked, avoiding the topic.

"We talked all about *you* and only about *you*," she teased.

"Very funny."

Looking down, he swirled his spoon in the soup, hesitating. "I saw Edgar today."

Leah slowed her chewing and looked up at Cole. "You did?" she asked. "Well, aren't you the social butterfly? How is he?"

Cole halted, pondering the truth. "He's, uh, doing well."

"What did you talk about?"

"All about *you* and only about *you*," he said, mimicking her mocking tone.

"Cole. I'm serious."

His brow furrowed, and his gaze dropped as he noticed her shifting in her seat, wringing her hands. "I'm worried. Did he seem fine?" she pressed.

He wanted to say, *No, he looked awful. He's the furthest thing from fine. You're right to be concerned. He needs help.*

Instead, he said, "He's okay. Really."

Cole's curt reply didn't appear to convince her.

Undeterred, trying to sound casual, he continued, "On the topic of making friends, Vel needs help with repairs to her place.

Since Edgar works in construction, and you said he hadn't been to work in a while . . . I thought I'd give him something small to get him going again. He seems like he could use the company."

Her eyes narrowed on him. "You want Edgar to help with repairs? At Vella's place?" she repeated.

Cole nodded, hoping she would buy it.

"And how does Vella feel about that? Having people over?"

"After some convincing, she came around."

"Right," she bit off. "If that's the case . . . I do agree he could use the company." He could see the struggle to let go written all over her face. "Did you find out what he gave you last night?" she asked.

"Oh, that. The cloth I tied around my ankle fell off, so he balled it up and threw it back. I was too drunk to see what it was. It was only when I got dressed this morning that I realized."

When he heard nothing in response, he glanced up to see her staring, unconvinced.

"I know when you're lying."

"I'm not lying."

She sighed and shook her head, then stabbed at a capsicum with her fork, ripping it off the skewer.

Cole thought she was letting it slide, opting for a passive-aggressive silence, which he would gladly take. He breathed out an internal sigh of relief. But without warning, she dropped her fork on the plate and glared at him.

Dammit . . .

"What are you hiding?" she pressed.

"Nothing."

She wanted to say, *Nothing, like your drawings.*

Not wanting to give away that she knew things she shouldn't know, she instead asked, "Are you still planning your stupid suicide mission?"

Leah had always worried about this. Since his parents' death, he'd been adamant about wanting to kill the monster that had taken them, declaring he would free them from Eden. He would clash endlessly with Leah about it, but this was when he was a young teenager; now he rarely spoke of it. Cole had come to his senses as he'd gotten older. He still wanted to leave Eden, but now he recognized the danger in making rash decisions. Then there was Vella to consider.

"Is that what you think this is about? I'm not a kid anymore. Of course not."

"I don't know what to think when you won't tell me the truth."

"You want the truth? Here it is: I'll attempt it one day. Might be my last day, but I will. Maybe . . . if I feel like it. Might even be tomorrow."

Leah shot him a death stare, making him flinch internally.

She took a deep breath, steadying herself. "And what about Vella?"

"What about her? What does she have to do with this?"

"Everything. What happens when you get yourself killed or, worse, get her killed?" Her voice increased in volume and intensity with each word.

"Guess what? She's going to die anyway—like you, like me. She's free to do whatever she wants."

"Are you stupid?" she snapped. "She does whatever you do. She'll do anything you say. You have a responsibility to her." She was almost shouting at this point. "You're going to get that poor girl killed before her time is up if you aren't careful."

Cole opened his mouth to argue, but nothing came. Somewhere deep down, he knew she was right. That was what scared him most.

Calmer, she said, "Let her die peacefully, not in there like . . ."

"Like what? My parents? At least they tried."

"Oh, Cole. There is nothing good about what they did. There's nothing in there but pain and suffering."

"It's better in Eden? Where she's experienced nothing but pain and suffering?"

"Things can change," she said. "But not if you die before they do."

He cast his eyes downward, his mouth twitching with bubbling frustration, but he said nothing.

"She deserves a normal life," she whispered.

"And there it is," he declared. "A normal life? You act like something's wrong with her. Like she needs your pity."

"You know what I mean. She needs to be around people. Not out there on her own."

"She's safer far away from these monsters."

"Monsters? Cole . . ." she said, shaking her head. "I don't even know what kind of conditions she's living in. I've been patient and given her space, like you asked, but this can't keep going on."

"Why would I want her to be around the same people that made her life a living hell? You want me to bring her back to that nightmare? Like Alex, for one. Let's talk about him."

She'd pressed a button, and it was all coming out now. Seething with rage, he continued, "Alex was one of those. He was in on it. He stood there laughing. On the surface, he's all nice, but when it comes down to it, he's just as bad as the rest. Those people like Alex did that to her. The ones you hang around with and exchange fake smiles with. The ones you think are the good ones. The real monsters are in here. I was there. You weren't. Day after day. No one was there for her. No one. They can go to hell. No! I'm not subjecting her to that." His body trembled with anger. "You don't understand! Never have!"

Leah stood up. She dragged a chair beside him. She reached for his hand, but he instinctively withdrew. Undeterred, she touched his arm and slowly moved her hand down to his, holding it tight, calming the trembling.

She leaned in and said, "I love that girl, you know that. I know you believe you're doing the right thing by her. You're keeping her safe and protecting her, but it's not helping her. It's not in her best interests for her to stay there. You must know that. She needs to be here with us, supported."

"I'm trying my best," he bit off.

"I know you are. And you know that I only want what's best for her."

He managed a small nod.

"You need to trust me. I know some people are cruel,

especially children. But those people are no longer children. They likely regret how they treated her. Like Alex. Give them a chance. They're not the monsters you think they are."

He stopped short of replying, swallowing his words.

"She's relying on you. I need you to help me help her." She made sure to avoid saying *save*.

"I don't know what to do. I don't want to see her get hurt again," he said.

"I know, it's tough. There will be times when she'll get hurt. That's life. But she'll be better off in the long run. Believe me."

"I know she had a good time at the party. I was happy to see her comfortable around people," he conceded. "I want her to have more of that, but . . ."

She leaned her head against his. "She's stronger than you think. Only you can help her make more memories like that."

Then, as she rose, she gave him a kiss on top of his head and moved back to where she'd been sitting. Cole sank into deep thought, trying to keep the feeling of helplessness at bay. He raked his fingernails up and down his thighs. The thoughts of those years at the orphanage still filled him with equal parts rage and sadness. He reminded himself there were still things he could do. He knew it would be hard, but he also knew she was right—he could do more. *Will do more. But those people . . . how could people capable of such cruelty possibly change?*

"It's not your fault," she whispered.

"What?"

"What happened to her wasn't your fault."

"I know," he snapped.

"You're lying again," she said, not looking up. "It's not . . ."

He said nothing, furiously wiping the edges of his eyes.

"Sorry," she said. "I just need you to understand that."

He tensed, scowling.

"I know what it feels like."

"What do you know?" he snapped.

She drew in a deep breath. "I knew her mother."

He looked up at her, eyes flashing with surprise.

"Not personally; it was more like I knew of her. She was a

copywriter at the library. I think she even wrote some books."

"What was she like?"

"She was very much like Vella. Although very different in some ways. Quiet, kept to herself, didn't have any friends that I knew of, a bit of a recluse, like Vella. I used to see her whenever I went to the library with Edgar; she would sit there, that distant look in her eyes," she said, her own eyes cast far away.

She swallowed hard. "I was just sixteen, but that's no excuse. I should've talked to her, gotten to know her. You could tell she was alone, suffering."

"What . . . happened to her?"

"I refuse to let her daughter suffer the same fate."

"What fate?" Cole asked. But he already knew; he hoped she would say something different.

"She took her own life before the end."

He watched as anguish spread across her face. "Why have you never told me this before?"

"It's not something I enjoy talking about. It's bad enough I let her daughter live out on her own for so long." Tears welled in her eyes, but she was quick to wipe them away. "She was only twenty-two. Twenty-two, Cole," she said. "That's on me."

Cole's face went blank. "You couldn't have possibly—"

"I knew. I saw it in her, and I did nothing. Same as—"

"What is it you said the other night? Isn't that wishing for things to be different?"

She glanced away. "Some things deserve to be different," she muttered. Then she looked back at him with intent. "Do as I say, not as I do, Cole."

He raised an eyebrow. "That's not setting a good example, is it?"

He had hoped to coax a smile out of her, but she remained unmoved, her eyes heavy with unspoken pain.

Cole's expression faltered. "In any case, that won't be Vella's fate," he assured her.

"I know. She has us."

11

Isara: Did we ever have a choice?

Drystan: No. Not with the life that was handed to us.

Isara: Does anyone?

Drystan: I don't know. But we can choose the lens through which we see it.

Isara: And how do you see it?

Drystan: I'm thankful I'm not alone. And of all people, I'm glad it's you here with me.

Isara: As am I. But why us?

Drystan: Why anyone?

—THE KNIGHTS OF ACIDALIA

Author Unknown

Restless, Cole left the house, knowing that he wouldn't find peace there. The conversation with Leah lingered, heavy in his thoughts. He found Vella sitting outside her home, her favorite book, *The Knights of Acidalia*, open in her hands. An empty plate rested beside her, warmed by the flickering light of a soft, crackling fire.

Without a word, he sat down next to her, staring into the flames. His expression told her he was troubled, but not knowing how to ask, she frowned and turned back to her book.

"Tell me the story," he said, his eyes still fixed on the fire. "The one you're reading."

"You haven't read it before?"

He shook his head.

Vella closed the book, glancing at him with a small smile. "Want me to read it to you?"

"No, I want you to tell the story. What's your version?"

"My version?" she said. "I'm not sure it'll be any good."

"I think it will be better," he said, his focus absorbed by the fire. "Please."

"Uh, all right. Let me think." She chewed her bottom lip, her eyes darting around as if piecing everything together from floating words in the darkness. "It's going to be a lot shorter, and many things simplified and cut out."

"I don't mind. I want to see it how you see it."

A sudden rustling of leaves behind them caught her attention. Startled, she turned toward the darkness, her eyes searching the shadows. Seeing nothing, she turned back around, vigilance still in her eyes.

"Want me to go look?" he asked.

"No . . . it's probably nothing."

She went back to her thoughts, playing with her bangs before tucking the hair behind her ear. "All right . . . I think I'm ready."

She shifted, crossing her legs, then began.

"Once upon a time, there was an island kingdom called Acidalia. In this lonely kingdom, there was a queen, the last mage of her kind. She was powerful, but she was also alone. Not long ago, she'd lost her husband, the king, to a terrible illness. Together, they had upheld a magical barrier that protected their kingdom from the three great chaos beasts roaming its borders. Now, that burden rested on her shoulders alone.

"The chaos beasts were legendary creatures of evil incarnate—Leviathan, the serpent of water and ice, Ifrit, the fiend of earth and fire, and Bahamut, the great dragon of wind and lightning. They circled the kingdom, waiting for the moment the queen's strength should fail so they could devour all she had sworn to protect.

"With each passing day, the queen's powers were fading. Keeping the barrier up placed great strain on her. She knew she only had about a month left before the barrier would collapse. Desperate, she decided to use her last resort. Beneath the castle lay the Cave of Night, a place of pure darkness, a void that devoured all light. It was said that a knight of pure heart would emerge from the cave, blessed by the gods of light, to save the kingdom."

Vella paused, glancing at Cole to see if she should continue. His eyes were still, captivated by the fire, his expression stern and unchanging.

"Go on," he said.

She continued.

"The queen sent out a call for anyone brave enough to enter the Cave of Night. Her most loyal guards went first—seven of the strongest and noblest. None returned. Then came soldiers of the Acidalia army. None returned. In desperation, she put out the call to any citizens brave enough to attempt it. Over fifty people entered. All were lost to the darkness.

"People stopped trying, feeling it to be futile. Hope dwindled. The queen's strength declined fast, and her despair deepened. But then, when the night was darkest, a rumbling echoed from the cave, which could be felt throughout the kingdom. She rushed to the entrance and saw something emerging from the darkness. Two figures, a boy and a girl, barely adults. To her surprise, the darkness was dissipating. It flowed and converted itself into an ethereal light, being absorbed by the two.

"The boy was clad in armor that seemed alive, shifting colors as though it were made from light itself. In his hand was a shield that radiated an abyss of light so deep, it could swallow you whole. The girl held a sword in her right hand that blazed orange one second and scarlet the next. In her left was a golden bow that shimmered as if it were crafted from the sun.

"The queen asked, 'Who are you?'

"The girl spoke first. 'My name is Isara. The last thing I remember was falling asleep in my bed. I was called here by a voice in my dreams, and when I woke, I found myself at the cave's entrance.'

"Then the boy spoke. 'I am Drystan. I, too, followed a voice that drew me here.'

"The queen was stunned. The prophecy had spoken of one knight, not two. The boy and girl looked at each other; they had never met, but they felt as though they had always known each other. Tied together by fate. Then, the queen heard a great commotion coming from deep within the cave behind the boy and girl. Many voices echoed from the depths. They turned and saw the people who had entered before them—those thought to be lost to the void—now emerging, all accounted for. The queen felt something she hadn't experienced in a long time: hope.

"The next day, the queen summoned Isara and Drystan. Their armor and weapons had disappeared. The queen's heart sank. 'Where have your gifts from the Cave of Night gone?' she asked.

"'They are not gone,' the boy said.

"'We can summon them at any time,' the girl added.

"The boy's armor materialized out of thin air, spreading across him from head to toe. Then he held out his hand and the shield radiated back into existence. At the same time, the blazing sword and bow of light appeared in the girl's hands. Filled with renewed hope, the queen asked if they would battle the chaos beasts.

"'It is a lot to ask. These beings are incredibly powerful. I can only ask that you attempt this willingly,' the queen said.

"The boy, Drystan, replied, 'We will. We do this because no one else can.'

"The queen said, 'I wish you all the best. I cannot help you. All my power is being funneled to the barrier.'

"'Rest, my queen. We will free you of this burden,' the girl, Isara, told her."

Vella told Cole in great detail about their epic battles with the first two chaos beasts, Leviathan and Ifrit, explaining how the boy and girl worked together as a team, learning to blend attack and defense as one. The boy protected the girl as she dealt damage with her bow, finishing them both off with her blazing sword.

She paused, thinking carefully before continuing. When she began the last part of the story, her tone shifted. This time there was a noticeable lack of emotion in her voice, and her animated gesturing had ceased.

"The final battle, against Bahamut, the dragon of wind and lightning, awaited them. Yet before that battle could begin, the queen's strength finally gave out, and the barrier fell. With the queen dead, Bahamut descended upon the kingdom, ready to destroy all. In a desperate final stand, Isara and Drystan combined their powers, unleashing a beam of light aimed at the dragon. Their final strike pierced the heart of the dragon, and Bahamut fell, defeated.

"Their gifts faded, but they saved Acidalia. The kingdom mourned the loss of the queen who had protected them for so long. Isara and Drystan became the king and queen of Acidalia, living happily ever after. Together, they ushered in an age of peace and prosperity that lasted long after they were gone. The end."

Cole sat seemingly unmoved by the tale, his eyes never leaving the fire. The crackling of the flames was the only sound that filled the silence. After a moment, he turned to Vella, a soft smile spreading across his lips.

"I like your version," he said at last.

12

When I was ten, I snuck into the orphanage cafeteria at night by myself. I ate a lot of cookies. Too many. I made myself sick. Then I took the rest and wrapped them in a cloth to save for later. I hid them behind some books in the common room. This way, if someone found them, they couldn't be traced back to me. The next day, I tried to sneak a few when no one was around. That's when Edgar walked in and saw me. So what did I do? I bribed him. Cookies in exchange for silence, though I doubt he would have ever told anyone. We had a signal. A raised eyebrow meant it was cookie time. Edgar was not known for his subtlety, so we got caught after the fifth time . . . Dammit, Edgar . . . Oh, Edgar . . . what did you do?

—"LEAH #8591"
CHILDREN OF THE PEACEFUL PASSAGE
by Aleister #8990

Late in the afternoon, the sun was descending behind the trees, casting long shadows across the field of grass, where Cole and Vella stood. The clearing lay near the doors, a few hundred meters away. Thick trees hid them from sight.

Vella paced around the edges of the clearing while Cole studied the orb in his hands.

"He isn't coming," Vella scoffed, hurling a rock that clattered against the perimeter wall.

"He'll come," he said.

"Probably still drinking," she muttered, throwing another stone.

Cole pocketed the orb. "He better not be."

Suddenly, hurried footsteps disturbed the foliage in the distance. The steps were quiet, but in the stillness, even the softest sound stood out. They snapped to attention, locking their eyes on the direction the noise was coming from. It was where they expected Edgar to come from, but something told them it wasn't going to be Edgar. Not with how he had been drinking yesterday.

A figure flashed through the line of trees and then emerged. They ran a few extra meters before noticing them. As soon as they did, they skidded to a stop. Vella instinctively stepped behind a tree; Cole stepped forward.

"Oh, Cole!" Alex called.

He was breathing heavily, sweat making his shirt stick to his chest.

"Alex . . . what are you doing?"

"Going for a run. Clear the head. Quieter out this way, no one else around," Alex said, still catching his breath.

"Right. Well, almost no one," Cole stated.

"Yes, true," he said, letting out a half-laugh. He leaned to the side, trying to get a better view of Vella. "Hey, Vella," he called, waving.

She ignored him, taking another half-step behind the tree, her eyes fixed on the ground.

Cole stepped to the side, blocking Alex's view.

"What are you two up to?" Alex asked.

Cole felt his patience waning but thought it would be easier to get rid of Alex by being civil. "Hanging out. Like you said, it's quiet here, no one around," he said, forcing a smile.

"Ah. I see when I'm not wanted." Alex laughed, trying to lighten the mood. "I'm joking. It's all good. I was just passing by anyway. I should get back to it."

He turned to leave the same way he had come, shouting over his shoulder, "See you around!"

"Sure thing," Cole shouted back, giving a half-wave. They listened to his footsteps fade into the distance.

"He never runs around here," Vella said, scowling.

"Yeah," Cole said. "Something's up . . . oh, Leah told me she spoke to him yesterday. Bet it was something she said. She wants me to *talk to him*."

"Uh, tell her to butt out," Vella said, ripping the bark from a nearby tree.

"She means well."

"Whatever," Vella retorted, turning away.

She rarely hid her feelings, so when she tried, it was way too obvious. It was clear this was one of those times. He didn't have to pay attention to notice the jealousy in her tone and body language. He knew she saw it as him taking sides against her. He considered making a playful joke to lighten the mood, but everything about her warned him that now wasn't the time.

They stood in tense silence, waiting. Luckily for Cole, they didn't have to wait long.

Unlike Alex, Edgar approached with no spirit or energy—just a noticeable hobble. Each step was a laborious effort. He winced every few paces, grabbing his head, telegraphing the severity of his hangover.

He didn't stop drinking after we left; that's for sure, Cole thought.

Irritation simmered in Cole, but Vella's frustration was more overt. She shook her head, every gesture laced with impatience.

Edgar grunted and wheezed his way over to them. "Sorry . . . I'm late," he said, taking a seat on the grass.

They joined him, settling down nearby. Vella shot a look of disdain his way, which Edgar caught. He shifted his focus to Cole, attempting to sidestep her glare.

"Well . . ." he began. He cleared his throat, causing him to cough several times.

"Are you all right?" Cole asked.

"Never . . ." He paused, putting a fist to his mouth, puffing his cheeks, taking slow, steady breaths through his nose. "Better."

"Yeah, I can see that," Cole said.

"Right," Edgar said. "Where to begin . . ." The question seemed more directed at himself.

Cole took the opening and asked, "Well, for starters, can you tell us what it was like? What did you see?"

Edgar's face tensed at the question. He took some time to consider it, then finally nodded.

"Let's start with the environment." He unfolded a crumpled piece of paper, smoothing it out on the ground in front of him. They shuffled closer to get a better look.

It was a crude drawing of a rectangle with several notes and spots marked. All the lines were uneven and had been traced over several times.

"Keep in mind, all the details are guesses from a man who thought he was about to die," Edgar said. "The whole area is huge. It stretched hundreds of meters into the distance and maybe a hundred meters wide. I couldn't get a grasp on the ceiling's height; too dark. There are several large pillars scattered around, but there are no other landmarks to speak of. It's all flat. There's a corner at the far end where it emerged from. I doubt it lives in there. Most likely it's contained elsewhere but gets released on cue. I suspect that they designed this place to be a combat arena or feeding pit, if you will."

"You think there's an escape route in there?" Cole asked.

"No chance. Even if there was, you would have to get past it first. It's *quick*. You'd never make it without it catching you. Even with another person creating a distraction, it wouldn't buy you enough time to cover the distance."

A wave of discouragement washed over Cole as he listened to all the details.

What did I expect? he asked himself.

"The whole place is dimly lit, making it hard to see the full area," Edgar continued. "It's filthy, with scattered objects everywhere. There is—"

He paused, grimacing at the thought of the dreadful details, then continued, attempting to skip over that part. "The smell is overwhelming. It physically hurt to breathe. We need to make face masks to at least stop it from being a distraction. The biggest advantages we have are the open space and pillars to create some space between us and it. At least for a few seconds."

"You've given this a lot of thought," Cole said.

"It's all I can think about," Edgar muttered.

"Tell us about *it*," Vella said.

Edgar grabbed at his shoulder without thinking; his breathing grew quicker and shallower. He looked down at his body and slowly withdrew his hand, his eyes darting cautiously around their surroundings.

Cole tried to change the subject. "Maybe tomorrow, Vel."

Vella almost pressed further but caught the warning glare in

Cole's eyes. She rolled her eyes and leaned back where she sat.

"Cole, let's go for a look ourselves."

"No!" Edgar blurted out, almost shouting.

Vella flinched, her eyes flickering.

Edgar swallowed hard and took a couple of deep breaths. "I mean, not yet. You're not ready."

Vella looked at him, perplexed. "Just a small peek. A few seconds," she argued.

Cole couldn't ignore how Edgar's eyes kept darting around. *He's clearly still not right. I better calm Vella down*, he thought. *And . . .*

"No peeking today, Vel. Small steps. Let's just talk for today. Okay?" Cole had almost opened his mouth to shut down Vella before Edgar did. His body trembled, breath coming in ragged bursts. The thought of seeing the Wolf was too much to handle.

Vella shook her head, turning her attention elsewhere in protest.

"One mess-up and we lose our only chance. We need to be careful. We need a plan," Edgar said.

"What do you have in mind?" Cole asked.

"Before anything, we need to be fit and fast before even taking the smallest look."

"We're already in fighting shape," Vella interjected. "You, on the other hand . . ."

"Maybe so, but I doubt you would come anywhere close to how quick it is," he countered.

He's definitely stalling us because he's afraid, but he's right. We can't mess this up, Cole thought. *Some time to breathe and think. That's what we need . . . what Vella needs . . . what I need.*

Vella's patience ran out. "You're a coward."

"I'm trying not to get you killed!" Edgar roared.

Vella recoiled, instinctively wincing. "I've had enough of this. Cole, we don't need him."

She jumped up and walked away, kicking a fallen tree branch as she stormed off.

"Vel," Cole called out. "Dammit."

Cole watched her pass out of sight, choosing not to go after her. He breathed out through his nostrils and turned to Edgar, glaring.

"Can you not yell at her?" It was a statement, not a question. "I know you're right, but be careful with her."

"Cole . . ." Edgar sighed. "Are you sure you want to involve her in all this?"

"I would do it alone if I could. I also know I can't stop her," Cole said. "Pushing her away would only make it worse. Who knows what she would do? We need to look after her. I'll take most of the risk."

Edgar gave a reluctant nod. "I should go apologize."

Cole stood up. "Don't worry about it. I'll talk to her. Edgar . . . why physical training?"

"It's more about discipline. This is life and death, not something we can take lightly. We need time to think through everything carefully and not rush in. Reason over emotion, Cole."

He nodded. "Do you have any ideas for training?"

"Some. I need to do some research."

"Research?"

"Don't worry. Just remember there is no doing this halfway. Tomorrow. Dawn. Here," Edgar said with a stern gaze.

"That's early . . ."

"That's the only way it works. We do it one hundred percent," Edgar insisted.

Cole gave a reluctant nod. "Speaking of one hundred percent," he said, his gaze boring into Edgar. "Remember, no more drinking. You're sober, or we do this without you."

"Sure," Edgar said. "One last thing. Never mention any of this to Leah."

"Wouldn't dream of it. I told her you're helping us repair Vel's place."

Edgar looked at him with a raised eyebrow. "I doubt she bought it."

"I know. I couldn't think of what else to tell her."

"It'll have to do. By the way, you don't have to do this. I can see how you react every time the Wolf is mentioned."

"I can manage."

"I know it can be tough, especially after what happened with your parents."

"I said I can manage."

Edgar sighed. "Alright."

Cole pulled out the orb, holding it up to the light. "How do you think it works?"

"I don't know."

"Why was it in there?"

Edgar stood up and brushed himself off. "I don't know. What does it matter?"

"I'm sure *they* would know about it, but why would they let us keep it?"

Edgar walked away. "Maybe they do. Maybe they don't. Again, what does it matter?"

13

I refuse to chronicle the events of today. But I will say this. In just one day, I've seen both the worst and the best of what people can offer. I almost missed the good because the bad was so horrific. We often take the good for granted, assuming it should be the norm, and it should be. But sometimes, we need to take a step back and appreciate those simple acts of kindness and courage. Otherwise, we risk getting lost in a world of apathy and despair.

—THE FIRST PEOPLE OF EDEN

Journal of Morgan #38

Day 10

Cole wasted no time heading to see Vella after leaving Edgar. Approaching the shed, it was quiet. Too quiet. He scanned the area, but there was no sign of her.

She must be inside, he surmised. *I hope she's okay.*

He knocked on the door. He finished his third knock when a sudden, sharp blow struck his shoulder, making him flinch.

"Hey! Stop." Cole threw up his arms, instinctively protecting his head. No follow-up blow came.

He turned, finding Vella holding her wooden sword, poised to strike again.

"What was that for?"

Vella held a vibrant grin. "Let's train. We don't need him."

Cole rubbed at the aching spot on his back, taking a moment for the pain to recede.

"We do. We can't do this on our own."

Her smile faded. "Who am I talking to?" Vella demanded. "Since when do we need anyone else?"

Cole tried not to get worked up, knowing anger would be counterproductive.

"Since this is no longer a game. This is life and death." He took a long breath. "I was wrong. We can't do this without help. You have to know this."

He wanted to grab her and shout: *Please, Vella, I can't do this yet. I'm not ready! Why can't you see that?*

"Why do we need his help? You saw him. He's useless." She swung her wooden sword at the ground, flicking up a mix of grass and dirt.

"He's the only person to go in and return. Ever. He must know some things that could help."

"So what? We can go look whenever we want."

"Yes, true. But I still think we need him."

"Why?"

Cole sighed. "Fine, we don't need him. But you saw the state he's in."

Vella paused, her expression softening. "What does that have to do with him helping us?"

"I'm worried he might attempt . . . something . . . if we don't look out for him."

"You're worried he's going to . . . try again. That's why you want to keep him around?"

"Yes. For Leah. I know she still cares about him. I can't sit back and let him die. Can you?"

Vella sighed and shook her head. "No . . ."

She paced back and forth, grinding dirt under her heel, looking deflated. "You really think he can be helpful?"

"You never know. It can't hurt to have his experience."

"He's not gonna report us, is he?"

"To Leah? No way."

Vella dropped her head, scrunching her mouth as her cheeks tightened, revealing her dimples. Cole couldn't help but smile a little as he watched her.

"So, he's just our responsibility?"

"For now. Until we know he's safe."

"Fine," she said, looking away.

"Also, go easy on him. You pushed way too hard. You could see how hard it is for him to talk about that stuff."

"What about him?" she argued.

"I already warned him."

She sighed. "All right . . . sorry. I got carried away."

"We can do this. For now, he's with us, but together, you and me, we'll do it. And we'll be free of this place. Forever."

Cole stepped closer, and without hesitation, he placed both hands on her shoulders. He felt her jump and take a half step back. But he didn't budge, looking her dead in the eyes.

"I need you with me. Do you trust me?"

The only other time he had touched her like this was on that terrible day. Which was why she hadn't instinctively pushed him away. The familiarity held her frozen in place. It felt comfortable and safe. As he held her gaze, the memory came flooding back, like a story that had been told to her rather than one she'd lived and endured.

Vella glanced up at the fifteen other empty seats in the classroom, then back down. Her pencil dancing across the paper. The image of a knight emerged, drawn from the pages of the book she'd recently read. Each line, each intricate detail, was carefully crafted. She lamented that she wasn't a better artist, able to do justice to the picture in her head. Outside, she could hear the laughter and shouts of her classmates and other orphans. But it all seemed distant, as if it belonged to a different world—one she wasn't part of.

Now thirteen, she'd once hoped the world might turn in her favor. That it might finally bring her some connection.

It's just around the corner, next year, don't worry, she would tell herself.

Instead, the world had only pushed her further away. Further isolation was all that was gifted to her.

She had made an effort, tired of waiting for things to happen, tired of feeling invisible. After her eleventh birthday, due to an unexpected gift, she'd felt a rare surge of confidence and decided to put herself out there, trying to make friends with some of the younger girls. But it only served to remind her why she never left the small, oppressive box. It suffocated her, but stepping out of it always hurt more.

Over the years, she'd tried many times to break free. To express herself. To connect. And every time, the other kids were there, ready to shove her back into that cramped space. Every attempt to reach out ended the same way. Rejection. Pain.

She stared at the finished drawing, the knight standing tall and proud, his armor and shield gleaming. She left the face blank, but she knew what she saw there.

As she looked around at the other desks, her eyes were drawn to Cole's, with its pen marks and carvings covering its surface. Other children running by broke her attention, their movement interrupting the light filtering through the windows, reminding her that she couldn't delay leaving forever. She would have to face the world outside, the one that always seemed so much more unjust and unfair than the ones in her books.

She sighed. Slipped the drawing into her notebook and stood up. There was nowhere she particularly wanted to go, no one she particularly wanted to see. Cole might be outside, but he was likely with Alex, or off by himself somewhere. The idea of joining him flickered in her mind, but she was quick to dismiss it.

He's had enough trouble because of me, she concluded.

She would go to her room and read—books never judged her.

She walked to her storage space to put away her notebook. Glancing down, she felt her heart race. A folded piece of paper sat inside. She hesitated, every instinct telling her to ignore it, to throw it away without looking. Nothing good ever came from notes addressed to her since they were almost exclusively messages or drawings from bullies. Still, she needed to know. There was a small part of her that still held out hope.

What if . . . ?

With trembling hands, she unfolded the note, one crease at a time. It wasn't a drawing, she realized with a mix of relief and dread.

The fear came from a particularly cruel drawing of her that was posted anonymously in the orphanage common room, titled *The One-Eyed Freak*. It sparked the nickname to spread, used widely to taunt her.

That was when she was ten. Three years later, she would still occasionally receive copycat drawings.

She tried to hide them, because if Cole ever caught wind of it, he went on the warpath and always wound up in trouble.

She took a deep breath and mustered the courage to fully open it. The message was simple: *Meet me behind the boys' dorms after class—Cole.*

Her heart leaped. *Could this be it?*

She found it hard to breathe, a smile creeping across her face despite her best efforts to remain calm.

"No way . . ." she whispered. A giddy squeal escaped her.

She'd heard about notes like this, knew what they usually meant. For a moment, she allowed herself to dream, to believe that it might be her turn.

She rushed out of the classroom, clutching the note in her hand. As she exited the building and stepped into the courtyard, the usual early afternoon buzz greeted her. Younger children played on the swings and climbed the playground equipment. The older ones clustered in groups, playing ball games or chatting among themselves. Her eyes darted around, trying to get her bearings.

"Dammit, I'm late," she cursed under her breath. "He might not still be there. Stupid Vella."

She didn't want to run, didn't want to seem too eager, but her feet moved faster than she intended. Weaving through the buildings, heart pounding in her chest, she pushed past scattered groups of children. When she finally turned the corner to the rear of the boys' dorm, her heart sank.

No one was there.

He'll come, she told herself, but the ache in her chest said otherwise.

She paced back and forth, her hope dwindling with every passing second. After a couple of minutes, feeling defeated, she slumped against the cold brick wall.

From above, she heard hushed voices. Before she could look up, someone whispered, "Now."

A trickle of liquid followed, drenching her from above. A warm wetness soaked into her hair, her clothes, and then the smell hit her. It wasn't water. She coughed and gagged, wiping her face with trembling hands. Above her, laughter erupted.

She looked up, horrified, to see two boys and two girls laughing at her from the windows above. Their faces twisted in cruel delight.

She sprang to her feet, furiously shaking and scrubbing at her clothes and skin in a desperate attempt to get the fluid off, but it was too late. It had already soaked into her clothes, and the stench of urine clung to her, impossible to escape.

"I can't believe she bought it," a voice said through laughter.

Vella's world narrowed to a series of snapshots: the laughter, the mocking faces, the acrid smell. And then, worst of all, a teacher turned a corner, watching the aftermath of the scene unfold. He didn't stop it. Instead, he smiled—a hint of amusement curling at the corner of his lips—before he turned and walked away.

Was he . . . laughing . . . ?

She couldn't move, couldn't think. The laughter continued to ring in her ears, the world spinning away from her as she stood frozen in place. Soaked from head to toe, she trembled as the liquid dripped from her hair.

No one . . . cares . . .

She ran. Voices called out, taunting her.

"Even Cole wouldn't like you, one-eyed freak."

"Loser."

"Die."

"Run, freak, run."

She ran and didn't stop. Beyond the orphanage bounds and into the woods she went, no one caring enough to follow. Where she was going didn't matter. What mattered was getting away.

Not until she reached the far edge of the woods did she finally stop, collapsing against a tree, tears streaming down her face. The smell of urine lingered on her, and her clothes clung uncomfortably to her damp skin. Peeling off her overshirt, she tried to wipe herself clean, but it was no use.

The note slipped out of her pocket and fluttered to the ground. She picked it up, her fingers shaking as she looked at it again.

"It's not even his handwriting . . ." she realized, anger and humiliation washing over her.

Idiot. This is your fault. Why would you think he likes you? Desperate loser . . . freak . . .

Truly alone. She cried. No one heard. No one cared.

It was only as the sun was setting that she looked around to see where she was. All energy and will had drained from her.

She didn't want to go back, didn't want to face anyone, but where else could she go?

Then she saw it: a way out.

She got up and ambled toward it.

All she could see was red, the blood-red of the door in front of her.

Her hand hovered over the glowing scanner next to the door. Ready.

What's the point? she thought. *Just do it. You deserve it. It's better this way.*

"Vel!" a voice called out from a distance, catching her at the edge. She froze.

"Vella! Where are you? Please, Vella!" It was Cole.

"I can't let him find me," she muttered, staring into the void.

Her hand inched closer. "Die . . . one-eyed freak . . ."

"VELLA!"

She jerked her hand back.

The desperation in the voice stopped her, drawing her away. Tears blurred her vision as she backed away from the door. It was calling her, and she had no choice but to follow it.

Head down, she followed the voice like a ghost lost between worlds, numbness closing in around her. Cole found her a moment later, his face pale with worry. He ran to her, pulling her into a tight embrace.

"I'm so sorry," he whispered.

She stood limply in his arms, her voice distant as she said, "I'm covered in . . . what are you doing?"

In response, he held her tighter and said "So?"

After a moment, he let go and grabbed her hand, pulling her. "Come on, let's get you cleaned up."

Her eyes were drawn to his hand and noticed the bruises and dried blood on his knuckles.

"Your hand," she said, voice weak.

Cole stopped and turned, giving her a look at his face, revealing several cuts and bruises.

He took a look down at his hands. "Oh, this."

"And your face . . ."

He ran his fingers along his chin, brushing against a fresh cut. He winced. "This is nothing."

"Did they hurt you?"

With a wide grin, he said, "I made sure Albin and Max couldn't piss for at least a month. You should see them." His voice was brimming with pride. "Though I might've broken my hand. Oh, well. Come on."

Vella felt tears well up again. This time, they were different.

"Hey, it's okay," he said.

She wiped her eyes and shook her head. "I'm fine."

A tight smile followed, and she was grateful she wasn't alone. That someone actually cared.

"Come on, let's get you cleaned up," he said.

But she pulled her hand away. "I'm not going back."

"Oh, we're not going back to the orphanage. I packed my stuff. I doubt they'll take me back anyway. Not after that," he said. "I stashed my bag. I'll get it later."

"Where would we go?"

"I'm going to find Leah so we can stay at her place tonight. We can trust her. Come with me."

Vella shook her head, still trembling. "No," she whispered.

"Vel . . ." Cole paused, thinking for a moment. "Actually, I have an idea. Come on."

He led her to a small, weathered shed. It was nestled down a gentle slope, hidden behind a thick tangle of trees and underbrush. Vines twisted up and through the walls. Grasses pushed up against the base, making it hard to tell where the shed and the ground separated. It felt like part of the woods, reclaimed by nature.

"We'll stay here tonight," Cole said, pushing open the door.

"No one knows about this place."

Vella nodded, following him inside. The shed was dusty, filled with old junk, but it felt safe. Cole left her for several minutes as she stood trembling. He returned carrying a pail of water and with a small bag slung over his shoulder.

"Wash yourself," he said, setting the pail down. "There should be some clothes in here that fit."

She looked up at him, confusion and gratitude warring in her heart.

"Why are you helping me?"

"Why wouldn't I?"

"I'm nothing," she whispered.

"Hey! Never say that," he said, placing both hands on her shoulders. "It's gonna be okay. You're safe. I won't let anything happen to you."

Vella looked into his eyes and, for the first time, believed it. She wasn't alone. Not anymore.

Presently, Vella felt the warmth of Cole's hands on her shoulders, grounding her in reality. Her face grew hot. Unable to hold his gaze, she looked down.

"Do you trust me?"

It was this exact spot where she'd chosen to trust him all those years ago. She had, and what followed had been the best years of her life by far, just the two of them. Faith in him had gotten her this far; she didn't want to doubt him. Other fears also went into her reasoning. Losing the only person that had ever cared about her weighed on her mind. To be alone again scared her unlike anything. No. There was no going back to life without him. It was him or nothing.

"Of course," she said.

Cole smiled, let go and took a half step back. His heel caught on a root. He stumbled, then fell.

As he hit the ground, the orb slipped from his pocket. His hand, bracing the fall, brushed against it.

He gasped and his eyes widened.

Vella stood over him, her hand outstretched.

His gaze locked on her hand.

"Here." Vella reached closer. "Did that hurt? Are you okay?"

He didn't respond, still staring at her hand. At her. Then he shook his head and let out a breath. He pushed the orb back into his pocket and got to his feet, but his eyes stayed fixed on her face.

"What is it?"

He didn't answer. Instead, he leapt forward and wrapped his arms around her.

"Hey! What are—get—uh—" she managed to utter. She didn't thrash or flail. Instead, she fell into reluctant acceptance.

"Now we're even for you hitting me," he said. "I will get us out of here. Depend on it. We're going to leave Eden."

Her resistance faded. Cole could feel the heat radiating from her face. Her arms hung at her sides. She wanted to reach out and touch him but couldn't bring herself to move.

Once upon a time, she'd been held lovingly. Those few times she'd seen her mother as a child, this reminded her of that feeling. Warm and safe. A feeling etched in her body. She couldn't forget such a feeling.

A thought occurred to her: *This isn't so bad.*

Her knight, steadfast behind his impenetrable shield and armor, lingered a moment longer.

"I won't let anything happen to you."

Not long after, Cole told Vella he had to leave to help Leah, but that was just an excuse. He stopped in the privacy of the woods halfway home, doubling over, mind reeling. His hands were shaking. He couldn't breathe. He'd been holding it together around Vella, but now that he was alone, he let it go.

What was that . . . ?

When he had fallen, the orb had slipped from his pocket and touched him. The instant they made contact, a surge of electricity tore through his body.

And then. He was somewhere else.

Dark. Vast. Silent.

The scene shimmered, out of focus. But one figure stood still.

Weapon in hand facing him.

Then everything sharpened.

It was her.

Vella.

Bathed in a soft blue light, she stood just far enough that the darkness blurred her face, yet it was unmistakably her. But she looked older . . .

Her gaze drifted past him, fixed on something else above him.

He tried to move. Tried to call out. But no sound came. He wasn't really there. Just a witness.

Vella braced herself, weapon raised.

Cole felt a fear unlike anything he'd ever known, like he was standing on the edge of death. A raw, primal terror surged through him, mixed with rage and adrenaline.

It didn't make sense. Why was he feeling this way?

Then it clicked: these weren't his emotions. They were hers.

An enormous foot stepped into view, spiked, heavy. Inhuman.

And suddenly, he understood.

The Wolf!

Everything happened at once.

He couldn't stop it. Couldn't move. Couldn't scream. Couldn't close his eyes or look away.

He watched, paralyzed, as the Wolf lunged.

And pierced her.

Blood spilled.

He felt it. The pain. The staggering loss of mind and body.

Then it all snapped away.

He gasped, finally able to breathe again. His eyes flew open.

Vella stood over him, her hand outstretched.

He remembered staring at her, terrified, but elated that she was alive.

The helplessness of being unable to reach her as she died had overwhelmed him. He needed to feel her, to make sure she was real. So he grabbed her and held her tight.

Presently, he tried to make sense of it.

What was that? Vella . . . she . . .

He'd daydreamed before. Even had vivid dreams. But nothing compared to that.

This had weight. This felt real. What he saw felt real. The pain felt real.

He took the orb from his pocket and stared at it. The sensation as it touched him. That was new.

Is that . . . was that . . . the future? No. Can't be. But . . .

He sat down and put his head in his hands.

I won't let that happen, he told himself. *That will never happen.*

14

Early on, I had a strange feeling about some of the people here. Many faces felt familiar. A few were too familiar. Laura's was one of those few. I felt like I'd known her before this place. Not just in passing, but as though I truly knew her. The first time I spoke to her, it felt like picking up a long-lost conversation. It took me far too long to work up the nerve. The thought of her rejecting me felt unbearable. There was a possibility between us, and I was terrified speaking to her would destroy it. Now a new, worse fear has replaced it. All I think about is the day I lose her, and it scares me more than anything. Even my own death pales in comparison.

—THE FIRST PEOPLE OF EDEN

Journal of Morgan #38

Day 250

No sparring session with Vella had ever left Cole this drained. Each step on his way home made muscles ache that he didn't even know existed. He knew things would only get worse—a lot worse—and there was no avoiding it. This was the path he'd chosen, and the point of no return felt long gone.

He groaned, stepping over a log. The physical pain he could deal with. The real issue was the tightness in his chest and stomach. It had become almost unmanageable over the past few days, after everything that had happened and with the knowledge of what lay ahead. He could feel it threatening to break him.

He wondered which would break first—the dread or his resolve. How easy it would be to just give up . . . Then he remembered what the orb had shown him yesterday. He didn't know what to make of it. Was it showing him the future? Something else? Regardless, it reminded him there was no yielding. The only direction he had was forward.

He craved solitude, some semblance of peace, and his only escape was work. He threw himself into it, hoping to wear out his body enough to burn off the physical symptoms of stress. Maybe it would quell the anxieties inside him that he had no real understanding of how to manage. But so far, it wasn't working.

The morning session had been brutal. Edgar had explored the library for physical fitness books, finding the most useful information in a soccer guide, particularly in the section on agility training. Vella and Cole were fond of the game. They had their own worn, makeshift ball and would spend hours volleying it back and forth without letting it touch the ground, never content until they set a new record. Their skills were decent, but they'd never played an actual game. In secret, they wanted to, but they wouldn't admit it, not even to each other. Now, doing drills designed for a game they would never play themselves was tough to stomach. All baking and no cake didn't sit well with them.

Edgar had explained that speed and agility would be their greatest assets for what was to come. He'd come up with a series of ten drills to do one after the other. He started them on two drills that day, using makeshift cones made of paper as markers. It didn't look professional, but it did the job. They did the two drills, followed by a minute's rest, sprint, and rest. After they finished that, they repeated the process.

Vella vehemently protested Edgar's nonparticipation, and after much argument, he conceded, joining them. Cole couldn't help but worry that Vella took a little too much pleasure in watching Edgar struggle.

And struggle he did. He was nowhere near as active as the other two, and it showed. After only a couple of rounds, his face had turned sickly pale and he seemed on the brink of passing out.

They trained for about an hour. By the end, Edgar was sprawled out on the grass, looking like he was knocking on death's door. His eyes seemed to fade in and out of consciousness. Vella watched on, no longer laughing, struggling to conceal her own shaking legs. She tried to lower herself to the ground as if she were trying to casually sit down and not because she could barely stand.

They had done nothing like it before, and their muscles made sure they knew it. Heavy with fatigue, they departed. Edgar struggled to bring himself upright, pausing to tell them there would be a second training session in the afternoon, after work. Cole winced at this. Not for his sake, but knowing Vella wouldn't take it well. And she did not. She didn't complain with words, but if looks could kill, then Edgar had suffered another brush with mass destruction.

The afternoon session was much lighter, focusing on upper-body strength. Push-ups, sit-ups, and exercises using tree branches Edgar had found. He had planned more leg training, but that wasn't possible in their current condition. It would be slow progress, he told them.

Presently, Cole ambled home after the session, contemplating Edgar's fitness program. *We don't need it, but it can't hurt to follow it. No rush. There are worse things than a little delay.* Then he thought about how he had struggled to do three sprints in a row. *It might be for the best . . .*

Cole, perhaps without realizing it, was more than happy with slow. Every part of him wanted to postpone the moment he'd have to face the Wolf for as long as possible. They still had time. Leah wouldn't turn thirty for a while.
But that time was a double-edged sword. The longer he delayed, the harder it would be to act. The higher the wall of anxiety would grow.

As he approached the front door—ready to eat anything and everything—he could hear the muffled sounds of conversation inside. He wanted nothing more than to avoid forced conversation with any of Leah's friends.

He struggled up the steps, pushed open the door, and braced himself.

"Cole. Hey."

This is worse than I could've ever imagined.

Alex sat at the kitchen table, in the middle of a lively conversation with Leah, who was managing two boiling pots.

Cole considered turning and leaving. Another consideration was grabbing the orb from his room and avoiding the interaction altogether. But then when would he eat? His throbbing hunger won, and he accepted his fate.

"Alex. What are you . . . ?" He trailed off, looking at Leah, who gave him a stern look.

"I invited him over for dinner. Ellie's working late at the hospital. Hope you don't mind."

It wasn't the first time Leah had invited Alex over for dinner, and Cole had managed to avoid him every time.

"Of course I don't mind," Cole said, forcing a smile.

He slumped into the chair at the far end of the table, doing his best to hide the involuntary wince as his sore muscles strained to lower his body. He didn't want to attract questions. Not with these two.

"Dinner's almost ready," Leah said.

Cole stared down at the table, hoping his existence would go unnoticed. He had no intention of initiating conversation. Unfortunately for him, he knew he didn't need to.

"Alex was telling me that he applied to be deputy mayor," Leah said, her tone upbeat, attempting to get Cole enthused.

"That's . . . great," Cole said.

Leah, standing behind Alex, shook her head, her eyebrows raised, motioning for him to say more.

"That's really good. I'm sure you'd make a terrific deputy," Cole added, a slight improvement in his tone.

Not enough, though. Leah looked up in disappointment, then returned to the kitchen counter.

"Thanks. Two others in the office have applied. But I think I have a decent shot," Alex said.

"I'm sure you'll get it," Leah assured him. "Then you'll be mayor in no time."

"And then Leah can fulfill her dream of controlling the dispenser schedules from the shadows," Cole said.

"About time," Leah said. "Because Alex understands I know what's best for Eden."

Alex chuckled. "You know I have to be impartial."

There was a brief, uncomfortable pause in the conversation. Leah gave Cole a wide-eyed look, pointing her head at Alex. Cole flicked his eyes to the ceiling and back to Alex.

"So, why do you want to be mayor?" Cole asked, unable to

think of what else to say.

He shrugged. "To help people. To make a difference."

"Help people?" Cole said with a wry grin. "And who are these people you'll be helping?"

Leah cut in. "Everyone. Helping everyone and make this place better. Isn't that right?"

Alex just smiled and nodded.

She served up their plates and took a seat. Life was treating Alex well. He had much of what you could hope for in Eden: a fulfilling job in the community, a loving partner, and respect from his peers. The more he talked, the more Cole grew tense. Anger simmered within him. Perhaps it was envy, but he would never admit that to himself.

"Alex has all these wonderful ideas he was telling me about," Leah said. "He'll really change things. Tell Cole."

"You're too kind. I don't want to get ahead of myself; I haven't even gotten the position yet. Enough about me. How are you, Cole?"

Cole labored through telling Alex about his life and work, trying to avoid mentioning Vella. Not much ever changed in Eden, and anything new, Alex likely already knew through Leah.

"Vella's well?" Alex asked.

He couldn't resist . . .

Cole gritted his teeth. "She is well," he said.

Leah jumped in. "She came out for my twenty-ninth birthday party. I'm so proud of her."

"That's wonderful. I do remember seeing her that night. What an amazing night it was," Alex said. "Amy's growing up so fast. She's adorable."

The mention of Amy caused Cole's stomach to clench. No one else would dare bring her up so casually. Leah was like a mother to Alex, as she was to Cole. She'd known him for as long as she'd known Cole, back when Cole and Alex were inseparable. Even after the two of them stopped speaking, Leah kept visiting him at the orphanage, wanting to keep an eye on him. Years later, they worked near each other in the town center, where they bumped into each other almost daily, making time to share the gossip of their lives.

Leah cleared her throat, choking up. "She is, isn't she?"

"I heard from the staff at the orphanage that she's quite the smart cookie," Alex said.

"She must get that from Edgar," she said with a small laugh.

"And very vocal."

"She definitely gets that part from me."

Leah and Alex shared a laugh, while Cole looked at his plate, smiling, thinking of a little Leah running around scolding the other children.

Alex took a long pause and cleared his throat. "There's something I want to tell you both." His face had a look of dejection, like he'd had a bucket of cold water dumped on him. Alex braced himself as if he were delivering bad news.

"Ellie's pregnant," he announced, wearing a smile that felt forced to Cole.

Ellie was seven years Alex's senior. The age gap had never seemed to bother them or bring many sideways glances from others in the community.

"Oh my! That's wonderful." Leah reached out and grabbed his hand.

"Yes, it is," he stated.

"Congratulations," Cole said, attempting a genuine smile.

"How far along is she?" Leah asked.

"Not far. We pretty much just found out."

It's good news. Why does he look so worried? Cole wondered.

"I'm so excited for both of you," Leah said. "What a week. Ellie's twenty-eighth birthday in a few days, a soon-to-be deputy mayor, and now finding out you're going to be a father."

Alex didn't share Leah's excitement; instead, he looked more despondent.

"Twenty-eight," Alex muttered under his breath.

A couple of hours later, Alex announced he was leaving. He explained that Ellie would be finishing up her shift at the hospital soon, and he wanted to have dinner ready for her when she got home.

"She's lucky to have you," Leah said.

Cole glanced sideways at her. "You jealous? Remember, he likes older women, so you might have a shot," he teased.

"Shut up." She slapped Cole's shoulder, which made Alex chuckle. Cole's expression shifted from playful to stern upon hearing Alex's laughter.

"See him out, Cole," Leah instructed. She hugged Alex goodbye and sent them out the front door.

She wants us to be alone. Wonderful, Cole lamented.

The soft light of the street shineballs guided them to the street. Cole trailed several steps behind Alex.

After doing his duty, Cole turned to go back inside, but Alex stopped him.

"I want in," he whispered.

Cole whirled around. "What?"

"I know about Edgar," Alex said, keeping his voice low.

Cole's body stiffened. *How does he know about Edgar?* His eyes narrowed as understanding dawned on him.

"You were spying on us?" Cole accused. "I should've known better. *Going for a jog,* were you?"

"Leah asked me to keep an eye on you, so I did. She's worried," Alex admitted without a hint of guilt.

"Unbelievable," Cole muttered, kicking the ground in frustration.

"Look, I'm not telling Leah anything. I want in, whatever your plan is," Alex said.

Cole glanced back at the house, then at Alex. Without a word, he walked down the street, motioning for Alex to follow.

Once they were beyond the streetlights, at the edge of the woods, Cole stopped. They were far enough to speak freely.

"There's nothing to be a part of," he stated, glaring.

Alex didn't flinch. "I heard everything. I know Edgar knows what's inside the doors, and it has something to do with that orb. It's a lot more than nothing," Alex said, his voice firm.

"Are you kid—" Cole broke off and a series of frustrated grunts and curses escaped him. He took a deep breath. "You heard nothing. You hear me?"

Alex just stared at him, unblinking.

"Goddammit!"

"I'm not going to tell anyone. Let me help," Alex pleaded.

"Why would we do that? Why would we even want you around?" Cole spat, any facade of politeness now long gone.

"Why do you hate me so much?" Alex finally asked, his voice tinged with years of unspoken pain.

It had been many years since they'd talked openly, ever since the day Cole had left the orphanage at thirteen. Seven long years of silence and simmering resentment had pushed them further apart.

"Why? Why?" Cole's voice rose with each repetition. "You act like this nice stand-up guy, but I know who you really are. How you really treat people."

"Vella?"

Cole clenched his fists and stepped closer, ready to hit him the moment he heard him utter her name.

"You never could forgive me for putting up that drawing, could you? But who was it that made the drawing?" Alex accused, his voice steady.

A flash of the memory of ten-year-old Vella's heartbroken face, streaked with tears, entered Cole's mind. And before he knew it, his fist connected with Alex's jaw. Alex took the blow without flinching, holding the side of his face and feeling for damage.

"Get the hell out of here," Cole warned, his voice low and dangerous.

Alex held his ground. "Did you ever tell her it was you?"

Cole clenched his jaw. "Leave."

"Of course you didn't."

Cole took another step forward, ready to strike again. "I made a mistake. You? You're just an asshole. What did you care? Everyone loved you. You could've stopped her bullying. Yet you made it worse."

"I-I was just a dumb kid. I'm sorry she had a rough time."

"Are you? I bet you still laugh at her with all the others. Her last day . . . I bet you got a kick out of that."

"Of course not. That was vile. It still makes me mad thinking about it."

Cole's anger faltered as he saw the sincerity in Alex's eyes.

"I'm not your enemy here," Alex pressed.

Turning his back on Alex, Cole asked, "How can I trust you to be around her?"

"I know you're trying to protect her, but I wouldn't do anything to hurt her. I never was that person. I may not have been there to stop things from getting out of hand, but I'm not capable of . . . do you think that little of me?"

He didn't answer.

"Look, let me talk to her. If she doesn't want me around, I'll stay away," Alex said.

Cole exhaled slowly and turned to face him. "I don't get it. You must understand what we're trying to do. Why would you want to join us?"

He studied Alex's face and saw the torment written all over it. Thinking about earlier in the night, he knew why.

"Ellie?"

Alex nodded.

"She's going to die soon, Cole," Alex said. "Two years. Two more years and she's . . . gone. Just like that. I know you want to protect Vella. And Leah. You're not the only one with people to save. If there's something I can do, I'll do it. I owe Leah that much as well."

Cole was moved to stunned silence. The sincerity in Alex's voice was undeniable. Cole had rehearsed this conversation in his head many times. None had ever gone like this. All these years, he had held on to hate he could no longer grasp.

"I can't imagine life without her. There is none. I'd rather die. I'll beg if I have to. Please."

"You're actually serious about this?"

"Very," Alex replied. "And I'm sorry I put up the picture in the common room. Truly. I hate myself every day for what she went through."

"Dammit, Alex," Cole muttered. He wanted to keep hating him, but now he didn't know what to think. He felt completely disarmed by his vulnerability. His mind whirled, seeing Alex—someone he had thought was impervious to adversity—standing before him, desperate and broken.

"Do you have any idea what we're trying to do?"

"Yes."

"You could die," he warned.

"I know. I don't care."

"This isn't a trick, is it?"

Alex shook his head. Cole mirrored the gesture, but in disbelief.

"Okay. Fine," Cole said. "Dawn. You already know where we meet."

"Thank you, Cole."

"But it's up to Vella. You're not in yet. First thing you do tomorrow is talk to her."

"You want me to apologize?"

"Couldn't hurt. Say you're sorry for how she was treated at the orphanage."

"But I didn't—"

"I know, just say it anyway. It would go a long way to make her feel better. And, who knows, she might even let you stay."

"All right. I will."

"Don't make me regret this," Cole said. "Actually, I already do. Can you let this go and pretend you heard nothing today?"

"I can't."

Cole shook his head and took a step back to leave but stopped. "Sorry about hitting you."

Alex touched his jaw. "Don't worry. Barely hurt. You've gone soft from being away from the chaos of the orphanage."

Cole forced a smile. "I still don't get it. Since when did you become so . . ."

"Reckless?"

"Yeah."

"Some things are too important to sit back and play it safe. You of all people know that."

They parted ways. At the front door, Cole watched Alex. He tried to compose himself as he walked past, disappearing into the night.

Cole paused, hand on the doorknob, as a heavy weight settled on his shoulders. Regret. Not for Alex, but for Vella.

The drawing . . . he had to bring it up. Should I finally tell her? Maybe it's time . . . no. She can't know.

15

My dad loved to cook. For my mom's birthday, he wanted to go all out and used most of his credits to buy a massive chicken, well, massive to a seven-year-old. He planned on cooking it in the backyard, and I thought I'd help by carrying it outside. But it was a heavy-ass chicken, and I dropped it in the mud. He didn't get mad. Instead, he laughed and that made me laugh. He even let me carry the new chicken home from the store . . . It might sound dumb, but I feel like they've been watching over me my whole life. Even death gives me something to look forward to—seeing them again. I can't tell you why. I have no proof. It's just something I've always believed.

—"ELLIE #8621"

CHILDREN OF THE PEACEFUL PASSAGE

by Aleister #8990

Click.

Cole jolted awake, his heart pounding. His sheets clung to him, soaked with sweat. He shot up and jumped out of bed, ignoring the pull of his overworked muscles.

"Where is it?"

He tore through the clutter of clothes, books, and junk scattered across his bedroom floor. It was still dark, and the faint glow of the approaching sunrise wasn't enough for him to see things clearly. The lack of visibility only heightened the pressure, fueling his rising panic.

"Where. Is. It!"

Finally, his hands grasped the orb buried deep in his closet, exactly where he'd left it. He held it to his chest, feeling how cool and reassuring it was to touch.

He exhaled, burying his head in his hands.

What happened?

Fragments of the nightmare clung to his mind. Those glowing eyes. Bodies everywhere. Vella lying dead. Blood, blood, blood. He shook his head, trying to dispel the images.

It's not real. Not real. Everything's fine.

It took him a while to compose himself and dress. His breathing remained labored. The images lingered in his mind. His legs, stiff and aching, made bending them to put on pants feel like a monumental task.

The first light of dawn crept into Eden as he trudged toward the clearing. The patches of bare ground were soft and squishy beneath his feet from the early-morning rain. Above him, the faint call of sparrows filled the air, mingling with the soft hum of insects.

He moved on autopilot, exhausted. He figured he would be the last one to arrive, considering how long it took him to walk a hundred meters.

When he reached the edge of the clearing, he scanned the borders of the wide expanse and saw no one.

He stood waiting, eyes half-open, his arms crossed high. Moments later, Vella appeared, dragging her feet, shoulders slumped.

I'm glad I'm not the only one feeling like shit, he thought.

He offered her a weary smile. She returned one in kind.

"So sore," Vella groaned.

She leaned against a nearby magnolia for support and slid down to the ground, her back pressed against the rough bark, a faint smile creeping onto her face as she got comfortable. It warmed him to see her smile at something so simple.

Edgar hobbled into view not long after. It took him a while to reach them. When he did, Cole raised a hand, signaling Edgar to give Vella a moment. Edgar was more than happy to oblige, collapsing onto the ground with a heavy sigh as his eyes closed on their own.

Cole paused, absorbing the moment of peace, a brief respite from the chaos of the past few days. The world stopped for a brief moment as no one moved a muscle and the slow movement of nature took center stage. Minute details became loud, important, earth-shattering events. A single drop of moisture from a leaf above landed on his shoulder, connecting him to the flow of nature around him. Each breath rose and fell with the pace of his surroundings. Effortless.

And he thought: *If only everything were this easy. I wish things could stay like this . . . not like the disaster that was yesterday . . . yesterday. Oh no.*

Cole's stomach dropped as the memory of last night surged back.

"Guys . . . there's a slight problem," he said.

Vella opened one eye, observing him with caution.

He braced himself. "We . . . uh . . . have someone else joining us."

Edgar sat up, shooting Cole a sharp, stern look. "Cole," he warned, adopting the tone of a parent reprimanding a child.

"Alex *may* have been spying on us yesterday."

Edgar let out a weary, annoyed groan, too exhausted to gather the energy to yell. "How much does he know?"

Cole shrugged. "Enough."

"What does he want?" Edgar asked, struggling to pull himself up.

Vella was wide awake to the news. Without him noticing, she blindsided him with a shove, knocking him off balance. "What the hell?"

"I didn't have a choice," he snapped.

Edgar repeated, "What does he want?"

"He says he wants to join us. I don't know."

Vella glared at Cole, threatening to do more than push him.

"Do you trust him?" Edgar asked.

Cole shrugged. "He seemed genuine. Trust? Not sure."

"Goddammit, Cole."

Alex came into view from around the tree line. He waved. No one waved back.

"Morning," he called out with a smile.

Cole shook his head. *Even at this hour, he still manages to find a way to be . . . him. Even his clothes are neat, hair perfect. This guy . . .*

They all watched him approach with no smile on their faces; Vella's gaze was particularly icy.

Edgar took a few steps toward Alex. "You want to join us, is that right?"

"I do," Alex said.

"Do you have the faintest idea of what you're signing up for?"

Alex nodded, unshaken.

"You do understand it means putting your life at risk?"

"Gladly," he said, meeting Edgar's gaze without flinching.

Edgar shook his head, a dark chuckle escaping him. "Why?"

"I have someone I want to protect."

Edgar glanced at the other two. Vella had turned her back, while Cole looked indifferent.

"For the love of . . . any more surprises?" he asked, glaring at Cole, his eyes filled with disdain. Cole avoided his eyes. Edgar turned back to Alex. "Does anyone else know?"

"No," Alex assured him.

"I don't know about them, but I'm not okay with this," Edgar said. "But I couldn't stop them. I doubt I can stop you." He walked off, muttering to himself, finding a log to sit on. He stared at the ground, deep in thought.

Alex looked past Cole to Vella. "Hey, Vella. Can I talk to you alone?"

She hesitated, glancing at Cole for reassurance. He nodded.

"W-what for?" she asked, her voice trembling.

"I need to tell you something. Just you, though."

She eyed him warily before looking back at Cole. "What is this?"

Cole gave her a reassuring smile. "It's okay."

His assurance did little to change her expression. "No."

Cole took her aside. "Trust me. It's all right. Give him one minute. Just one."

"Whatever. Fine," she conceded.

Alex led the way deeper into the woods. Vella trailed behind at a distance. Alex stopped when they were out of earshot. Cole watched with intent, anxiety gnawing at him.

"What's this about?" Edgar called out.

Cole ignored him, his attention fixed on Vella. He was just far enough away that he couldn't quite read her face. *Don't mess this up, Alex!*

He watched as what he thought was confusion spread across

her face. Then, abruptly, she took a step back, her expression shifting to one of shock. Moments later, she shook her head violently before turning and running off.

"Dammit," Cole muttered, sprinting toward Alex.

When he reached him, Alex stood there looking defeated.

"What happened? What did you say?" Cole demanded.

He sighed. "I tried to apologize. She thought I was messing with her," Alex said. "I guess I don't blame her. Sorry."

"It's all right. I'll go talk to her. Go see Edgar. He can bring you up to speed," Cole said. "I should've seen this coming."

He looked back toward Edgar, who was already walking off. "Actually, go home. I'll catch you up this afternoon. Same spot."

Not waiting for Alex to respond, Cole took off after Vella.

He found her pacing frantically in front of her place. The moment he arrived, she rushed over and shoved him to the ground.

"What the hell was that?" she yelled.

He tried to keep his voice calm and steady. "He's sorry. He isn't playing a prank."

She shook her head, still pacing. "Why did you bring him?"

He pushed himself up off the ground and dusted himself off. "Like I said, he wanted to apologize. I know you have every right not to trust him."

"Are you in on it?" she accused.

"In on what? There's no trick," he said.

"I don't believe you," she yelled.

She was getting more manic by the second. Cole knew he needed to intervene and fast. He jumped in front of her pacing. He placed a hand on her arm. She swatted it away.

"Stop," he pleaded, trying to meet her eyes. "Look at me. Believe me when I say he's being sincere."

She looked away, trying to avoid his gaze, but he wouldn't let her.

"Hey. It's me. Come on."

Her expression finally softened. "He's really not messing with me?"

"You're safe," he assured her.

"He's sorry?"

He nodded. "He is."

She backed away, her demeanor much calmer. She turned away, hesitated, and then turned back, eyes cast down.

"Do you remember that drawing? The one that got put up about me when we were ten?"

Cole felt a sharp contraction in his chest. He nodded, dreading where this was going.

"The one that made everyone start calling me the one-eyed freak?"

Cole swallowed hard. "What about it?"

"He told me he made it and put it up."

And he thought: *He took the blame for me? Why bring it up at all? What was he thinking!*

A wave of nausea washed over him. The guilt was almost too much to bear. He had to get it out now, or it would eat at him forever.

"No. He didn't. I—"

Stop! an internal voice screamed. Another voice rose: *She deserves to know the truth. You can't keep going on like this.*

He trembled as he spoke. "I did it."

The words escaped his lips almost on their own. Now it was out. There was no going back.

There was almost no physical reaction to the words. "What do you mean?"

"I did it. I drew the picture. Alex put it up. I didn't mean—"

Her face drained of all color, and her mouth fell open as she struggled to process what he had said.

"What? Can't . . . be . . . y-you? Is that a joke?"

He could say nothing.

"Tell me you're joking. Say you're joking."

He could only shake his head, his guilt plastered on his face. He left no doubt, yet . . .

"Say it! Say you're joking!" she yelled, almost begging.

Again, he shook his head.

"You . . . ? You did it? I-I don't believe it." Her eyes flickered. She felt as if her whole world was slipping away.

"I-it's not what you think," he said. He could feel his own world slipping away, powerless to do anything.

The weight of his words sank in. "How could you? I thought you were different," she said, her voice weak and distant.

"I'm sorry. Every day I regret it. I hate myself for doing that to you."

"I thought you cared."

"Of course I do. You know I do."

Vella shook her head, feeling like she was stuck in a bad dream, numb to everything around her.

"You? You called me the one-eyed freak. That's where it started. Everyone called me that because of that drawing. Every . . . single . . . day. Why would—" She stopped, still processing the revelation.

"Go away," she whispered.

"Vel . . ."

"I trusted you."

"I'm so sorry."

"Go away!" she screamed.

A wild panic gripped Cole, his hands shaking as he struggled to think. He'd left the orb at home. There was no redoing this moment, no second chance. He was teetering on the edge of a precipice, and he couldn't afford to fall. *I can't lose her now. Not now, not after everything.*

"I'm not going anywhere . . . because . . . because . . . I love you," he blurted out, the words escaping before he could stop them.

Vella froze. Her eyes went wide, breath catching in her throat.

Cole stood motionless, as if time itself had come to a standstill. The words lingered between them, thickening the air with unspoken emotion.

Why did I say that? Cole shouted within.

They stood in awkward silence, both scrambling to make sense of what had been said.

Finally, Vella spoke, her voice trembling and fragile. "You do?" she asked. Her gaze fixed on the ground.

"You know I do. I would never do anything to hurt you."

"Then why did you do it?"

"I was a dumb kid. I didn't know any better." *Dammit, I sound like Alex*, he realized. He shook his head. "Actually, there is no excuse. I'm sorry. For everything."

"Has it all been a lie? Is that why you stuck around? Because you feel bad for me? Have the last ten years meant nothing to you? Was it all just pity?" she accused.

"No. Of course not." Then, without thinking, he said, "I mean it. I love you more than anything. I can't live without you."

What are you doing, Cole? his mind screamed, but the words were out, irreversible.

Before he could say anything else, she turned and ran inside, slamming the door behind her.

"Vella?" Cole called, his voice barely above a whisper.

He stood there staring at the door as time slowed to a crawl.

A drop of moisture from a leaf above landed on his shoulder. He had never felt so disconnected from the world. Everything had never felt so difficult. Even drawing a single breath felt impossible.

What have I done . . . ?

Vella lay curled up on her bed, staring at the wall an inch from her face. No tears came. She didn't know how or what to feel. The only thing she did feel was numbness and a bottomless pit in her stomach.

Her mind replayed the scene from that day, over and over, like a scab she couldn't stop picking at, keeping the pain flowing.

She walked into the common room to find a huddle of kids, snickering and whispering, their eyes fixed on something on the notice board above. She edged closer to get a glimpse of what they were looking at. Peering past another child, she saw it.

A cruel caricature of her. It was drawn with exaggerated features, with large letters scrawled across the top: *The One-Eyed Freak.*

Her mind went blank.

Several kids turned and noticed her.

"Hey, look! It's the one-eyed freak," one boy exclaimed.

More heads turned to look at her. Then came the laughter. Shouts of the mocking name and rising laughter rippled through the throng.

Vella stood frozen, her throat tightening as the tears welled. Snapping to action, she shoved her way through the crowd, reaching up to tear it down, but it was too high. In desperation, she tried jumping to grab it, but her fingers couldn't even brush the bottom edge, leaving it just out of reach.

The laughter only intensified as they began chanting the name. Tears blurred her vision and prevented her from seeing the drawing she was reaching for.

It was too much. She had to get out.

Turning, she shoved her way through the crowd, pushing past the tormentors. On her way out of the common room, she bumped into Cole at the door and pushed past him. She kept running until she reached her room, slamming the door behind her.

She collapsed in the corner of the room, sobbing uncontrollably.

After some time, the tears stopped, but the pain was still tender and raw. She sat huddled in the corner, her eyes far away.

There was a knock at the door. She flinched, curling up tighter into herself. Another knock came, but she remained silent, hoping they would go away.

The door creaked open, and someone stepped inside.

She squeezed her eyes shut, bracing for more ridicule. When nothing came, she glanced up to see who it was. It was Cole standing at the door.

His voice was soft. "Vella. Are you okay?" he asked.

She said nothing.

"I'm sorry about the drawing. I took it down." He took a half step back. "If anyone calls you that again, I'll make sure they regret it," he said with venom in his voice.

He lingered, his hand hanging on the doorframe. "It looks nothing like you," he said. Then he was gone.

He did that. That same person. My Cole did that.

Someone had once told her, months after it had happened, it was Cole who'd done the drawing, but at the time, she'd refused to believe it. *They're just messing with you*, she'd told herself. It wasn't possible. Not him. He was the only one who ever seemed to care. If that was possible, that he could do such a thing—what was the point? There was nothing else. Every day she suffocated under the weight of her tortured existence, and he was the one light that kept her going.

But there was one thing she had quietly buried, something she'd never let herself fully consider: the handwriting of the title. Written in all uppercase letters: *THE ONE-EYED FREAK.*

Then, one day years later, he was writing a list of what she wanted from the town store. She watched his hand move, the letters in all uppercase, and it clicked.

The image she'd tried to repress surged back into her mind. She'd never paid attention to the title before, to the way it was written. But the letters were the same. The handwriting matched the heading on that drawing.

Suddenly, it was all she could see.

There was no more denying it.

She didn't speak to him for a week. She didn't tell him why. She didn't know if she could ever talk to him again. Definitely not ask him about it. The last thing she wanted was to hear him confirm it out loud.

But after days of hiding away in her shed, she came out in the middle of the night to use the restroom and found him huddled under the oak tree, asleep. She had heard him out there every day during that time. Waiting for her.

She looked at him lying there and knew, with painful certainty, that she would never find anyone else who cared like he did. Maybe never find anyone who cared at all. And that thought scared her more than anything. To be alone again.

So she decided: even if he had done it, no one had ever tried so hard to make up for wronging her—or even tried at all. Deep down, she knew the drawing wasn't the cause of her pain in the orphanage. The other children were. With or without it, not much would have changed.

She swept a blanket over him and went back inside.

Over the years, she still thought about it, and every so often, a rare wave of anger toward him would rise. She never fully accepted it. She asked herself constantly why he stayed. Was it guilt? When she finally asked him, "Why do you hang around me?" he looked thrown off but simply answered, "Do I need a reason?" It didn't ease her doubts. How could anyone possibly like her?

So she kept pressing those doubts down. Eventually, she found ways to forgive him by rationalizing it however she could. *It was a mistake. Someone made him do it. He clearly regrets it. It wasn't that bad.* Whatever she needed to tell herself. In the orphanage, he had defended her, over and over, getting into trouble on her behalf. Found her safety. He brought her what she needed from town. He kept her company. And one day, without even knowing it, he saved her. Regardless, she felt she owed him her life—on the days she believed that her life had value.

She couldn't sustain hatred toward him. So she chose to let it go. Pretend it never happened.

The gnawing doubts about why he was still around haunted her. On her worst days, she told herself it had to be guilt. That was why he stayed. Not love. Not choice. Just guilt.

But now, with Alex and then Cole finally admitting to the drawing, something visceral broke open inside her. Her mind flooded with the pain of those days in the orphanage. It was too much. She didn't know how to process it all. It became real. Too real. And at the same time, not real at all, the whole exchange between them felt like she was never in control.

But eventually, the storm of memories quieted, and she could think with some clarity. She focused on the part that mattered most—his words. The way he said them. The way he looked at her.

His words played in her mind: *I love you more than anything. I can't live without you.*

She'd dreamed of hearing those words from him for as long as she could remember. But not like this.

The drawing taunted her: *This is how he really sees you. As a freak.*

She wrestled endlessly with the conflicting truths. There was one reality. But the doubts were so deeply rooted, she couldn't shake them.

But what if he was telling the truth? She could feel her heart racing. *You have to do something.*

A chorus of familiar voices fought inside her head.

One voice said: *Why would he love you?*

Another said: *Of course he cares about you and loves you.*

The loudest voice said: *No one could love someone as hideous as you. He only pities you.*

Cole walked right past Leah, who was standing by the hallway door.

"What happened to you? You look like death," she teased.

He ignored her, heading straight to his room and collapsing onto his bed.

Cole pressed his face into the pillow, letting out a muffled scream. This was the day he'd feared the most. His mind whirled, torturing him with the image of Vella brushing past him. Those eyes filled with devastation as she ran out of the common room. The distress on her face had followed him everywhere since that day, permanently pressed into his mind's eye. Forcing its way into his head almost daily.

Knowing he was responsible for all her pain and suffering tore him apart. He had given himself no respite since, doing everything he could to try and make up for it. But deep down, he knew there was no making up for it. He'd ruined her life, and nothing could convince him otherwise.

It had all started hours before Vella saw the drawing. Cole and Alex were holed up in their room, admiring Cole's artwork. They lay sprawled on his bed, giggling as Cole drew a picture of their teacher, mocking her after she had scolded them the previous day. Alex laughed hard, egging him on.

They continued, moving on to a girl in class who never hid her disdain for either of them. Then they made their way through the rest of the kids, one by one, their sketches becoming harsher as they went. Not thinking anyone would see them, he let his creativity and cruelty run free.

Then came Vella. Cole, thoughtless and caught up in the moment, drew hers without hesitation. It was the most refined, the most vicious, making Alex laugh the hardest.

Once they finished and the novelty wore off, Cole tossed them aside. They got ready to go outside. Alex ran ahead, eager to leave. He didn't notice that Alex had taken the drawing of Vella, among others, with him.

Cole packed away his things and headed outside to find Alex. Unable to find him anywhere near the dorms, he went to check the common room. That was when he bumped into Vella and saw the expression on her face, the one that would haunt him forever.

Thinking about that day made him sick. And now that she finally knew the truth, those feelings were only magnified.

Then there was the matter of his confession that did nothing to resolve the issue. In fact, it did the opposite, only vastly complicating things.

He had no idea how to move forward, no idea how to undo the damage he'd caused. He wanted no forgiveness—he had convinced himself he deserved none—but the thought of losing her crushed him.

A chorus of familiar voices fought inside his head.

One voice said: *She's never going to want to talk to you again.*

Another said: *She'll come around. It'll all work out. Give her time.*

The loudest voice said: *You're worse than all of them. You don't deserve her. You deserve to be alone. To die alone.*

16

Name: Cole

Age: 10   Number: 8745

SUBJECTS

Language Studies: Average   Social Studies: Poor

Math: Poor   Science: Above Average

Art/Recreation: Excellent   Physical Education: Above Average

JOB EXPERIENCE

Cole tried working as a library assistant, and it was a disaster. He was sent back to us on the first day. Next time, we need to find something that suits his nature. Maybe something more hands-on.

FINAL OBSERVATIONS

Cole has difficulty maintaining attention, especially during activities he doesn't find personally meaningful, which applies to most classroom tasks. He often draws instead of completing work. When asked to pay attention, he argues that I'm wasting his time with useless information. He talks too much and keeps distracting other students, particularly Alex, who seems to be his only friend due to his standoffish nature. Cole can be somewhat combative towards some students and staff at the slightest provocation. Group activities are a challenge. He has plenty of potential but no clear outlet or path. Whoever takes him on next year must help him learn to work with others.

Cole ignored his body's relentless pleas for rest. He kept working, clearing and sowing cabbages, refusing to stop. He worked through the lunch break, not giving himself a second to think. If he did, the weight of his thoughts threatened to crush him.

The double bell signaling the end of the workday rang through the stillness of the fields, but it didn't register in his mind. He kept feeding the last of the livestock. When he finished, the thought of going home crossed his mind for a fleeting moment, only to be discarded just as quickly. He figured Edgar might have canceled the afternoon session, but the idea of more self-inflicted physical torture was too appealing to ignore. He walked to the clearing, knees buckling several times, but he pushed on, ignoring the pain.

When Cole arrived at the clearing, Edgar and Alex were already there. They stared at him as he arrived, concerned by his sorry state. His clothes were filthy, covered with dirt and sweat, as was his skin. His eyes were distant, half-open. Every movement seemed like a struggle just to keep his legs under him. Without bothering to greet them, Cole muttered to Edgar to get them started.

Noticing Cole's decrepit state, Edgar suggested they skip the session and talk instead. But Cole was in no mood for advice and brushed him off, urging him to hurry up. Sensing it was useless to argue, Edgar set up the markers in silence.

As they were about to begin, Vella appeared from the tree line. She fixed her eyes on the ground as she approached the starting line, her expression unreadable.

Cole's eyes lit up for the first time since that morning. A mix of relief and anxiety warred in his chest. Breaths came in ragged bursts as he tried to read Vella's expression, but she didn't even glance his way.

"Are you participating?" Edgar asked.

"Of course," Vella said, her voice flat, betraying no emotion.

Edgar expelled all the air from his lungs. Not wanting to be the odd one out, he reluctantly joined them at the starting line. Vella's eyes flickered toward Cole, who met her gaze with trepidation. She looked away in an instant. Cole's throat clenched; her silence was more unsettling than any outburst could have been.

Edgar gave a few quick instructions to Alex, and they started the drills.

Cole made it through two rounds before he collapsed. His legs no longer listened after all the neglect. No matter how hard he willed it, his legs would not move. He punched the ground in frustration.

Edgar offered a hand to help him up. Cole brushed him off, dragged himself to the nearest tree, and collapsed against it.

As soon as he felt the bark on his back, his eyes closed on their own.

Vella stood off to the side, catching her breath, her eyes fixed on Cole, who was still out cold.

"Hey."

She flinched, jumping away from the voice, instinctively falling into a defensive stance. Edgar stood next to her, a hand up to show he meant no harm.

"Sorry, I didn't mean to . . . scare you."

She exhaled heavily and said nothing, fixing her eyes back on Cole.

"I wanted to apologize for the other day," Edgar said.

"It's fine," she muttered, not bothering to look at him.

Edgar glanced between her and Cole. "He'll be all right."

She glared at him. "What do you want?"

Edgar cleared his throat. "Can we start over? I was hoping we could be friends."

Vella remained silent.

"Ah . . . well . . . okay, then," he said. "Just . . . let me know if you need anything."

Friends?

She flicked a glance at Edgar, then at the doors.

He had done what she would've done—if it hadn't been for Cole. *But he had no one.*

She'd spent a lot of time thinking about what Cole had said, about how they needed to look out for Edgar.

When she'd first met him, she'd sensed something, a familiar feeling she hadn't been able to name. Now she understood why she'd resisted accepting him.

The way he avoided eye contact, his guarded stillness, and the quiet tension in how he carried himself. He reminded her too much of herself.

And why should someone like her be worthy of anything but rejection?

Friends?

She finally spoke up. "Can you go over and hit him for me?"

Edgar smiled. "I don't think he would learn anything. We need something more severe for him."

"Any ideas?"

He glanced around and pointed to a nearby tree. "We could put him on that low branch over there so when he wakes, he'll fall off and get a scare he won't forget."

She stifled a laugh. "That's a good one."

"Actually . . . I think I saw him twitch. He'll be up soon. Too . . . late . . ."

"Shame."

Edgar walked away but stopped upon hearing her call out. "We can be friends."

He turned around. "On one condition," she said.

"What's that?"

"You help me keep Cole in check."

He smiled. "Deal."

She watched him walk over to Cole. *Friends? No one's said they wanted to be my friend before.*

Cole eased his eyes open in time to see Edgar approach and flick him on the forehead.

"We're leaving," Edgar said.

Cole groaned and rubbed his head. "How long was I out for?"

"Couple of hours." Edgar crouched down next to him. "I don't know exactly what's going on, but you can't do this to yourself."

Cole glanced away to see Vella gathering her things.

Edgar followed his gaze. "Talk to her."

"Shut up."

Edgar stood up and sighed. "If not for yourself, then take care of yourself . . . for her. It's obvious she was worried sick."

Cole kept his eyes fixed on Vella as Edgar walked off.

His mind, now a little more rational after the forced nap, knew Edgar was right. He had to talk to her. The orb was in his pocket, a safety net if things went wrong.

It couldn't hurt to try, he reasoned.

"Vel," he called out, hobbling over to her as she was about to leave.

She stopped but didn't turn.

"Sorry about that . . . I didn't mean to leave you alone with Alex and Edgar."

"Edgar's not so bad. We . . . talked. And Alex is fine," she said, keeping her back turned.

"Well . . . good."

He swallowed, bracing himself. "Do you . . . want to come over for dinner?" he ventured.

"Sure," she replied, without a hint of anger or hesitation.

She agreed . . . just like that?

"Great. Uh, did you want to walk with me now or come by later?"

"I-I'll walk with you," she stammered, her voice trembling with the first hint of emotion.

They walked in silence. Vella kept her head turned away from him.

His mind raced: *So, she's not mad? But she's avoiding looking at me or talking to me . . .*

He replayed her reaction from the day before and it hit him like a brick. *Oh no, she's not mad. She's embarrassed.*

Of course. You slow moron. Still, why is she not mad?

"Time?"

The words, a gentle whisper, shocked him into awareness. His chest heaved, and the world tilted around him.

Why would she ask that? I asked her to come over. Come on. Dammit. Do something!

He raised his hand in front of him, holding up three fingers: *Up to you.*

Looking down at them, he felt uneasy, so he put two down, leaving one finger up: *Stay.*

He caught her glancing sideways and thought he saw a faint hint of a smile.

As they entered the house, Leah's face lit up at the sight of Vella. "What a pleasant surprise," she said. Leah wanted to welcome

Vella with a hug but, not wanting to ruin a good thing, she let her be.

Neither of them said anything as they walked inside.

"You two look half dead. Come, sit. Food's almost ready," Leah said, trying, and failing, to contain her excitement.

She stopped to look Cole up and down. "What in the world . . . Cole, you're disgusting. Go wash up. Now."

Still half dazed, he nodded and sauntered off to the bathroom. When he returned, Vella sat at the table, and she gave him a small smile that faded.

Cole sat across from her, studying her to try to gauge her mood, but her head was down, expression unreadable.

Leah placed a plate in front of them, breaking him from his thoughts. The mouthwatering aroma brought tears to his eyes, while Vella's face lit up with joy. They ate like they'd never seen food before. Leah watched them with quiet amusement and let them eat for a while before deciding to start with the antagonism.

She turned to Vella. "How's everything at home?"

"Good," Vella replied, voice flat.

"She wants to know if you'd like to come live with us," Cole said, still chewing. "Isn't that right, Leah?"

Leah shot him a glare, annoyed by his bluntness. But Cole and Vella had expected the question regardless, leaving Leah at a disadvantage. Still, she pressed on. Undeterred.

"You know how I feel about you living alone. We have a spare room—"

"I'll think about it."

Cole almost choked on his food. *Think about it? What! Maybe she's too exhausted to fight, or she's just being nice? Or maybe she's serious? I don't know anymore . . .*

Leah was also taken aback by the casual response. "Wonderful," she said, trying not to betray her excitement. She shot Cole an exuberant look, thrilled by the unexpected victory.

"You won't hog the bathroom like Leah does, will you?" Cole asked with a dry smile.

Leah didn't miss a beat. "Oh, I'm sorry. Someone needs his

mirror time to make sure his hair is perfect."

"I do not," Cole shot back, a bit too quickly.

Leah glanced at Vella and mouthed, "He does."

Cole sighed and shook his head, his frustration apparent. But then, Vella's laugh broke through, light and genuine.

Even Cole couldn't help but chuckle at himself. As his laughter faded, he caught Vella's eye, and for a brief moment, their gazes met. But, in the blink of an eye, she looked away, a faint blush coloring her cheeks.

Leah, sensing the positive turn, seized the moment. "You know, your hair would look beautiful with a proper wash, Vella. I have the perfect idea for how we can cut your hair. We can make him wait for hours."

Vella's light expression faded, embarrassed by the attempted compliment.

Leah continued, unaware of the effect her words were having. "I remember your mother had long, flawless hair. It always made me jealous."

Cole gave her a warning look, but the damage was done.

Vella's head dropped, her unkempt hair hiding her face. "That's not me," she whispered.

Leah reached out, gently taking Vella's hand. "It always has been. Right, Cole?"

Vella yanked her hand back and stood up. "Thank you for dinner," she muttered, rushing out the door with her head down.

Leah watched her leave, powerless to do anything. She threw down her fork and cursed herself under her breath.

Cole stood up, shoulders slumped. "I'll make sure she's okay."

"Everything was going so well. I had to bring up . . ." Leah shook her head and pushed her plate away in frustration.

Cole went over and placed a reassuring hand on her shoulder. "I know she appreciates what you said."

Without looking up at him, she touched his hand. "Go."

Vella was halfway down the street when he emerged from the house.

"Vel, wait up!" He caught up with her and fell into step

beside her.

She kept her face turned away.

"Are you all right?" Cole asked. "Sorry, she was just trying to help. She can be a bit much sometimes."

She stopped without warning, and Cole halted beside her.

"Cole . . . do you think I'm beautiful?"

The question hit him like a punch to the gut. *Where did that come from?*

He stared at her, stunned, mind racing as he realized he couldn't afford to hesitate. "I don't think. I know you are."

After a moment, she turned to face him, her expression still unreadable. "What you said . . . this morning . . . that you . . . uh . . . In what way did you mean it?"

If the previous question was a punch to the gut, this one was a kick to the temple.

In what way . . . ? He was lost. He needed time to think, but there was none.

His chest felt like it was caving in, suffocating him, as his mind scrambled for an answer. He loved her. There was no denying that. But how did he feel about her, really? He'd always seen Vella as family, like Leah. He would jump into any danger for her, would give his life for her in a heartbeat. But physical attraction?

That's where things got complicated.

He understood the source of his turmoil, and it filled him with disgust. The people around her, those she'd grown up with, had shaped not only her self-image but also how Cole saw her. *Just look at her. She's not good enough; she's ugly,* a cruel voice in his head whispered. The guilt of such a vile thought pierced him over and over. She had many charming qualities. He adored her smile and her eyes, the unique way she kept her hair, her laugh, and the other little things that made her Vella. Her enthusiastic attitude and vibrant personality always brought light into his world. There was no life without her. Yet there was a perception of her lodged deep within him, a perception that battled against him. He'd been captivated by the conventionally attractive girls his age, despite how much their personalities repelled him. But never Vella.

She'd faced ridicule and belittlement all her life. As much as he hated to admit it, he cared about what others thought. This concern tainted his view of her. Was he repulsed by her? No. The revulsion was directed inward, toward himself. The more he had those thoughts, the less worthy he felt of her and of love in general.

He'd considered the possibility of them being together many times. Several years ago, he had almost broached the subject with her, but he'd hesitated. How could he bring it up naturally? How would she respond? So, he'd let it go. There was also the risk of ruining the simple, uncomplicated bond he shared with his best friend. What they had was easy, effortless. Why disrupt that? Would they end up resenting each other like Leah and Edgar? Why jeopardize their relationship? All these thoughts piled up until he'd abandoned the idea altogether.

Presently, all he could think about was how he could get out of the situation.

I don't want to upset her, but I can't do this right now, he thought.

His hand slipped into his pocket, feeling for the orb.

The orb was there. How simple it was. All he had to do was press it.

"Vel," he stammered, "I—"

"I've always wanted to tell you how I feel," she said, her voice low, unable to meet his eyes. "I was afraid you wouldn't feel the same way. Then you said it. I've never felt so happy." She hesitated, taking a deep breath, then added, "I love you too."

Cole's worst fears were realized in four words. His heart sank. The words he'd blurted out in desperation had spiraled into something he wasn't prepared for.

She peered up to see the shock on his face.

"Did y-you not . . . m-mean it?"

Press it, press it, he urged himself, but his body and mind halted.

"Oh . . . no . . . of course not," Vella said, her voice cracking with distress. "What was I thinking? I'm so stupid."

She turned and ran. The pain in her voice cut through him

like a knife.

"Vel!" he called after her, but she didn't stop.

You've done it this time, he berated himself, watching her disappear down the street.

He stood there, hands on his head. *I can't leave it like this.*

Without a second thought, he pulled out the orb and pressed the button.

A sharp zap seared through every nerve in his brain, followed by sudden silence. When he came to, he was standing in front of the house again as Vella walked away.

This time, his feet stayed rooted to the ground. Paralyzed by a flood of guilt, he watched her retreat, every fiber of his being longing to vanish, to sink into the earth and never resurface.

Why would she be in love with a monster like me?

17

SCHOOL REPORT FOR YEAR 436

Name: Vella

Age: 10   Number: 8749

SUBJECTS

Language Studies: Above Average   Social Studies: Poor

Math: Average   Science: Above Average

Art/Recreation: Excellent   Physical Education: Excellent

JOB EXPERIENCE

Vella excelled in furniture making. Rather than asking for help, she prefers to figure things out on her own. She didn't speak much, but this wasn't seen as an issue. They liked her regardless.

FINAL OBSERVATIONS

Vella is a quiet, introspective student who strongly prefers to work independently. Getting her to speak in class feels impossible, and the other children aren't helping. I am genuinely concerned for her well-being. She is self-conscious about her eyelid and is often teased by other students. Rather than retaliating, she withdraws further. I've tried talking to some of the children who are giving her a hard time, but I fear my words are falling on deaf ears. Vella struggles to engage in group activities and generally avoids social interaction. She is quite talented and has the potential to excel in whatever she chooses, but her reluctance to connect with others is limiting her growth. She doesn't appear to have any friends, and I believe having just one would make a significant difference. I have only a few months left here, and I hope that whoever takes over next year will be able to reach her in ways I could not.

Edgar canceled the morning training. He said their muscles needed time to recover, as was evident from how stiffly they were all moving. He told them there'd be no meeting in the afternoon, so they could rest. He added an extra warning for Cole to make sure he got the message.

He then introduced them to a stretching routine, apologizing for not having done it sooner. He ran them through the important stretches to do before and after sessions.

They had a quick chat, bringing Alex up to speed about the

orb. Cole did a couple of tests with him. After he tried it out, his usual calm, confident expression was replaced with one of shock. He wanted to speak, but his mouth hung open and he stared at them. He walked off in a daze, bumping into a tree before disappearing from sight.

Cole noticed how Edgar had improved over the past few days. His face had regained some color, though it still lacked spirit. He wanted to ask if Edgar had returned to work, now regretting that he hadn't made it a condition of his participation. But he decided to leave that question for another day, content for now with Edgar getting clean. At least, Cole thought he was.

Vella kept her distance, her eyes avoiding Cole's. She hovered on the outer edge of the group, peering in. Neither said a word to each other, and Vella said nothing at all.

Cole spent the workday wrestling with the memories of last night's disaster. The guilt gnawed at him with each passing hour, wearing him down. His body ached from pushing himself beyond his limits. But the pain in his muscles was nothing compared to the self-inflicted mental torment.

He refused any respite. To escape his thoughts, he busied himself. He managed to take some of Edgar's advice and gave himself light duties. He kept his hands busy with tool cleanup, maintenance, and inventory work, but it wasn't enough to keep his mind distracted. His thoughts kept drifting back to the way she'd looked at him when she'd run off. It was no longer part of their reality, but he'd experienced it all the same.

Last night, when sleep had finally come, it was only because his muscles had demanded it, but even then, he'd dreaded the dreams that would follow—vivid, relentless, and malicious.

Vella's feelings weighed on his mind. Now that he knew how she truly felt, he realized it was only a matter of time before she confronted him again. There was no running this time. He had to be ready. No solution came to him, and he wasn't searching for one, hoping it would appear out of thin air.

His unchecked thoughts spiraled, no matter how hard he tried to focus on his work.

When he got home, he found he needed another distraction.

Preparing dinner seemed like a good idea. He got to work, chopping and dicing.

Leah arrived shortly after, sinking herself into a chair at the dining table with a heavy sigh. She dropped her head to rest on her folded arms.

"Why are you home at this hour?" Her question was muffled, but he got her meaning.

He said nothing, focusing on bringing the wood-fired stove to a steady flame.

She lifted her head and attempted to answer her own question. "I pushed her too far, didn't I?"

"She knows you meant well. She just needs time alone, and I need an early night," he lied.

Leah groaned, burying her face in her arms again. "I was so close. How is she?"

He paused, placing a pot of water over the flames.

"She's fine. Don't worry."

Silence stretched between them, but it felt more oppressive than comforting. Needing to break it, Cole took the initiative.

"Busy day?"

Before Leah could answer, there was a series of rapid knocks at the door.

Leah held up a hand, signaling him to stay as she got up to answer. Cole wiped his hands and turned, leaning back on the bench, waiting to see who it was.

It wasn't what either of them expected. Vella stood at the door, a box in her arms and a bag slung over her shoulder. Cole's breathing stopped altogether.

"What's all this?" Leah exclaimed. She attempted to contain her excitement, but rising fluctuations in her voice betrayed her.

Vella cleared her throat. Her eyes flicked to Cole for the briefest moment before settling back on Leah. "Is . . . is it still okay . . . if . . . to stay—"

Before Vella could finish getting across what she wanted to say, Leah enveloped her in a hug. The box slipped from her grasp and thudded to the floor, narrowly avoiding their toes.

"Of course!" Leah planted a kiss on Vella's cheek, her grip

tight and suffocating.

Vella projected distress, but it seemed to fade as she accepted Leah. She shot Cole a desperate look for help. He smiled and mouthed, "Sorry." Despite everything, the small interaction eased the tension in his chest, allowing him to breathe a little easier.

When Vella had endured enough, Cole stepped forward, placing a hand on Leah's shoulder. "Release her, demon," he said, his voice deep with mock severity.

Leah whirled around, accidentally smacking him but not letting go of Vella. She pulled Cole into the embrace, squishing the three of them together. In that moment, with their heads touching in the forced group hug, all the guilt and fears that had plagued Cole faded.

Vella and Cole's eyes met for a brief moment, their faces inches apart. They shared a glancing smile as he felt the comfort of their warmth. He closed his eyes, savoring the moment and tucking it away as a quiet reminder that there was nothing to worry about.

Leah's excitement only grew—to Cole's growing concern—as she rushed to show Vella her room, not finishing one thought before jumping to the next. Vella followed, her expression light, not appearing overwhelmed by Leah's frenetic enthusiasm. In fact, she seemed amused, much to Cole's relief.

Vella was given the smallest of the three rooms, tucked between Cole's and Leah's. That didn't bother her. In fact, she was surprised by how spacious it felt. It was nearly the size of her shed, and the high ceiling made it feel even larger. A window overlooking the backyard was a welcome addition, and the smooth flooring was a clear improvement over the rough boards she and Cole had laid themselves.

After unpacking, she drifted into the living room. Leah kept talking as she browsed the bookshelf, half listening.

By the time they sat down for dinner, the initial elation had faded, replaced by a more subdued atmosphere. The room was quiet, with Leah occasionally glancing at both of them, smiling as she ate and letting out a relieved sigh every now and then.

Vella's spoon clinked as she set it down. Her eyes darted between Cole and Leah, her hands rubbing anxiously up and down her thighs.

Cole was watching her fidget and mouthed, "What's wrong?"

She ignored him and turned to Leah. After taking a moment to clear her throat, she asked, "C-can I come work with you, Leah?" Her voice was soft, almost a whisper.

Leah stopped chewing and froze. Cole also froze, his spoon hovering at his lips.

She swallowed. "You want to . . . come work with me?" Leah asked, her voice even, somewhat doubtful.

Vella nodded, her gaze fixed downward.

Leah's eyes brightened, glancing at Cole as if to say, *Isn't this amazing?*

Cole's thoughts raced, trying to process the unexpected development. Vella had never held a job before, having been self-sufficient in her secluded little pocket of space.

Where had this person come from? Moving in and now wanting to work with Leah? Not just that, but in the center of town!

"Of course! We can always use extra help. It shouldn't be an issue," Leah assured her.

Vella smiled, her eyes meeting Cole's. He returned her warm smile, even though his mind churned with new worries.

Is she doing this for me? To impress me? Is this what she thinks I want?

The logic tracked, now knowing her true feelings for him. He was happy for her, but doubt gnawed at him. Is this too much for her? *Is this what she actually wants?*

A heavy weight settled on his chest as the memory of last night reached out and dragged him down. He still didn't have a plan for dealing with Vella's feelings, and he knew he couldn't keep running. Not with how naturally unwilling she was to back down. Panic bubbled up again; the vise in his chest gripped him tighter.

Presently, Leah was rambling to Vella about her job, the good, the bad, and the mundane. Vella listened with a mix of nervousness and newfound confidence, her posture straighter than Cole had ever seen.

He pushed his fears aside for a moment, admiring her newfound strength. She needed his support now. If things went wrong, there might not be a next time.

He looked at her to grab her attention. Catching her eye, he smiled, and she responded with a wide, confident grin—one unlike any he'd seen in all their years together. It filled him with a warmth that made him believe, if only for a moment, that everything might just turn out okay, even if he didn't have all the answers right now.

He tapped one finger to his shoulder: *Stay.*

18

Resistance has given way to acceptance. For the majority, at least. Time has eroded any hope of leaving Eden. Maybe that's for the best. As a collective, we can focus on building something meaningful with the short lives we have left. But no matter how much I try, something deep down refuses to accept this place. And I think it always will. I'll continue documenting our struggles here, but unless a miracle happens, there probably won't be any more mentions of the doors or escape. All I can do is accept the six years I have left. Or try to. It's a really nice place. And it's filled with people I care about. So, there is that. It could always be worse.

—THE FIRST PEOPLE OF EDEN

Journal of Morgan #38

Day 200

Cole waited outside the house, looking down the street. The evening sun cast long shadows across the path. He could see Leah walking with someone who looked familiar but vastly different—Vella.

At first, he almost didn't recognize her. Her long black skirt and white semiformal blouse were so unlike her usual clothes that it felt like seeing someone else entirely. The outfit didn't quite seem to fit her, not just in size but in spirit. He had to stifle an amused smile. Her hesitant strides alongside Leah made it clear that Vella was trying, but this wasn't her world.

He held up a hand to greet her, trying to suppress the flutter of nerves in his chest.

She waved back, then, glancing at her outfit, shifted uncomfortably, suddenly self-conscious.

In that moment, he was caught in déjà vu as the vision returned to his mind's eye. She was in the same position, the same distance away, just like when he saw her facing off against the Wolf. And dying. The pain of it hit him again, and he grimaced. He drew a sharp, shallow breath and forced a smile.

Reaching the edge of the property, she took off into the house. "I need to change!" she called out, already halfway to the door.

He chuckled, giving her a thumbs-up. His hand trembled, but he held it firm until she was gone, then turned to meet Leah. She stood watching the house, a light, easy smile on her face.

Before speaking, he cleared his throat, hoping to steady his voice. "How'd she do?"

"Amazing. She's trying so hard," Leah said, brimming with pride.

"I'll admit, I didn't see her working in clothing," he said.

"I have no doubt once she gets the hang of it, she'll be quite good at it."

Cole nodded, his expression tightening with concern. "Did anyone at work give her a hard time?"

Leah smirked. "That's not going to happen," she assured him. "I went around and made sure everyone understood that if they so much as looked at her funny, they would have to deal with *me!*"

Cole couldn't help but smile at the thought of her marching around, putting the fear of Leah into them.

"She'll have her challenges," Leah admitted, her voice softening. "But I'm confident she can manage."

"I'm worried it might be too much, too soon."

"Trust she knows what she's doing. You mean well, but you have to have more faith in her. You can't protect her forever."

"You're right. Sorry."

Leah placed a reassuring hand on his arm. "And if it is too much for her to handle, we'll be there for her."

He nodded.

She stared at him for several seconds with a mix of amusement and disbelief.

"What are you looking at?"

"God, you're both adorable. You know, she wouldn't stop talking about you. It was 'Cole and I this, Cole this, Cole that.'"

His face heated up, and his hand instinctively reached up to scratch the back of his neck.

"I'm kind of jealous, you know," she said.

Seeing his uncomfortable, bewildered expression, she cut in.

"That's not what I mean, dummy," Leah teased. "To be in love . . . it's the most wonderful thing, Cole. It can make you feel like you can do anything. Leaving her place to come live with us, working with me. You know how hard that must've been for her. Only one thing could've pushed her to do that."

Her words hit him like a wave. He swallowed hard, feeling the added weight pressing down on his shoulders. He nodded, not trusting himself to speak.

"Don't you dare break her heart. You hear me?"

"I don't mean to."

"Then don't. That girl would do anything for you."

"I never wanted her to do all this for me."

Leah wrapped her arms around him from behind, resting her chin on his shoulder. "You love her just as much. I know," she whispered.

"It terrifies me."

"Love will do that. As it does to most people. Terrifying and wonderful at the same time." He felt the experience coming from those words. She exhaled, her breath warm against his ear. "So many people here are afraid to get close to anyone because they know that either someone they care about or they themselves will die soon. What's worse—leaving someone behind or being left behind? To hurt or be hurt?"

She sighed, a sound steeped in years of unspoken sorrow. "What's worse is never experiencing it at all. Letting the fear stop you. Don't be one of them."

"Where do you fall?"

"Somewhere in the middle," she replied. "I had my time, and I'm grateful for it."

"Do you ever regret leaving Edgar?"

She added weight to his shoulders as she slumped. "Sometimes," she admitted. "But we didn't have what you two have. I thought we did. Maybe we did. But by the end . . . we just made each other miserable." She paused, taking in their surroundings. "Things change, Cole. We need to appreciate what we have while we have it."

She let out a small unexpected laugh. "You know what? I've

come to be grateful for this place."

Cole couldn't help but laugh as well. "What? Why?"

"Knowing I'll die soon, I look around and see how beautiful everything is. I feel blessed. Every day's a precious gift. Do you feel it? Look around. *Really look.*"

Cole did as she asked. His gaze swept over the house, the trees, the flowers, the people he loved—all safe, all together. The sun dipped lower in the sky, casting a golden glow over everything. For a moment, there was no fear, no doubt, just the simple beauty of the world around him. Not a single problem to be found.

"Are you scared?" he asked.

"Of course I am. I'm human after all."

"I'm scared to lose you," he whispered.

She gave him a squeeze and kissed him on the cheek. "I love you too."

Vella burst out of the front door, still struggling to put on her shoes. Leah straightened up, giving Cole a gentle push toward her.

"Don't be afraid."

They walked side by side in awkward silence. The weight of unspoken feelings hung between them. Vella had her eyes down, stepping on dried leaves as they walked, which he already knew was a bad sign.

He cleared his throat. "So . . . how was your first day?" he asked.

"It was . . . good. I did some simple clothing repairs. I need to work on my stitching," she said. Her voice was steady, though her eyes betrayed her nerves. "Leah was helpful, and everyone was friendly. I'm just not used to being around so many people." She let out a weary sigh. "And the clothes she made me wear were so uncomfortable."

A teasing remark about her outfit flickered in his mind, but he suppressed it. Her confidence was paramount, and it currently balanced on a knife's edge.

He thought to himself: *She would've made fun of herself for wearing that only a few days ago.*

Instead, he let out a soft laugh. "It looks good on you," he said, then, scrambling, added, "I mean, whatever you wear looks good on you."

Vella puffed out her cheeks, trying to hide the smile tugging at her lips.

"She wants to cut my hair," Vella murmured, fidgeting with the ends of her bangs.

When did she care about her hair? Stupid question, Cole.

"What did you say?" he asked.

"I said I'd think about it," she replied. "What do you think?"

He hesitated, sensing the importance of the question. "I like the way it is now, but it could be worth a try."

"Yeah, if you think so."

She fidgeted more, biting her bottom lip and tapping her fingers by her side, her movements growing more restless by the second.

It's coming, he thought.

He screamed to his unresponsive body, *Do something!*

Then, without thinking, he bolted forward.

"Come on! Last one there has dish duty!" he shouted over his shoulder.

It was a desperate, childish move, but Vella's competitive spirit took over, and she chased after him, grinning.

He cursed under his breath. *I need some help. I can't keep doing this to her.*

19

The people of Eden could've broken under the weight of our hopeless situation. It would have been easy. But instead, they resisted in the only way they could: by living. By choosing peace. Joy. Connection. They built a community, almost out of spite. They said, *If your plan was to watch us destroy ourselves, we won't give you the satisfaction. We will love. We will carry our scars without shame.* A quiet rebellion. A civil act of disobedience. Or maybe just a way to stay human. Either way, sometimes it's easier to pretend that's what happened. Not that they had no other choice. And maybe that's enough.

—A PEOPLE THAT SHOULD HAVE NEVER BEEN
The History of Eden
by Luke #4342

"Vella, where are the other cones?" Alex asked, holding the other half.

She stopped stretching and pointed to a patch of grass behind him where she had left them.

"Thanks."

That's an improvement, Cole thought.

He knew it would take a little more time for them to become friends, though he could only hope they'd get that far. On the other hand, things were different with Edgar.

Vella watched Edgar struggle to bend down to get his water bottle. With a final, strained grunt, he managed to grab it.

"You all right, old man?" Vella called out.

Edgar straightened, shot her a look, and grinned. "At least I'm not passing out."

They both glanced at Cole and shared a laugh at his expense. His mind was too far elsewhere to worry about the jab. Once he caught up, he was left confused. The way they talked to each other felt too casual.

After a moment of Cole not saying anything in return, Edgar looked at him with a worried expression. "Cole . . . you good, bud?" he asked.

"Fine."

Cole felt lost in a feeling of unease. The walk home, the inevitable moment of being alone with Vella, was where another uncomfortable encounter loomed. He needed help from someone, and the choice by process of elimination was—Edgar.

"Vel, you go ahead; I want to talk to Edgar," he told her as they parted ways.

Vella eyed him suspiciously. "Why?"

"There's something I need to ask him about . . . his experience. It's delicate. Better if I do it alone," he lied.

Vella's mouth tightened. "Whatever," she said.

Her disappointment was clear, laced with agitation. She turned and walked away, looking back a couple of times before disappearing out of sight.

Cole let out a relieved breath and caught up with Edgar as he was leaving.

"Hey, Edgar."

"What is it?"

"What's up with you and Vella?"

"Are you upset about the joke?"

"No, no. It's just . . . a big change between you two."

"Ah . . . yeah, we had a good talk when you were out. We just . . . had a bad start."

"I see."

Edgar looked at him with squinted eyes. "I get the feeling that's not what you wanted to talk to me about."

"No, it's not . . . mind if we sit?"

"One of those talks, is it?"

Cole shrugged.

"All right, come on," Edgar conceded.

They sat down on a nearby fallen log, coarse and moss-covered, nestled between a few low-hanging branches. Cole fidgeted with the bark.

"Edgar, when you had the orb . . . did you . . . experience anything unusual?"

"What do you mean?"

What he wanted to say: *Did you have waking nightmares that were so vivid you experienced real pain? You know, seeing loved ones die. Possible futures. That sort of thing.*

Instead, he said, "Just anything out of the norm."

"Apart from time travel?"

"Yeah."

"No. Nothing that comes to mind. Why?"

"Never mind. That's not what I wanted to ask."

"Well, go on."

"That night . . . when you gave me the orb . . ." Cole began.

Edgar let out a deep breath. "What about it?"

"That night you told me you had 'already heard what you needed to.'"

Edgar sighed, having his concerns validated.

Cole pressed, "When you talked—"

Edgar raised a hand to stop him. "Yes, I talked to you before, and I said and asked things of you I shouldn't have. That's all you need to know."

Cole shook his head. "That's not the part I care about." He paused, the guilt creeping into his voice. "I may have used it . . . like you did . . . to erase something."

Edgar's face hardened. "That's part of why I didn't want it anymore. To stop myself from abusing it." He sighed. "This is my fault. I should've warned you. You can't keep it on you. Hide it somewhere or give it to me to hide."

Cole gave a subdued nod.

"You have to let things happen, Cole. No matter the outcome. It's not fair to them . . . and to yourself," Edgar added, his voice softer now.

Seeing the turmoil etched on Cole's face, Edgar asked, "What did you do?"

"It's not about what I did . . . it's more that I don't know what to do."

"You think I would? You want advice from a guy who screwed everything up and couldn't even succeed in taking his own life?" Edgar's laugh was bitter, tinged with self-deprecation.

"Maybe. No. I don't know . . . I thought you might understand."

"What happened with you and Vella?"

"Is it that obvious?"

Edgar chuckled. "She can't look at you, and when she does, she immediately turns away. It's like watching a child with a crush. It reminds me of how I used to be around Leah way back when. It's clear she's enamored with you."

The image of Edgar being like that brought a flicker of a smile to Cole's face.

Edgar continued, "It wasn't like that a few days ago. What happened?"

"I told her I loved her."

"And you don't?"

"It's not that."

"You didn't mean it the way she's taking it?"

Cole shrugged, nodded, and shook his head all in one motion. "It's too much to handle right now. It was simpler before. Easier. I wish things could go back to how they were."

"Too late for that, pal." Edgar stood and faced Cole. "But I think it's clear. You meant it. Trust me."

Cole stared at him, puzzled.

Edgar felt tempted to smack Cole for the stupid look he gave.

"You're overthinking it," Edgar said.

He stepped closer and poked Cole in the stomach. "What does your gut say?"

"Run away," Cole answered without thinking.

Edgar felt a twitch in his hand but again resisted the urge to smack him. "Wrong voice. Deeper."

Cole frowned, looking even more lost. Edgar glanced around, thinking about how to explain it. After a moment, he snapped back to Cole.

"Close your eyes," Edgar commanded.

He obeyed. "What now?" Cole asked.

"Stop talking," Edgar barked.

He watched, waiting for indications of calm in Cole before continuing.

"Now. Focus."

Edgar waited a minute, watching Cole's expression. "What

does your gut say? Don't say anything out loud. If you do, I will hit you."

Minutes passed, the silence stretching, as the soft sounds around him grew louder. Slowly, the chaos in Cole's mind quieted, and he could feel something deep within him shift.

Edgar stood with his arms crossed, waiting patiently. "Sometimes you need silence. Let your mind sort itself out. It might bring up some ugly things, but it also reminds you what's truly important. Listen, everyone else can see the answer as clear as day except you, so I'll let you figure that out for yourself."

The turmoil within Cole diminished. The voice within grew clearer as the other noises faded, receding into the distance. He could start to feel something. A warmth spread through him, enveloping him.

Edgar observed as a small, genuine smile spread across Cole's face.

"Looks like you got it," Edgar said. "And those concerns? They don't seem so important now, do they?"

Cole nodded.

He kept his eyes closed, choosing to sit with the feeling a while longer. It crawled under his skin, consuming him entirely. He felt it flow through him, from his fingertips to his core.

And in that feeling, there was only one person.

20

When I was young, I had this stuffed animal I loved. I called her Robin the robin. I know. Very original. One day, I was out playing, and she got ripped on a tree branch, losing a bunch of stuffing. I left her in my room and went back outside. When I came back, she was gone. My mom said she had to throw her away. I cried for days. Then, weeks later, on my birthday, I woke up to find Robin sitting at the end of my bed. As good as new. This Robin.

—"ASTRID #8719"

CHILDREN OF THE PEACEFUL PASSAGE

by Aleister #8990

Leah knelt in the garden, brushing damp soil from her hands. She carefully separated the tangled roots of the marigolds. Without noticing, her mind wandered, and her hands went still, flowers held loosely between her fingers. Then she dropped them, startled by the trembling in her hands. Familiar thoughts crept in, and with them came a rush of emotion. Her breathing grew shallow. It was surging too fast for her to get ahead of.

Out of the corner of her eye, she spotted Vella approaching the house. A sense of relief washed over her. She wiped her eyes and waved her over. Leah gathered herself, grateful for the distraction, but she could tell something was off. The tension in Vella's posture and walk gave it away. But it didn't seem serious enough to worry her. *Just a little lovers' quarrel,* she mused.

Vella wandered into the backyard, her eyes drifting over the flowers without much focus. A small scowl hung on her face.

"I could use some help," Leah said, motioning to a cluster of marigolds. "These were growing too close together. Help me spread them out?"

Vella didn't reply. But she obliged, kneeling beside Leah, her movements slow and mechanical.

"You okay?" Leah asked.

Vella nodded, though her eyes seemed distant, the usual spark absent.

Leah marked out spaces for the marigolds, handing four to

Vella. They worked in silence, but Leah couldn't ignore the heaviness in Vella's demeanor. It was eating at her with each passing second.

"What's wrong?" Leah pressed.

"I don't know," Vella said, her voice barely audible.

"Is work too much?"

"It's a lot. Exhausting," she conceded. "But it's not that."

Leah paused, watching Vella trembling as she fiddled with a marigold. "You can talk to me, you know. Just between us girls."

Vella hesitated, putting down the flowers and picking at her nails. "Do you think . . ." She trailed off, her gaze dropping to the ground.

Leah stayed silent, waiting for her to continue. "Is there anything . . . you think I can do about . . . ?" She made a vague motion to her eye.

Leah took off her gloves and moved next to her. "Oh, my dear girl. If there were, I wouldn't. I'm sure it gives you trouble seeing at times, but I wouldn't change it, nor any other part of you."

Leah's tone was firm but gentle. But Vella flinched as if struck.

"Why would you say that? I look like a monster."

"Don't say that."

"I know you're thinking it. Everyone is."

"No, they're not. I'm not."

Vella stood abruptly, her eyes brimming with tears. Leah reached out, grabbing her wrist. Vella flinched and yanked it away, stepping back.

"Wait," Leah pleaded.

"I know what you all think of me," she cried. "I saw it in everyone's eyes today. How they looked at me."

Before Leah could respond, Vella turned and stormed inside. A moment later, Leah heard the faint sound of her bedroom door shutting.

Leah stabbed the trowel into the dirt, muttering a curse under her breath. She only felt slight relief that Vella had chosen to go inside instead of running back to the shed. After washing her hands, she followed her inside.

Pausing outside Vella's door, Leah waited and listened. She could hear the muffled sounds coming from within but couldn't make out what they were. Leah sighed, her own heart heavy with guilt. When all noise subsided, she took care in opening the door and stepped inside.

The room was dim, the curtains half drawn, leaving her to retreat into the shadows. Vella lay huddled in the corner of the bed, face buried in a pillow, facing the wall.

Leah sat down on the edge of the bed, careful not to startle her. She reached out, resting a hand on Vella's shoulder. Vella recoiled, wriggling away, pressing herself deeper into the corner. Leah withdrew her hand. She sat in silence with Vella, waiting it out, her presence a quiet offering of support.

"I didn't mean to make you feel worse," Leah whispered. "I'm sorry for all the trouble your eye has caused you. You didn't deserve any of it."

Vella didn't respond, her face still hidden.

"I'm sorry you had no one. But I'm here now," Leah said.

More silence. Leah's words hung in the air, unanswered.

"Let me help you," Leah whispered, her appeal full of desperation. "Please."

"What can you do for an ugly freak?" Vella choked out, her voice muffled.

Leah winced, feeling her heart sink, and for a moment, she was speechless.

"You wouldn't understand," Vella added. "You're perfect."

Leah squeezed her eyes closed, feeling a heavy lump in her throat. She got up, leaving the room to gather herself. When she returned, she lay down on the bed beside Vella, facing the opposite direction.

Time dragged on; the room grew darker as the sun set.

They heard Cole enter through the front door and rummage around in the kitchen for a few minutes. Then he left the house.

"Where's he going?" Vella asked, her voice small.

"He's running an errand," Leah lied. She'd left a note for him to get something to eat and to leave the house for a while.

Vella didn't respond. The quiet stretched between them once more. Night crept over everything, its presence freeing them from the harsh light of day.

Leah broke the silence this time, speaking into the still air, hoping someone would hear her. "I remember your mother. She sticks in my mind. I can still see her sitting there, haunting me."

Vella's head lifted off the pillow.

"I only saw her at the weekly gatherings once, when it was her birthday. She sat by herself, not smiling, not talking to anyone." Leah brushed her nose with the back of her hand. "I wish I had gotten up and sat next to her. Spoke to her. But I just sat and watched . . . like a damn fool." And Leah thought: *Not only that but openly laughed at her.*

Leah could feel Vella shift behind her.

"And then you'd come out to see her. It was like a switch flicked inside her. In those few minutes, seeing you, she was the happiest person in all of Eden. She loved you more than anything. It breaks my heart that you didn't grow up with that love, the love you deserved."

Vella turned around to face Leah.

"Your mother . . ." she began. "She had you when she was quite young."

"But . . . if she had me when she was young, why did she stop seeing me when I was seven?"

"That's because . . ." Leah felt the words caught in her throat, writhing and cutting her up. "She had her struggles . . . and she could no longer take it. Being here. Alone."

"She . . . ah . . . but I was here."

"She wasn't equipped to raise a child. She needed someone to help her; she needed a friend. I should've helped . . . instead . . ." She wanted to add, "I only made it worse." But she couldn't say it, not to her.

Vella remained silent, her body tense.

"I want you to know, I'm far from perfect. I'm a monster. And inside me is an ugly mess," Leah said. "I know it's way too late, but I'm here for you. I'm sorry I left you alone out there on your own for so long."

Vella shifted closer, resting her head against Leah's back. Feeling Vella's warmth caused something inside Leah to crack.

"I hope you can forgive me," Leah whispered.

The silence that followed was heavy, but this time, it was a shared silence filled with understanding.

"Cole said he loved me," Vella finally said.

Leah rolled over to face Vella, wrapping an arm around her and pulling her close. She gently cupped Vella's face, lifting it to meet her gaze. Leah ran her thumb along her skin and forced a smile. "I'm surprised it took him this long," she said.

Vella cast her eyes down, as Leah sensed the "but" hanging in the air.

"I ran away," Vella said. "It feels like he's been avoiding me ever since, like he didn't mean it . . . I just don't understand how he could love me."

"That boy . . . I think he shocked himself just as much as he shocked you. But he meant it. That much is clear to everyone but you two, it would seem."

"I'm scared," Vella admitted, her voice a soft murmur. "I'm scared that if I don't do something, it'll all just . . . disappear."

Leah pulled her closer. "Be patient. He'll come around. He can be *a little slow*," she said, letting out a small laugh. "So that's why you've been pushing yourself so hard?"

"Why would he like me as I am? Look at me," Vella said. "Even he thinks I'm ugly. When we were kids, he made a drawing making fun of my eye. That was the first time someone called me the one-eyed freak. I bet he's still disgusted by me."

Leah felt a painful squeeze in her chest. "Kids can be stupid and cruel, but that doesn't excuse what Cole did," Leah said. "He told me about what happened several years ago. I see how much it affects him, knowing how much pain he caused you. I don't think he has ever forgiven himself."

"Is that why he's always looking out for me?"

"I don't want you to get the wrong idea. It's part of it. But only a small part. I know how much he actually cares. He truly loves you. As for your eye, if Cole doesn't like it, it's only because of how much torment it's caused you. Don't hate him for it. He bears enough of that for the both of you."

"I don't . . . I can't."

She brushed a stray hair from Vella's vision, giving her a flicker of a smile. "My dear girl, you're too good for him, believe me. He—" She paused midthought. "Wait . . . should I?" she muttered. "Screw it. I have something you need to see."

She got up, pulling Vella to her feet. "Come on, before he gets home." She hurried Vella to Cole's room. "He thinks I don't know about his stash. Never mention this to him. He'll kill me," Leah said as she rummaged through his closet.

She pulled out a notebook overflowing with sheets of paper. The notebook had different colored tabs.

"I think it's the blue one," she muttered to herself. She sat on the bed with Vella, flipping to a section marked by a blue tab. "This is your section."

"What do you mean *my* section?"

"See for yourself." Leah handed the open notebook to Vella.

The tab was filled with dozens of loose sheets of paper. On the first piece of paper was a rough drawing of Vella gardening.

"What's this?"

"Keep going."

She moved the page aside. The next was another sketch of Vella, more detailed this time. And the one after that. On it went. Each page showed progression. The drawings improved as Cole's skills developed. Vella was speechless as she flipped through the pages, the details becoming more vivid, more expressive. She stopped at one of the last drawings. A detailed portrait of her smiling, brimming from ear to ear, eyes squinted, showing no trace of her eyelid problem.

Leah watched with quiet elation at Vella's stunned expression. "Go to the last one," she urged.

Vella was still captivated by the smiling, carefree, joy-filled version of herself on the page—a version she didn't recognize.

"You should keep this one," Leah said.

"I don't know . . ."

"It's a good keepsake. A reminder. That's what Cole sees. And you need to see it too."

Vella set the portrait aside and turned to the final drawing. The page was crinkled and worn. The drawing from all those years ago. But it was different now as Cole had reworked it over the years. He'd added scores of details and shading, transforming it into something unrecognizable from the original. The cruel title at the top had been ripped off, replaced with a simple heading: Vella. The drawing focused on her smile, her eye only a small detail in the overall visual. A ten-year-old Vella stared back. One she'd never known.

"I . . . look . . ." Vella whispered, "happy."

"He doesn't see your eye," Leah said. "He sees all of you."

A tear dropped onto the page, and Vella hurried to wipe it away. She stilled when Leah's hand gently brushed her face.

"I didn't know he was this good. He never does any drawing around me."

Leah remained silent, knowing Vella would understand why. After a moment of the unspoken answer, Leah said, "I need you to help him let go and move on."

She nodded. "I'll try."

Leah embraced her, kissing her on the head.

"What's in the other tabs?" Vella reached for another section, but Leah put a hand on hers to stop her.

"Maybe he can share that with you one day."

Leah closed the notebook, and as she did, a page slipped out, gliding across the floor. It landed before them. The page was consumed by thick lines of shading. In the middle lurked a pair of burning eyes, full of malice, staring at them from the dark shadows.

"What's that?"

As soon as it fell, Leah snatched it up and slid it back into the notebook. "Don't worry about it. Some of them aren't as kind as your section."

"Wait . . . was that . . . ?"

"It's nothing. We've invaded his privacy enough." She put the notebook back in its place and rearranged the closet as it had been.

"Keep this. It's yours." She handed Vella the portrait she'd set aside. "Now, how about something to eat? I'm starving."

Vella nodded and followed her to the kitchen.

As Leah was working away, Vella played with the ends of her hair, still tied up in a ponytail in her usual style.

"You said I might look better if it was cut differently. Can you cut it?"

Leah paused, turned, and smiled. "I've changed my mind. I don't think I will. Not yet. I need you to see yourself as Cole sees you. When I see that, I will. Besides, I think it looks good as is."

Vella let slip a slight scowl and dropped her head.

Leah noticed and put her left foot on a chair for Vella to see. She pulled up her pant leg, exposing the number and countdown on her ankle. Vella couldn't help but stare at the ticking clock, noticing the zero where the years should be. Leah motioned to her four identifying numbers.

"Should we be embarrassed or ashamed of these numbers? Do they bother you?"

"Not really," Vella said.

"Branding us with these numbers seems pretty intentional. Why give us numbers at all if not to make us feel small and worthless? But that's not what we accept. We could be ashamed of them, but we're brought up to embrace them. It's part of who I am."

Before Vella could respond, Leah added, "I know it's not fair to compare it to your eye because no one's going to make fun of me for it because we all have it. But the point remains. You have to learn to love every part of yourself. It's a choice. It might not feel like it, but it's a choice you have to consciously make every second of every day. Then it becomes natural, automatic."

Cole returned shortly after. As he walked in, Leah and Vella exchanged a glance filled with hidden conspiracy. Then, turning to him, their eyes softened, as though they were admiring a baby lamb.

"Why are you looking at me like that?" Cole sat down at the table, eyeing them with caution. "What did you do? What happened?"

"Nothing," Leah said, sharing a knowing smile with Vella.

"No. What's that? Stop it."

"Really. It's nothing."

"Don't give me that. Tell me!"

"Enough, Cole."

"What was that look, then? Vella? Come on."

She shrugged, struggling to keep a straight face.

He turned back to Leah. "That confirms it. Now I know something is definitely going on."

The argument dragged on, stretching well past the point of it making sense. Vella couldn't stop laughing, watching on as if they were putting on a show just for her amusement.

After things settled, she remembered the drawing of the eyes filled with malice. She had seen reports on the Wolf and had seen the same distinct eyes drawn across many of the pages. He wasn't the only one whose life it had touched.

They'd never talked about that day Cole had lost his parents. She knew enough about it from overhearing other kids talk about it, but she had no idea how deeply it affected him. She thought he was fine, that it didn't bother him. How could it? Now, she could piece together some idea of the truth, and it was far worse than she'd imagined.

The longer she stared at him, the more she could see the cracks as plain as day. He wasn't okay. Never had been.

She always thought of him as untouchable, impervious to all harm. Her infallible knight who allowed nothing to penetrate the armor and shield. But it got through all the same; the armor was just hiding the damage underneath, blinding her to the truth.

He'd refused to let her see past it, and she had done nothing to strip it away. Did she ever notice? Did she see it and choose not to acknowledge it? She didn't know. Either way, it didn't ease the guilt. He'd needed her, and she hadn't been there.

Cole noticed her staring, and he just smiled; a slight flicker in his eye betrayed him, and she saw it all.

21

Isara: What voice drew you to the cave?

Drystan: It sounded like my own. Who did you hear?

Isara: It was me . . . but not me. Calling out.

Drystan: What did it say?

Isara: It told me to follow it into the darkness. It pulled me in . . .
until I heard someone else. You. Dragging me back.

—THE KNIGHTS OF ACIDALIA

Author Unknown

The moon hung high in the night sky, bathing Eden in its cold, indifferent light. Cole stood at his window beneath it, eyes fixed on the distant mirage, as if the pale glow might offer some answers. Restlessness gnawed at him, an urge he couldn't shake off, a longing he could no longer ignore. Sleep was impossible. His heart pounded on top of his skin, each shallow breath making the invisible hand in his chest grip tighter.

He knew what he needed. Something deep inside was calling him, beckoning him, but his surface reactions fought against it. His conscious mind screamed in protest.

The orb had changed everything, making it possible to do things he had never even dreamed of. It brought him closer to the moment he'd imagined and dreaded all his life—the moment he would face the monstrosity that took his parents. That moment was within reach anytime he wanted. The thought made his stomach drop. His breathing grew more ragged as the anxiety tightened its hold.

He clutched the orb tightly in his right hand, as though it could anchor him. The longer he put it off, the worse the dread became. It was driving him mad. Dragging him down, affecting every second of his life.

What chance did he have against the Wolf if it had already mentally broken him? There was only one way to move forward. Only one way out.

It's time, he told himself. *Just one look. That's it.*

A familiar voice whispered: *Do it. Hurry up. Now. Now. Now. Face it, coward.*

He slipped out of his bedroom window, careful not to disturb the stillness of the night. Not to wake Vella.

The journey to the door was fraught with hesitation; more than once, he froze midstep, wanting to turn back. But something pushed him forward, a determination stronger than his fear, an obsession with freeing himself from his mind's prison. It was a call echoing in his mind, drawing him closer.

Before he knew it, he was standing before the crimson door. The orb rested in his hand, its smooth surface cold against his clammy skin. He stared at the red door, its color a stark contrast to the night around him, then lowered his gaze to the orb. To his right, the green door stood closed, the only one that hadn't opened. They believed it would be the door that would lead them to freedom once the monsters behind the other two were slain. At least, that was what they hoped. It was what he desperately held fast to.

Click, click, click, click. The sound echoed in his ears, building his anxiety. He peered into the orb, hoping that it would answer him, that something, anything, would emerge from the depths of its black void. Cole lost track of time, standing at the precipice of the abyss.

Click. This noise was real this time.

Now! Go! Do it! He attempted to psych himself up to give himself the final push he required. The door loomed before him, a barrier between him and the void. His hand hovered over the scanner, trembling.

Do it! The command echoed in his mind. A desperate plea for courage.

He took a deep breath, gathering his resolve, and slammed his hand against the scanner.

The door slid open with a hiss, releasing a wave of foul air that hit him like a punch. Cole recoiled, gagging as the stench filled his nostrils. Edgar had warned them, but nothing could have prepared him for the reality. He hurried to pull off his shirt, wrapping it around his mouth and nose to try to block out the smell. It didn't help. Still, he pressed on into the putrid smell of death.

The darkness beyond the door pulsed with a life of its own, pushing back against him, repelling him, urging him to retreat. His legs quaked with each step, every muscle fighting him, screaming at him to turn back. But one step at a time, he forced himself forward. His breathing quickened. Each inhale was a desperate struggle for the oxygen he needed just to remain standing.

The door thundered shut behind him, making him flinch. He gathered himself, forcing down the panic, and pushed further into the oppressive darkness. Above him, distant blue lights flickered. They grew brighter, gradually revealing the area around him. He turned his head, taking in the scene. A small solid green light blinked above a glass sphere. Its lens was fixed on him, broadcasting his image back to Eden.

The scene felt disturbingly familiar. This was the place from his vision of Vella. The knowledge only heightened his unease, dragging his thoughts somewhere he didn't want to go. What he hadn't noticed at the time was what surrounded him. Scattered across the ground were broken weapons, scraps of clothing—and bones.

He froze, his heart skipping a beat as his gaze locked on a fragment of a human skull beneath his foot. His eyes darted around the metallic floor, and what he saw made his stomach churn.

A low growl stunned him, rippling through the air and vibrating through every bone in his body.

Cole slowly turned his head, dread crawling up his spine. The blue lights above cast eerie shadows. They revealed the beast as it emerged from the darkness. Its eyes glowed with malevolent intent.

He was no longer in control of his body; he might as well have been watching himself on the screen from the outside. His fingers tightened around the orb, thumb hovering over the button. Sweat slicked his palms, the orb slipping in his trembling grip.

Those eyes.

The same ones from his nightmares. Finally, here it was. Ready to devour him. His breath caught in his throat, his heart pounding so hard it felt like his chest would burst.

This is where they stood. I'm here.

The floor quaked with every footfall of the beast, sending vibrations that reverberated through him.

Just a little longer, Cole! Hold on, he commanded himself.

Behind him, a voice called out.

"Cole!"

Startled, the orb slipped from his grasp. *No!*

He dove to the ground, scrabbling through the debris. The thunderous footsteps were growing louder.

He managed to grasp it in the darkness, his fingers closing around the orb. He squeezed it in both hands, making sure he wouldn't miss the button.

Nothing.

Dammit. Come on!

He turned it over in his hands and squeezed again. In that split second, he looked up, and it came into full view. But all he saw was the bright blue eyes, seizing him.

And it was gone in an instant.

The moon and stars returned, the ground solid and familiar beneath him. He gasped and fell to his knees, pressing his hands to his head as he tried to calm himself.

His hands dropped to his side, brushing the grass as his mind reeled.

I'm alive . . .

But the relief was short-lived. *I'm a fool. I can't do it, it's too much. We don't stand a chance.*

His body bore no evidence of the horror he'd just faced. It was as if it had never happened. But the dread, the guilt, clung to him like a shadow.

A soft voice pulled him from his thoughts.

"Did you go in?"

Cole hung his head, unable to turn and face her. *I can't believe I almost got her killed.*

He remained still as soft footsteps approached him. They stopped, leaving a gap between them.

"Time?" she breathed.

In that moment, he wanted nothing more than her. Desperation rose in his chest. He could no longer bear the gulf between them.

He lowered his hand, holding out his finger and thumb: *Stay and never leave me. Ever.*

It was out of his control now; he'd given all he could. The rest was up to her.

Vella took several careful steps and knelt behind him. Then a hesitant hand touched his back before retreating.

After a moment, he felt it return, trembling ever so slightly before another joined it. Her hands crept around to his chest, fingers tentative. Her arms tightened, pressing against him. He felt the warmth of her body sink into his back, the steady rise and fall of her breath as she embraced him. Finally, her head pressed against his back, and with that light touch, something inside him settled. His chaotic breaths slowed, evening out as her touch anchored him back to safety.

"I'm here now," she said.

One thing was clear in his mind: *I don't deserve her.*

His next words left him effortlessly, like an easy breath.

"I love you."

She lifted her head for a moment. Then she strengthened her embrace and pressed her forehead against his back.

"I love you, too."

The tension drained from his body, leaving only a profound exhaustion. *Mom, Dad, how were you so strong? How did you face that with a smile?*

In that moment, he felt the answer.

"Why don't you hate me?" he whispered.

"After everything we've been through, how could I be mad at my Cole?"

"I don't deserve your forgiveness."

"Take it anyway."

He turned to face her and, with a finger, he gently lifted her chin to meet her eyes. The gentleness of her dark green eyes filled him with a deep ache.

"I should have never hesitated. You're the most beautiful person I know."

He leaned in, pressing his lips to hers in a gentle, lingering kiss.

22

ORPHANAGE ADMISSION FORM

Mother: Leah [8591]   Father: Edgar [8598]

Child: Amy [8977]   Age: 1 year, 10 months.

Authorization: Rachael [8491], Head of the Orphanage

Date: 07.09.442

REASON(S) CITED

From the mother: Both parents are unfit to raise Amy.

PARENT STIPULATIONS

• Visitation rights are limited to birthdays present presentations.

• As per the mother's request, both parents are to be turned away if they attempt any visits to Amy.

• Any changes to stipulations need to be approved by both parents after a meeting with the head of the orphanage.

NOTES

A letter from both parents to Amy is attached to give to her on her fourteenth birthday.

The sun had only just begun its slow climb, casting long shadows across the dirt path as Cole walked beside Vella. Exhaustion from the sleepless night was overshadowed by a renewed sense of purpose permeating his every nerve. As they made their way to the clearing, Cole took a chance and reached for Vella's hand.

She flinched at his touch but was fast to recover, holding it out for him to grasp. Her delight was palpable in the way she wriggled with excitement at his touch, bringing a laugh to Cole's lips. Suddenly, she jumped in front of him. Grabbing his shirt, she pulled his face close to hers. With a smile, she pressed her nose to his, lingering for a moment before kissing him.

He smiled against her lips and gently pulled her closer. Returning the kiss with a tenderness that made time melt away. They lost themselves in the moment, making the world feel irrelevant and small by comparison.

By the time they reached the clearing, Edgar and Alex had already done several rounds. Seeing Cole and Vella hand in hand, their shift from exhaustion to amusement was apparent.

Alex shot Edgar a sly grin. "Told you."

Edgar chuckled. "It's about time," he remarked. And they all knew he didn't just mean their lateness.

Vella, suddenly self-conscious, let go of Cole's hand, looked away from them and hurried ahead.

"Lovebirds, you're behind—catch up! Go, go, go," Edgar said, clapping his hands as they passed him.

Running alongside Vella, Cole felt a surge of energy he hadn't felt in a long time. The session passed in a blur, the exercises barely registering as they moved into their wind-down stretches.

"Good luck getting back your fifteen-stage circuit record," Cole boasted.

"I guess I'll have to settle for my twelve-, ten-, seven-, five-, three-, and two-stage records," Vella said.

"There are some concerns as to the legitimacy of some of those records."

"Are you questioning my integrity as Timekeeper?" Edgar asked.

"What integrity? We all know you fudge the numbers for her."

Edgar and Vella glanced at each other, trying to keep a straight face.

"That's what I'm talking about. Cheaters, the both of you," Cole protested.

"You're being paranoid," Edgar said.

"Don't get me started about cheating. I saw you didn't go all the way around on the third one," Vella added.

"Who cares about records," Alex cut in.

Cole and Vella both sniggered, then burst out laughing.

"I think someone's jealous," Vella said.

"Why would—" Alex cut himself off, lips pressing into a hard line as a sharp breath escaped through his nose.

"There's no shame in being fourth," Cole said.

"Fourth! No way Edgar's beating me."

Even Edgar couldn't help but laugh. "The numbers don't lie," he said.

"Whatever. Doesn't matter," Alex muttered.

"Sounds like it matters to you," Vella prodded.

Alex just grunted, returning to his stretching.

"I think we should add a twenty—"

Cole froze. A twig snapped under a footstep behind him. He turned, and his stomach dropped.

"Edgar?" he called out. It sounded like it was a plea for help because it was, his voice tight with dread.

Leah stood there, arms crossed, her morning robe billowing in the soft breeze. The stoic way she held herself only made the tension in the air thicker.

"Leah," Edgar managed to say, his usual composure shattered.

Leah glanced at Alex, who immediately looked away from her. Then at Cole, who did the same. Vella was the only one she offered a small smile.

"Go home, children. I want to talk to Edgar. *Alone*," she said, her voice controlled and commanding.

The three exchanged nervous glances, sensing impending disaster.

"Leah—" Cole started, but it only took a simple look from Leah to shut him down. He shot Edgar an anxious look. Edgar returned a calm nod.

Even if Cole had the orb, he knew it wouldn't help them here. After last night, he had taken Edgar's advice a little more seriously and hidden it away to prevent it from being misused by himself or anyone else.

Cole turned to Vella. He motioned with his head for them to leave. Along with Alex, they gathered their things and scurried away.

This left Leah and Edgar alone.

Leah remained motionless with her arms crossed, studying Edgar. He moved closer, his eyes darting around, unable to remain on her. He had to compose himself and fast. If she found out what they were actually doing, she might kill him herself. Any danger to Cole and Vella, real or perceived, would be met with her full wrath.

"What's all this?" she asked.

He cleared his throat. "This? Cole's idea. He thought some exercise would do me some good," he lied, though the nervousness in his voice betrayed him.

"Uh-huh." Leah's eyes narrowed. "And Alex?"

"He kinda just . . . inserted himself."

"I see." Her eyes sharpened. "How are the repairs with Vella's place going?" she asked with an eyebrow raised.

Fortunately for him, he didn't miss a beat. "Didn't take too long. Actually, I don't think it was a real problem. I think Cole made it up."

"Why would he do that?" she asked, her tone still firm and probing.

He sighed, glancing around. "He's trying to help."

"Who?" she pressed.

Edgar looked up and away, mouth tight.

Leah read the cue, and her expression softened. Her mouth contorted as she thought, then, after a moment, she cleared her throat. "H-how have you been?"

"Great."

It wasn't lost on her that the wear of the past several years had taken its toll on him, adding an extra ten years to his face.

"Seriously, how are you?"

"We don't have to do this, Leah."

"Answer the question," she said, a little more forcefully than intended.

He shook his head, staring down.

"So, nothing's changed?"

He shook his head again. "What did you think would change?"

"I don't know. I thought if I weren't around, maybe you would . . . feel better."

A chuckle escaped him. "Having you around wasn't the issue."

"What is it, then?"

"It's just . . . nothing I feel like I can control. You already know this."

"Not because of Amy?"

Her name hit a nerve. He winced. "No."

Swallowing hard, he said, "I've told you before. I don't blame you."

"Shut up," she snapped. She turned away, moving her eyes around, blinking. "Dammit . . ." She took a deep breath and faced him.

"I'm sorry," she whispered. "I should've come to see you . . . sometime in the last five years."

"I'm not your problem."

"Oh, Edgar . . . you never stopped being my problem. I've just been pretending you aren't."

He looked at her as a soft smile formed, drawn into awe as if he were looking at a ghost from the past.

"Don't look at me like that," she said quietly.

"Like what?"

"Like . . . you're seeing something that's no longer there. It's gone. Even I don't see it anymore."

"It's still there. Trust me."

"Shut up," she muttered. The full weight that had been building in her hit her, dragging her down.

"It's good to see you," he said. "I missed talking to you."

"Edgar . . . why haven't you moved on? Forget about me."

Edgar let out a bitter laugh. "Move on? Look around. Who's left?" he scoffed. "They're either dead or with someone else enjoying their remaining days together, and I'm stuck here. Watching. Come on, Leah. I know why no one wants me, but you? I was never under any illusions about my standing. I was lucky to have you. I don't understand why you chose me in the first place. What excuse do you have? From what I've heard, you haven't even been trying."

"That's none of your business."

"Well, take your own advice, then. I'm none of your business."

She took a moment, feeling herself sinking. "I don't deserve it. It wouldn't be fair. After I let her go . . . I let go of any hopes of . . ."

"You deserve to be happy," he said.

She squeezed her eyes, trying to refocus. To get away from the topic, she asked, "What's really going on?"

"What do you mean?"

"Why didn't Cole or Alex tell me about this?"

"I don't know. Maybe they didn't want to worry you . . . about me."

"No," she said. "It's more than that."

Edgar shrugged. "I wouldn't worry. At least try not to. It's just a bit of fun . . . Maybe not fun most of the time, but it's good for me and I feel like it is for them as well."

Leah took a moment to consider and gave a small nod.

"Those two . . . Cole and Vella. You did well with them." A smile spread on Edgar's face. "They—" He broke off.

"They what?"

He shook his head, regretting his words. "Don't worry."

"What did they do?" she demanded.

He swallowed and met her eyes. "It feels like they saved me. I don't really get out of the house much these days . . . but they've given me something. In a way, they're saving me from myself."

Leah's face froze, her gaze dropping as her fists clenched at her sides.

"You need to stop blaming yourself. You put up with all you could."

"I didn't try, Edgar."

"It's all right."

"It's not." She took another moment to study the ghost of her past. Unable to bear it any longer, she looked past him. "I'm gonna . . . go . . ."

"Sure."

"Is this a regular thing?"

"Morning and evening."

"Okay."

Before she could leave, he cut in. "The other night . . ." He started but faltered, letting out a heavy sigh. "I—" He stopped himself again, shaking his head. After taking a moment to take a deep breath, he smiled. "Amy's growing up so fast. It was good to see her again. She's looking more like you every day."

Her eyes lit up for a moment, an almost conditioned response to hearing her name. "I can't believe something so good came from me . . . I just hope she takes after you," she said. "Wait . . . how do you know? I didn't see you that night. Where were you?"

"I was around."

"You could have come and said hello and wished me a happy birthday if you were *around*. That would have been nice."

He lowered his head and nodded. "I know. I'm sorry."

"Don't be, it's fine."

She took a step back, but he stopped her.

"Leah . . ." He hesitated, letting out a slow breath. "It's a tough time for them. You remember what it was like . . . waiting for the people you love to die."

"What?"

"Cole. He isn't taking it well; I can tell."

She thought back to the days spent waiting for Cole's parents to die, counting down each one with dread filling her heart. She would have done anything not to lose them. Anything. But there was nothing that could be done, and it tore her apart.

"I don't know what I'm supposed to do."

"I don't think there is anything you can do. I just wanted you to know. Don't be too hard on him."

Leah nodded and turned to leave, then paused. "I was watching for a while . . . . it looked like they were enjoying themselves. I'm glad. They could do with someone like you in their lives."

23

I wonder what it's like to live past thirty. That's what everyone asks themselves. No one is exempt from their day of death, so there's never any reason to get upset with anyone else. Unless you think about them: the humans who exist, or once existed, outside Eden. How much did they squander what we would kill for? The trap is to covet what can never be obtained. And if you do become trapped, ask yourself: What are you missing that's right in front of you?

—REFLECTIONS ON EDEN

By Simon #9067

Dinner the night before had been eerily quiet. Leah didn't speak or touch her food. Every so often, she shot Cole a measuring stare. Each time, he averted his gaze. He knew Edgar gave nothing away, but rather than tempt fate, he kept his distance.

Presently, during the lunch break, Leah tore small pieces from her sandwich, eyes scanning the park. The anxiety from the morning before still clung to her, making her restless.

Vella sat beside her, silent and thoughtful, her eyes on the people playing ball games. Leah's gaze caught on a familiar figure across the park—Alex.

A harsh breath escaped through her nose. She set the sandwich aside, fists tightening as she rose. "Back in a minute," she muttered to Vella.

Alex, spotting Leah approaching, took a hesitant step back, like a helpless deer sensing danger from a predator. Every instinct screamed at him to run, but he stood his ground, knowing that running would arouse further suspicion. And where could he go? He would only be able to elude her for perhaps a day. At best.

Might as well get it over with, he thought.

"Hey." Leah's voice was sharp, cutting through the playful noise of the park.

Alex's eyes flicked around nervously. He knew he could put her mind at ease if he could remain calm and composed.

"Why didn't you tell me about your little exercise group?"

Leah demanded, closing the distance between them.

Alex swallowed hard, scrambling for what to say. "Sorry, I was, it's just . . ."

"What?"

"Wasn't sure if I wanted to keep joining them," he lied.

"And?"

"I'll keep going."

Her eyes narrowed. "So, you and Cole are getting along now?"

"He still has his reservations about me, I can tell, but we were able to talk . . . it's a start."

This, at least, was something she could smile about. "Good. That's great."

He tried to return a smile, but it didn't quite reach his eyes. She noticed it but said nothing.

The smile faded from Leah's lips. "I should be happier . . . I just can't shake this feeling he's up to no good."

"Like what?"

"I don't know. It's just that boy . . . I know when he's hiding something."

"You worry too much," he said.

She shifted her focus to Alex's face, her eyes narrowing. "Speaking of which . . . Alex, what's going on with you?"

"What do you mean?"

"You're not yourself. What's happened, Alex?"

"Nothing's happened. Nothing's going on. Honestly."

He tried to deflect, but Leah wasn't having it. "Cut the crap, Alex. I can see it in your eyes. For weeks I've seen this shadow of a person. What's bothering you?"

"Nothing," he said in a faint voice, diverting his gaze.

"Alex. What's going on?" she continued to press. "Hey. What. Is. It?"

Leah's unwavering gaze finally broke through his defenses and the words were torn from his throat.

"It's Ellie."

"What about Ellie?"

Leah's expression softened as the realization hit her.

"Of course. I should've seen it sooner," she muttered. "You're afraid of losing her."

He nodded.

Edgar had warned her that Cole wasn't taking looming death well, and now she understood it wasn't only him. Leah shut her eyes and silently cursed. When she opened her eyes, she offered a softer expression.

"Come on." She took his arm and guided him to a quieter corner of the park, away from prying eyes.

"You're focusing on the wrong part," she said. "You have two years left with her. Make the most of that time."

Alex nodded but didn't look at her. "I can't imagine how she must feel, knowing how little time she has left. She tries to hide it, but I can see it," Alex said. "Like I see yours."

"Mine? I'm at peace with—"

"Now who's not telling the truth?" Alex cut in. "I see it. I help people transition to the final stages all the time and it's as plain to see on them . . . as it is on you and Ellie. Stop trying to act tough. I can't stand it. Be real with me for once."

"What do you want me to say?" Leah demanded.

"That you're not okay. I want someone, anyone, to admit it!"

"I'm fine. Besides, it's none of your concern."

"Unbelievable . . ." Alex drew his eyes away from Leah and looked around. "Every day I hate this place more and more. I can't stand it."

"That doesn't sound like the Alex I know."

"Apparently we don't know each other."

"Enough, Alex. Have you spoken to Ellie about this?"

He shook his head. "Everything was a lot simpler before Ellie. Don't get me wrong, I'm happier with her. But why does the bad have to feel so horrific when what you have is so amazing?"

"That's what love does," Leah said. "You don't get one without the other."

"When we first got together, I told her I'd be okay with the limited time we'd have together," Alex said. "But I'm not. And I know she isn't either."

"Oh, Alex." She pulled him into a hug, pressing him close. "None of us are okay. But we keep going. Try our best. That's all we can do."

He gripped her sleeve. "Life here doesn't feel worth it without her."

She held him tighter. "It's always worth it, Alex."

Giving him a moment to settle, she let go and looked him in the eye. "Talk to Ellie. Don't let your emotions get the best of you. Keep your head. And don't let the fear win."

He nodded, his resolve shaky but present.

"And this stuff with Cole and Edgar, does it have anything to do with Ellie?"

Alex turned away, unable to meet her gaze, and shook his head. "It's helping to distract from all that."

"Talk to her," Leah reiterated, with a stronger tone. "Okay?"

He gave a faint nod.

"Remember, you can come talk to me anytime."

"Yeah, I know."

Returning to the bench, she found Cole sitting where Vella had been. Vella was on her way to sit with Edgar when she stopped and looked back at Cole.

He was frozen, eyes fixed ahead.

They could only hope Alex didn't break.

As Leah approached him, she thought, *I should have no reason to fear, but that boy. I know him. All too well . . . Cole's not dumb. But why does it feel like he's doing something reckless and dragging them in? He can never leave well enough alone.*

Vella flashed two fingers to Cole repeatedly to try and warn him: *LEAVE! Save yourself!*

Leah sat down beside him, her agitation etched in her eyes.

She turned to Cole, staring a hole through him.

He dared not look at her.

Alex crossed the park, his steps heavy, the conversation with Leah still weighing on him. He spotted Ellie sitting on a bench on the far side. Her face lit up when she saw him. She reached down, rummaging around in her bag to take out their lunch. As

she was doing that, he sank back, head tilted up, staring at the
sky.

Ellie put their lunch to the side and slid across, tucking herself
under his arm. He let out a long breath in and out, allowing
himself to take in her scent to ground him.

"What's wrong?" she asked.

Alex dropped his head, meeting her eyes with an easy smile.
He pulled her closer and kissed her on the forehead.

"Nothing."

"What was that about, with Leah?"

"Oh." He took a moment, eyes pulling away from her to look
ahead. His eyes clouded, and his expression faded.

He forced a chuckle without a smile. "She's upset about the
dispenser schedule."

Ellie studied him for a long moment, the silence stretching
between them. Then she turned forward, her eyes scanning the
distance, trying to find what he was looking at.

"Right . . ."

24

In the early days, it was assumed Eden would simply empty itself of all people because no one would willingly have children. But that theory was proven wrong sooner than anticipated. They didn't count on humanity's greatest trait: adaptation. And adapt we did. A lifespan of thirty years became relative. If that was all we had, we would make it work. Eden wouldn't stop us from building lives, relationships, and families. Without available contraception, having children became inevitable. And, over time, as society evolved to care for all its citizens, the guilt of bringing children into this world began to fade. They knew their children would be cared for, just as they had been. Still, debates about the ethics of having children persist. There will always be objections and people abstaining from having children. Going forward, I can see the number of objections shrink as our culture will simply see it as a part of life. It only took a couple of years for the outside universe to fade into irrelevance. This is where we would live and die. The human spirit exists to preserve. Not to give up and go out quietly. And then there is the hope that one day yours will be the children to escape this place and live the long lives you could only dream of. There is always a reason to keep going.

—A PEOPLE THAT SHOULD HAVE NEVER BEEN

The History of Eden

by Luke #4342

Alex woke before dawn, lying in bed with his eyes fixed on the sterile white ceiling. Its starkness offered no details he could focus on and relax his eyes. The haze of white made him nauseous, a constant reminder of their reality: rats trapped in a maze with no exit.

He glanced at the wall above his head, where the same oppressive whiteness seemed to close in on him, mocking him with its cold uniformity. And he thought: *No wonder why people don't want to live in these places* . . .

There used to be a waiting list for Permahomes. Now, with the population dwindling, there were always dozens left unoccupied. Ready at anyone's request. It wasn't just a population problem that caused so many to be left empty.

He couldn't help but feel amused as he pictured Cole trying to accept living in one of the Permahomes. Cole wasn't alone in his rejection of them; much of the population chose Crafthomes. They came with extra maintenance problems, but they were made by human hands, not cold and alien like the Permahomes.

He rolled to his side, and his expression softened as he watched Ellie. He ran his eyes over each little wrinkle around her nose and eyes. Strands of dark brown hair spilled across her face, half hidden beneath the blanket as she lay lost in the quiet peace of dreams.

It had been a week since Leah had confronted him, and he still hadn't spoken to Ellie about what plagued him. The days blurred together, unchanging, except for the wall between them, which only seemed to grow thicker.

Her slow, rhythmic breathing was interrupted by a brief half-snort before returning to normal. He stifled a laugh and shifted closer to observe her. The longer he stared, the harder it became to tear himself away from the comfort of their bed.

With a reluctant sigh, he forced himself up. He dressed, casting one last look at Ellie before heading out.

The deserted streets and early-morning silence brought him a sense of peace he couldn't find within himself. The crisp morning air flowed through him, helping him brush off the early morning fatigue.

Alex made his way toward a particular spot along the perimeter wall, and his favorite place in all of Eden. It was the one spot that offered him time for quiet reflection and where he could attempt to gain some perspective on his life.

His feet first brought him to the Eden memorial. As he approached, a mechanical servant of their captors passed by in the opposite direction, startling him.

A surge of anxiety overwhelmed him; instinctive fear flared into anger. He resisted the urge to turn around and kick the machine. He wanted to destroy it but knew he would die before he even put a dent in it.

"Damn Ghost," he muttered.

He came to a stop, closed his eyes and took a deep breath. Then, opening them again, he fixed his gaze on the wall ahead.

The names and numbers of everyone who had ever lived in Eden were etched into it. He made sure to come here at least once a day to remind himself what he was fighting for. A little over nine thousand names stretched before him, a sobering reminder of his place in the grand design. But also, a reminder he wasn't alone. Nine thousand souls—past, present, and future—shared in what he was experiencing. He brushed his fingers across the indents in the wall.

Thousands of people no longer alive understood him, and he wanted to understand them.

How did they do it?

Once, the population had thrived at over a thousand people. But now it was teetering on the brink of falling below four hundred within a generation or two. The decline felt inevitable, like a slow, unrelenting spiral. Alex couldn't help but wonder if this place would simply empty itself, running out of people before anyone uncovered the truth. *What number on the wall would mark the end of it all?*

Alex looked up. The immensity of the wall was the only thing to greet him. It loomed above, cold and oppressive. He sighed and lowered his eyes to the ground.

Putting the thoughts aside, he turned to the left, where the installation known as the Children of Eden stood. The wooden wall, now hundreds of meters long, was covered with clay handprints preserved behind glass, each belonging to a child who had grown up in Eden. At five years old, they added their mark to the wall. Rather than allowing the numbers that marked their identities to be a source of shame, they marked them next to their handprints along with their names, proudly displaying them. It was a symbolic act of reclaiming their identity. It asserted that these numbers were theirs, not tools to diminish them.

Alex walked the length of the wall at a steady, slow pace. He scanned the mass of handprints, the last traces of those who had come before, each one a reminder of the fragile innocence that was buried within each of Eden's citizens. He stopped at a different spot each time he came, imagining the lives behind the small hands printed into clay. The ghosts of the thousands of hands reached out to him, telling him, "I was here. Where you're standing. We're no different."

He drew on their collective strength, proud to stand as one of them. He could feel himself reaching into the future, offering the same support to those who would come here, seeking strength in their hour of need.

He neared the end of the wall, where his own handprint resided. But that wasn't what he was looking for. He scanned the wall until he found the name Steven. A few years older than Alex, Steven had also grown up in the orphanage, and the two had known one another well enough that Alex considered him a friend.

Steven had recently taken his own life, the weight of Eden's reality too much for him to bear. He'd lost everyone close to him, leaving him alone and isolated.

Alex's chest ached as he stared at the handprint. He'd tried to help, but it hadn't been enough. *I could've done more. Should've done more.* Those were the words he had scolded himself with many times since that day.

He looked up and down at all the other thousands of handprints. How many had felt like Steven had in his last days? How many had succumbed to the pressures like he had? How many had pressed on despite all of it?

It's not too late. I'm still here. I can change things, he repeated to himself.

He eyed Vella's, Cole's, and his own. He shook off the dark thoughts and pressed forward.

At the end of the line, he saw the latest additions, including Amy's handprint, and it brought a smile to his face. Then he looked at the unoccupied area, where his own child's handprint would soon be. A small reminder that hope remained.

As he left the memorial and approached the clearing, the distant sound of an argument reached his ears. He recognized the voices immediately—Cole and Vella. They'd been at it for at least half an hour. It annoyed and amazed him that they had the energy to be this boisterous this early.

When he arrived, he saw them sparring with their wooden swords. Edgar sat off to the side, eyes half closed.

Of course, it's about their stupid game, he thought, shaking his head.

It meant everything to them, though he could never quite understand why.

Cole called out to him. "Help settle this."

"No! He's just gonna side with you," Vella groaned.

"Oh, and Edgar didn't just side with you?"

Alex had no interest in getting involved. Not in the slightest. But something deep down told him it would be worth it. Not for the argument itself. But for something far more important.

"Go on. What is it?"

25

Bernard: When I was twelve, Ryan and I thought it would be a great idea to stay up all night. We did. And instead of going to class, we slept. Our teacher stormed into our room, banging a wooden spoon against a pot. He dragged us out of bed and into class, and every time we tried to rest our heads, there he was, pot and spoon in hand, ready to wake us up. Kathy sat back, laughing at us. My friend Ryan became a teacher, and guess what? He did the same thing to one of his students. Ah, the circle of life.

Kathy: It was very funny. Oh, that reminds me! The day before that, Bernard farted in class. He tried to cover it up by coughing. Way too loudly and not even in time with it, drawing more attention to himself. Then the smell hit. I hated him for months after that. That's why I enjoyed his suffering so much.

Bernard: I forgot about that. She did the same years later, but covered it a little better with a cough. It wasn't well enough, though; she went beet red as all eyes turned on her.

Kathy: Oh, shut up. At least mine didn't smell.

Bernard: Sure it didn't.

—"KATHY #8591 & BERNARD #8593"
CHILDREN OF THE PEACEFUL PASSAGE
by Aleister #8990

"What are you thinking about?"

Ellie's voice broke the silence, pulling Alex back from his thoughts. Ignoring his breakfast, he traced the rough wood grain of the table, feeling the small imperfections beneath his fingers, trying to anchor himself to the present.

"Actually, trying not to think," he said, not looking up.

Ellie's eyes narrowed. "And what are you trying not to think about?"

"Work," he lied.

Before she could press him further, Alex stood, gathering their dishes. He rinsed them in a rush, the clatter of plates punctuating the unspoken friction. He bent to kiss her on the cheek before heading out.

"See you for lunch?" he called from the front door.

"Sure," she said. She hesitated, as if wanting to say more, but let him go.

Stepping outside, the perfect weather did little to lift his spirits. The short walk to his office, past the identical houses lining the street, added to the suffocating sense of monotony. Eden's city center loomed ahead, bustling with people commuting to their respective jobs.

Approaching his building, he saw Leah entering one of the manufacturing buildings down the street. He waved and she returned a hard gaze with a small wave. With a sigh he went inside.

His office, located on the second floor, sat at the heart of Eden. It was part of a shared workspace, where his desk faced another within a cluster of four. To his right was the mayor's office, closed off but ever present. To his left, a window that encompassed most of the wall offered a view of the busy street below.

Alex surveyed the papers strewn across his desk and blew out a sharp breath. Sitting down, his hands hovered over the dispenser schedule. He needed to get to that soon, but he decided it was a job for another day. He placed it on top of the stack of death reports and pushed them aside. He pulled a small stack of citizen complaints closer. A single file sat to the right of them.

He gripped his pen, staring at it. He glanced up at the clock on the wall and tossed the pen aside and put his head in his hands. After taking a breath, he cast his eyes to the window. The constant flow of foot traffic below often became his distraction. A way to drift away from the problems that accompanied his work and life.

The fragility of their makeshift society terrified him. He sensed that they were always walking a fine line between order and chaos. As if at any moment the curtain could be pulled back and everything would descend into turmoil.

He had one particularly gripping fear. As he watched the street below, the nightmare would unfold before his eyes in real time. It always started the same: a man, erratically sprinting down the street, eyes wild with manic panic, wailing and raving. All the fears, anger, and hopelessness that had been long suppressed deep inside were finally unleashed.

Then it would spread. One person would become ten, ten would become fifty, and soon there would be hundreds. Before long, the entire place would be infected, engulfed in a swarm of madness. People turning on Eden and each other. Violence and destruction would spread like a disease, all ignited by that single person. That one person would shatter everything, allowing everyone to let go of their fragile hold on hope. Buildings would burn. Death would ripple outward. And he'd remain sitting there, frozen, powerless to stop the inevitable.

Because that was how it wanted to be.

How it demanded to be.

People passed below, their skin transparent to him, like glass. Their calm exteriors scarcely concealed the chaotic beings lurking underneath. Those entities stared back, sneering at him, taunting him. That fragile glass shell could crack at any moment. And when one cracked, it would crack them all. Despair taking root and spreading was one small catalyst away.

Tearing his eyes away from the window, he calmed his breathing. He knew it to be nothing more than mere fantasy, yet he couldn't shake the feeling that it was inevitable, given their situation trapped in Eden.

And yet, despite those moments of looming dread—which were, in truth, few and far between—what he witnessed every day defied those fears. The strength people showed far outweighed any reason they had to stay headstrong in the face of such pressure. Each day was filled with small victories: the reward of helping others in his role and witnessing others support each other as they navigated life in their confined world. It amazed him at what people could accomplish when they worked together, making hope rise above despair.

Today, though, the burden felt heavier, tipping the scales the wrong way. The file on his desk was the culprit. Death was the one constant in Eden, an inevitable force that demanded his attention all too often. An appointment was scheduled today, a couple, both twenty-nine, their time nearing an end. Their reality. His responsibility.

He pushed through the minor paperwork first, anything to delay the meeting. But eventually, the time came, and he couldn't keep them waiting any longer. Snatching at the file, he left the office.

Their house, indistinguishable from his own save for the garden and the number eight on the door, greeted him with a stark familiarity. They welcomed him in, guiding him to the living room where they sat together on the sofa, hand in hand.

"Would you like some tea?" the woman, Kathy, offered, her voice steady.

Too steady, Alex thought.

Alex shook his head. "No, thank you." He paused, steeling himself for what he had to say. "First, I want to check in. How are you both holding up?"

The man, Bernard, spoke first. "We've been preparing for a while, so . . . we're ready. As ready as we can be, I suppose. Not sure how else to put it." He let out a nervous laugh, squeezing Kathy's hand.

Alex nodded, his throat tightening. "I understand Kathy has two weeks and, Bernard, you have two months."

They both nodded as the reality of their situation sank in, blanketing the room in tense silence.

Before Alex could continue, Bernard cleared his throat, his voice firmer this time. "I've been thinking a lot about it, and despite her protests, I've decided we'll go together. I want to be with her during that time."

Kathy turned to him. Her eyes glistening with unshed tears. Alex could see the love and the pain in her eyes, and it took everything in him to maintain his composure.

He swallowed hard, his throat dry. "You do? Well, there's nothing to say you can't. I need to make sure that's what you want."

Bernard didn't hesitate. "It is."

Kathy looked away, blinking rapidly to hold back the tears.

When she spoke again, her voice trembled. "I keep telling him he doesn't need to, that I'll be fine, but he won't listen."

"Personally, I think it's a beautiful gesture," Alex said.

She leaned into Bernard, pressing her head against his shoulder. He wrapped his arm around her, planting a kiss on her forehead.

Bringing herself back upright, she met Alex's gaze. "Do you have a special someone in your life?"

"I do."

"Would you let them do that?"

Alex paused, considering his answer. "I could try to stop her. But . . . it would ultimately be up to her. Hypothetically, she might be afraid to go it alone later, so I would understand."

"I never thought of it like that." She looked at Bernard, eyes softening with a sadness she couldn't hide, before turning back to Alex. "Is she younger?"

"Several years older."

"Would you . . . ?" Kathy's voice trailed off.

Alex glanced away, the words sticking in his throat. "She wouldn't allow it. Not even to entertain the thought." He looked out the window behind them. "But if she did . . . I'd gladly go with her."

"She must be a special lady."

"Very."

He accepted Bernard's request and moved on to the practical details of their passing—boxing possessions, the recycling process. Then, finally, came the difficult part.

"When it's time, our designated life transition specialist, Riley, will come to escort you to the Peaceful Passage."

Kathy's grip on Bernard's hand tightened, her knuckles whitening as her fingers clenched.

"Will it hurt?" she asked, her voice trembling.

This was the part that made everyone anxious, and the part they wanted the most reassurance about. He explained that while there were no guarantees, the aim was to make the process as painless as possible. The procedure involved inducing unconsciousness in a way that minimized discomfort, followed by a careful method of ensuring a gentle and serene end.

Alex did his best to explain everything thoroughly, being mindful not to heighten any fears about the sensitive subject.

She nodded, trying to find comfort in his words. "That doesn't sound too bad," she said, looking at Bernard.

"Together, it'll be nothing," he replied, a sad smile tugging at his lips.

"Yes. Yes, you're right."

Their courage warmed Alex, but it also deepened the ache in his chest. He tightened his grip on the clipboard, Bernard's words echoing in his mind. Looking down, he took a steadying breath, marking off items on the form.

Only one remained.

"Do you have any final wishes or requests?" Alex asked.

"You can't give us an extra twenty years, can you?" she asked, adding a light laugh.

Maybe, he thought.

"I wish I could," Alex said with a bittersweet smile.

"It's all right," she said, shaking her head. "I was joking. All we need are these last weeks. Together."

Alex nodded. "Well, if there's anything, let us know. You're entitled to any request, within reason."

He finished the meeting and took his leave, his steps heavy as he walked back to the office. The pit in his stomach threatened to swallow him whole. He passed by the office building, choosing instead to wander aimlessly.

He spotted a bench overlooking a flowerbed and sat. Beyond it, the woods stretched out. Ignoring the scenery, he tilted his head back, eyes tracing the artificial clouds.

"Skipping work?" Ellie's voice broke through his stupor as she sat down beside him. "I saw you walk past. You look like you're having a rough day."

Alex's eyes wandered down to Ellie's face, then to her stomach.

"Should we have brought them into this place? Did we make a mistake by deciding to have a child?"

She narrowed her eyes, more confused than concerned.

"Do you?"

"Sometimes . . . to put them through all the pain and suffering. Knowing that, like us, they'll only have a short life. It feels cruel."

"Well . . . would you trade it all for never being born? All the things you've been lucky enough to experience. Despite all the pain and suffering." She swept her gaze around. "Look around, Alex. Would you trade it?"

He followed her eyes, taking in the explosion of color that surrounded them.

"Feel me." She took his hand and stroked his palm. "Would you trade this for your worst day never to happen?"

Alex closed his eyes, feeling her soft touch.

"Think about your life, Alex. Tell me you wouldn't still take the limited time you've had, despite all the bad. Even if you were to die today, would you honestly wish you'd never been born?"

Alex smiled faintly and shook his head.

"Thought so."

He turned his head forward and his smile faded.

"Alex . . . what is this really about?"

He sighed. "Remember when we first met, and I said I wasn't bothered? That I'd be okay when you . . . eventually left before me?"

Ellie shifted closer. "Oh, dear . . ." she whispered, her voice full of understanding.

"I'm having a hard time accepting it."

"That's what's been troubling you? I'm relieved. I thought you were cheating on me," she teased.

"Of course not—"

"I was joking, dummy," she said, squeezing his hand. "I always knew this would happen."

"From the beginning?"

"I've seen it . . . and experienced it too many times. It's happened to me with people I've lost." She sighed, feeling the weight of her past pressing down on her. "I just didn't think it would happen this soon."

"Do you feel it, or is it just me?"

"Every day since we met."

"And you still wanted to be with me?"

She ran a teasing finger up his arm. "It's like putting a cake in front of a child and telling them not to eat it. It's getting eaten. And what a good cake it is," she said with a sly grin.

He smiled, but the sadness in his eyes didn't fade.

"You're not having regrets, are you?" she asked.

"Of course not. I just never thought . . ."

"It would be this hard?" she said, reading his mind.

"Yeah. This place without you feels . . . empty. Pointless."

"I hate doing this to you. I know it's selfish of me. Sometimes I think I should've left you alone."

"Don't say that."

"Then I remember how I wouldn't trade the days with the people I lost for anything. Even with all the pain that came with it."

Alex sighed, looking around. "This damn place . . . we could've had sixty to seventy more years. It's hard not to think about it. The what-ifs are killing me."

"Even if we did, I still would've gone first, and you'd have many years without me."

"I'd be sick of you by then, so it wouldn't be a problem," he said, forcing a smile.

She dug a playful elbow into his chest, a small smile tugging at her lips.

"You ever think about it? You know . . . dying?" he asked.

"Too much," she whispered.

Alex thought back to the couple he'd met with earlier and their decision to go together. The idea of not facing the end alone.

"Would you let me go with you? We could go together, so you wouldn't need to be alone."

"That's the sweetest, but dumbest, thing I've heard you say."

He chuckled, knowing her answer before he even asked.

"How about . . . we go out in a blaze of glory?"

"Like your friend's parents did?"

"That's something I could live with. At least we could say we tried. I never used to think I could do something so insane, but now I have something worth fighting for . . .”

“If we were the same age, I might entertain the idea.”

“No, you wouldn’t.”

“You’re right. I’m not much of a fighter. And most importantly, that’s not our reality.”

“Our reality?” he mused. “Are we fools? Do you think we gave up too easily on trying to leave this place?”

“Not at all. We’re doing our best. There are some things we can’t control.”

“But don’t you think we could try for future generations? It may take a million years, but one day, that generation could be free thanks to what we started here. Did we give up too soon?”

“It’s a noble thought. But it’s just that, a thought.”

“I can’t sit here and do nothing.”

She pressed in closer, resting on him. “Be with me here and now. That’s not nothing to me. That’s everything.”

26

The young are not psychologically equipped to handle the death of someone close to them, especially that of a parental figure. Proper mental development is essential for processing trauma, and children under fourteen fall far below that threshold. In these vulnerable children, the mind runs wild. If left unchecked in the wake of life-altering events, it can cause irreparable damage to the psyche. As time passes and more children are left here with nowhere to go, this place will become the cornerstone of Eden. It is our responsibility to ensure we support them, or we risk losing them.

—THE ORPHANAGE COUNSELOR HANDBOOK
By Brendan #924

"Quit stalling," Cole called out.

Vella dismissed him with a wave of her hand.

It was nine-all—next goal wins. Cole watched from across the clearing as Vella whispered something to Edgar. He glanced at Alex, but neither of them had anything to say. So, they stood in silence waiting on them.

No one was in the mood to train. Instead, they'd decided to play two-versus-two soccer. To even the teams, Vella and Cole had to be on opposite sides: Alex and Cole against Edgar and Vella.

It was mainly Cole and Vella playing against each other, while Edgar and Alex effectively played as full-time goalies.

Vella walked to the middle and dropped the ball. She looked back at Edgar and nodded. He returned a thumbs-up.

She dribbled the ball up, taking Cole wide. She slipped past him, dribbling even wider. Cole motioned to Alex to come out and double-team her in an attempt to trap her and force her to give up the ball. She waited a moment for them to get closer, and then flicked the ball up to herself and kicked it high over Alex and Cole. To their dismay, Edgar was waiting at the goal face to receive it and tap it in.

Vella gave Cole a sly grin. "Game over."

He rolled his eyes and turned to glare at Alex.

"What did you want me to do about it?" Alex protested. "You called me out of the goal!"

Vella laughed, running over to Edgar, and they high-fived, adding a slap with the front and back of their hands.

Cole sighed and shook his head. He turned to find Alex walking away without a word.

The trip home was quieter than usual. Cole hadn't heard a word from Vella as he drifted off, lost in his own thoughts.

He expected some gloating, not that it would have bothered him. He had let go of any frustration about losing. Any frustration he felt was about what the game represented. They were getting comfortable. Too comfortable.

The decision to play soccer instead of making meaningful progress was a symptom of that. And yet, he couldn't deny how much fun it had been for everyone. Just to let go and enjoy something simple.

Is it so bad? he wondered.

He had no thoughts of giving up, but he wrestled with a choice: force things forward or let them continue at the current pace?

I'll give it a week or two, he decided. *If we haven't made any progress by then, I'll do something.*

The other concern was: *How serious would everyone be about the mission when it came time for real action?*

Edgar was an unknown. And Alex? When things got real, would he still be standing with them, ready to fight?

But what about himself? Could he stand and fight? The Wolf's hold on him still remained. He was secretly glad for every day they delayed, or at least his body was. It reacted violently whenever he even considered it. Still, the vision the orb had shown him of Vella's death spurred him into action. There was no choice but to keep going.

He was pulled out of his mind by Vella. She kept glancing at him, obviously wanting to say something but unable to find the nerve. He'd felt the same glances during the morning walk, but now they were more frequent and unsettling.

He'd had enough and decided it was time to help her.

"What is it? Something on my face?"

Vella's mind was not on the game or the mission.

Since the day Leah had shown her Cole's sketchbook, she hadn't been able to stop thinking about what she'd seen. The depths of her ignorance had been exposed, and it was a painful thing to face. She'd only glimpsed a single page, but that had been enough to reveal the ongoing struggles he'd kept hidden from her. She dreaded what lay on the rest of the pages. And the full extent of what he'd been enduring.

Alone. Without her help.

It all pointed back to that one day. The more she stewed on it, the more she realized how it had shaped his life. They had never spoken about that day before. She'd never asked, and Cole had never volunteered any information. It hadn't bothered her until now, since she hadn't realized it was an issue.

The thought of him suffering alone pressed a constant invisible weight on her chest, especially knowing how often he had been there for her during her darkest hours. Even if he had caused some of that pain with the drawing, he had still shown up for her.

She had always believed he didn't need help, that he was untouchable, invincible. But that illusion had shattered. Now she could see the truth. There was a distance between them, a quiet gap she had been blind to. How far did it reach? What else might he be hiding from her? If she wanted to be with him, truly be with him, she would have to bridge that gap. They would be together but remain alone until then.

"What is it? Something on my face?" Cole asked.

"No, no. I just wanted to ask about . . ."

"What? It's all right, tell me."

She had no idea how or when to bring it up. It didn't help that they were rarely alone these days, and the more she put it off, the more it ate at her. There might never be a good time or place, so she decided to force the issue.

"You don't have to talk about it if you don't want to . . . that's fine, but . . . if you ever wanted to talk about the day your parents . . . passed away . . . I wanted you to know, I'm here."

Cole's only reaction was a brief sideways glance at her. He seemed unfazed as they walked on. He opened his mouth to say something, but nothing came out.

When he finally spoke, he said, "There's not much to tell."

She wanted to pry, to break down whatever wall he was holding up. But she knew if he didn't want to talk about it, there was no point making him do anything he didn't want to.

They walked back in uncomfortable silence. Cole kept his eyes fixed forward. His fists clenched, and his mouth twitched, making her keep her distance.

Vella jolted upright, breath catching in her throat. A shout rang out, followed by the sound of heavy impacts against the walls and floor. Her heart pounded in her ears. It came from somewhere outside her room, but she couldn't tell exactly where. She held her breath and listened.

The quiet that followed was thick and unnatural, pressing in against the walls. She braced herself and waited. And when nothing happened, she slipped from beneath her blanket and tiptoed toward the door. She cursed under her breath as every floorboard seemed to give way and creak beneath her.

She stuck her head out of the bedroom door.

Leah's door was slightly ajar. Inside, Leah lay still with one eye open. She raised a hand, beckoning Vella in. There was no panic or surprise in her face.

Vella knelt by her side and whispered, "Was that you?"

"It's Cole," Leah murmured. "It happens every now and then."

"Why?"

Leah sighed. "Don't worry."

"Shouldn't we check on him?"

Leah shook her head. "Better to let him be. Go back to bed."

Vella looked down as her lips tightened. She gave a reluctant nod, backed out of the room, and closed the door behind her.

Instead of going back to her room, she hesitated. Cole's door stood closed, quiet. She crept closer, each step slow and muted, then leaned in to listen. Floorboards shifted inside.

She pulled back from the door. "Cole," she whispered. "Is everything all right?"

Nothing.

Then, after a moment, there was movement. The door creaked open a sliver.

Cole poked his head in the gap, sweat dampened his forehead, his breathing shallow. "Sorry, did I wake you?"

"Don't worry. Are you okay?"

He nodded, betrayed by a rigid, stuttered movement of his head.

"What happened?"

"It's nothing. Bad dream."

"Want to talk about it?"

"Go back to bed."

"Cole . . ."

"I'm fine. Really. Sorry."

The door closed before she could say anything else.

She returned to her room, sat on the edge of the bed, but sleep was the furthest thing from her mind. Restless, she pushed herself up and crossed to the window.

A voice called out: *You will always be useless to him. To everyone.*

She pressed her forehead to the glass, a lump forming in her throat.

No! There must be something I can do, she told herself.

Lifting her head, she gazed out at the backyard, her mind racing. Her eyes landed on the lone apple tree in the corner. She stared at its base, and a memory flashed in her mind: the two of them, years ago, lying under a different tree.

An idea formed. If he wouldn't let her in, she'd have to find another way.

She stripped her bed of its sheets, grabbed her pillow, and slipped out the back window. The cool night air brushed her skin as she stepped barefoot onto the soft grass. She laid a sheet down near the tree, settled the pillow, and lay back. The stars sprawled across the sky, capturing her attention.

With her left hand, she felt along the ground for a small stone. When she found one, she sat up and threw it at Cole's window.

It made a soft clink against the glass.

A moment later, his curtains fluttered. His head poked through, a bewildered look on his face when he finally noticed her. He opened the window and whispered, "What are you doing?"

She waved him over.

"Vel . . ." Cole took a moment, sighed, and climbed through the window.

He crouched next to her. "Why are you out here?"

"It's a nice night," she said, patting the space next to her. "Join me."

She shuffled over and took one side of the pillow.

Cole looked around, still showing signs of agitation.

"Just for a minute," she urged.

He sighed. "Okay . . ."

He lay down beside her, his head touching the edge of the pillow, arms crossed. They lay in fragile silence, staring up at the night sky.

"What does this remind you of?" she asked, shuffling closer.

He closed his eyes. "I don't know, Vel."

"The night we left the orphanage."

Cole let out a semi-amused huff. "Right. We couldn't sleep in the shed because it was too cluttered and dusty."

"And we slept under a tree with clothes for pillows."

She recalled that night with clear detail. She couldn't rest, so she watched him sleep, her eyes drifting to and from the cuts and bruises on his face and hands. That same feeling of powerlessness to help him gnawed at her.

"Yeah . . . this is much nicer." He unfolded his arms and let them rest by his side, wriggling around to get more comfortable.

She reached out and placed her hand over his. Immediately, she felt the damp clamminess of his skin.

He shuffled closer, getting his head comfortable on the pillow, and let out a long, weary breath.

She inched closer until their shoulders touched.

"I know what you're trying to do," he said.

"What's that?"

He didn't answer.

They lay there, neither close to sleep, their minds too restless. Vella could hear his short and sharp breathing. Cole turned onto his side, facing away from her.

She opened her eyes, staring at his back. He was right there, but he felt so far out of reach. The frustration built, causing her throat to constrict.

Curling up behind him, she pressed herself gently against the warmth of his back. Tears stung her eyes. She sniffed, wiping her nose with the back of her hand.

Cole stirred, then turned to face her. She turned her face down, unable to meet his gaze.

"What's wrong?"

She shook her head, wiping her eyes.

He moved an arm over her without touching her. Then he lightly placed his hand on her back. She stiffened, then relaxed to his touch. He brought his arm down and pulled her closer.

"Too much?"

She pressed her face into his chest and gave a faint shake of her head.

After a moment, Cole whispered, "I'm okay. Really."

"No, you're not."

"Even if I'm not, that's not your problem."

She sniffed again. "Of course it is."

He kissed her on the forehead. "I'll tell you about it someday. I promise."

"Okay."

They lay there, the silence warm and protective, until sleep finally claimed them.

Cool droplets danced across their skin, stirring them. The predusk rain began, catching them off guard.

They scrambled up, leaving the pillow and sheets behind as they hurried through Cole's window.

Once inside, they brushed off the moisture on their skin. Cole sat on his bed, head down, still half asleep as Vella made her way to the door.

"Stay. Please," Cole said.

She froze, her hand hovering over the doorknob.

"What're you going to sleep on? A bare bed?"

He lay down on his side, facing her, and patted the space in front of him.

Her heart thundered in her chest. Taking her time, she crossed the room and sat down on the bed. Trying to steady her breathing, she gripped the edge of the bed. She flinched when his hand touched hers. Slowly, her fingers relaxed. She eased back and lowered herself, lying against him.

She hesitated for a moment, then shuffled backward, nestling into the warmth of his body.

He slid an arm around her waist, pulling her close, his touch cautious but firm.

"I'll always be okay with you around," he whispered.

She gripped his arm, and let out a long, quiet breath.

"Was this your plan all along?" he asked.

"Let's just say it was."

27

SUMMARY

Due to repeated behavioral infractions, Leah [8591], age thirteen, is being placed in a household one year ahead of schedule. This decision follows her fifth major offense this year, indicating a concerning lack of respect for authority and community standards.

PLACEMENT DETAILS

Leah will be placed under the guardianship of Rose [8454] and Rory [8430], effective immediately. The couple, already familiar with Leah through her job placement under Rose, has agreed to take her into their household.

APPROVAL

This has been reviewed and approved by Central Administration in accordance with policy guidelines.

Authorization: Alicia, Head of Orphanage [8375]   Date: 12.06.429

Leah sat on the front porch with a steaming cup of tea in hand. Vella sat beside her, waiting for Cole to finish cleaning up so he and Vella could leave for their "exercise" group.

It had been several weeks since she had found out about it. While she tried to let go of her nagging concerns, they lingered. She didn't have any evidence, no real reason to worry. But something still ate at her. A gnawing feeling that they were hiding something, and Cole was the main culprit behind it.

Leah took a sip and leaned back. "Your stitching is getting very good," she said, turning to Vella. "And in such a short time."

One thing that softened Leah's internal irritation was Vella— her little project.

"I don't like it that much, though," Vella said.

"Well, you're free to do whatever you like. We just might need your hands every now and then."

"Thanks. I want to do some woodwork tomorrow. Finish off some chairs."

Leah kept herself busy helping Vella adjust to work life. Vella was naturally dexterous, so the technical side was easy for her. It was on the social side of things, where Vella had the most difficulty, where Leah focused her efforts.

"Maria is having a party tomorrow night. You should come; everyone from work will be there," Leah said.

"Ah, I don't know . . ."

"Just think about it. No pressure."

Vella nodded, and all of a sudden, she went quiet, seeming to shrink into herself.

At work, Vella only spoke when necessary. Leah knew that someone with Vella's background would have difficulty fitting into her boisterous, close-knit workgroup. Progress was slow, but there was progress, and that gave Leah hope. Still, there were days when no amount of encouragement could get Vella to open up. On those days, Leah would let her be. She watched as Vella stuck to her task, head down, showing no joy and withdrawing further into herself. It was the same kind of hole she'd seen Edgar sink into many times.

Cole burst through the front door, stumbled on the steps, and nearly lost his balance, which sent Vella into a fit of laughter.

Leah watched, not for the first time, as Vella's entire demeanor changed. It was like a switch flipped when she was around Cole. Her face lit up, and the quiet, withdrawn girl became someone who seemed to radiate warmth. Leah was aware that the two of them had started sharing a room. Most of the time, she was happy for them as they found joy in growing closer. But other times, she watched them with a sinking emptiness for what she'd missed. A hollow ache she refused to acknowledge, forcing it aside however she could.

Vella got up and went over to Cole. "Nice one, dingus."

"Thanks for the concern." Cole inched forward and kissed her.

As they walked away, Cole called out to Leah, "Am I doing dinner tonight?"

He was met with a cold stare. "Yes."

"Okay . . ."

At the edge of the street, Cole glanced back to see her eyes still fixed on him. Yesterday, he'd suggested she join them, saying the exercise might do her some good. A single look was enough to convince him never to mention it again. But her watchful gaze had started long before that. Ever since she'd found out about their little meetups, he'd felt her eyes watching, silently warning him.

He quickened his pace, feeling her breath on his neck.

Cole watched Edgar as he prepared to ask the difficult question. He'd waited a week as planned, but he could wait no longer. Dread or not, he had to force things.

He noticed Edgar's light expression, and he thought about last night and how Leah had asked how he was doing. Every so often, she would ask about Edgar, and he would say he was doing well. In many ways, he was. It was night and day from when Cole had first found him on the couch a few weeks ago. But as Cole measured him now, his eyes still seemed to lack something, and any smile felt forced—unless it was with Vella.

Edgar and Vella would talk with ease. They would still argue at times, but they were light, trivial arguments that Vella would provoke to get a reaction out of him. Cole felt an odd sensation seeing them together. They shared something he couldn't quite understand. A natural connection he didn't have with either of them. He felt himself getting jealous that Edgar bridged a gap with her he couldn't. It was a petty jealousy he dismissed as fast as it came. At the end of the day, they got along, and that was plenty. They'd found something in each other they both desperately needed, and he was happy for them.

In the afternoons, they continued their two-on-two soccer matches: Vella and Edgar versus Cole and Alex. Vella and Edgar usually won, much to Cole's growing frustration. He would end up taking it out on Alex, sparking heated arguments while the other two watched in amused silence.

The teams were evenly matched in terms of skill. But Cole and Alex lacked the connection that Vella and Edgar had. It wasn't just teamwork; it bordered on telepathy, the way they moved in sync with glances and small gestures. They even had their own flashy plays. Making it look so effortless it bordered on disrespect, like they were showing off just to rub it in.

Vella had suggested another game today, but Cole had shut it down. Not because he wasn't in the mood—he had something else in mind.

Everyone was consistent with training. They pushed through every session, six days a week, taking Sundays off to rest. Edgar increased the difficulty as time went on, but Cole knew the real test was yet to come. And now it was time to step things up.

Presently, they were catching their breath, winding down after a particularly grueling session. Cole braced himself to ask the question that had been weighing on his mind, a question that he knew the others were also silently contemplating.

"Bring your chess set next time. I'll definitely beat you," Vella provoked.

"My set is missing a few pieces," Edgar said.

If Cole had been paying attention, he would have told Vella not to go down this route; he knew Edgar was *really* good. That was one thing he knew about him. He'd learned the hard way after playing against him a few times when he was younger, before Leah and Edgar had split.

"A likely excuse," she said.

"Bring yours, then."

"Ours is broken . . ."

"Is that right—"

"Hey." Cole cut in.

Edgar stopped and turned to face him. Vella and Alex were forced to pay attention, sensing the seriousness in Cole's tone.

"What's up?" Edgar asked.

"When are we going to . . . uh . . . you know?" Cole looked around and knew he didn't need to explain further.

Edgar hesitated, jaw clenched, choosing silence over an immediate response.

Cole glanced around at the others. "We're ready. Are we not? At least go in and have a look around."

Ever since that night, when he'd faced his mind's tormentor alone at the crimson door, Cole hadn't dared to return. The nightmares had eased since he'd started sharing a bed with Vella, but the mere thought of going back left him fighting for breath. He wanted to make progress by himself, but he knew he couldn't face the Wolf alone. He thought about starting with the Bear, but it stirred up just as much resistance. Now, here he was, finally admitting that he needed help.

"Yeah, it's about time," Vella said.

"I agree," Alex added.

Cole turned back to Edgar. "We have a majority."

Edgar surveyed the group. His gaze lingered on each of them before he nodded, albeit reluctantly. "Tomorrow. We can use our day off."

They agreed, and he turned to Alex. "Can you gather all the records Eden has about the Bear?"

The Bear. That was what they called the monstrosity behind the dark blue door. They called it that because it was the closest thing they could compare it to, but it only somewhat resembled an Earth bear. It had two legs, two arms, claws that protruded from both its hands and feet, and fur covering its massive body. But that was where the similarities ended. Its exact size was hard to pin down; some claimed it stood as tall as two buildings, others said three. Whatever the case, they knew that nothing of its size had existed on Earth.

"I already have all the accounts on both the Wolf and the Bear," Alex said. "I've skimmed through them, but I'll double-check the archives to see if I missed anything."

Cole eyed him, surprised. *Maybe he's more serious about this than I thought.*

"Is that why I couldn't find anything at the library?" Vella asked. "You had them?"

Alex just smiled and shrugged. "There's a reason I haven't brought them earlier. Well . . . . you'll see for yourselves tomorrow."

"Thank you, Alex," Edgar said.

"Why the Bear, why not the—" Vella started. She was going to ask why not the Wolf but caught herself in time as she glanced at Edgar. She cleared her throat. "What about weapons?"

"We need to figure out a plan first. We don't know what kind of weapon we want to use against it. Short-range, long-range? A spear, knife, hammer? Sharp, blunt? We don't know how we're going to try to kill it until we learn more about it."

"Yeah, I guess . . ."

"We have the fitness foundation; next is information."

Vella groaned. "Sounds lame. Let's just go in."

"In time, Vel," Cole said and thought, *Research is going to be useless. No one with a firsthand account of the Bear has ever lived. That's the information we need, not what some people saw flash across the screen for a second.*

"We could go in and think we're safe and out of reach, but the Bear could have tricks we don't expect, and it could kill us without us having time to reset," Edgar explained. "Then no more orb . . . or us."

An almost believable excuse, Cole thought. *If I had to guess, he needs a day to prepare himself. I don't blame him. Or maybe his plan is that if we have a night to stew on it, we'll pull out?*

"Didn't think of that," Vella said. "So, what's next?"

"Recon and training with the orb. Once we know from the reports exactly what it can do, then we can go in and take a look ourselves. Start out small, see what we're up against and figure out weak points."

"All right," Vella conceded.

Edgar shot them a stern look. "It should go without saying, but tell *no one.*"

They agreed with a shared glance.

Given everything, I was expecting more resistance from Edgar, Cole thought to himself as they parted.

Cole noticed that Vella seemed more subdued that evening, lost in her own world of thoughts. The others, including himself, shared a similar anxiety. Even though they faced little immediate risk, the thought of coming face-to-face with that thing was enough to make them second-guess everything. None of them slept well that night.

They reconvened the next day at the agreed spot. True to his word, Alex brought all the records he could find on the Bear.

They sat in a circle, sifting through the files, jotting down any details they thought might be useful. The records covered a four-hundred-year history of deaths at the hands of the Bear.

Cole's assumption was right—the accounts were not going to help. They varied wildly, often contradicting each other, and many seemed exaggerated, if not outright made up. They found a few sketches, but there was no consistency among them.

"This is all useless," Cole muttered. "Like, what is this? This one claimed it breathed fire. What kind of—" He stopped in frustration, flinging aside the final report he could stomach.

Vella sat to the side, tossing the orb up and down like it was a child's plaything.

Edgar looked up from his notes. "Just get the general stuff. We'll get the important details ourselves."

"So many deaths." Alex sighed. "I didn't think this many had tried. And these are just the recorded ones. How many more were there?"

There were accounts of around fifty attempts, which surprised them. Cole took heart in the fact that so many hadn't given up. They had dared to face it. He paused, glancing at Edgar. How many of them, recorded and unrecorded, had gone in with the right intent and mindset? He tried not to think about it.

Alex tossed the pile of papers aside, exhausted.

When they finished, Cole compiled a page of handwritten notes while Alex filled two pages and Edgar filled one and a half. Edgar gathered them, adding several dozen blank sheets behind them.

He wrote in large letters on the front page: *Project Stupidity*.

"Everything we learn goes in here. No detail is too small," Edgar said, tapping the pile. "Alex, can you take this home and bind it?" he asked. Alex nodded, taking the stack and flipping through the notes they'd gathered. It wasn't much to look at.

Edgar motioned for Vella to join them. She stopped playing with the orb and sat next to Cole.

"So, what did you learn?" Vella asked.

Cole chuckled, Alex shook his head, and Edgar let out a long, weary sigh.

"Not much," Edgar said. "There shouldn't be any surprises. Keep a safe distance. That's all."

"Wow. Productive."

"Very."

"So . . . is it time?"

"It's time," Edgar said, straightening up. "As you know, only two are allowed to enter at once, so here's how it'll go. Two will go in, and the other two will be on standby in case something goes wrong. Only the person with the orb will remember the encounter, so they'll need to relay the information clearly and concisely. Write it down while it's fresh in your mind. We'll take turns to get the most accurate information. What one person notices but others overlook could make all the difference. But information isn't the most important thing. Staying alive is. Don't stay longer than you need to."

They exchanged hesitant glances. The gravity of the situation was sinking in.

Cole broke the silence. "I'll go first."

"Any objections?" Edgar asked.

No one spoke.

They walked over to the dark blue door situated to the right of the central green one. Cole glanced at the red door on the far left, thankful it wasn't that one. His eyes lingered on the green door, yearning for the day it would open. He didn't dare look up at the board counting down the time left for everyone.

"I'll go in with him," Edgar said, beating Vella to the punch. She tried to object, but Cole assured her he would be fine.

"Vella, Alex, you're on standby," Edgar continued. "You two are our last hope if things go wrong. If you see the green light change to red, you need to move fast. If we die, we die together. Are you ready for that?"

They exchanged uneasy looks. This wasn't a possibility they had considered.

Edgar's trying to scare us off, Cole mused. *Not doing a bad job, either.*

"It won't come to that," Cole assured them. "We'll play it as safe as possible." He directed the last part at Vella, who nodded, almost as if to shut him up.

"What happens if you get injured? Do you remain hurt when you reset?" Alex asked.

"No," Cole explained. "You could be dying, and it could . . ." He hesitated and glanced at Edgar, then continued with caution. "Save you. Your body will be in the same condition as it was at the reset point."

"Well, that's good."

Cole eyed the orb as it went eerily quiet around him. "We've got a couple of minutes," he relayed.

Edgar took a deep breath. "Cole, as soon as you get back, tell us everything you can. I'll distract it for as long as possible . . . Even if it kills me, you keep going until you feel like you're in danger. Don't let it get anywhere near you."

"But—" Cole protested, but Edgar cut him off.

"It doesn't matter about me. I won't remember. I can run distraction for everyone."

"Even if it can be undone, I can't let that happen," Cole said.

"The decision's yours."

"Edgar, what the hell! I agree with Cole," Alex interjected. "We don't let anyone die, no matter what."

"No getting yourself killed, Edgar. I don't want to watch anyone die. On second thought, maybe Alex," Vella said with a grin.

Alex glared at her, then smiled, knowing she wasn't the type to take pleasure in something like that. But her grin lingered a little too long, making him nervous.

"Stop," he said, nudging her.

"Make me."

"Vella, no killing Alex," Cole said, then added in a low voice directed to Vella, "Just this once."

Alex shoved Cole. In retaliation, Vella spear-tackled Alex, causing him to stumble to the ground.

"Hold him down, we're gonna throw him in," Cole said, jumping on Alex.

"Enough!" Edgar barked. "This isn't a joke."

Their smiles dropped, and they scrambled to their feet, hurrying to stand around Edgar.

"Unbelievable," Edgar mumbled.

He cleared his throat and picked up where they'd left off.

"Come on, let's vote," Edgar said. "Raise your hand for a 'no one dies' rule."

Cole glared at Edgar. "What seriously isn't a joke is having such reckless abandon when it comes to your safety. Why is this even a vote?"

"I won't—"

"You won't remember. I get that, but come on."

"Just vote."

Cole and Alex raised their hands first, followed by Vella.

Edgar relented, raising his hand. "It's settled, then. If you see the decoy about to get hurt, press the button."

"The decoy?" Vella asked.

"Yes. Our roles will be the observer, the decoy, and the backups. We'll rotate the roles. As the decoy, is there anything you'd like me to do, Cole?"

"What do you mean?"

"The decoy will need to follow the observer's instructions to get the information they want. Maybe not now, but say you want me to run in a certain direction or throw something—anything."

"I'll keep that in mind," Cole said.

"Not that it will matter for now. We just need to get a better picture of what we're dealing with. Everyone will get one reset, yes?"

"One?" Vella grumbled. "How about five?"

"One," he affirmed with a stern look.

She rolled her eyes and nodded.

"I doubt anyone will want to go a second time after their first attempt anyway," Edgar muttered under his breath.

Is that why he hasn't been stalling more? He thinks this will get us to give up? From one look?

"Speaking of which, is there a limit on the number of times you can use a single reset point?" Alex asked.

"If there is, I haven't found it. I pressed it around two hundred times, and I couldn't be bothered doing more than that," Cole said. "I'd say it's infinite."

"Thank you for your thorough testing," Alex said, the sarcasm not lost on Cole.

"Before I forget, Cole, here." Edgar handed him a long, thick cloth. "Use this as a face mask."

"Oh, for the smell," Cole said, trying not to reveal that he had already experienced the oppressive smell.

"I hope it'll be enough."

They stood around, anxiety deepening as they waited for it to tick over.

"Whoa . . . we get to see it," Vella said, shaking her arms.

"Crazy, right?" Cole affirmed. "How're you feeling?" he asked Alex.

Alex nodded, gathering his words. "A little nervous . . . danger of dying aside, it's pretty amazing we get to be the first ones to see it and live to tell the tale . . . to no one."

Cole bounced up in an attempt to shake off his nervous energy. "When we kill it, then we can tell as many people as we like."

In an instant, a change washed over them as the reality struck them. None of them could stay still. All of them felt their breathing becoming shallower and more irregular.

Edgar turned his back to them, looking out into the woods.

"Nervous Leah's watching?" Cole asked.

"I wasn't thinking about that, but now that you mention it. Very."

Cole glanced around the woodland area. "I've made myself paranoid now . . ." He forced himself to turn away. "How long do you think we'll get in there before we're forced to reset?"

"If it's like the other one, around thirty seconds. Not long. I don't expect anyone to last half that."

Click.

"It ticked over," Cole said.

"No time to waste, let's go."

Cole put on his face mask, as did Edgar. He glanced back at

Vella. Her concern was evident. Her arms were crossed, and her fingers were tapping nonstop.

"You won't even remember this. Weird, isn't it?"

Her eyes narrowed at him. "I'd better not."

Cole's heart raced at the thought of revisiting the nightmare beyond the doors. That night, he had entered the red door alone. This time, he wasn't. Having the others with him gave him a small buffer against the fear.

Edgar took the lead, touched the scanner to open the door, and motioned for Cole to follow.

Cole looked back once more. Vella's eyes softened with concern as she gave him a nod, urging him forward.

Taking one step forward, he suddenly hit an invisible barrier. His body seized up, the horror of past memories flooding back. Trembling, he screamed inwardly, *Move!*

Edgar, noticing Cole's hesitation, offered him an out: "We can let someone else go first."

That was all the motivation Cole needed. Not wanting to give Edgar the satisfaction, he forced himself to move forward. He shook his head and motioned for Edgar to continue, knowing that if he spoke, it would shatter the weak façade he was barely holding together.

I can leave whenever I want, he reminded himself.

He slammed his hand on the scanner, braced himself, and stepped into the abyss.

The smell was the same overwhelming stench of death, immediately making Cole gag. Edgar winced, struggling with the stench as well.

"Damn that smell . . . still getting through," Edgar muttered, pressing on.

Despite knowing he was, by all accounts, safe, Cole's body screamed in violent protest. Every muscle tensed, fighting the urge to flee.

The lights above grew brighter, illuminating the space.

This place looks the same as the other one, Cole thought. *It might as well be.*

He glanced at the small green dot behind him and gave a

hesitant wave to Vella on the other side.

A low growl echoed from the distant darkness ahead. A cold shiver swept over his skin.

Here we go . . . hold!

A paw, then an arm, emerged from the shadows.

It stood in full view now, and what a sight it was. Beyond anything Cole could have imagined from the sketches. He froze, gripped by fear and awe at the behemoth before him.

The first thing he noticed was its eyes, bright yellow, with a narrow slit of black in the center, like a cat's eyes. It opened its mouth and roared, revealing a second row of sharp teeth behind the first row of massive, jagged fangs. Its fur was brown with patches and smears of red and yellow. A long, scaly tail poked out from the fur, ending in a pointed barb. The tail, which had been wrapped around its torso, unfurled as the beast drew closer.

Edgar stood about twenty meters ahead. The monster loomed hundreds of meters beyond him. When it emitted a second, louder roar, Cole lost all control of his muscles, and for a moment, his vision blurred.

It had Edgar in its sights and charged, but Edgar didn't move.

"Edgar!" Cole shouted.

He didn't turn. Cole wasn't sure if he hadn't heard him or if he was frozen in fear.

The thunderous footsteps of the charging beast almost knocked Cole off balance.

"Dammit," Cole cursed.

He looked the beast over, taking in whatever details he could. After a few more seconds, he realized there was nothing more to gain from this expedition.

He reset.

The all-too-familiar brain shock surged through him, and he was back. He let out a sharp breath, realizing only then how long he'd been holding it.

The others stared at him, waiting.

"So?" Vella asked.

Cole wanted to speak, but no words came out. He tossed the

orb to Vella and paced a few steps away, trying to gather his thoughts.

He wanted to tell them all about it, to warn them, but how could he? There was no way to prepare someone for that.

Maybe Edgar's right . . . this is all we need to experience for us to give up. But I can't show weakness now. We must continue. It's part of the process. What did I expect?

He returned to the group, grabbed the document, and wrote down everything he could remember, ignoring their concerned looks. The eyes, the size, the stench, and the roar were the only things present in his mind. Everything else around him meant nothing.

Vella looked down at him with a worried expression.

"Cole . . . ?"

"Yeah?"

Vella knelt beside him, placing a hand on his shoulder. "You're safe now."

"I know. I'm—" Only then did he realize his hands were shaking uncontrollably. He finally took note of what he was writing down. All scribbles.

She grabbed his hand, easing the pencil out of his tight grip.

"Take a minute," she said. "I'll go next."

Cole rocked back, pulling his knees to his chin, and stared off to the side, trying to focus on his breath.

His thoughts darted all over the place: *It's too much. We can't kill that. It has to be possible. Has to. We're going to die. No. Stop. It can be done. No. It's hopeless. But for Leah, it has to.*

His thoughts bounced around from one extreme to another, wrestling with the reality of the situation.

"We have time to wait for the next reset point," Edgar said. "I'll go with you."

"No, I will!" Cole blurted out, then caught himself and said in an even tone, "No . . . I'll go with her."

They waited in silence for the next few minutes. During that time, Cole managed to steady himself. He wrote down some actual words before it was Vella's turn.

She paced around, glancing at the orb every few seconds.

"Vella, maybe—" Edgar began but stopped. He took a moment to consider his words. "Just be careful. Count to ten and reset."

She glared at him, thinking he was going to try to stop her, but her face softened seeing how worried he looked. She nodded. "Ten."

"Come, sit," Cole said, diverting her attention.

She sat with him as he explained what he saw and what to expect. "Try not to get too startled by the—"

Click.

He heard the soft click of the orb. He jerked around to face her, watching and waiting as she stared at the grass.

Suddenly, she jumped up off the ground and looked around at each of them with wide eyes.

"Whoa! What the hell, that's ridiculous. How freakin' big was that thing? It had a mouth within a mouth. Crazy! And that roar . . ." She was buzzing with manic energy, pacing around with a wide grin. "I want to see it again."

Cole caught up with her, placing both hands on her shoulders. "Are you good?"

"Yeah, yeah. I just can't stay still. That was insane! I want to see it again."

He noticed her trembling. "Maybe another time, when you've calmed down," Cole said with a smile.

She glanced down, noticing the shaking. "But—"

"I know. Another time."

She paused, glancing around as if catching herself. Then she nodded and handed over the orb.

They sat as Vella continued to ramble. Cole gave her his full attention, smiling and nodding, trying to keep her balanced.

Next up was Edgar. He appeared unfazed, walking away like he was taking a casual stroll, but Cole knew better.

Alex was last; Cole went with him.

As the orb ticked over to the next reset point, Alex was standing one moment and the next, he stumbled back, collapsing to the ground.

He scrambled backward, his body trembling, wide-eyed. He

stared ahead, drawing short, frantic breaths.

After a few seconds, he glanced around and noticed their eyes on him, the terror still raw in his eyes. He shot to his feet, trying to collect himself.

Without a word, he dropped the orb and walked away. He slumped against the perimeter wall, staring ahead in silence.

No one blamed him for how he reacted. They all would have done the same if they hadn't been paralyzed by their own fear.

They all sat with similar thoughts, doubts plaguing them about the impossible task they'd undertaken.

Cole lay on his back, vacantly staring up, pulling grass with his fingertips. Under his breath, an occasional curse escaped him.

Beside him, Vella lay on her stomach, watching Edgar sketch the Bear. Her chin rested on her hands and her expression was blank. She intermittently pointed things out for him to add and change.

Alex sat away from them, eyes fixed on the sky above. Time was of no consequence; only the comfort of each other's presence grounded them in the moment.

The orb sat beside Vella. Cole, still lying on his back, reached out and grabbed it.

A familiar sharp jolt shot through him the moment his fingers touched it. Electricity surged through every nerve in his body.

Then he was gone. Back in that place again.

He saw her. Vella, older, facing the Wolf.

No! Not again!

The same vision. The same moment.

Nothing had changed. Events played out the same as before.

Even the pain returned exactly as before.

But this time, it didn't end there.

The reality shifted.

Alex appeared. Older, like Vella was. He didn't seem to want to fight. He was running, looking around for something. A way out? Was it even his choice to be there? Cole watched helplessly as the Wolf tore through him—shoulder to torso. He felt it. The agony. The helplessness.

A second strike followed. Ending it.

Still, it wasn't over.

Edgar came next. Unlike the others, he looked almost the same as he did now.

But like the others, death came swiftly.

He was on the move. Cole could feel he was afraid, but much calmer than the other two. He managed to dodge a lunge. Another claw came his way, but he stepped on something on the ground and lost his balance, and it was over in an instant.

Then darkness. A distant tunnel of light appeared, rushing toward him. The world snapped back like a door slamming shut.

Cole gasped, shooting upright. He clutched his hands to his mouth, dragging in rapid, shallow breaths through his nose.

Vella and Edgar turned to look.

"What's wrong?" Vella asked.

Cole forced a cough and pulled his hands away. "Swallowed—a—bug," he said, voice strained, trying to smile as if it were nothing.

Any other day, it might have been amusing to them. But neither of them reacted. Their attention returned to Edgar's sketch.

Cole stared at the ground, then at the orb.

It happened again.

Only this time, it wasn't just Vella. It was Alex and Edgar too. He knew Edgar's death wasn't from the past because he had survived that encounter. Barely. But what he saw now . . . there was no surviving that. Edgar had died.

He might have assumed those deaths were from a failed attempt he would reset, one that hadn't even happened yet. But he wasn't in any of the visions. No one was. They were alone.

He couldn't play it off anymore. He saw it. Felt it. This was how they would die.

Unless he stopped it.

He pulled his knees up and wrapped his arms around them. His eyes and throat burned as tears rose.

It wasn't just the pain. It was the terror he felt with them in those final moments. He couldn't put that feeling away so easily. The rawness of it clung to him. Three deaths.

Three agonizing ends. All in the blink of an eye.

His gaze flicked to each of them.

Can I even stop it . . . ?

Aching loneliness made him want to reach out, to say something.

I can't do this by myself.

But how could he possibly explain what he'd seen? So he gritted his teeth and remained silent, bearing the pain.

"I'm heading home," Alex said, with no sign of emotion.

None of them bothered to look up at him. Edgar was the only one to offer any acknowledgment, a small groan at that.

Alex ambled away, his movements slow and without purpose.

Cole's mind was still elsewhere as he thought, *The Wolf . . .* "What are we supposed to do against that?" he muttered.

Edgar paused his sketching. Thinking Cole was talking about the Bear, he said, "We take it one day at a time, one step at a time."

"Is that it?" Cole asked.

"It's all we can do."

28

The self-proclaimed resistance group folded after witnessing what happened to four of their members who entered the doors. As obnoxious as they were, no one approached them with an "I told you so." Instead, people showed sympathy; several even tried consoling them. I do pity them. For all their false bravado, at least they were trying. I've seen what those monsters have done to people, and I know exactly how they feel. Now I fear for what comes next. They have two choices: true acceptance or despair leading to self-destruction. I hope it's the former.

—THE FIRST PEOPLE OF EDEN
Journal of Morgan #38
Day 165

Cole and Alex walked in strained silence, the morning air heavy with the tension from yesterday's encounter.

As they gathered the makeshift training cones, Cole noticed the frustration in Alex's movements—jerky and uncoordinated.

Vella left early, saying it was her turn to make breakfast. Edgar excused himself, claiming he wasn't feeling well. This left Cole and Alex alone with no buffer.

Alex forced the cones into Cole's arms and turned away immediately. The weariness on Alex's face was unmistakable, dark circles under his eyes and furrowed brow permanently etched into his features.

He looked like he was carrying the weight of the world on his shoulders, every muscle tense, every breath labored. Cole had seen similar signs before, back when they were kids. It told him that Alex was on edge.

Cole felt no better. But a stubborn fire inside him kept the despair at bay. For now. He wouldn't let the future he'd seen come to pass. Not while he still had the power to do something about it.

One step at a time, he reminded himself. *Did you think this was going to be easy? No. This is what it's going to take.*

As Alex walked away, he felt a compulsion to say something.

Just let him go. Leave him alone, he told himself.

But concern got the better of him, and before he could stop himself, he called out.

"Hey."

Alex stopped, turning to face him. "What?"

"Uh, how are you holding up? Want to talk about it?"

"About what? What do you want to talk about?" His voice was weary, laced with irritation.

"Uh . . . yesterday."

Alex's eyes narrowed. "What's this? Checking up on me?" Alex asked. "*Now?*"

"I—" Cole broke off.

Alex shook his head. "Too late, *friend.*"

Cole sighed. "I'm trying here."

"Yeah, way too late," Alex said. "About seven years too late. Do what you do best. Keep pretending I don't exist."

"Like you did before I left?"

Alex's face flared. "Is that what you think?"

"You had your friends. You didn't need me."

Alex scoffed and stifled a laugh, smiling in disbelief. "You always were clueless," he said. "You up and left the orphanage without a word. I was your best friend, and you just disappeared on me. Never came to see me or even check on me. What? I ceased to exist?"

"You know why," Cole muttered.

"So, that means we were never friends?"

"No . . . I don't know. You spent all your time with the others."

"Because that's what we're supposed to do. Be friendly, be social. I tried to bring you in."

"They didn't want to look at me. It was all about you. Besides, I hated them."

"You hated everyone. Even me, right?"

"Cut the crap, Alex. You're the victim all of a sudden?"

"No, Cole. All I wanted was my friend. I didn't care about the others. After all we went through . . . what? Nothing? And you want to check on me now?" Cynical laughter escaped him. "You don't get to do that."

Cole swallowed hard. "Vella needed me."

"I understand that, but other people existed. What's the point of explaining this to you? You've always just done whatever you wanted."

Alex's breaths came quicker, his chest rising and falling as the pent-up frustration spilled out. "I had to hear it from Leah. Cole, Leah! You couldn't come tell me. For all I knew, you were dead."

"I didn't think you cared," Cole said, the words tasting bitter.

"Of course I did. After everything we went through, how could I not?" Alex snapped. "But not to you. No. Not you. We live so close to each other, and yet I've only seen you four times in seven years. Three of those times I saw you, we never spoke. What the hell is that?"

Cole's shoulders slumped, feeling something inside fade. The illusions of hate he'd built over the years fell away, leaving behind nothing he wanted to accept. All that remained was a deep shame, forming a heavy pit in his stomach.

"I'll admit you didn't deserve most of the hate I felt toward you. It's . . . just . . . that whenever I saw you, I was reminded of all the bad parts of growing up in that place. You had it easy. Everyone loved you. You didn't seem to have to try for people to like you. I . . ." Cole breathed out sharply through his nose. "I was . . . jealous."

Alex's eyes widened. "Jealous? Of me?"

"Don't make me repeat it," Cole grumbled.

"I didn't think you were capable of such an emotion."

"Well . . . you learned something new today."

A small, warm smile tugged at the corner of Alex's lips. "I always wanted to be carefree and wild like you were. Stupidly fearless. You took no shit."

"Bullshit."

"I cared too much what others thought . . . still do," Alex continued. "But you? You didn't care. It was amazing. Didn't matter who or what it was, they were getting the unfiltered, no-BS Cole."

Cole chuckled, shaking his head. "Believe it or not, I cared. A lot."

"Well, it didn't show. Yesterday, when you were with me in there . . . it reminded me of those nights after Tom's death. I felt safer with you there. And when you left . . . those nights felt unbearable. I knew what it was like to be truly alone."

"Now you know how Vella felt all the time," Cole said, then winced at his own harshness and was quick to add, "I wasn't doing much better myself, if that helps."

Alex nodded, a faint smile still lingering. "Yeah, you're right. I have no right to complain." He dropped his head. "Still . . . it hurt. I missed having you around. It wasn't the same. You're the closest thing I had to real family. That's what hurt the most."

Cole felt a lump in his throat build. "I didn't think about it like that," he said. "You're right. I . . . didn't think of anyone but Vella. Sorry."

They stood in silence for a moment, the air between them growing a little lighter.

"I'll admit I could and should've done more. And I should've known how thick-headed you are," Alex said.

"We were just dumb kids, right?" Cole flashed a smile.

"Right," Alex whispered.

"For what it's worth, it's good to hang out with you again," Cole said, his voice softening.

"Life was way too boring without you."

They exchanged a knowing laugh.

"Look, if you want to give up on all this madness, I don't blame you," Cole said.

"My mind's telling me to quit, but every fiber of my body screams, stay and fight."

"Why?"

"I don't need to explain to you of all people," Alex said. "I feel it. That fire, that rage. I know you do too. I'm sick of being told about our limitations. I refuse to accept them anymore."

Cole smiled, knowing someone understood him. "But it's completely stupid to continue. You saw that thing."

"But you're not giving up."

"Of course not. If you'd rather focus on becoming a big-shot mayor, don't worry, it's all under control. I got this. Isn't that the goal?"

Alex's expression turned serious. "Before, you asked why I wanted to become mayor."

"To help people, right?" he quipped.

Alex's solemn look silenced him. "Do you know what happened to Vella's mother?"

Cole's expression darkened, a warning for Alex to tread carefully.

"Huh, you do . . . I see. Well, when I was fifteen, I did work in public records. I found they had all the information on lineage and the whole history of everyone who has lived here. They keep track of everything. I found files on my parents . . ." Alex breathed out slowly. "I found out they killed themselves when I was two. It was my mother first and then my father a month later. Both hung themselves."

"Wait—what?"

Alex brushed over his comment and continued, "I kept looking and found Vella's mother. And so many more. Last year, seven. Nine the year before that. You know how many there have been this year so far? Five. Five, Cole! Three this month alone."

It would've been six with Edgar, Cole thought.

"At the time, I didn't understand. Why would anyone resort to that, especially when we only have thirty years? But as I got older and met more people through working in administration, it started making sense. People lose the ones they care about all the time, and who's there to help them make sense of it? Sometimes, the people they lose are all they had, and when they're gone, there's nothing left. Just emptiness. Isolation. And that's only a small part of the pain people carry, the struggles they're left to face alone."

A look of faint disgust crossed his face. "Hell, Vella could very well have been another one. The way she was treated . . . if she didn't have you . . . I hate to even think about it." He paused to take a steadying breath. "I know too many that we grew up with in the orphanage who have . . . there shouldn't be any, Cole. We already have it bad enough with our limited lives, and yet a lot of people can't enjoy that small time they have. People are suffering. And no one's helping them."

Cole remained silent, absorbing Alex's words.

"That's why I want to be mayor. Change things."

"Dammit, Alex." Cole looked down. "I'm sorry about your parents. You should've had the chance to at least meet them."

"Don't worry about me. Other people have had it a lot worse."

"So, what are you going to do about it?"

"I've tried to raise it with Owen, but he says it's only a minority and there's nothing we can do. We should focus on the majority. It's not worth the resources. Can you believe that?"

"I can."

"Yeah. I guess you can. Sometimes this place and these people—it gets to me," Alex said. "There's a fine line between someone in the majority and becoming part of the minority. What's the point of going on when you have no one? The people you loved are gone, and so are multiple parts of you. No one's there to help pick up the pieces because everyone's having a hard time keeping it together themselves. Then you are all alone. No one knows you exist. I wonder if anyone even tried to help my parents."

"You can change that now," Cole said.

"I don't know. I feel powerless to help anyone. I can't save Ellie . . . what's the point? I can't do anything."

"You're trying. That's more than most people do."

"It feels futile."

"It might be, but that's not going to stop us. We don't give up."

"We?"

"Yeah," Cole said, grinning. "Is there a problem with that?"

Alex smiled and shook his head in amusement.

"Then I don't want to hear it. If you, of all people, give up on this place, what hope do we have?"

"God . . . being lectured by Cole. How far have I fallen?"

"If you decide to give up on what we're doing here, that's fine. Because I won't."

"That's what worries me."

Cole shrugged and smiled. "I have my own way of doing things."

"By throwing your fists at it."

"Basically."

They shared a laugh, finally able to relax around each other.

"But you can do something important. Make a real change," Cole said, his voice sincere.

"Maybe." Alex turned, took a few steps, then froze, staring at the tree line. To him, the obscured doors beyond it were perfectly clear. Waiting for him. "Cole . . ."

"Yeah?"

Alex turned back. "What if it's a mistake?"

"What is?"

"What if we're not meant to leave Eden?"

"Vella asked me the same thing a few days ago."

"And?"

"Do you ever get the feeling this place shouldn't exist? Like, deep down, you know it's all wrong?"

"Uh, yeah. But what if . . . worse things happen because we succeed?"

"We don't know that."

"I get the feeling it's not going end in peace and harmony."

"Maybe. Who knows? We could name a hundred possibilities. All I know is this sick game needs to end. No matter the result."

Alex said nothing, contemplating Cole's words.

"It's worth the risk. Isn't it? We're all going to die soon anyway," Cole added.

Alex couldn't help but laugh. "Well, when you put it like that."

"Either they'll end this place one day, or we will. And I think we should be in control of our fate for once. Don't you?"

"Do you have a plan? Thought about countermeasures? In case things go bad?"

"How do you plan for something you know nothing about?"

"Yeah . . . I guess."

"I didn't need to tell you any of this, did I? You already knew. You just needed to hear it from someone else. Some kind of affirmation to quiet that overthinking mind of yours. Right?"

Alex gave him a faint smile, then took a deep breath. "You wanted to know how I'm doing? I'm not okay. Everything's compounding, piling on top of each other. I feel like I'm being crushed."

"You're not the only one. Try to rest and it'll get easier. One day at a time," Cole said. "I'm sorry for not reaching out. That's on me. Also, I might not have been there before, but I'm here now. If you need anything, let me know."

Alex nodded and walked away.

"Hey," Cole called after him. "We still have a third of our lives to make up for lost time."

Alex took a few steps and stopped. "By the way, when I found out what made Vella leave the orphanage, I made sure those two got another . . . lesson. After their cuts and bruises healed, of course. They wouldn't even dare look her way again. They'll remember the consequences," Alex said. "I always had your back."

29

The phenomenon of suicide (as far as records indicate) has persisted since the early days. How does one explain it? We only have thirty years to begin with. Why shorten that? For some, it can feel like the real question is why try at all? Why press on when it all feels meaningless since the future leads nowhere? Why go on living when you have lost the people you care about? Why go on when there is no hope? The challenge is not explaining the phenomenon but understanding the underlying cause of why those affected are asking themselves these questions. Only then can we begin to help those most at risk.

—THE SOCIAL SERVICES HANDBOOK, SECOND
EDITION
By Simon #9067

Edgar sat alone in the quiet of his home, the silence as suffocating as the stale air. Each scrape of his spoon against the bottom of the bowl echoed through the empty house. The sound amplifying the isolation that had become his constant companion.

His hands trembled as he lifted the spoon to his mouth. He swallowed without tasting, the actions driven more by habit than hunger.

Tears slipped down his cheeks, falling unnoticed into his soup. Not bothering to wipe them away, he put down the spoon. The bouts of uncontrollable crying had been less frequent since Cole and the others had come into his life. But they still remained a part of his daily routine. When he was alone, as he often was, the tears came freely. A simple thought or memory about Leah or Amy would push itself to the forefront of his mind and trigger them. Sometimes they would come of their own accord. The sheer weight of being alone was enough, ready to snatch him at any moment.

Even when he'd had both of them, there had been stretches where he'd struggled to pull himself out of bed. The simplest of tasks had felt impossible as he was caught in a heavy haze for days at a time. Leah, facing her own difficulties, had had no understanding or care for his struggles, causing a rift to grow between them.

Today marked the final milestone—one year left. But it wasn't the ticking clock that weighed on him; it was the struggle to get through each day that truly tested him. He put down his spoon, resting his head in his hands as a wave of despair washed over him. He tried to push the thoughts away, but they only grew louder, more insistent. His frustration mounted until he couldn't suppress it any longer.

"Stop," he groaned, the sound growing into a desperate scream. "Please . . . stop . . ." His voice broke into a whisper. Fighting only made it worse. He knew that, but what else could he do?

Pushing himself out of the chair, Edgar stumbled to the cupboard, pulling out a bottle of shine. He'd promised Cole he would quit drinking, but it was a promise he couldn't keep. He only managed to cut back enough to avoid a visible hangover. He took a long swig, feeling the burn as the alcohol slid down his throat. Setting it aside, he dragged himself to bed, even though he knew he wouldn't be able to sleep.

A knock at the front door startled him. Considering the day, it was one he'd expected and prayed wouldn't come. He considered ignoring it. Wiping his eyes with his shirt, he tried to compose himself, though the raw redness around his eyes was still evident, not that he was aware or cared. The knock came again, louder this time. Edgar sighed, forcing himself to the door, knowing it wouldn't stop. He hesitated before opening it a fraction.

He expected Cole, but instead, it was Vella standing alone, trying to hide a bigger smile than the one on her face.

"What're you doing at the moment?" Vella asked.

Edgar held the door partly closed, hiding his face from her. "Nothing," he muttered.

"Ah, good, good. Leah wanted me to invite you over for dinner."

"I just ate," he mumbled.

Vella chuckled. "Not a problem. Come on. I'm not taking no for an answer."

"I'm not ready."

She paused, hearing how small his voice was. "Are you okay?"

"Fine."

"All right . . ." Vella cleared her throat. "It would mean a lot to me if you came. There's something I want to show you."

Edgar sighed, defeated. "I'll come."

"Great," Vella replied. "Come around when you're ready. And before you say anything, just know I'll come back if we don't see you soon. I'm serious. I will."

He nodded, inching the door closed. When he heard her leave, he leaned against the door and let out a weary sigh. More than a hint of annoyance was directed at Leah and Cole. He groaned and lightly punched the door.

Why did they have to send her?

He went to the kitchen and slumped into a chair. Across the room, his eyes drifted toward the bottle of shine sitting on the kitchen counter. He pulled himself up, crossed the room, and wrapped his fingers around the base. He stared at it for a long time, tightening his grip around the glass. The thought of having to face them was too much to bear.

Out of the corner of his eye, he spotted the cones for their training. Beneath them sat their scouting report about the Bear. He brushed aside the cones and stared at the front page. Where he had first written *Project Stupidity* in large letters, Vella had crossed out *Stupidity*. In its place, she'd put the word *Victory*; each letter was in a different color and size.

Scattered around the rest of the cover were multicolored drawings of whatever random things came to her mind, childish doodles filling every corner—a stark contrast to what lay inside.

Near the bottom was a caricature of her standing triumphant over the slain Bear. Below that was a stick figure drawing of the four of them. A light laugh escaped him as he looked over the chaotic absurdity of it all.

His eyes drifted away and his face went sullen at the realization that he couldn't let her down now. He was going to have to go, like it or not.

Closing his eyes, a smile crept across his lips. That single page reminded him of everything she had given him. Her boundless energy and enthusiasm for the little things had brought joy to his life that he'd thought was long gone.

The only smiles and laughter he could remember from the past few years, he could directly attribute to her. She made life unpredictable in the best way. Her spontaneous words and actions never failed to brighten his days.

He pushed the bottle of shine away, stepping away from the counter. After changing into some fresh clothes, he left the house.

As he approached their front door, a different kind of dread settled in his chest. He knew Leah would remember it was his birthday. Did she actually care, or was this Cole's doing? It didn't matter; what he feared most was the warmth he knew would greet him inside.

Forcing a smile felt impossible, but he didn't want to worry Leah. He steeled himself by taking short, sharp breaths as he opened the door.

"Happy birthday," they shouted in unison.

The sight of Cole, Vella, Leah, Alex, and Ellie around the dining room table hit him hard and heavy.

The warmth of their welcome threatened to overwhelm him. He stood frozen, jaw clenched, balling his fists to stop them from trembling.

Not here. Not in front of her. I can't let her see it, he reminded himself.

He forced a smile and stepped inside. Vella was the first to greet him, pulling him into a hug.

"Come on." She took his arm and led him inside.

Cole was next, forcing him into a strong embrace. Edgar felt as though he was a lifeless body, being passed around without any control. He couldn't help but smile.

Alex shared in the fun, offering a handshake only to pull back at the last second and engulf him in a hug. Edgar's greeting with

Ellie was more reserved, as they'd never spoken to each other before, but her warmth was no less genuine.

Finally, he reached Leah. Wearing a soft smile, she wrapped her arms around him. "Happy birthday," she whispered.

She pulled away to get a better look at him. Her eyes scanned his face. For a split second, she flashed a half-grimace as she assessed him, then faded back into a warm smile.

Vella tugged at his arm, feeling some relief as she broke him away from Leah.

She held an arm behind her back. "I made you something," she said, brimming with excitement.

He glanced at Leah, who gave him a flicker of raised eyebrows. "It's all her," she said.

Vella revealed a rectangular package wrapped in crisp paper. As she handed it over, Edgar could hear the faint rattle of wood inside.

"Don't tell me . . ."

Her smile widened. "Open it."

Edgar peeled away the paper, revealing a smooth, polished wooden box. The top of it was covered with squares made from contrasting types of wood, one a rich, dark brown and the other a lighter, almost golden shade. He stared at it, his expression frozen in disbelief.

"When you said you could beat any of us in chess, I took it personally and I thought you needed to prove it. And since neither of us has a complete set . . . well . . . now you've got no excuse."

What did I do? he wondered. His eyes remained fixed on the board, afraid to lift them.

"Open the drawer," she implored.

He twisted it in his hands to find a small knob for a pullout drawer on the side of the box. He hesitated for a moment with his hand on the knob before opening it. Inside were the chess pieces, each one meticulously hand-carved.

"You did all this?" he asked, still unable to look at her.

"Uh-huh. Well, I had to get a little help at work, but for the most part, it was me. Cole did the pawns."

He picked out one of the queens, feeling it in his fingertips. The attention to detail in it, in the whole thing, amazed him. Feeling a lump in his throat rise, he pleaded, trying to will himself not to break.

What did I do to deserve this . . .

"Why . . . did you . . ." He glanced up at her but was quick to drop his head, feeling their eyes on him. "It's . . . I love it. Thank you."

She stepped forward and wrapped her arms around his chest.

There was no stopping it now.

He broke.

They sang, had cake, and spent the night drinking, talking, and playing games. Cole entertained Ellie with stories about growing up with Alex, none of which were particularly flattering. Most of the memories were ones he thought he'd forgotten, and they made Cole laugh like he hadn't in years.

Vella and Edgar were engaged in their fifth game of chess. Predictably to everyone but Vella, Edgar had beaten her every time, but she wouldn't give up, demanding they play again until she won. She fell for every trick in the book. At first, she thought he was letting her win, offering her favorable openings. But they were soon revealed to be traps. They were traps she kept falling for until she became wary enough to avoid them. And the one time she didn't take his bait, he revealed with a wry smile that it wasn't a trap at all. He kept up the mind games throughout, ramping up her frustration.

"Vel, I warned you," Cole said, glancing over after Edgar dealt her another loss.

Leah, off to the side, watched Vella and Edgar in their never-ending struggle. Now and then, she looked over to see Cole smiling and laughing, taking heart at seeing him and Alex together, getting along.

Cole caught her gleeful glance and rolled his eyes, mouthing, "Shut up."

As the night neared its end, Alex and Ellie were the first to leave.

Cole and Vella struggled to stay awake through their own game of chess. Vella finally conceded after her tenth loss to Edgar. Undeterred, she turned to Cole, challenging him instead. It was a desperate move in an attempt to get at least one win that night and salvage some dignity.

Sensing the night winding down, Edgar took the opportunity to leave. The night had revitalized him in a way he hadn't thought possible but was exactly what he needed. He felt like he could finally find some sleep now.

Leah saw him out, insisting he take the leftover cake. She walked with him to the end of the property, the night air cool and still.

"Well . . . ah, thanks for tonight," Edgar said, shifting the cake and chessboard in his arms.

"You're welcome," Leah said.

"Was this your idea?"

"I was thinking about doing something for your birthday. But before I could even float the idea, those two came to me and insisted. Especially Vella," she said with a small laugh. "Not that I was opposed to it."

"I didn't think they liked me that much. I can be a bit hard on them."

"You wouldn't put in that much effort for someone you didn't care about," she said. "I've never seen them doing so well. Regardless of everything, I'm glad they have you. You've made quite an impression on them."

It was true. He'd changed their lives as much as they did his. How had he not seen this?

A smile crept over his face. "They're something else."

"Look," Leah began, her tone shifting. Edgar braced himself, knowing something was coming. The last time he had heard that tone, his life had fallen to pieces.

But it wasn't what he expected.

"I don't think it's good for you to live on your own. Cole and Vella have *progressed*, shall we say, and are sharing a room now, which leaves a spare room."

Edgar blinked, caught off guard. The tension in his chest

eased a little, and he let out a small laugh.

"Their idea?" he asked, though he already knew the answer.

"Mine," Leah said, resolute in her tone and expression. "I'm not proposing anything more than that. I don't like the idea of you living alone. It's not good for anyone."

"You'd be okay with that?" Edgar asked.

"Of course."

He wondered how much Cole told her about his state of mind after his failed suicide attempt, thwarted by the orb.

No, Cole wouldn't have told her more than she needed to know. This was all Leah.

Of course it was. She lived a little too much for those around her, which was what worried him.

"I don't know, Leah. It's a nice idea, but I don't think I can accept the pity," Edgar asserted, though his voice wavered.

"Pity? We live beyond stupid concepts like *pity*. Stupid, idiotic pride. Let it go," Leah said, frustration rising in her tone. "Why won't you let anyone help—"

"I can look after myself," he said, cutting her off. He immediately regretted it, taking a half step back.

She stepped toward him, staring him down, her gaze piercing. Edgar faltered and looked away, unable to hold her stare. She took another step, twisting her head to look at him.

"Fine," he muttered.

She leaned in closer. "What was that?"

"Thank you," he whispered.

"Good," Leah said, stepping back, satisfied. "You'll be here tomorrow, right?"

He nodded, feeling a strange mix of relief and apprehension.

"If I don't see you, I *will* send Cole and Vella around. You know how annoying they can be."

"You always were a bully," he said with a soft smile.

"I do what I must. I'm just happy you're letting me help . . . since I never did before."

"You put up with all you could."

She paused to look him over, then shook her head. "You picked the wrong person. You deserved so much better. Why not pick someone else?"

"There was . . . no one else."

She unconsciously scowled hearing the words. "Do you think you deserved punishment? Is that why?"

"I just . . . I don't think we get to choose," he said. "You were everything I wished I could be. I admired you."

She took a moment to study him, taking in his words, before she finally nodded. "I think that's it . . ." she said, looking off into the distance. "I thought too little of you because you thought so highly of me."

She looked back into his eyes, and with every passing second, it felt like the knife was twisting deeper.

"I wish you could see what I see," he said.

"That's what I'm talking about," she said with a hint of frustration.

He took a moment to let her settle before saying, "I don't blame you for giving up Amy."

"Stop saying that," she said, through gritted teeth.

"You need to hear it."

She shook her head, scowling.

"You did the right thing," he added.

"Shut up." She hurled the words at him. "Just . . . enough."

"Do you think you deserve punishment for it?"

"I don't deserve your forgiveness," she said. "I know how much you loved her. She was the only thing that made your bad days better."

"I love her more than anything and that means doing what's best for her. And . . . letting go . . . of her . . . is w-what's best for her."

Leah squeezed her eyes closed. "Can we not do this? Please."

A silence fell over them as they both had nothing more they could add. Leah took a few deep breaths and glanced at him, noticing his relaxed expression. Her face softened in turn.

"Well . . ." She cleared her throat. "See you tomorrow. I plan on making it my life's mission to make you smile again now that I've got Vella and Cole taken care of."

He shook his head. "I'm happy enough."

"Cut the crap," she snapped.

"What about you? How are you?"

"Great."

Edgar chuckled. "Remember, I can see through you too."

"Can you? Tell me, then. How am I?"

"I know you're not fine. I know you're hiding a lot."

"How could you possibly know that?"

"Like I said, I know you."

She shook her head and turned to walk away.

"Wait," he called out. "Here." He held out the chessboard to her. "One less thing for me to bring tomorrow."

She smiled and accepted it.

"How do you manage?" he asked.

"I make sure I'm not alone."

30

There are things you can't unsee, and things you can't unhear. I can't say which has kept me awake more nights.

—THE FIRST PEOPLE OF EDEN
Journal of Morgan #38
Day 21

At breakfast, Leah mentioned that Edgar would be staying in the spare room for a while. Cole and Vella accepted the news with no objections.

"Does that mean . . . you two . . . ?" Vella asked, her face lighting up.

Cole gave Leah a sly grin. "Well? Does it?"

"Shut it, Cole," Leah said. "No, it doesn't, Vel."

"Oh . . ."

Leah smiled at her genuine reaction. "Maybe you can help find someone for him," Leah said with some playfulness.

Vella's mouth tightened as she returned to her food, saying nothing.

Later that afternoon, Edgar arrived with only a single bag. Leah frowned at the light packing, but Edgar just shrugged it off and laughed along with the other two.

Cole had always imagined that a full house would be suffocating, but he found himself enjoying the extra company. The initial phase of living together was pleasant. Everyone made the extra effort to accommodate one another.

They attended the weekly party together. This time around, Cole and Vella joined Leah and everyone else on the dance floor, no longer needing to hide away. They could share the moment with the others, but it still felt like it was just the two of them, lost in their own world.

For Edgar and Leah, it was a special night. They got to see their daughter once more. She presented Edgar with a handmade self-portrait, which he hung with pride on the living room wall when they got home.

The next morning, Edgar joined them on their walks to and from training. Only a few weeks ago, Cole had been alone in this routine, but now he couldn't imagine it any other way.

The breeze was light, the woods quiet. Peaceful. He felt like he was exactly where he needed to be. He kept pace with Vella, with Edgar a few steps behind.

All of a sudden, Vella's pace faltered, then stopped altogether. Her entire body stiffening as she stared through the trees. Cole noticed and stopped as well. His eyes followed hers to see what caught her attention.

She had her eyes fixed on a Ghost removing a rotting tree. The automaton took no notice of them as it effortlessly cut the tree into pieces and placed them neatly in a cart with fluid, unnatural smoothness.

He instinctively took a step back to be closer to her. Edgar, sensing something was wrong, hung back a few paces, giving them space.

Cole didn't need to ask what she was thinking about. They never talked about it. No one who was there that day ever did.

"Come on," he said. The words were hollow as his eyes remained glued to the Ghost. The white sphere of its head hypnotized him, keeping him trapped.

Out of the corner of his eye, he could see that Vella's hand was shaking. It took him a moment to realize that his own heart was beating erratically, his hands and jaw trembling, his breathing labored. His feet felt rooted to the spot, no longer under his control.

"Try not to think about it," he said. His own voice felt distant, not his own.

"I-I can't . . . Tom . . . I can still hear him," she said, her voice fraying.

"Me too," Cole whispered.

Tom had grown up with them in the orphanage. They hadn't known him well since he'd run with a different crowd, being a few years older. In Eden, they were taught from a young age how to avoid death. The rules were clear: don't dig too far down, don't try to remove implants, don't tamper with the dispenser, and never interfere with a Ghost. These were a few from a longer list, warning them that disrupting the status quo led to disaster.

Doing any of these would often result in instant death—not instant in the sense that it was quick, but instant because it began without warning, and once it started, there was no stopping it.

That day, the kids of the orphanage were playing outside like usual. Cole and Alex were kicking a ball around while Vella sat off to the side, hoping to remain invisible.

Tom and his friends were known troublemakers. They had been hanging around the fence line when a Ghost passed by, carrying waste out of Eden. Tom sensed an opportunity to try to impress his friends.

The warnings about Ghosts were clear: Don't touch them, don't hit them, don't hinder any of their work. But the problem with the warnings given to the younger generations was that they had never experienced the reality behind the words. The brutal consequences. The ruthlessness. It was one thing to be told; it was another to experience it. None of them had ever seen, firsthand, the truth of Eden or what they were up against.

"There is no way that would happen."

"For that?"

"They're lying."

"Not a chance."

"Kill you? What a joke."

"They're trying to scare us."

"I heard someone hit a Ghost and nothing happened."

Kids would often mess around and touch the skin around the implants. The result was always the same: searing, intense pain for up to a minute. Not deadly. But it was unlike anything they had ever experienced, a pain so intense it felt as if their arm was literally on fire. Everyone could see that nothing was happening in a physical sense, no burns or injuries, but their brains screamed otherwise.

Many were left in tears. Some would attempt to laugh it off despite the distress they couldn't hide. All would be left clutching their arms, the torment still at the forefront of their minds. Anyone who did it remembered that pain for the rest of their lives. It became a test of courage for certain groups of children. Alex had gotten tricked into it, while Cole had done it on a dare, and neither of them had ever wanted to put their hands anywhere near it again.

They assumed the pain was coming from the implant somehow manipulating them within. If it was just some pain, even if it was incredible, eleven-out-of-ten pain, it wasn't damaging them. So, what did it matter?

"Nothing bad will happen."

"Double dare you. Do it and I'll touch my implant."

If there were going to be consequences, they would expect it to be intense pain, but it would be short-lived and isolated. Like touching an implant. No big deal.

Tom picked up a small rock, a grin spreading across his face as his friends urged him on. Without much hesitation, he threw it over the fence at the Ghost. Just to be cautious, he threw it in a high arc, hoping it would land on the Ghost.

It didn't matter that the rock was too small to harm the Ghost.

It didn't matter that he hadn't thrown the rock directly at it.

It didn't even matter that the rock he'd thrown missed by several meters.

And it didn't matter that he was a twelve-year-old child.

The moment it left his hand, it was over. They knew what he was trying to do; they always did. And there was no forgiveness.

Tom's raw, violent screams tore through the air as he collapsed, his muscles tightening in agonized spasms. Everyone froze and could only watch in horror. He convulsed and writhed; the pain seemed to come from anywhere and everywhere. It was one thing for it to be your arm; another to have every part of your body consumed by agony beyond comprehension. The orphanage staff rushed over and ushered the children to their rooms.

There was nothing anyone could do for Tom.

The screams continued. He pleaded and begged for it to stop. His agony dragged on for what felt like an eternity. Vella would later say it went on for twenty minutes; Cole thought it was closer to ten. Some said it was longer; others, shorter. Time had warped in those moments, distorted by the sheer terror that gripped them all.

Cole remembered huddling on the floor, his hands clamped over his ears, eyes squeezed shut, every muscle tensed as hard as they could. Alex curled up beside him, his body trembling as tears streamed down his face. Cole dared to open his eyes once, catching a glimpse of Alex. He wanted to reach out, to offer some comfort. But he felt paralyzed, his own tears soaking into his shirt. Tom's screams pierced the air, shooting through every nerve in his body.

Everyone was desperate for it to stop. The screams and cries were broken up by attempts to muffle the sounds, but it never lasted. The shouts came out louder, the cries piercing their flesh. Finally, it did stop. Tom's suffering ended when they decided he had endured enough to send a message. A message to the people of Eden. Remember who is in control.

Minutes after the noise stopped, against his better instincts, Cole felt the urge to check if it was, in fact, over.

Cole stood and crept to the window. Behind him, Alex remained huddled, eyes shut and hands covering his ears. Slowly, he shifted the curtain to peer outside.

It was over.

He trembled, watching as the Ghost carried Tom's lifeless body in its hands.

They'd learned a brutal lesson that day, one that none of them would ever forget. Every time they saw a Ghost, they were reminded of that feeling of helplessness, the screams echoing in their minds as vividly as they had on that day.

Now, standing there frozen, Cole felt like that same helpless child. Trapped in the past, as if every experience since had been just a dream. The Ghost brought it all back, locking him in that small, agonizing window of time.

He squeezed his eyes shut, trying to ground himself in the present.

Words from somewhere else reached him: "Are you okay?"

A hand on his shoulder made him jump, snapping him back to reality. He flinched, causing Edgar to stumble backward.

"Sorry. Yeah, I'm . . . fine."

"I heard about what happened with Tom, but I never knew you two were there that day. I'm sorry. That must've been tough," Edgar said.

"We were just nine," Cole said vacantly, still staring ahead.

He wrenched his eyes away and turned to Vella, who was still lost in her waking nightmare. He took her hand, giving it a gentle squeeze.

She blinked, the haze lifting from her eyes, and she turned, burying her face in his chest. She held onto him fiercely, her body trembling. He put an arm around her, and she let it all out.

"Don't worry. You're safe," he whispered, rubbing her back.

Cole had Alex with him during that painful time, making him feel less alone. But who did Vella have?

She has me now.

He felt a reignited anger burn within. *We're getting out of this damn place.*

When they reached the clearing, Alex was waiting. Cole released Vella and jogged over to him, the corners of his eyes burning. Alex took a half step back, caught off guard by Cole's approach. Without a word, Cole pulled him into a hug.

31

I liked to sit and read during the lunch breaks. I didn't like playing with the other children much. I was used to being alone, then one day, a volunteer at the orphanage sat next to me with a book and read beside me. She would sit with me every day after that. We would swap books and discuss them. She even had this one book she wrote and gave it to me to read. It was called *The Knights of* . . . something. I can't remember. It was nice to have someone to talk to. But that's not the part I cared about. It was the feeling I've kept with me, comfort, security. Someone was with me. I wasn't alone. Then, out of nowhere, she stopped coming. I was devastated when one of the staff finally told me what had happened to her. Her name was Rebecca. I remember how she would glance up every now and then and smile. There was one little girl she always watched, though she never went near her. I've always wondered . . . did my mother love me as much as that?

—"SOPHIA #8664"

CHILDREN OF THE PEACEFUL PASSAGE

by Aleister #8990

Cole sat alone on his break, choosing the solitude of Vella's shed over joining Vella and Leah in town. He rarely found time for himself these days, so he relished these quiet moments in the woods, with only the shed, her garden, and the slow rustling of leaves for company.

The shed had been left unattended for weeks now, and signs of neglect were beginning to show. Grasses were growing through the garden and creeping up the walls of the shed. It wasn't bothering him, but for Vella's sake, he wanted to keep the place tidy for her. That was a job for another day; presently, his attention was pulled elsewhere.

After another scouting trip, he'd looked through the sketches Alex and Edgar had made of the Bear. And it bothered him how bad they were. Something itched at the back of his mind at the knowledge that he could do much better. Drawing wasn't their strength, but he held himself back from doing his own for

Vella's sake, lest he remind her of their painful past. He avoided drawing around her entirely, afraid there might be something in his style she would recognize, something that could connect him to that old, cruel image. She knew now, but the guilt still weighed heavily on him.

She could have made peace with it, but it was a risk he wasn't willing to take. The last thing he wanted was to trigger any pain for her.

Things between them were better than they had ever been. There was no reason to compromise that with a careless insensitivity.

What should have been a source of pride had become something he associated only with shame.

He would slip his version in within the other pages, hopefully unnoticed. Then again, she might see it, so maybe he wouldn't. Regardless, he was adamant about doing the real thing justice. He pulled out his sketchbook and pencil and drew the Bear.

With each stroke, he captured the scale, detail, and essence of the creature in ways the others couldn't. When he finished, he flipped the page, satisfied.

His hand moved absently over the new sheet. Soon, the page filled with eyes—dozens of them, all the same, each one staring back at him with the same malice.

The nightmares hadn't haunted him as frequently or as intensely lately, thanks to Vella's presence beside him. Her warmth seemed to keep the horrors at bay. Most of the time. There were still nights when he'd wake up drenched in sweat, in a state of heightened panic. Then there were the nights he would lie awake, afraid to close his eyes, trapped in a similar state of dread.

He was able to hide some of these episodes from Vella. During the times he couldn't, she was there to comfort him. Over time, he was finally able to tell her about the day that haunted him, revealing it in bits and pieces.

Almost as if snapping out of a trance, he looked down at what he had drawn. He cursed aloud and tore out the page. It was a compulsion he couldn't break since childhood, following him ever since he'd seen those eyes.

He flipped the page again, searching for something else to draw. His thoughts drifted to Vella and Leah, imagining them sitting together, eating, and watching the play of people around them. He drew that image.

A couple of strokes in, he stopped. A memory pushed itself to the forefront of his mind. One of him and Leah. He turned to a new page and put pencil to paper. It popped into his head now and then, but he'd never understood why. He thought that if he drew it, he could make sense of it.

He'd tried before, but none of his attempts were able to capture the moment. This time was no different. Frustration crept in as he stared at the latest attempt. *Not even close.* Annoyed, he ripped the page out and tried again. But again, still nothing close to the memory. He tossed the sketchbook aside, frustration simmering, but beneath that, a determination to finally capture it.

One day . . . he thought.

A sudden clicking sound made him flinch. He jerked his head up. The shed door creaked open, leaving a narrow gap. He breathed a sigh of relief.

After gathering his things and closing the door, he returned to work in the fields.

When the workday finished, Cole made sure to arrive home before anyone else. He went into his closet and hid his sketchbook behind a false panel in the back of the bottom shelf. He realized his old hiding place had been compromised when he'd seen several pages poking out, likely by Leah, he surmised. So he'd created this new spot for extra security.

Luckily, she didn't find the orb, he thought with relief.

He was already thinking about moving the hiding spot outside the house, just in case Vella went looking around.

He placed the sketchbook inside with the others, stopping short of reinserting the panel. The orb sat beside the sketchbooks. He froze, caught in the abyss of the surface, watching it intently and bracing himself for the inevitable click.

A minute passed. Nothing. Feeling foolish, he finally decided to put the panel back in place.

Click.

He winced and muttered a curse under his breath. After packing the shelf to cover the panel, he walked outside and sat on the front steps, his head in his hands.

He looked up to see Leah approaching. She called out to him, her voice strained.

She was alone. An uneasy feeling settled in his gut.

Where's . . . Vella?

Leah's expression told him everything.

He ran out to meet her. "Where is she?" he asked, fists already clenched.

"I let her go home early. She had some . . . trouble," Leah said, choosing her words with care.

Trouble. His heart rate spiked, anger rising to the surface. "Who was it?" he demanded, making a mental list all the possibilities he could think of. "Who?"

"Someone her age visited the office and ran their mouth. Don't worry, I dealt with them," Leah explained, gripping his arm.

A harsh, wordless scream of frustration escaped his lips as he broke away from her and ran inside. He hoped she was hiding and he hadn't noticed her.

But there was no sign of Vella. The emptiness of the house only fueled his panic. He rushed back outside, his eyes wild.

"She's not inside!" His voice cracked with frustration.

He wanted to lash out. Blame Leah for letting this happen. But when he saw her pacing the edge of the street, distress written all over her face, muttering to herself, all the anger drained out of him.

What am I doing? Why would I even think of blaming her?

He walked over to Leah and pulled her into a hug.

"It's not your fault," he said.

Before breaking away, he gave her an extra squeeze. Then he took off, already knowing where Vella would be. He sprinted to the familiar place, dread twisting in his stomach.

Nothing stirred as he arrived.

"Vella," Cole called out.

No answer.

He approached the shed and eased the door open.

There she was, huddled in the back corner, knees tucked under her chin, arms clasped around her legs, her eyes puffy and red. She stared blankly forward.

"Hey," Cole breathed in a low voice.

He moved closer to sit beside her. She didn't respond, keeping her eyes fixed ahead, unblinking. The silence was killing him.

"What happened?" he asked. Vella remained silent, her body closed off and unyielding.

Cole's concern deepened. He reached out to wrap an arm around her.

"Don't!" she snapped.

He recoiled, dropping his arm.

Frustration ravaged him, tearing at his throat. She was hurting, and he was powerless to help.

He tried again, his voice almost a plea. "Do you want to talk about it?"

Still, she said nothing. The silence stretched on, heavy and oppressive.

"Time?" he whispered.

She tapped two fingers and a thumb to her shoulder: *Leave. You can't ignore me.*

He didn't move.

"Leave me alone," she warned. "You have to."

"I can't," he said.

"Now!"

"But—"

"Leave!" she screamed. "Leave me alone. Get out. Get out! Get out!" She pushed him, driving him back until he scrambled and staggered to his feet.

The force of her words disoriented him, but the look in her eyes—those eyes filled with pain and suffering—hurt him more than any words could.

He stumbled out of the shed, closing the door behind him, his mind reeling. Every instinct screamed at him to go back inside, to hold her, comfort her. But he knew he couldn't force her to accept help. She needed space.

"I'll be back later," he said to the door, hoping she was listening.

He lingered outside, pacing in circles as helplessness gave way to anger. Anger at the people who'd hurt her, at Leah for letting it happen, and most of all, at himself for being unable to protect her.

His thoughts whirled between sorrow and fury, revenge and concern. It was a maelstrom of emotions, each one fighting for dominance.

On his way back, he saw Edgar walking his way and considered taking a detour, but he held his ground, letting Edgar approach.

"How is she?" Edgar asked.

Cole shook his head, trying to hide his frustration.

"I'll watch her. Rest and clear your head."

He nodded. "Don't go in; let her be."

"Sure."

As Cole passed, Edgar grabbed his arm, pulling him close. "Keep your head. For her."

Cole looked up, anger flaring, but when their eyes met, Edgar's intensity caught him off guard. His expression softened, and all he could manage was a small nod before continuing on his way.

When he finally returned home, Leah was finishing dinner. The scent of her stew filled the air, but the last thing on his mind was eating.

"Is she okay?" Leah asked.

Cole collapsed into the nearest chair, his head falling back as he stared up at the ceiling. Leah watched him, her hands gripping the counter, already knowing the answer.

"I don't know what to do," he whispered.

Leah approached him from behind, placing her hands on his

shoulders. Her face filled his view.

"I'm sorry," she said. "I promise you, I'm going to spend my remaining days making their lives a living hell." Her words were fierce, but Cole knew they were ultimately hollow.

Cole flipped his head forward. "Can I get dinner to go?"

"Of course." She slapped his chest lightly and left him to think.

He sank further into his seat, eyelids growing heavy.

"Does it get easier?"

"What do you mean?"

"I'm only twenty, and I feel . . . exhausted."

She let out a laugh. "You have no idea how good you have it now."

"Don't tell me that."

"Sorry. That's just how it goes."

"How can it possibly get more complicated?"

"For starters, parts of your body start aching in ways you didn't think possible. But I'm guessing that's not what you're asking about."

"No, but thanks for giving me something to look forward to."

"You're welcome." She let out a soft laugh. "The thing is you have a better perspective on your life as a whole, but you also realize how much of those years were wasted on things that don't matter, how you focused on the wrong things, and missed what's right in front of you. As you get older, you spend less time making new mistakes and more time trying to make up for the old ones, even though you can't change the past." She paused to breathe. "It all wears on you more, weighs you down. It feels more complicated. It's a long-winded way of telling you no, it doesn't. Sorry. You've got it easy now. Appreciate it."

"What a joke . . ."

"I do wonder sometimes how overwhelming things would be if we were to make it to fifty."

Cole chuckled. "Maybe it's for our own good that we don't."

She went back to prepare the stew. "Maybe . . ." It sounded as if the life drained out of her with that one word.

Leah's words made him feel like he was sinking further down, helpless to help her as well.

"Cole, we knew this was going to happen sooner or later, right?"

"Yeah, I guess. Still doesn't make it easier."

"She's in a much better place than she used to be, so I've got no doubt she'll bounce back, stronger than ever. Give her some space and be there when she's ready. All right?"

"Yeah . . . all right."

"Did you know she made a friend at work? And all on her own!"

"She did?"

"I'm so proud of her. That girl can do anything. She just doesn't realize it yet."

His eyes wandered to the bedroom door. The thought of the orb crossed his mind. He could use it, find the right approach, and guarantee success. But the thought of betraying Vella's trust again made him think better of it.

Still, the idea of having a safety net, just in case, was tempting. So he decided to take it with him for peace of mind.

He ran into his room, grabbed the orb, and headed back out.

This time, he was determined to help her. The right way.

32

It is time to review the outcomes five years after implementing the new laws and justice system. A sheriff and a deputy have proven sufficient to maintain order, and it is my recommendation that we continue with this two-person law enforcement model. Abuses of power should still be monitored closely, though none have been reported so far. The officers appear more interested in spending their time enjoying their own lives. Most arrests have involved rowdy drunkards needing a night in a holding cell to sleep it off. Occasionally, an extra day or two has been added to have them rethink their actions. In five years, there has been only one serious act of violence requiring an extended sentence. The mayor and sheriff coordinated to determine the penalty: one year in a five-by-five-meter cell. Since serving the sentence, the offender has shown no signs of reoffending. They now have just two years left to live, and losing more than that seems to be deterrent enough. This reflects the broader reality of crime in our community and why it remains low. When people know real consequences follow violations against each other, why risk losing what is already small and precious?

—EDEN ANNUAL REPORT
For the Year Ending 20
Page 34

Cole sat with his back against the door, sleep a distant thought. The crisp night air passed across his skin, cool and refreshing, but it did little to calm the storm in his mind. After several failed attempts to talk to Vella, he slipped the container of stew inside and left her alone.

Even if he couldn't reach her right now, he resigned himself to knowing she was safe.

It wasn't the hard ground that kept him awake. It was the relentless torture of his thoughts, the endless search for a solution that refused to come. He felt small, weak, helpless, like a leaf caught in a whirlpool, unable to escape the pull of his own mind.

The orb, cold and smooth, passed between his restless hands, a manifestation of the turmoil inside. He brought it up to eye level, staring into its black, reflective surface that seemed to stretch without end.

What are you? The question echoed in his mind, unanswered.

For a moment, the moonlight caught in the orb, making it gleam like an eye staring back at him. The sight startled him, a sudden reminder of the demon that haunted his nightmares.

He flinched, causing him to drop the orb. Even now, the terror lingered. Much like the memory of Tom, he was trapped in that brief moment in time, helpless to do anything.

Shaking off the unease, Cole reached down to retrieve the orb.

The last time he'd tried to get a glimpse of the Wolf, it had almost ended in disaster. He hadn't even considered going back since, despite feeling the same call reach out to him every night. The anxiety continued to eat at him, and he was desperate to find a way to conquer it.

He had no intention of killing the Wolf. Not yet, at least. He just needed to see it, to be able to look it in the eyes. Until he could do that, he knew he'd remain forever trapped. A helpless child. Powerless.

He knew it couldn't harm him so long as he could remain in control of his body, but he was afraid he couldn't even manage that.

The fear he experienced around the Bear had lessened over time as they did more tests. But enough for him to stand up to the Wolf?

If I can't even do this, how am I going to kill it? I can't . . .

He stood up and immediately reconsidered. The longer he stood there, the tighter the knots in his stomach became.

Do it.

No, don't.

You have to.

You don't need to.

Yes.

No.

Go.

Stay.

Dammit!

Enough of this. Just go to the door and figure it out then.

He could work with that, so he walked.

Soon, he found himself in front of a familiar red door. The walk had given him enough time to calm down and find the nerve he required.

His breath quickened despite his attempts to keep it even and steady. He wrapped his shirt around his mouth and nose, a flimsy barrier against the stench that awaited him.

Staring at the crimson red door, hand at the ready next to the scanner. He waited. Keeping his mind on his breath. He couldn't control much. But his breathing was something he could work on, even if his body viciously fought him. His chest was constricting, choking him. Still, he fought.

It can't hurt me, he repeated over and over to himself.

He heard the familiar click—the sound he had been waiting for. It sent a jolt of adrenaline through him.

He jerked his hand forward but stopped it short of touching the scanner, sensing something was off. He checked the orb. There was still a minute before it would tick over. He squeezed his eyes shut, pressing the bridge of his nose.

I'm losing my mind. Wonderful.

When he regained his composure, he focused on the orb. He watched it with care, making sure there would be no mistake this time.

Click.

He felt his insides jolt at the sound. He bolted into action, stepping into the darkness. The dread was immediate, wrapping around him like a vise. His heart hammered, and his hands trembled as the familiar low growl echoed in the darkness.

This time, he swore not to break. Anger held him together— at the Wolf for the deaths he'd seen, both past and future; at the people who had hurt Vella; and at himself. He braced, planting his feet.

The ground trembled as the beast approached. Its presence was more imposing than he remembered. It moved slowly, deliberately, almost as if it knew there was no escape for its prey.

Cole's breathing halted as the creature came into full view. Its massive form dwarfed even the size of the Bear. Spikes instead of fur covered its body, with horns protruding from its head and claws that looked capable of rending steel. The low growl reverberated through him, a constant reminder of the danger he faced.

But Cole didn't move; his rage forced him to hold his ground.

Just get a good look at it, he told himself.

It moved on all fours, its massive body making the ground tremble with each step. Its back arched, but it kept its head lowered, showing off its larger spikes on its back and head. It crept forward carefully, edging into striking distance, ready to pounce.

Rather than roaring, it maintained a low, guttural growl. Its eyes were fixed on Cole. He stared back, almost losing himself in the blue abyss of its eyes but snapped out of the trance just in time to reset.

The world whirled back to the familiar sights, but he wasn't done. Again, he went in, staying a little longer each time, committing every detail to memory. The teeth, the claws, the spikes. He cataloged them all, piece by piece, no detail too small. He lost track of time, each encounter blending seamlessly into the next. He went on and on, drinking from the infinite well of time until he quenched his thirst.

Again and again, and again, and again, and again.

What had once been life-threatening became routine, even mundane. His breathing and pulse steadied, but not his desire.

He wanted more.

He craved it.

There was only one thing left. The eyes. He met its gaze, staring into the depths of those wrathful blue oceans of dread. Those eyes burning with intensity, with anger, and—*fear?* The thought startled him.

Fear? No. Surely not.

He reset again, trying to make sense of what he saw in its eyes.

The Wolf's eyes wavered ever so slightly, a subtle hint of vulnerability beneath the malevolence.

It's afraid? How? Why? Maybe I'm seeing things.

He took another look. There was no mistake. It was there.

The logic didn't add up, so he tried working backwards.

Freeze or run, fear chooses one or the other. No. That's not right. He thought back to earlier this afternoon. *When Vella is afraid, she'll lash out. If it feels fear, then anger is a reasonable response. So, there's the third option. Fight. Attack. Protect. Does it fear that I threaten its home? Does it see me as a threat to its existence?*

Then he noticed its posture. *It's trying to intimidate me by showing off its spikes. It's a defensive stance. Head down, back arched, growling.*

He now realized he had seen similar traits in the animals he tended to when they were afraid.

It sees me as a threat. It's trying to intimidate me, as any cornered animal would. It's alone, living in darkness, isolated. No wonder it's hostile.

Again, he went in, staring at it; a strange feeling stirred within him—pity. How could he pity such a monstrous creature? He reset, but the feeling wouldn't go away. The hate he'd carried for so long melted away, replaced by a deep empathy. The Wolf wasn't his enemy. It was a victim, like him. Trapped in its own tiny world, as they were trapped in Eden.

We're the same.

The realization hit him like a wave, and he found himself laughing. It started as a chuckle but soon grew into a full-blown fit of hysterical laughter. He collapsed to the ground, tears streaming down his face. He clutched his sides as the absurdity of it all washed over him. The fear, the anger—it had all been for nothing.

As the laughter subsided, Cole felt a weight lift off his shoulders; his body felt as light as a feather. Breathing had never felt so easy, his mind clearer than it had been in years, and life never felt so simple.

He thought of his parents, of the brief moments of warmth they'd given him before they were taken away. He'd buried those memories under layers of hate, but now, they resurfaced, bringing with them a sense of peace. Experiencing such unconditional kindness changed his life, both for the better and for the worse.

He felt glad he had gotten to experience all of it regardless. He lay on the ground, staring up at the sky, elation fading, feeling the world shift around him.

Eden, the people he knew, and even the Wolf all seemed different now, seen through the lens of empathy. He couldn't hate them anymore. Even the people he labeled irredeemable. He could no longer hate them.

I wish everyone could have this experience, he mused.

Cole knew what he had to do. But first, there was one more thing.

He entered the door one last time, standing firm as the helpless animal appeared before him.

"Hey," he called.

It approached, bristling with the same familiar hostility. Its growl echoed in the stillness, but he didn't flinch. Instead, he lowered himself to the ground, crossing his legs, his gaze steady with it.

He smiled with ease; its rage could no longer touch him. The creature hesitated, inching closer, its movements sharp and wary, until finally, it stopped a good distance out of reach of Cole. It still growled, low and angry.

"I'm sorry," he whispered. "It's not your fault."

He waited a few more seconds, feeling a deep sense of contentment as he reset for the final time. Back outside, the night air against his skin felt extraordinary.

He thought about Vella, about the drawing that haunted him. The one that had triggered the nickname used by others to taunt her. He'd sat at its genesis, so every time they'd called her "the one-eyed freak," it had felt as though he was the one saying it. It was a small part of their history, yet it consumed so much of his life.

Did that kid know any better?

He'd paid for that sin tenfold. Now, he wondered if he could finally forgive the last person he still harbored hatred for.

If only it were that easy. But I'll try, he thought.

He saw lights in the distance flickering. Two figures entered the Peaceful Passage building. His heart sank; only one would come out.

There are some things I can't forgive.

The brief euphoria he felt faded, replaced by a heavy sorrow. For the person who would never return to their loved ones. And for the reality that demanded he kill the Wolf, for whom he had newfound sympathy.

He knew it was them or the Wolf. He would have to come to terms with that. Another day. He was suddenly tired. So very tired. It could all wait. His life, however, could not.

He hurried back to the shed, not wanting to miss another moment.

Inside, he found Vella fast asleep, her body curled up on the mattress, facing the wall.

Cole lay down beside her, wrapping an arm around her. Vella stirred, grabbing his arm and snuggling closer.

33

When I was little, my mom was a supervisor on our field trips. It meant the world to me because I didn't see her much growing up. So when she came along, it made me so happy to be able to spend time with her. I remember one night when we got to sleep under the stars. I'll never forget lying on her lap until I drifted off to sleep, feeling warm and safe. If I ever had trouble sleeping, I would picture being in that moment with . . . [She lost consciousness before she could finish, but her smile remained.]

—"IVY #8756"

CHILDREN OF THE PEACEFUL PASSAGE

by Aleister #8990

"Do you mind?"

Cole halted his whistling but still held an unnaturally easy smile that bothered Vella.

Early-morning light filtered through the trees as they walked back home. Vella had woken in a softer mood, which simplified things for Cole. With little effort, he managed to convince her to come back for breakfast.

His steps were light and effortless, his gaze drifting around her as if she weren't there. She watched him, a sense of disquiet creeping in, as if she were looking at a possessed man. It unsettled her to see him this relaxed. He was too calm. This wasn't like him. He should be fuming. Something was up.

"All right! Enough. What's wrong with you?" she snapped.

"I went in the red door last night and—"

Before he could finish, Vella elbowed him hard in the solar plexus, dropping him to his knees. But even crumpled on the ground, wheezing, he couldn't wipe the smile off his face.

"Without me? What were you thinking!"

"There's something . . . I need to show you . . . after breakfast," he managed between gasps of air.

"Idiot," she muttered, taking off without him.

When they reached the house, Leah greeted Vella with a hug. Vella willingly leaned into her, bringing a smile to Leah's lips.

"I'm so sorry," Leah whispered.

Vella looked away. "It's not your fault. It's fine."

Leah pulled back, fury in her eyes. "It's not; I'm going to destroy that girl."

Cole cut in. "No need. It's all right."

Leah eyed him, dumbfounded, unsure whether to feel proud or concerned. "What the . . . ?" She glanced at Vella, eyebrows raised. Vella shrugged and shook her head.

Edgar lingered behind them, and when he got the chance, he gave her a comforting hug, whispering, "Just say the word, and their septic tank will have an unfortunate malfunction." Vella stifled a laugh. It tempted her, but she shook her head.

They got through breakfast with minimal talking. Edgar sat off to the side, absorbed in a book, now and then glancing up at them with a content expression. Leah, warmed by Cole's relaxed demeanor, smiled at him, proud of him for bringing Vella back without losing his cool.

After the meal, Cole ushered Vella out of the house. Swarms of people greeted them in the streets. They carried supplies and food, set up decorations, and hung signs.

"What's going on?" she asked.

Cole pointed to a banner fluttering from a light pole. "People's Day," he said.

"I forgot it even existed. I haven't exactly been around," she said. "What's it for?"

"Us. Those still alive."

"Cool . . ."

"I know you're being sarcastic, but it's an important reminder to celebrate life while we have it."

"Who's the person standing next to me saying these things?"

Ignoring her, he said, "Think they usually have a whole festival in the south park."

"Is that where we're going?"

"No."

Without another word, Cole took her further into town, greeting everyone with a smile. For once, Cole was the one initiating these interactions, waving and asking how everyone's day was. It was a departure from his usual reluctance to engage. Today, the world felt different to him—the sun seemed brighter, and the day warmer. It was as if he'd stepped into a new reality.

Vella, hanging back half a step, was still unable to understand what had gotten into him.

They were nearing the center of Eden, and Vella was starting to panic. "Cole, where are we going?"

"*You* tell me," he teased, his smile widening.

She stopped, crossing her arms. "Cole," she warned.

He turned to her and grabbed her hand. "We're going to face your monster."

"What?" Her eyes widened in realization. "No, Cole." She pulled her hands free and took a few steps back. "Whatever you are planning, I'm not doing it."

He moved closer, standing within a breath of her. "I want you to experience what I did last night."

"What exactly did you do?"

"I got my life back."

She felt her frustration bubbling over at his cryptic words and actions. "What are you talking about?"

"This isn't going to be easy, but I need you to do this."

"You haven't even told me what we're doing."

Cole met her eyes. "I need you to trust me."

Her heavy, ragged breathing intensified. The thoughts of yesterday threatened to push her to breaking point.

"I need you to see what I see. Please." He placed the orb in her hands, wrapping her hands with his own. "You have nothing to fear."

She resisted, her hands tense in his. "Cole, I'm warning you," she said, voice trembling. "I don't want to."

"Any other day I would say, 'Let's go home and hide. Just you and me,'" he said. "But there's no more hiding. Not today. Not anymore."

Vella watched him, hoping he would break into a grin and say he was joking, that they could go back to the shed and waste the day together. But his steady gaze never wavered. He meant it, and that scared her the most.

She accepted the orb, her eyes filled with uncertainty.

"Was it Ivy?" he asked.

Her face tightened, and she looked away, confirming his suspicion.

Ivy, one of her childhood tormentors, still had a subconscious hold on her. Even the mention of her name stirred a deep-seated, involuntary dread.

"I see. Come on." Not waiting, he walked off.

"Cole, stop." She called after him, but he didn't even turn. She glanced around, uncertain and frustrated.

"Dammit." With a groan, she jogged to catch up with him.

Cole brought them to Alex's house, and he came out to greet them. "Leah told me—" Alex began, but Vella's glare stopped him. "Uh, I wanted to make sure you're okay."

Cole answered for her. "She's well and appreciates the concern."

Vella rolled her eyes, arms crossed. Alex looked at them, trying to understand what was happening.

"We're looking for someone," Cole said.

"Who?"

"Ivy."

"Ivy?" Alex repeated. He glanced at Vella, then back at Cole.

Cole shook his head, warning him not to press further. "Right, Ivy. Next street over, house six." He pointed in the direction. "Wait, Cole, you're not going to do anything . . . drastic, right?"

"Of course not," Cole said, still smiling.

Alex eyed him warily. "Okay . . . just try not to make any trouble."

"There won't be any," Cole assured him. "See you around midday?"

"What? You're . . . coming?"

"I think we will."

Alex looked at Cole with squinted eyes, mouth agape, then turned to Vella. "What happened to Cole? Why's he so calm? I was expecting scorched earth Cole. It's freaking me out."

"He's been like this all day; it's annoying me, too," Vella said.

"You didn't burn down her place or anything, right?" Alex asked.

"I would never," Cole replied, playing up his smile.

Vella gave him a shove. "You're creeping me out. Stop."

"I can't believe I'm saying this, but I miss cynical Cole," Alex said.

They left Alex's place and made their way to Ivy's home. The front was neatly curated, with a vine-covered archway leading down a tiled path to the door. A wooden trellis mounted on the front wall, also draped in vines and dotted with hanging potted plants, added a touch of color to the otherwise painfully white and bland exterior.

Across from Ivy's house, they found a bench at the edge of the park. People behind them were playing games and enjoying the morning.

Vella's leg quivered erratically. "Cole, I can't do this."

He placed a hand on her thigh, calming her shaking. "There's nothing you can't do."

"That doesn't make sense."

Cole didn't respond; instead, he turned his attention to the orb. There was still a third of the rotation left.

He brushed up against her. "Here's all you need to do," he said. "Get as close as possible to her front door. If you feel like it's getting too much, reset and start again. Keep going; try to take more steps each time. Even if it's just one."

"Then what?"

"When you make it, knock on the door. When she answers, you don't have to say or do anything. Watch her, observe her. From her feet up to her eyes. Note every detail about her. Do this over and over, as many times as it takes, until you're comfortable looking her in the eyes."

"Why? What's the point?"

"You'll see," he said. "The next five minutes are yours to repeat as much as you like. Only you exist. Your own little bubble, safe in your pocket of time. No one else can intrude. Think of it like your personal space at home. Soon, it'll come to feel like that. Remember, she can't hurt you; she's just an illusion. I will be here with you every step of the way, guiding you through it. You have all the time in the world. Nothing can hurt you while I'm around." He held her hand. "One step at a time."

She nodded, her shaking growing worse.

Click.

It could take one reset, or a thousand. He would only know the last one.

Vella's body trembled; tears welled at the corners of her eyes. Cole's worry grew, but then, unexpectedly, a smile spread across her face, followed by a sudden sharp laugh.

She closed her mouth and tried to take a breath through her nose, but she couldn't contain the cascade of giggles from escaping her.

The sound grew, bordering on hysteria. People nearby glanced over with concern. Cole gestured to them, reassuring them that she was okay.

She clutched her sides, tears welling. Before long, her uncontrollable laughter got in the way of her breathing, making her cough and sputter.

Cole patted her back, whispering, "You see?"

She nodded, still catching her breath. After a moment, she wiped her eyes and spoke, her voice light and free.

"I lost track of how many times I did it. But I kept going back just to see her stupid expression when she saw me."

She burst into laughter again. "How did I ever care what she thinks? I'm such an idiot."

Laughing herself breathless, she collapsed back into Cole's chest, exhausted but elated. He explained his own experience from the previous night and how they related.

"You were right," she said. "Her eyes . . . she's scared too. Just like . . . me."

"Like everyone is."

"Is that right . . . ?"

"You can see it everywhere. You have seen it everywhere; you just didn't know what it was."

She cleared her throat, still coming down. "I saw ridicule,

laughter, and for a moment, I wanted to slap her. I did once. Not a slap; I flicked her on the forehead. Sorry. I had to. But it was the other times when she saw I didn't flinch, I saw it—she's scared. Her confidence, it's all an act. Then I noticed other things, like her house, her life . . . it's sad."

Cole wrapped his arms around her. "I'm proud of you. I knew you could do it."

"I couldn't have done it without you. You walked me through the hard parts."

"No, that was all you."

"I wish I could believe that."

"Well, I don't remember any of it, so believe it."

"I'll try," she said. "So, what did you see last night?"

"A helpless animal trying to protect itself," he said, his voice soft. "It might be in my head, but I feel certain. I saw fear. Almost like it was crying out for help."

"Don't tell me you feel bad for it?"

"In a way. Don't you feel bad for Ivy?"

"In a way," she said. "Funny, that."

"You know, I used to hate that no one was trying to escape Eden. I thought they'd all just given up. I despised them so much. But they haven't given up. They're trying. In their own way. And it takes more courage than I ever gave them credit for. It's more courage than they have a right to show."

They sat in silence, soaking up the sun and the atmosphere of Eden. People flowed all around them, and they remained unmoved, undisturbed. Cole and Vella watched them as they shared their invaluable time with the people they'd chosen or had chosen them. The world felt different now, warmer, more alive. Every sound, every smell, every touch seemed miraculous.

This must be what it feels like to actually be alive, she thought.

Vella let out a satisfied sigh. "We're so stupid."

Cole shared a silent agreement.

"Anything you want to do?"

"No. Not . . . a . . . thing."

She felt his chest rise and fall with each breath; how curious it was. His breath, his life, everything felt precious.

As they sat there, Ivy stepped out of her house. She spotted Vella and drew half a step back.

Vella smiled and waved.

"Actually, there's one thing I want," she declared. "I want you to show me your sketchbook. I want to see you draw in front of me."

"How do you . . . ?" He trailed off and groaned as the realization hit. "Leah . . ."

Vella pulled a folded piece of paper from her pocket. She unfurled it, revealing the sketch of herself that Leah had told her to keep. The paper was now wrinkled and worn from overuse.

"I might need a new one."

"You got it. Can you grab my sketchbook for me? There's a false panel at the back of my closet, bottom shelf. I'll find us a place to sit in the south park."

"Ah, nice hiding spot. See you there."

Vella jumped up and took off but stopped abruptly and turned back.

"Here," she said, tossing the orb to him.

He caught it, and the instant it touched his palm, it happened. Again.

A violent surge tore through him, stronger than before. He felt every muscle, every nerve, every fiber of his being activated.

Then the visions returned. Vella. Alex. Edgar.

The same deaths he had experienced. Brutal. Inevitable.

But it didn't end there.

One after another, more faces appeared. Dozens. Hundreds.

He watched their deaths. Felt them.

The majority were people he'd seen around Eden.

Ivy. Ellie. The mayor. Coworkers. Children he'd grown up with. People he passed in the market. Names he'd never learned but faces he'd never forget.

Most deaths came quietly, gently, in the calm of the Peaceful Passage. Others were less fortunate—activated implants, freak accidents, and, in rare cases, deaths at the hands of the Wolf.

And then there were strangers. People he'd never seen before, dying in places he couldn't recognize. Places that shouldn't exist.

Finally, he saw the person he had most hoped to avoid. Leah, resting comfortably inside the Peaceful Passage. She was looking at someone, then her eyes briefly shifted to another figure nearby. One of them held her hand. He couldn't hear anything, but from her reaction, he knew one of them was speaking to her. She smiled and nodded. Tears fell.

He felt every part of her distress and wanted nothing more than for it to end. He couldn't take any more.

Slowly, her senses dulled. Her muscles relaxed. The dread eased. Her mind drifted, and she passed in peace.

The stream of deaths went on and on, yet his own was nowhere to be found.

The flood of lives and losses overwhelmed him. Each one layered on the next, each one adding to his burden.

He wasn't sure it would ever stop.

And then a flash of light.

He was back, still sitting on the bench. No time had passed in the real world, though it felt like he had been gone for hours.

Vella was jogging away toward the house, unaware.

Cole sat frozen, staring straight ahead, chest heaving.

"Vella . . . help . . ." he uttered.

He turned, but she was long gone.

His hand brushed against his cheek. It was wet.

Tears streamed uncontrollably down his face, blurring his vision.

"Vel . . . come back," he whispered. "Please."

34

My friends and I used to play this game where we had to keep a soccer ball in the air by volleying it. If it hit the ground and you were the last to touch it, you were out. One by one, someone would be eliminated until there was a winner. The catch was the losers had to stand in a line against a wall while the winner got a free shot at them. I remember getting a bruise on my ass once. It hurt to sit for days . . . To be fair, I gave as much as I took. Crude as it was, it was some of the most fun I've ever had. They're all gone now. I'm the only one left. I guess that makes me the winner. I'll get my free shot at them soon.

—"OWEN #8640"

CHILDREN OF THE PEACEFUL PASSAGE

by Aleister #8990

Alex sat hunched over his desk, pencil in hand, trying for the third time to draw the Bear. Each line felt wrong, proportions not even close. Each attempt failed to capture the horror etched in his mind.

He had work he could do, but nothing seemed important enough to take him away from his incessant sketching.

The memory of the third and most recent scouting mission scraped at the back of his mind. Every time he thought about it, his stomach twisted in knots, making him seize up.

To distract himself, he focused on the other problem: Was it even possible to kill such a thing? The thought dragged him down, drowning him in doubt. His mind worked overtime, trying to convince him that it was possible, but every voice inside whispered that it wasn't.

Yet something inside him refused to give up. He had something to fight for, and he couldn't let despair win. Anger was his best defense. It kept him pushing through all the grueling exercise sessions and forced him to get out of bed day after day. Then there was Cole, who never seemed to waver, so he couldn't.

They had made more trips into the Bear's lair, and the

document they were working on had grown as a result. Pages on pages filled with observations, plans, and sketches. But none of it made the task seem any less impossible.

He grimaced as the memory of the recent scouting mission forced its way to the forefront of his mind—the memory of breaking the rule. The one rule they'd all promised never to break, and he'd broken it.

He stared at the sketch, trying to focus on the details. But the pencil slipped from his hand as the memory took hold, replaying in his mind. The moment he froze, lost in the void, watching from another world.

A claw flashed ahead of him. It cleaved through Cole, spraying his blood in a wide arc in his direction. Vella's hands gripped his shoulders, yanking him out of his shock. But her eyes, filled with scorn and betrayal, seared into his memory. He'd barely registered Cole's death; it was Vella's eyes that had bored into his mind.

He hadn't told them. He couldn't.

"Unforgivable," he muttered.

"Alex."

The voice startled him, and he instinctively shoved the drawings under a pile of papers. Owen—the mayor, his boss, and the person he aspired to be—stood over his desk. Owen looked lost. The weight of authority and other burdens etched exhaustion into his face.

"Are you free?" Owen asked.

"Uh, yeah. What's up?"

"We've got a situation. I thought I could handle it, but we're running out of time, and I need someone else . . . a fresh voice."

"What is it?"

Owen sharply exhaled. "It's Terry."

Alex left the office in search of Terry. He wasn't at home, so Alex spent most of the afternoon asking around and searching the public common areas.

Finally, he found Terry on the outskirts of town. He sat alone, knees pulled to his chest, staring at the cold metal of the perimeter wall, his gaze fixed and unblinking.

Alex approached and sat down beside him. He followed Terry's eyes, hoping to get a read on him.

"How are you, Terry?"

Terry didn't look at him. "Here to tell me what to do as well?"

"No one's telling you what to do. We're here for you."

Terry's voice came out flat. "Uh-huh. So Owen gave up and now it's up to you?"

"I'm here to help. Terry, you know what will happen next."

"How do you know?"

"I've seen it firsthand. It's not something I'd wish on anyone. You've heard it too, those nights. It's long; it's torturous. There's no mercy."

His words didn't seem to register. "I'll take my chances," Terry said.

Alex sighed. "Help me understand. Why resist?"

Terry lifted his pant leg, revealing his death timer. Seven hours left and counting.

"Why do they get to dictate when I die? No. I refuse to let them win."

"I get it. It's not fair, but it doesn't change our reality."

Terry's eyes grew more distant. "I wonder what their reality is. What do you think it looks like?"

"I don't know. I try not to dwell on things I could never know."

"Yes, you're right. It doesn't matter." Terry took a deep breath and looked at Alex. "I do this for God."

"God? What're you talking about?"

"Humor me," Terry said. "Do you believe there's a God? An afterlife?"

Alex knew the concept of a god, or gods, was foreign to most in Eden. Some referred to their captors as gods, but without reverence. Others had tried to worship them, hoping to earn favor, but those groups never lasted long, just like their ephemeral existences.

In the early days of Eden, references to gods, messiahs, and prophets were scattered throughout books about Earth. The first people of Eden read of the atrocities committed in the name of gods, and it hadn't taken long for Eden's leaders to decide to remove and burn any references to Earth's religions altogether. They wanted a united community, not one fractured and divided by hatred as Earth appeared to be in the books.

Still, some spoke of and believed in a higher power. It was a god without identity. Nothing more than a comforting figure in their minds to help them feel less alone.

God, the refuge of the suffering and hopeless, should have swept through Eden, spreading like fire through their community. But the idea of God, the highest power, became synonymous with their captors. And that power inspired only hatred. To the people of Eden, they were God—cursed, day and night.

So, the people of Eden turned to what was real, what they could rely on: each other. They built their lives and community around making things better for the people who shared their struggle. The worship of everyday life became all that mattered. They had no gods to call upon, no divine force to look to for hope. No savior. They only had themselves.

Alex paused, recalling the sleepless nights spent wrestling with such questions. He wanted to believe there was more. Ever since he was a child, he'd spent countless hours staring up, hoping for answers—a sign, divine intervention, anything to reassure him he wasn't alone. But the only thing that ever came was the screams, the cries—real and remembered—of those God had abandoned.

"It's hard to believe a God would allow a place like this to exist." Alex shook his head. "No, I don't think so. As for an afterlife . . . I don't know."

Terry's voice grew cold and hard, anger lacing every word. "I see your point. But I believe. In service of God, I want them dirtied. I want them dragged down beyond forgiveness, beyond salvation. So that when they meet their final judgment, standing at the foot of God, there'll be no mercy for them. We'll be there, passing judgment—condemning them. For eternity."

"I agree they'll face judgment someday," Alex said. "But it's not for us to get involved in. That's what I think, anyway."

"Why not? We've lived in passive inaction our whole lives. I refuse to accept that we're powerless. I know what I feel, and it's telling me, 'Don't let them win! Do something!'"

Alex felt it too, that burning fury that had driven him to join Cole and the others in their hopeless mission. He was under no illusions about their chances. But the fire kept him going. The desire to fight back, to do something, anything, that would make a difference.

"I feel it too," Alex admitted.

"Then you understand I must do something."

"Do what, Terry?" Alex asked. "Fill your final moments with so much pain and suffering you'll be pleading for death? What exactly are you going to do? Tell me."

Terry remained impassive. "Not accept their reality. I refuse to acknowledge them. If they want to kill me, fine, but I'll not be part of their reality. I'm not going to have some poor soul burdened with having to kill me. They will have to do it themselves."

"This isn't the way. And you know it."

"We all have our own ways," Terry said, his tone flat and final.

They sat in silence that felt more comfortable than not. Alex understood him. He couldn't fault him for not wanting to go out quietly. But he couldn't let it end like this. Not with the consequences of Terry's death looming. He struggled to find the right words, to change Terry's mind. If an appeal to reason wouldn't work, he'd have to appeal to something else.

"Think of everyone else," Alex said. "You've heard those cries. You've lost sleep over them, haven't you? Felt your soul tortured for days after? I have. My partner has. My friends have. If not for you, do it for us. Please . . . Terry . . ."

He didn't respond, his eyes fixed on the wall as if someone were waiting on the other side.

It was then that Alex knew he'd lost him. Nothing would pull him back now. They couldn't force him, or could they? It was out of his hands; it was up to Owen now.

Alex stood and walked away, his legs feeling heavy, his whole body weighed down with fatigue. There was too much to deal with. He couldn't help Terry. He couldn't even help himself, let alone anyone else.

"I won't scream," Terry said.

"You will. Everyone does."

Alex kept walking, making it to the clearing. He rested against a log on the fringes and waited for the others to arrive.

Would I face judgment for letting Cole die? he wondered. *If there were a god or gods, they would be the ones who had to answer to us. Face our judgment. But, no, there's nothing. We have each other, and that's it. If there is something after, so be it. But Ellie, Cole, Edgar, Vella, Leah, Amy—they're all that matter now.*

Alex woke to a hand on his shoulder. Cole stood above him with an amused smile.

"Tough day? You all right?"

"Yeah, yeah," Alex muttered.

He pulled himself to his feet and stretched to wake up. Cole, Vella, and Edgar went about setting up the drills.

It's now or never, he thought, glancing around at them.

"I need to tell you all something," Alex said. "It's kind of serious."

They stopped, their eyes darting between one another, sensing the gravity in his voice. Then, gathering around him, they waited.

"Well, out with it," Vella said, losing patience with Alex's hesitation.

He couldn't meet her eyes, so he instead focused on Cole.

"During our last time inside, I-I . . . dammit. I don't know how to say it."

"Just say it; you can tell us anything," Cole said.

"I . . . let you die . . ." He flicked a glance at each of them. "I let Cole die. I screwed up. I'm sorry. I don't know what happened. My body just stopped working . . . I killed him. I broke the rule . . . I . . . I'm so sorry. I . . . dammit."

Vella shot him a look full of venom, while Cole glanced at Edgar with concern.

All of a sudden, Cole let out a relieved breath. "I'm glad I'm not the only one. I got Edgar killed. I felt like I left my body, and by the time I snapped out of it, it was too late." He laughed. "Vella did too. She told me she got you killed."

Vella gave Cole a sideways glance. "No—"

Cole poked her from behind his back, interrupting her.

Finally catching on, she cleared her throat. "Yeah . . . sorry, I didn't actually mean to."

"Yeah, I got Cole killed as well," Edgar said.

People died . . . Why are they being so casual about this?

"Oh, that's not fair, being killed twice," Cole said, still wearing an amused smile. Vella burst out laughing, too. Even Edgar chuckled.

"No one's gotten me killed, that's all that matters," Vella said.

"I'll have to fix that," Cole said, nudging Vella.

She punched him in the shoulder. "Don't you frickin' dare."

Alex's mouth hung open, his eyes darting from face to face, looking for someone to give him the reaction he expected. Not this.

Edgar raised an eyebrow at him, then clapped him on the shoulder. "I expected it to happen. No harm done. But we appreciate the honesty," Edgar said. "Don't beat yourself up about it."

Alex shook his head and finally joined in the laughter. He felt air return to his lungs and his body grow lighter.

I was worrying for nothing.

But as the laughter faded, the repressed images came flooding back. Cole being slaughtered. Blood streaked across his face.

Cole's blood.

His smile slipped away; the feeling of being crushed returned.

They can't be okay with this. Can they? Am I overreacting?

Then he caught a glimpse of Vella shooting Cole an angry look, which he tried to dismiss with a subtle hand wave. Cole looked back to Alex and smiled.

Oh . . .

35

Have you ever thought about death? Really thought about it? If you are reading this, of course you have. To know you'll die so soon. And the exact date and time. It might as well be tomorrow in your mind. It's not just that; what happens? You're just gone? You close your eyes and what? Nothing? How do you even fathom such a concept? It's overwhelming. Inconceivable. To experience it is the only way to comprehend the unbearable weight of finality.

—THE FIRST PEOPLE OF EDEN
Journal of Morgan #38
Day 601

Cole woke to the sound of screams, sharp and raw, piercing the stillness of the night. They didn't come from anyone in the house, though it offered little comfort. His heart raced as he squeezed his eyes shut, praying that the screams were a figment of his imagination.

A few agonizing seconds of silence passed. He braced, waiting. Then another visceral scream tore through the night. Cole cringed, every muscle in his body tensing at the terrible implications. Someone had tried to resist their fate, to escape the inevitable. Their time was up, and the implant was killing them. Slowly, cruelly, without mercy.

Growing up, Cole had heard these screams for as long as he could remember. They always sounded the same; different voices but the same desperate, anguished cries. The quiet nights only intensified the horror, making it impossible to escape their reach.

Even when he was a child, those cries had etched themselves into his memory. And every time he heard them, they pulled him back into being that helpless child.

Ever since Tom's death, the screams carried an extra unbearable weight. The first time he'd heard the screams after that day, he had woken to the sound of children crying in the next room. Then the screams had followed, freezing him in place. He'd tried to make himself as small as possible, pressing his head into the pillow, as if that could block out the terror. An invisible grip squeezed his chest and stomach, suffocating him.

He remembered checking on Alex afterward, panic rising when he saw that Alex wasn't in the bed beneath him. It wasn't until he saw Alex that he felt a small measure of relief. He was gripping his pillow, staring out the window, shaking.

Alex had told him he felt safer with Cole around, and the truth was, he felt the same way. And those nights after he left the orphanage—serene nights filled with distant screams—were some of the loneliest of his life, with only dread as his companion.

Now, lying in the dark, his thoughts drifted to Vella and Alex. They had faced the same horror. Alone.

He opened his eyes to see Vella. She was curled up in a tight ball, facing away, her body trembling. Cole reached out, placing a gentle hand on her arm. She flinched violently, flinging her arm back and catching him in the face.

He let out a soft cry of pain. It was almost a relief, as this was pain he could handle.

Vella whirled, eyes wide. "I'm sorry. You scared me."

"I'm fine," he said, rubbing his face. "Are you all right? You're shaking."

She shook her head, shifting closer until her head was resting against his chest. The screams echoed in the distance. Someone's torment was still unfolding somewhere out there.

"We should help them," she whispered, her voice barely audible.

Cole tightened his hold on her. "What can we do?"

"I don't know . . . anything."

He wished he had an answer, wished he could offer her even a shred of assurance, but the truth was, there was nothing they could do. The screams would end soon—perhaps in another five or ten minutes—but not soon enough.

"I-I don't want to die, Cole," Vella said. Her lips quivered speaking it out loud.

"I know. Me either."

His thoughts turned to Leah. She was likely lying awake,

battling the same fears that gripped the rest of Eden. He wanted to check on her, but the same fear kept him frozen where he lay.

"We'll stop this, right?" she asked.

Cole wanted to promise her that they would, but the words wouldn't come. He could only manage a low, noncommittal sound, hoping it would be enough.

At last, the screaming stopped.

But the dread lingered, hanging around like a thick smog blanketing them. With Vella nestled against him, he found some solace. They stayed like that for hours, until her trembling subsided and she drifted back to sleep. Only then did Cole allow himself to follow her into uneasy rest.

The morning light carried with it a dark shade of gray. It offered no warmth.

A cold chill covered Cole's skin, one he wouldn't be able to shake that day.

It was a somber day, weighed down by the memory of the night before. No one went to the clearing at dawn. At breakfast, no one spoke. Even Leah, usually the one to start a conversation, sat mute. She stared off into the distance, her eyes heavy and dark with exhaustion and distress.

Edgar wasn't doing any better. He didn't bother eating, and after failing to focus on his reading, he bitterly threw the book aside. There was no hiding what lay beneath today, nowhere to bury it or keep it locked away. It was futile to try. Everyone's inner turmoil and hidden anxieties took hold. They were on full display, etched on their faces.

Cole wanted to say something—anything—to break the troubling silence. But all life had been sapped from him, and he wasn't even sure he could verbalize the smallest of noises.

The early morning bell rang out. Normally, this would get them up and moving, ready to start the day. But no one moved. Not even to wind the clock. They remained stuck seated at the table for hours. Cole and Vella left the house around midday and went to hide away in the clearing. Soon, Edgar and Leah joined them.

The clearing was calm, a stark contrast to the storm of

emotions that swirled inside them. The sun bathed them in its light, but it did little to warm the cold dread that still gripped them.

Edgar lay in the middle of the field, eyes closed. Leah joined him with an arm draped over her eyes. Vella sat with them, picking petals off the wildflowers around her. Cole sat off to the side with his back to a log, watching them. Only seeing them, everything else was an unfocused haze.

They remained silent, each lost in their own thoughts, hoping it would all pass.

Alex ambled over and wore the same distant expression as Leah, as they all did. Edgar asked if he knew the person they heard last night. Alex just shook his head, unwilling or unable to talk about it. He collapsed next to Leah, lying on his stomach, staring at the perimeter wall.

They spent the rest of the day in the clearing, listening to the rustling leaves, the distant buzzing of bees, and the soft chirping of birds. They tried to return themselves to the simple world that surrounded them. But it was one they couldn't feel a part of; it was distant, lost to them.

They shared another world. It was brutal, painful, and unforgiving.

But at least they shared it.

Together.

36

Our baby girl was born today. She's perfect in every way. I can't begin to describe how incredible it feels to hold her in my arms. But I can't help staring at the number and death timer on my baby. When the Ghost delivered her and put in the implant, Laura screamed and thrashed in protest. By the end, she was inconsolable. It was as if they'd already taken our baby from us. Normally, Laura would have been killed for attacking a Ghost. But nothing happened. It's like they understood that watching your child receive a death sentence is punishment enough. The worst part was the way Laura looked at me afterward. The scorn in her eyes, as if I was supposed to stop it . . . Her name is Amelia. She is number 1255.

—THE FIRST PEOPLE OF EDEN

Journal of Morgan #38

Day 821

"What's wrong?" Cole whispered. "You keep moving."

"Can't sleep," Vella said.

He groaned and rolled over to face her, keeping his eyes shut.

She lay on her back, staring wide-eyed at the ceiling. "Sorry."

"All . . . good. What's up?" he mumbled.

For weeks now, the fragile peace they'd known was fraying. Each of them grappled with the weight of their own fears and the ever-present ticking down of the clock. The encounters with the Bear, the terrifying glimpse into the hell that awaited them, had left a mark on each of them—some more visible than others.

She played with her lips: biting them, pursing them, then blowing out air as she pressed them together.

"I know you want to say something," Cole said, eyes still closed. "Tell me or I'm going to sleep in the hallway."

She sighed, tapping her fingers on her hand.

Cole had always been the one to push forward, to charge headfirst into danger with a reckless determination that bordered on self-destruction. But even he couldn't deny the creeping sense of dread that ate at the edges of his resolve. The recent nights, punctuated by the screams of that person who had run out of time, reminded him of the frailty of their existence. It pushed him to think more about the daunting task in front of them. Not tonight, though; his muscles ached for rest. Vella, on the other hand . . .

Once a silent shadow in their group, she'd emerged with a new sense of purpose. She'd always been a survivor, hardened by a life of solitude, but something had shifted in her. The bond she formed with the others, particularly with Leah and Edgar, opened her up in ways Cole hadn't expected. She had seen how their lives intertwined and how their fates linked to the fate of all in Eden. And it scared her how much she was starting to care.

But that wasn't the only thing that scared her.

Fear, she realized, was something she could no longer afford to give in to. The time for passive resistance had gone on for too long. Now, there was only action—dangerous, life-threatening action.

The orb had given them an edge. A way to fight back against the forces that sought to crush them, but it wasn't enough to continue to just observe and survive. Vella knew they had to take the next step, to strike at the heart of the beast that loomed over them.

She puffed out her cheeks, wanting to tell him what she really wanted to get off her chest. But she couldn't. Not now. So, instead, she braced herself to set events into motion. Events she might not be able to stop once started.

"Vel," Cole warned. "I'm about to get up. Talk to me."

"I want to show you something."

"Now? Can't it wait?"

She sat up. "No."

Cole groaned and rolled over to face the wall.

She pulled herself out of bed and grabbed Cole's arm. "Please."

He pulled his arm away and wrapped himself in the blanket, forming a protective cocoon.

From the bedside table, she grabbed the shineball, tapped it five times, and threw it on top of him.

"Vel!" Cole recoiled, shielding his eyes from the blinding light. He quickly unwrapped himself and turned it off. He sat up, rubbing his face. "This better be good . . ."

She led him through the woods to nowhere he cared about. He trudged along behind her, his arms crossed, eyes half-closed. After bumping into a tree, he forced himself into a higher state of awareness.

He glanced at her. "Why are we going to your old place?"

She didn't turn to answer. "Don't you think we've waited long enough?" Her voice was flat and distant, as though she were speaking to herself.

"What?" He caught her expression, and he didn't like what he saw.

Recently, Cole had sensed a change in her. One he couldn't quite understand. They'd shared their fears, their hopes, and their dreams in the quiet moments between battles, but now Vella was becoming something more, an independent force to be reckoned with, a warrior in her own right.

And that terrified him as much as it inspired him.

He knew now what this was about, but saying it out loud would make it real. It would mean crossing a line they might never come back from.

Without another word between them, they reached the shed. A place that had once been their sanctuary, a retreat from the harsh realities of Eden. Now, with no one to maintain it, the area had taken on a wilder feel. She used to keep the grass and plants in check, but now they ran free, growing and tangling together, doing as they pleased without her.

"Can you tell me now? What're we doing?" Cole asked.

"Wait here."

She dashed inside, closing the door behind her with a hurried thud. Cole heard a series of clattering noises, like she was tearing the place apart from the inside.

The door creaked open, and Vella emerged. Her arms strained with the weight of two objects draped in cloth. She kicked the door shut with the back of her heel, careful not to drop what she was holding.

"Here," Cole said, stepping forward to help her.

"Watch the ends," she warned.

He withdrew his hands and stepped back. "What is it?"

Vella laid the objects on the ground. She exhaled, weary but smiling, a determined smile.

"Go ahead," she said, nodding towards the cloaked objects.

Casting her a wary look, Cole knelt down and unwrapped the cloth, revealing what lay beneath. His eyes widened.

"Weapons!"

Two spades, their ends filed down and reshaped into instruments of death. One had been crafted into a spear, its sharp tip catching the moonlight. The other was shaped like an axe head, with edges that looked just as sharp as the spear's point.

"So, you're the one who stole the spades from my work. They tried to blame me, you know," Cole said.

"Sorry," she said, though her smile never wavered.

"You don't sound sorry."

"Because I'm not."

He shook his head in amusement as he bent down to inspect them closely.

"Why didn't you tell me?"

"I figured it wouldn't come up for a while. I made them just in case."

Cole frowned.

"I also didn't think you would be too happy . . ."

"Uh-huh."

He picked up the axe and gave it an experimental swing. The weight, the balance—it was impressive. He paused, putting the weapon down, and turned to face her.

"Why are you showing me this now?"

Vella's smile faded and gave him an exasperated look, telling him he should already know.

"Don't you think it's time we got serious?" she asked. "We have everything we need; we always did. It's time we stopped messing around, killed those things, and found out who's behind the walls. Put an end to this. We can do it. Just the two of us.

We were never getting anywhere with Edgar and Alex. But you already know that."

He did. And he couldn't deny the truth in her words. If they were ever going to attempt to kill the Bear, the conditions couldn't be more ideal. They had trained, prepared, and gathered all the information they needed. They were fit, fast, and agile. All it would take was someone brave—or reckless—enough to push further than they had dared before.

He was ready; he'd always been ready, but several things held him back. One was how hopeless the task seemed, and he still had no real plan. Then there was his newfound sympathy for the Wolf and Bear. He didn't want to kill them, but what other choice did he have? Let everyone else die instead? But more than that, it was Vella. Her life was on the line too. For the first time, things were going well, and everyone seemed content. *Why risk everything now? Can't what we have just be enough?*

The vision of the hundreds of deaths he'd witnessed—that was the reason. Something needed to be done.

He stared at the weapons she'd crafted. "Do you think these will do the job?"

"With what resources we have, these are the best we've got."

"What about something with a longer reach?"

"You really think that's going to matter? With a thing that big?"

He allowed himself a smile. "No, you're right. Something sturdier, with a little more power, will give us a better chance." He chewed his lower lip. "So . . . how would we attempt it behind their backs?"

"We can sneak out in the middle of the night."

Deep down, Cole knew they could find a way. That wasn't the issue. He desperately wanted to press on. Yet he was stalling, more out of fear for Vella than anything else.

"We can save people, Cole."

He looked up at her, seeing the conviction in her eyes. "Like the person from the other night," he murmured.

"Exactly."

"What's gotten into you? Why the eagerness now?" he asked.

Vella pointed down to her ankle, where her death timer and number were visible. Cole realized, only now, that she hadn't bothered to hide them for weeks. The ticking down of the numbers stared back at him. "Eight-seven-four-nine. Over eight thousand people—soon to be nine thousand—have died here. And who knows how many countless more. I was reminded it's not just Leah and Edgar we're trying to save. It's everyone. That person who cried out for help. No one saved them. A person at work is about to die. Shouldn't we try to save them? People are dying all the time. Who's thinking of them?"

A smile spread across his face as he saw the fire in her eyes. And he thought to himself: *She's right. The longer we delay, the more people die. Alone, scared, helpless. If I can stop one of those deaths I should try.*

"Since when did you start to care about the people here?"

"Since you, Leah, and the others made me care, I even want to save that damnable Ivy. This is your fault."

Her words warmed him, but they also tightened fear's grip on him.

This is your fault, her words echoed in his head.

He didn't want to risk her life, but he knew that if he could do it alone, he would.

"It's about damn time we left this place," she said.

He stared at the axe. "Are you sure?"

"Are you?"

With Vella now pushing for action, he knew there was no more putting it off. She wouldn't stop, not now that she had a goal. A push over the edge was just what he wanted. He was done with the days and nights spent wallowing in dread. He no longer wanted to watch Leah suffer, or see Alex torture himself over Ellie, or let Edgar keep throwing himself into danger. He didn't need any more reason than the people around him. He felt the fire rising, blood boiling. "Never been more ready."

"Good."

"In two days, Sunday," he said. "We take it slow."

"Slow," she agreed.

There was no turning back now. Soon, they would face

whatever horrors awaited them—together.

No, not together. I'll figure out a way to do it myself. No matter what. I'm sorry, Vel. This is my task, no one else's.

He clenched his fists around the handle. He knew he could sneak off during the lunch break and try as much as he liked by himself. For now, he'd humor her.

Even if I have to betray her trust, I can live with her hating me . . .

I can't live with the alternative.

37

Nothing new to report to you. Actually, there is something. The roses I planted bloomed. They are beautiful. Today was a good day.

—THE FIRST PEOPLE OF EDEN

Journal of Morgan #38

Day 470

Cole and Vella threw themselves into their training with manic intensity. Tomorrow they would begin attempting the impossible. So they pushed themselves to the limit. Not to prepare, but to calm their anxious minds by tiring their bodies.

They sparred before and after sessions. What was once a source of joy now turned into a serious game of life and death. They fought for dominance over each other—for each other's sake. Who would carry the burden? Neither would relent.

By the end, they were spent, physically exhausted but mentally relieved, at least for the moment. The future, with all its uncertainties and dangers, was something they couldn't afford to dwell on, but it still happened of its own accord. They played out scenarios in their heads, losing track of the real world. The two of them didn't speak about it, but they knew the other was playing through the same mental game.

That day, Alex had been noticeably different, not happier or sadder, just different. As they wrapped up, he approached them, his usual calm demeanor leaving behind a sense of quiet unease. He shared the news that they had selected him for the role of deputy mayor. They congratulated him with great enthusiasm, swarming him in a huddle and roughing him up, leaving his clothes and hair in a mess. He took more joy in their reaction than in the news itself.

Ellie decided to host a small party at their place that evening to celebrate. Alex extended the invitation to them, also asking them to let Leah know since he hadn't seen her that day.

By the time the four of them arrived at Alex's house, the small gathering was already underway. Ellie greeted them with a warm welcome at the door. A couple of Alex's coworkers and friends were already inside, with several more on the way.

Leah, ever the supportive figure, was excessively animated in her congratulations, making Alex wince in embarrassment. She presented him with a shirt she had made in preparation for his promotion and insisted he try it on at once, much to his dread. Cole made sure to fuel the awkward situation by encouraging Leah.

Things calmed down after that, and as the night went on, the atmosphere grew lighter and more boisterous.

A few hours later, Cole found himself alone, surrounded by the buzzing hum of animated conversation. He leaned back against the wall, feeling a cozy, pleasant naivety brought on by the alcohol.

Across the room, he watched Vella throw her head back in laughter, a far cry from the withdrawn girl she once was. She was engaged in a lively exchange with Astrid, a friend she had made at work who also happened to be a friend of Ellie's. Pride swelled within him as he observed her at ease among others. It was a far cry from the girl who once preferred to be invisible. Her natural effervescence was now on full display, no longer his secret to behold and adore.

Despite the warmth of the scene, Cole felt a familiar sense of discomfort in the social setting. Needing a moment to himself, he slipped out the back door to get some fresh air.

He stepped into the cool night air, catching sight of the scenic sky with its lively pulsing of scattered stars and the moon radiating a yellow-tinged hue. He took a deep breath and felt a sense of freedom and the endless possibilities it held.

Leah was already outside, leaning against the wall with a drink in hand. He took a few more steps, trying to distance himself from the noise of the party. He took a moment, letting the serenity of the night wash over him.

"Lovely night," he said.

Leah murmured her agreement.

"It's strange . . ." she mused.

"What is?" he asked, still looking up.

"I've never heard you say anything like that before," she said, her eyes distant. "I'm happy for you. It almost feels like I'm not needed anymore."

"You will always be needed."

"The last thing I want is to leave and still be needed."

Without a word, Cole moved to stand beside her, his eyes tracing the constellations above.

"You're not thinking of leaving, are you?" he asked.

"Shut up."

"I think that would be rude. Why would you do that?" he asked, as seriously as he could manage.

She shook her head with a faint smile, remaining silent and refusing to engage.

"We'll be fine," he said. "Still, it feels like you, of all people, aren't allowed to leave."

"I can do whatever I like. I might even leave tomorrow," she prodded.

"Now that *would* be rude."

The silence between them stretched, comfortable and warm.

"What was it like for you . . . losing my parents?"

Leah's expression softened, her eyes filling with a distant sadness. "It was tough," she admitted.

"I'm sorry I never asked before," Cole said, his voice low. "You were more of a child to them than I ever was. You actually knew them. I didn't. I think about losing you, and I struggle to imagine an Eden without you. It would feel hollow. How did you deal with it?"

"I didn't. Well, not well. It took time. And I still miss them." She exhaled, a long, weary sigh. "I took it out on Edgar, on whoever was around. I wish they were still here . . . I don't know what to do sometimes. It still feels like I'm fumbling around in the dark without them."

"What made it easier? Did it get any easier?"

"It got easier with time. It felt like an important part of me was ripped out by an invisible hand . . . never to be returned." She shook her head. "Actually, I don't think it has gotten easier."

Cole swallowed. "I don't want that."

"No one does," Leah agreed. "But we all have to deal with it. Everyone you look at has dealt with it in some form. But I was lucky; you showed up on my doorstep years later, and it felt like someone returned a missing part of me. A gift in the form of a little shadow of them to tell me everything would be okay." She smiled at the memory. "I wouldn't change a thing . . . Actually, I would change one thing. I should've taken you in right after they passed away. I shouldn't have waited for you to come to me."

"You had your life to live, not look after some brat. And besides, you always came to check on me. A little too often."

"Still . . ."

"Did you know your real parents?" he asked.

"I only remember seeing them a few times," Leah said, her voice tinged with sorrow. "The last time was when I was nine. Two times a year, I saw them to give them their birthday presents, and one year it just . . . stopped. I had no idea what happened. I was just a child. I thought they no longer wanted to see me. That they hated me. It was a terrible thing for a child to go through. It took me years to learn the truth, but the damage was done. I'm glad Amy won't be old enough to go through what I did. I want her to have a normal life where she's not hung up on me. She'll have enough pain losing people when she grows up, but her childhood should be for her."

"I'll tell her all about you."

"Just tell her I love her."

"I will."

"Did I ever tell you that your parents did?"

"Didn't need to."

"I spent so much time with your parents," Leah said. "And for the longest time, I still didn't understand why they chose the path they did. There was never any hint that they would do that."

"I never doubted for a moment why they did it," Cole said. "But now I'm not so sure."

"The thought of dying without trying . . . ," Leah said, her voice growing firmer. "Knowing there's something you can do and doing it. Even if it feels useless. I don't feel that way, but I understand. They had each other, and it gave them the courage they needed."

Cole thought about them, the smiles they wore in those final moments. It still amazed him how they managed to do that, knowing they were about to die. The memory warmed him, giving him strength.

Then he thought about it more, and it started to bother him: *Their smiles* . . .

"Were they . . . *well?* You know, before the end?" he asked.

"I don't know," Leah said. "They always kept me at arm's length, especially in those final months. I never actually knew what they were going through or how they were feeling."

"They were smiling, but they must've been terrified. Did they really feel no fear because they had each other? Doesn't feel possible. They were just people. Courage and love alone can't hold those feelings of dread at bay."

"I think they refused to let anyone else see it . . . Let us see it."

Cole wanted to ask, *How much are you not letting us see?* Instead, he said, "At least they didn't have to deal with whatever they were feeling alone."

Leah glanced sideways at him. "I know you're up to something. I can see it all over you; you've been distracted. I know you wouldn't do anything lightly. But still . . ."

He let out an amused huff. "Nothing scares me like you do."

"Nothing?"

"Well . . ." He paused, his voice growing serious. "Losing you and Vella."

"That's what worries me. Don't do anything stupid," she warned.

"I'll try."

"There's no way I can accept living longer than you. Or Vella, Alex, or Edgar. My time's almost over, and I've accepted that."

"You think anything comes after this?" Cole murmured. "After death?"

Leah took time to consider the question that weighed on her

mind through many lonely nights. "Part of me doesn't want anything to be after this. I'm all worn out. I can't take much more," she said with a light tone. "But it feels like there has to be. This can't be it. Surely . . ."

"What do you think happens? An afterlife? You get born as someone else? Or is this it?"

"I don't know how, but I think we'll all be together again, somehow, some way."

"In what way?"

"Like I said, I don't know."

"Maybe we'll get another shot at a full life with everyone in another time and place," he added. "Maybe we already have."

She slid over and leaned her head on his shoulder. "One where we aren't doomed to make the same mistakes. In that case . . . I'd like that."

Feeling her soft warmth, a warmth that made him feel impervious to any danger. That warmth drove an overwhelming force to rise within him, tearing at his throat. He swallowed hard and closed his eyes to calm himself, struggling to push it back down.

"It's all right. I'm not going anywhere," she whispered.

"It's not fair."

"No. It's not."

"I can't do it without you. It's too much."

"Hey. I'm not dead yet."

He wiped his nose with his hand. "I can't believe you're crying."

"I know . . . I'm sorry," she said, rubbing his back.

They rested on each other in comfortable silence, soaking in the atmosphere of the night. Cole couldn't help but think about how many more times he would get to spend a night like this with her.

"It's been a while since it's been just the two of us," Leah said, breaking the silence.

"Does that bother you?" he asked with a chuckle.

"No, no," Leah said. "It's just . . . strange how everything can change in just a couple of months. Before, we would sit in silence in fear of argument. Then along came Vella and Edgar, and now it feels like a real home, full of life."

"It's nice," Cole agreed, his voice soft. "We're like a real family."

"Not 'like'—we are," she said.

He let out a slow breath, knowing she was right. It eased his mind, knowing he had their support. But one worry still lingered. He spoke to try to air this concern.

"Well, like any family, we worry about each other. I'm worried about you. How are you doing? You can tell me—"

Without warning, Vella came stumbling out of the back door. "There you are."

Leah lifted her head off Cole's shoulder and motioned her over, wrapping her arm around her as she joined them.

"What are you two doing?" Vella asked.

"Enjoying some peace and quiet," Leah said.

As she spoke, Edgar and Alex emerged into the yard, their faces lit with the soft glow of the evening.

"Well, *we were*," Leah whispered into Vella's ear. The two of them stifled their laughter.

"I have something I want to share with you," Alex said, holding up a bottle of whiskey. "It's a twenty-five-year-old one I've been saving. I've got some glasses inside."

"Who do you think we are? Just pass the bottle around. It's nicer out here," Cole said.

"It's one of Ruby's, though."

"*The* Ruby?"

"Shut up, Cole. It means it's good," Leah said. "She died twenty years ago. From what I've heard, she was the best there's ever been. Before her, alcohol was nowhere near as good as it is now. She improved our distilling capabilities tenfold. But no one since has been able to make alcohol—whiskey in particular—like she could."

"Wow," Cole said, voice flat and cold.

"Who do you think you are?" she snapped. "Appreciate the heroes that came before you."

"Give him the bottle," Edgar said. "Show him."

"But I got glasses inside . . ." Alex pleaded with a faint voice.

"Gimme the bottle," Cole said.

"But—"

"The bottle, Alex."

Alex relented, handing it over.

Cole opened it and took a swig. He smacked his lips. "It's all right," he said, short and sharp.

"All right?" Leah fumed. "Just admit when you're wrong."

"Fine," Cole said. "She must have been an amazing person. If it tastes this bad, imagine how awful it was before her."

"You little . . ." She reached over and slapped him on the back of the head. "No respect."

Holding a smirk, Cole sidestepped, avoiding a second slap. Alex took the opportunity to squeeze between him and Leah, taking the bottle from Cole.

"Thanks for coming, everyone," Alex said with quiet gratitude.

"We wouldn't miss it for anything," Leah said.

"Not much else we could do instead," Cole said.

"He's joking, Alex."

"I know," Alex said, giving Cole a shove with his elbow. "I didn't want to have a party for this, but Ellie insisted."

"Why wouldn't you? This is a big deal," Cole said.

"Nothing really changes; it's just a dumb title," Alex said, his voice dismissive.

"Well, regardless, you have to celebrate the little wins," Leah said, her voice firm. "They don't come as often as we think they do." She took a drink and let out a sharp exhale as the liquor burned its way down her throat.

Edgar sat down, leaning against the wall beside Vella. She took the bottle from Leah's hands and, without a word, passed it down to him.

Edgar eyed the drink in his hand, taking a small sip. He felt a rare deep sense of ease, a feeling that arose from being surrounded by the people he cared about. He had concerns about the future, about the others, but for now, he knew he still had time. Everything was under control, and he could savor this final period of his life a little longer. He felt grateful for the second chance he'd been given, thinking that maybe something out there was looking out for him, telling him he still had more to do. His purpose was right in front of him. There was nothing higher or more meaningful that he needed or wanted. Death, while still frightening, no longer felt like the worst thing that could happen. Allowing Cole, Vella, or Alex to come to harm, *that* was his worst fear. Cole was the main concern, but he seemed content with things for the moment. So, there was no urgency in him. *I'll steal the orb if I have to. Do it myself.* It had always been his plan when the time came, but that moment still seemed a long way off. He wanted to save Leah and Amy, but it wouldn't be Cole or anyone else to do it for him. It had to be him. He could breathe easy for now and enjoy the moment. *Even if I die tomorrow, there's one thing I'd want to carry with me. This.* No matter what happened, this memory of warmth and companionship would outlast the darkness of loneliness. With quiet resolve, he passed the bottle to Vella, his smile soft and fleeting.

Vella felt an unexpected surge of emotion as Leah wrapped her in a warm embrace—the mother, sister, and role model she had always longed for but never had. As Vella fingered the tip of the bottle, tracing circles around the top, a deep-seated worry brewed in her mind. She was keeping a secret, one she wasn't ready to share, and the thought of revealing it filled her with unease. It didn't feel fair keeping it from them, especially Cole. *I want to tell them, I want to shout it, but telling them now would ruin everything.* It excited and scared her unlike anything she had ever experienced. She exhaled, trying to expel her doubts. She glanced around at the people she was with. And the worries subsided, replaced with a sense of belonging she had never known. *What would I be doing without them?* she wondered. *At home, alone. Reading? Crying? Lying awake wishing I'd never been born.* A small smile broke through as she thought, *I don't deserve them. I'm not good enough.* As far as she had come, those thoughts of inadequacy hadn't left. It was too much a part of her for a few weeks to simply erase. Her thoughts turned to Ivy, and she wondered, *Does she think the same? Are they all thinking the same thing? Maybe. Probably. How stupid.* But as long as she had them, she felt it like it would all turn out all right. How could it not? She could keep going without any fear. She pressed the bottle to her lips before withdrawing it and handing it to Leah.

Leah fixed her eyes on the stars above, losing herself in rumination. Thinking, wondering, hoping. She was thinking of her daughter, Amy. Wondering if Cole's parents would be proud of her. And hoping that whatever Cole was planning wouldn't end in her worst fears realized. With under a year left in her life, she felt as though her life's work was near completion. Her purpose fulfilled. Still, she prayed for the strength to see out the remaining time with her head held high—confident and unshaken. Like Cole's parents. Smiling to the bitter end. But were they without fear? *No, Cole's right. There was no strength that could've helped them then. Did they know that? Were they well enough to make the correct decision? Oh, how the terror must have gripped them in their final moments. Did they have to watch each other die?* The thought was almost unbearable. *I just hope they died quickly and without pain.* Growing up, she'd mythologized them in her mind, but the myth had fallen apart as she'd gotten older. She knew this from her own experience, stepping into their shoes. They were just people, no different from anyone else. Fears and doubts would have plagued them. Like her own anxieties did. Every day it got harder as the voices within got louder and stronger, pleading: *I'm scared. I don't want to die.* She yelled back, trying to force them back down, but that only made them come back stronger. Resisting what demanded to be acknowledged was a losing game, but she didn't know what else to do. She swallowed hard, forcing herself back to the present. Around her were the people she would do literally anything for. *This is all the strength I need,* she told herself. She took a drink from the bottle and passed it to Alex.

Alex appeared calm on the outside, but inside, he felt a lingering hollowness. He'd achieved what he wanted—deputy mayor— but it hadn't brought him the satisfaction he'd hoped for. Nothing could fill that void, except perhaps . . . something more. Something foolish and risky. He still held out hope for ambitions only Cole could understand. Cole would never quit, no matter the odds, and that gave Alex a strange sense of comfort and strength. As he stood shoulder to shoulder with them, the warmth of their presence consumed him, easing the hollow feeling inside. Ellie stepped out to join them, nestling herself under Alex's arm. She made the emptiness inside feel like it had never existed. He held her closer as he took a long drink before handing the bottle to Cole.

Cole felt the fire inside him burning hotter than ever. He had the power to do something, but he knew it would take an immense effort. How long would it take? Was it even possible? He had no doubt that he could make it possible; it was just a matter of how much he would have to give in return. Would it take hundreds of loops, thousands, millions? He was prepared for all of it. This was his time to rest and to focus. Moments like this only added fuel to his fire. To keep this. To have more of this.

A vibrant energy ran through and over his skin, making it impossible for him to stay still.

He pushed himself off the wall, picked up a half-deflated soccer ball from the ground, and faced them.

"All right, up!" Cole declared.

The others didn't react, except for Alex, who raised an eyebrow. Everyone else kept staring forward, content.

"Alex, do you know what I feel like?" Cole asked, raising his voice to make sure the others paid attention.

Alex eyed Cole for a moment, then it dawned on him. "Absolutely not, Cole."

Cole smiled and nodded. "Oh, yeah."

"We're too old for this," Alex protested.

"That's where you're wrong."

"Midnight tag, really?"

"You know you want to," Cole teased. "I think you've forgotten how to have fun."

"You're a grown man suggesting this. An adult. A twenty-year-old person."

"Your point?"

Alex shook his head, eyes darting up.

Cole and Alex had played the game with other kids at the orphanage. They'd snuck out after dark to play until midnight or later, or until they got tired. It was a tradition passed down through the generations for hundreds of years. So it was said, but like the children who played the game, the estimate was not to be trusted. All they knew was that children before Leah and Edgar's time had played it. Alex and Cole had many good memories of running around after dark, unsupervised, savoring the exhilarating breath of freedom that the game provided. But Cole had one regret: Vella had never been part of it. She'd never been invited.

She would watch through the window as the other children snuck out without her. Kids often played without being asked, but that wasn't what held her back. The fear of becoming a target for further bullying kept her safe inside.

"We're playing for Vella; she's never played before. I think we owe her that," Cole said.

"I thought this was my night," Alex said.

"You're a man of the people now, and this is what the people want. We owe her," Cole insisted.

"I think it would be fun," Vella said, soft but hopeful.

Alex sighed in resignation, then looked at Leah. "You're playing as well."

"I've played before, but . . ."

Alex raised an eyebrow at her.

"I'm old," she said in weak protest.

"Rubbish. Let's go," Edgar added. "Leah had a streak of three games straight of not getting tagged once."

"Yeah . . . I just hid."

"Leah's in, then," Edgar declared.

She shook her head, resigned to her fate.

Cole tossed the ball up and down. "Well. Looks like we're on," he said with a grin. "Ellie, can you play?"

"I'll sit this one out. I'm feeling a little nauseous," she said.

"Very well. Everyone else, let's go. You know the rules. North side only. No hiding in and around houses. If you're touched with the ball, you're it. You have to give a sixty-second head start . . . And . . ." He paused, thinking for a moment. "To add to the fun, when you're it, you have a drink. The one to finish the bottle loses. What shall the penalty be? Alex?"

"Let me think." He let go of Ellie, walked up to Cole, and took the ball from him. "How about a shit shake?"

Leah groaned.

"Great idea," Cole said, staring at Leah.

"Just . . . go easy," Leah said.

"What's that?" Vella asked.

"Don't worry, no one's going to make you drink literal shit," Cole said.

"Might as well be," Leah muttered.

"We start with a milk base, but this time I think it should be shine. Everyone gets to add one ingredient to the shake, and the loser has to drink it."

"Well, I won't lose," Vella boasted.

"No, not shine," Leah groaned.

Cole and Alex took great pleasure in her discomfort, feeling like they were back in the shoes of the two ten-year-olds who hadn't had a care in the world. Back when the only thing that had mattered was deciding how to have fun with their free time.

"Vodka. I'll meet you in the middle," Cole said.

Leah rolled her eyes. "Great. I just won't lose then."

"That's the spirit. I'll start," he said, taking the ball back from Alex. "When the moon reaches the diamond-shaped patch of stars or—"

"It's called the Southern Cross, genius," Alex interrupted.

"Or!" Cole continued. "When the bottle empties, whichever comes first, the game ends, and we meet back here. Ready. Go!"

Alex and Vella shot off toward the back gate, while Edgar and

Leah took their time walking.

"You two don't seem to be in a rush. One . . . two . . . three. Four, five, six. Seven, eight, nine." His count quickened, and they quickened their pace in turn.

Alex stopped and called out, "Ellie, let anyone inside know who might want in. I know for sure Josh would."

"Yes, all right. Go." She had a good laugh at the rare sight of Alex's childlike exuberance.

Alex and Vella were already lost to the darkness, while Edgar and Leah had just picked up a slow jog.

"Leah's hiding spot is the sunflower bed," Edgar shouted.

"Oh, come on. What am I supposed to do now? I don't want to run," she groaned.

She leaped, giving Edgar a shove in the back. Edgar swayed sideways, trying to block her path in retaliation. They vanished from sight, laughing and taunting like the children they once were.

When Cole finished his count, he took a deep breath and walked out into the night. Grateful to be free.

They played for over two hours, completely caught up in the game. Along the way, they encountered children from the orphanage who had snuck out to play their own game. They teamed up, sharing information and hiding spots. Chaos erupted as bodies appeared from every direction, heightening the fun and excitement.

In the end, it was Cole who finished the bottle and faced the consequences of a disastrous "shit shake."

He didn't mind; his stomach did.

38

My job as the designated life transition specialist is, by far, the worst Eden has to offer. I wonder if I even had a choice. They needed someone, and given my history, they thought I would be a good fit. My predecessor, Riley, told me this job requires a certain mentality. But when Riley's time was up and I was left on my own, I quickly learned that I didn't have it. It almost broke me. When I thought I could take no more, a special person found me sitting on a park bench in my darkest hour. To say she saved me would be an understatement. She told me, "You're allowed bad days. Just don't give up. Rest if you need to, then keep going. The people passing on need you. And believe me, Aleister, you are needed." I said, "Anyone could do what I do." She just laughed. "No, they can't. They wouldn't last a day in your shoes. You carry a special responsibility. You look after people. You make them feel safe. That's not something just anyone can do. It may not be what you wanted, but it's what you can do. Be there for them." Now she's gone. I watched from the shadows the day she walked through that door and vanished from Eden. I remember she saw me and smiled. I don't know how she put on such a brave face. This book is for her. Vella.

—"MY FOREWORD"
CHILDREN OF THE PEACEFUL PASSAGE
by Aleister #8990

The silence was unnerving; not a sound disturbed the stillness. Cole sat on the edge of the bed, his thoughts heavy with the colossal task they were about to undertake. To distract himself, he drew. Across the room was his subject.

Vella stared out the window, lost in her own thoughts. The moon hung over her, casting a soft glow around her. Cole couldn't help but smile, but his expression faded into a frown. Frustration welled as he failed to capture the moment as perfectly as he saw it.

The longer they waited, the more the weight of expectation pressed down on them. He glanced at the orb sitting on the bedside table. Each click of the orb wound his anxiety tighter.

Cole hadn't realized how tense he was until a creak echoed

through the house, making both of them flinch. Vella glanced at him, exhaled in relief, then turned back to the window.

"Can I see it now?" she asked.

"Almost done."

She looked down at the orb to her left and sighed.

"Cole . . ."

"Yeah," he responded, not looking up.

"Have you ever used the orb without me knowing?" she asked.

"Have you?"

"No."

Cole hesitated and put aside the sketch of Vella. "Morning after Leah's party . . . you seemed like you needed space, so I used it."

She said nothing, betraying no signs of emotion.

"Actually." He sighed. "I have a confession to make. There was another time. The night you left dinner early. The day before you moved in. You told me how you felt, and . . . I panicked."

"Was that it?" she asked, still not turning to face him.

"Yes. I couldn't forgive myself if I did that to you again," he said. "I'm sorry."

She tilted her head down, wanting to look at him, but stopped herself.

"When you told me you loved me," she said, "I couldn't tell if you meant it or if you just said it because you were panicked that I was upset about the drawing. I desperately wanted to believe you meant it. I can't tell you how long I've wanted to tell you how I felt. Then when you did, I'd never felt so happy."

Cole cringed, remembering she had used the same words during her confession that he had erased.

"I rushed things, thinking that if I waited too long, it would all go away. But I still wonder if you actually love me, or if it's just pity," she said.

"You can't think, after everything, it's pity that keeps me around," he said.

"I know it's not, but that feeling never leaves. It keeps telling me 'You're not good enough' and 'No one could ever love you.' Like one day you'll vanish just so you don't need to be with me."

Before he could speak, she added, "I know it's crazy. I just can't get rid of this feeling that everyone's going to leave me."

Cole stood up, his legs feeling heavy as if they might give out beneath him. He moved behind her, wrapping his arms around her waist, pulling her close.

"Everyone feels that way . . . I think. But I love you more than I could ever love myself, and I wouldn't leave you willingly. Let's just say it would take a lot to keep me away."

She leaned back into him, her body relaxing under his touch.

Cole spoke in a low voice. "After I used the orb that second time, I kept thinking . . . how could you possibly love a monster like me?"

A chuckle escaped her. "You say some dumb stuff, but I didn't know you thought even dumber things," she teased.

Turning, she kissed him, then playfully shoved him onto the bed and climbed on top.

Reaching over, she picked up the sketch he'd been working on. It was of her, standing by the window, with an enlarged moon encircling her head from the shoulders up.

"I love it."

With a grin, she flung it aside and kissed him again. She pulled back an inch and spoke into his mouth. "You're making it hard to leave."

"I'm not doing anything," he said, smiling.

"If you hadn't kept those drawings from me . . . I would've had no choice but to force myself on you."

"Well, if I knew . . ." He leaned in and kissed her.

She drew back and sighed. "We should go."

He tapped one finger to his shoulder: *Stay.* Adding, "We don't have to do anything."

She laughed. "If we don't go now, we'll definitely wake them."

"Are you sure about this?"

Her eyes searched his. "Are you?"

He nodded, unable to verbalize an answer.

"Who will do it if not us?" she asked, more to herself than to him.

He looked at her as if seeing her for the first time, his gaze tracing the details of her face. A soft smile tugged at his lips.

"What will you do with your extra time?" he asked.

She considered it and smiled. "Raise a family."

"Tell me about it. What does it look like?"

"I have a daughter and a son. I watch them grow. I can talk to them, hug them, and kiss them whenever I want. I'm there for them through the good and the bad. The tears and laughter. They leave me for their own life's adventures, but they're not too far away. They find love of their own, have kids of their own. And I have a loving partner by my side as we grow old together. Live happily ever after."

"Like Isara and Drystan."

Her smile and eyes wavered. "Just like them," she said under her breath.

"Did you have someone in mind? This loving partner?"

"There's some jerk who I can never seem to get rid of."

"That sounds nice," he whispered, giving her one last kiss.

In that moment, Eden and all their worries melted away.

Hand in hand, they walked, saying nothing, feeling everything. When they reached their destination, Cole's hidden resentment flared. The sight of the doors enraged him, forcing him to confront the unjust burden that weighed on their shoulders.

Above the doors, the blue glow of the countdown screen and its ticking numbers filled him with a different kind of resentment.

Remember why you're doing this. Who you're doing it for, he told himself.

Vella climbed a large oak tree nearby and untied the weapons she had stashed there. She dropped them down, letting Cole choose first. He opted for the one with the spear end. The bundle included improved face masks made by Vella. They tied them around their necks, letting them hang down for the moment.

Cole went to move toward the door before Vella stopped him.

"We should talk about it," she said.

He tensed up at the implications. "What to have for breakfast tomorrow?"

She showed no signs of amusement. "The rule, Cole."

"I know. Can we discuss it another time? Keep it in place. For now."

"We can't ignore it forever." She stared at him, trying to get him to engage.

"I know. Just not today."

"I don't like it any more than you do, but we can't ignore it forever."

"Not today," he reiterated.

"You can let me die if it'll let you explore other possible—"

"Vel, not today." He tried his hardest to keep himself from yelling the words.

She eyed him, not wanting to drop it.

"I'm sorry, I just can't deal with that . . . yet."

She nodded in frustration and understanding.

There was the other issue neither wanted to speak about. Who would do it? Who would be the one to take the final responsibility? Only one could. Both thought it would be them, and they knew the other thought the same. An argument would come out of it, one they weren't ready to have.

"I'll go first," she said. "How many attempts?"

"Start with fifty," he suggested. "Then we can discuss what we find. Repeat. Do a few hundred resets tonight. Then call it a night to process things. We can work our way up from there."

"All right."

"We both need to reach a point where we're as comfortable in there as we are anywhere else."

"Like with Ivy?"

"Exactly."

She eyed the axe in her hand as it threatened to slide through her clammy grip.

"No being a hero," he warned.

Her head snapped up. "I should be saying that to *you*."

A sly smile touched his lips as he handed her the orb. She saw it and shoved him.

She turned her attention to the orb, watching it in silence as they waited.

Click.

He watched as a subtle shift washed over her, her expression softening into one of deep contemplation. She handed the orb back to him and, without a word, she walked away and lay down on the grass, staring up at the sky.

Cole watched her, sensing the depth of her thoughts. Not wanting to disturb her, he leaned back against the wall, his gaze shifting between her and the lights in the sky.

The real question that plagued him was how he could avoid having to watch her die at all. He would need to act soon before she took things into her own hands.

I could do several hundred runs with Vella and as many as I like tomorrow. Would I have to actually kill it tomorrow? On my own? I might.

He tried to think of the effort that might take, and he could already feel himself grow weary.

The click of the orb brought him back to the present.

"It ticked over," he said.

Vella jerked back to the real world. They pulled themselves up and secured their masks over their faces.

She led them into the lair of the Bear.

The foul air stung his nostrils, and he grimaced. *I'll get used to it*, he told himself.

He stood ready as the lights faded in. Vella was several steps ahead of him. He took a look down at the makeshift spear in his right hand. The weight of it felt right, light and evenly distributed, yet strong and deadly. The tip looked remarkably sharp.

What an amazing job she did. Even now, she still manages to surprise me, he thought.

He looked at her and smiled in admiration. She glanced at him, confused by the stupid grin she could see in his eyes.

She turned back around, shaking her head.

"What're you smiling about?" she asked.

"Nothing."

He pulled the orb from his pocket, ready in his left hand.

A familiar snarl rose from the shadows. Vella moved forward to get the beast's attention and create a safe buffer for Cole's protection.

Then, there was another noise.

Click.

"What . . . was that?"

39

It's hard to describe what I've seen. The monitors only show fragments of what's on the other side of those doors, and even those fragments are enough to haunt me. Flashes of massive feet, claws, horns, and eyes. The implications of what it all means are deeply disturbing. I can't fully put it into words, but one thing is clear: we're not leaving. I pressed my ear to the door. I shouldn't have. I could faintly hear them. Screaming. Begging. I can still hear them. To be there, trapped and helpless, just waiting for death to come. I can't imagine it.

—THE FIRST PEOPLE OF EDEN

Journal of Morgan #38

Day 2

Cole thought he heard a faint clicking sound. A sharp, cold flash swept over and through him, sending his mind and body into pure numbness.

No. It can't be. I heard the click not a minute ago!

He tried to convince himself it was nothing—just a trick of his imagination. But he knew better. The real trick of the imagination had happened before he entered. Knowing that, he didn't want to look at the orb sitting in his left hand and confirm his worst fears.

No . . . it's just in my head, he kept repeating, clinging to the fragile hope that he was imagining things.

Without looking, he pressed the button. He should have been outside, back in safety. He should have been sitting with his back against the wall, under the serene night sky, watching Vella lying on the ground. But he wasn't. He was still standing in the exact same spot. *No . . .*

Cole pressed the button again. And again. Nothing changed.

His panic flared into full-blown terror. At last, he looked at the orb. The indentations had recently converged and were only now drifting apart. He was falling, and there was nothing to catch him. Staring in disbelief, his mind scrambled to make sense of what he was seeing.

This can't be happening. What've I done?

His thoughts spiraled out of control, self-recrimination echoing in his mind. *How could you have been so careless? We're going to die here. All because you didn't check the damn orb. Vella trusted you. She was too far away to hear if it actually ticked over. She trusted you! And you chose to trust a noise that came from inside your head. ARE YOU JOKING?*

He stood frozen, paralyzed by the realization of what this meant. Unwillingness to accept this new reality threatened to destroy him as the uncaring universe continued to move around him.

Vella turned back and saw his expression. "Cole, what's wrong?"

He couldn't bring himself to answer her. The grip on his throat, chest, and stomach was suffocating him. Instead, he reset to escape the question. But he couldn't escape the grim reality of their situation.

Do something!

His mind screamed at him. But his body refused to obey. He remained rooted to the spot, eyes darting around their tomb. The scattered bones and tattered remains of clothes littered the floor. A grim reminder of how it would end if he failed.

No escape. No escape. No escape. No escape . . .

He focused on Vella, desperate to try and calm his racing heart. *I can't let her die here.*

Closing his eyes, he pressed the button again, hoping to wake from this nightmare. But when he opened them, nothing changed.

Leah's words settled into him: *You're wishing for things to be different.*

Why can't they be different? Why?

Her words came back in response: *What purpose does it serve to think like that?*

None.

The finality of their situation settled over him, heavy and unbearable.

What can I do?

His mind finally grasped a sense of rational thought. *There's only one thing to do. Either we die here, or the Bear does. There's no room for hesitation. It will kill us without a second thought. I have to be prepared to do the same.*

Cole knew he was alone in this fight. Vella was there in the flesh, but she couldn't help him. His resolve hardened. *It has to be it, not us.*

He forced himself to focus, adrenaline kicking in, pushing him toward action. Drawing a shaky breath, he tried to steady it, willing his body back under control.

Then came Edgar's voice in his head, a memory from that first glimpse of the Bear: *One step at a time.*

One step at a time, he repeated. So he did. He watched each step of the Bear, timing its movements. After taking a few resets, he estimated ten seconds before it reached them. *Ten seconds to find a way to kill it.* He needed to make every second, every fraction of a second, count.

As his muscles remained paralyzed with shock, he didn't know what to do. So, he watched for what felt like hours. His mind became more composed and analytical. He had to be cold, calculating. There was no room for emotion.

You have one job. Do it.

His breathing evened out. The shaking lessened over time. But the stress never subsided. One mistake, one slight miscalculation, and it would all be over.

He looked down; the fate of those who had faced this monster before him lay at his feet.

At least I can die as one of them. But even as the thought crossed his mind, he rejected it. *No, I can't. I have to do this—for Vella.*

Unlike his encounter with the Wolf many weeks ago, there was no laughter to release the tension. No outside to retreat to. There was only cold apathy that spread through him.

How easy it would be to let go . . . to let it end . . . oh, how easy.

One step at a time, he reminded himself, watching the Bear with added focus. The one thing he had to his advantage was time. A vast ocean that never ended; he could swim endlessly, but there would be no land, no shore, no salvation in this endless abyss.

Endless time in the form of the same ten seconds. This was what his life had been reduced to. The monotony wore on him, his frustration bubbling into rage. He screamed over and over, venting his anger, but it offered little relief. His best defense, he knew, was holding tight to the fire raging within. It could keep him going, but for how long?

Think. He forced himself to consider the Bear's weak points: the head, the eyes, the heart, the throat. But getting close enough was a risk. The tail and stinger posed a deadly threat, extending the beast's reach by thirty meters.

It's too much.

Vella was so close, yet she felt unreachable, frozen in time. He was truly alone.

Let go, a voice whispered. Freedom was within reach. He just had to surrender to it.

Enough!

To anchor himself, he hummed a tune. It was a song that had been stuck in his head ever since the band had played it at Leah's and Edgar's parties. Vella hummed it once in a while, and it had burrowed into his brain, playing nonstop for days.

How did it go? He recalled the beat. The rhythm. The words.

His mind filled with images of those nights, and all the people there. How easy life had felt in that short time span. It made him feel foolish that he had kept all that at bay for so long. All he wanted was to see and talk to Leah again. Vella. Anyone.

He hummed louder, drowning out the unhelpful chatter of his mind, and returned his focus to the Bear's movements.

Hours passed, resetting the same few seconds over and over. Eventually, he reached a dead end. There were no more details to ingrain, nothing left to memorize.

His thoughts turned; now he was forced to come up with a plan of action. He decided it was time to run some tests and start moving. But where to begin? Vella was the obvious choice.

"Sprint forward, right hugging the wall, and run back at the second pillar," he barked to Vella. She obeyed without question, the Bear charging after her. He reset.

He repeated the process, adding his own movements as an

extra variable. Every possibility was tested, over and over. He made sure they stayed at least three seconds clear of it at all times, ensuring their safety.

Taking a break from countless tests, he ran through everything he knew.

One: Ten seconds is the maximum amount of time I have without risking harm to either of us.

Two: I can't come to harm or even risk myself if we both want to escape.

Three: If Vella comes to harm, that loop is irrelevant, even if I kill it.

Four: Taking Vella out of the equation and meeting it head-on is out of the question. It's too quick to dodge, and if I mess up once, it's over.

Five: A sneak attack is the best option, taking everything into consideration.

Six: At around seven seconds, the Bear will turn its full attention to Vella if I move in the opposite direction.

Seven: I need at least fifteen seconds to get close enough from behind to reach a vulnerable spot.

Now the hard part . . .

Problem: She needs to buy me an extra five seconds.

Solution: Find the perfect path where she survives long enough, and repeat it.

Cole knew she was quick enough to avoid some attacks and buy him the time he needed. But how many times would it take for him to find that one path?

He hadn't risked her coming to harm once, and now there was no way around it.

The truth of what was about to happen finally sank in, and in that moment, he felt all the warmth drain from his face.

I have to risk her and . . . be willing to let her die.

He'd been avoiding it while running tests, delaying the inevitable. But now, there was no other option.

I can't, his mind screamed in reflexive rejection.

She'd said she would be okay with it no more than five real minutes ago. Even so, the idea of having to sacrifice her disgusted him.

To watch her die like his parents . . . It was too much.

There was no one stopping him this time.

No force holding him back.

He had to let it happen.

Let her go.

Let them go.

I must.

He could feel bile forcing its way up his throat even thinking it.

The thought of passing the orb to Vella crossed his mind, but he dismissed it as soon as it appeared. That would be taking the easy way out, he knew. He thought her capable, but she would put his own welfare above her own. *I can't let her. I need to be the one.* This was the mess he'd created; there would be no one else to fix it for him.

So, it's finally come to this. Goddammit . . .

He let out a deep breath and readied himself. This was the first time he went past ten seconds, and it was the worst few seconds of his life. On pure reaction, he almost reset but managed to stop himself. Staying his shaking hand, he kept count in his head.

Ten . . . eleven . . .

It lunged at her. She couldn't avoid its claw.

He turned away. Visceral noises consumed him, shredding his insides.

All of his life, he had done everything he could to protect her, and now her blood stained his hands.

You killed her . . . unforgivable. Murderer.

Then the screams stopped; other, worse sounds didn't.

His thumb hovered over the button as the sickness in his stomach rose, threatening to reach his throat.

I can't let it be for nothing. Again.

40

As I come to my end, my only piece of advice to you is this: Life is a matter of acceptance or action. If there's nothing you can do about obtaining something you want, refusing to accept reality only leads to pain. So, you're always better off accepting. Believe me. It's a waste of energy to fret about what you can't control, no matter how unnatural or difficult it feels. Although, if there *is* something you can actually do—fight. And never stop. All we have is what we can control. If you won't even put in enough effort to fight for what you want, especially when it is within your sphere of control, what's the point of living? If you can't find the strength, you've forgotten what you're fighting for in the first place. And if you can't find a good enough reason, it's not important enough to waste your time on. But when you come across those rare things you *truly* want, but feel too afraid, unworthy, or incapable of pursuing, remember this: you only have a small amount of time, and you'll never regret trying. So, fight and rage until your last day. Not for anyone else but for your own sake.

—THE FIRST PEOPLE OF EDEN
Journal of Morgan #38
Day 1944

Cole lost count of the resets, but he knew exactly how many times Vella had died: *forty-five*. And there would be many, many more.

He was still nowhere near finding the timeline where she survived long enough for him to sneak up from behind. The lack of progress wore him down, planting seeds of doubt. Was it even possible? The thought dragged him down with every failed attempt.

Alternatives? None that didn't risk his life. And his life was both of their lives.

He took a steadying breath. Though the aroma of decaying death filled his nostrils, the smell didn't register in his mind. The stench that had once made his stomach churn faded into the background. It was as familiar now as the scent of his own bedroom.

The hum of the song still lingered in his head, though now it was a faint shadow of what it had once been. It was fragmented by the constant brain zaps. Fear of worse pain made him accept them. In fact, he was thankful—they kept him focused.

But the mental strain was wearing him down. Eden felt like a distant memory, almost as if it were someone else's life and this endless loop was all he'd ever known. The fear of physical breakdown wasn't a concern; his body remained as fresh as when he'd entered. But that was about all he had going for him.

He had a sick feeling of déjà vu. In recent years, it wasn't the memory of his parents being killed that woke him at night—it was what he saw in the nightmares.

What he saw now.

In those dreams, it was Vella and Leah he was forced to watch being torn apart while he stood by, helpless. Every time he tried to intervene, something held him back. An unseen force. All he could do was watch as he lost everything he had left.

And always, the blue eyes stared back at him—mocking.

There was nothing here to taunt him but his own lack of control.

But those nightmares paled in comparison to the knowledge of the hundreds of people who would die if he failed. He had lived all their deaths. He knew what was at stake.

Hours and hours passed as he counted her deaths.

Four . . . hundred . . .

If he did keep track of the full tally of resets, it would likely add up to a hundred times that. Nothing he did or said to Vella worked. Each subtle inflection in his tone, even when using the same words, caused events to play out differently. He needed to test each variation with painstaking patience.

Often, he could foresee inevitable outcomes, resetting before they played out, sparing himself from witnessing countless more deaths. He'd heard every scream. Every plea. Seen every possible death. There was a time when it had nearly driven him mad, but now it was just white noise. Nothing felt real anymore. It was as if he'd ceased to exist in their world at all, merely peering in from outside, like watching a screen from a distance. It felt like he was playing a game. Nothing more. A repeated game of chess with no correct series of moves.

He constantly heard her calling his name. She begged him to save her, but he was powerless to help.

He'd had another fear when he'd started this—and it wasn't watching her die.

It was going numb to it.

Losing her to indifference.

And now, he felt dangerously close.

Time passed on and on with no end in sight.

He was sinking, losing himself.

Falling.

The fire faded; the rage gone.

He allowed his eyes to close.

How did this happen?

What are we doing here?

This is what you wanted.

No, it's not.

What do you want?

I want to go home.

You know what you have to do.

What's that?

Open your eyes.

No.

There's another option.

Not that either.

What do you want, then?

I want it to stop. Why won't it stop?

You know why.

When will it stop?

When you stop.

It's not possible.

Are you giving up?

Leave me alone.

You're talking to me.

Why can't you ever leave me alone? Why is it whenever you come, it's just to torment me? Just shut up and leave me alone for once. I know what's happened in the past. What do you want me to do about it, huh? I can't do anything to change it. You know this. Leave me be. Please . . . stop . . .

No.

Goddammit. I know about the drawing. I get it.

Do you?

Of course I do! I know about all my mistakes. All of them! Why can't you let me be? Stop reminding me. I can't do anything about them.

You can.

What the hell do you want me to do?

Die.

Shut up . . .

Open your eyes, Cole.

I'm tired . . . can't you do it?

No.

Why not?

I don't exist.

Useless.

This is your chance.

For what?

Be the savior you always wanted to be.

I never wanted to be . . .

Who are you trying to convince?

Not like this, though.

Admit it, you were happy that you messed up.

Of course not—

No need to care about others' safety because you messed up. You don't have to do it alone because you happened to make a careless mistake. Now you have Vella to die for you. She gets to feel excruciating pain, over and over, while you remain clean.

There's no other way. I can't have her do it.

How convenient.

What would you have me do?

Admit it.

Admit what?

You wanted this. Regardless of your intention.

Fine. I knew I couldn't do it alone. It doesn't mean I would intentionally put her in danger. It doesn't make me a bad person. Does it?

The fact that you have to even ask: what does that tell you?

I'm not a bad person.

Of course not. You're completely innocent. You're the hero.

I don't want to be the hero.

Come now. You do. Did you think it all came free? People will get hurt for your reckless ambitions. You charge in headfirst, but what of those who follow? You can tell yourself all you want that you'll do it alone, but they'll follow your lead. You're responsible for them. Leah was right. You'll get her killed.

I won't.

Even if you don't, you'll inflict pain on all of them in one way or another because that's who you are. You're a curse to those around you.

Shut up.

It's not enough for you to accept that the people around you will die. You have to spread death and pain yourself because you cannot accept reality.

Stop it.

You might change things, but you'll destroy everything for the sake of moral righteousness. You're *so* brave. What of the bodies left in your wake? The lives you've ruined.

I won't let that happen. No one will die.

How do you think it will go? Everything will work out?

Why can't it?

You know better than that.

Go away.

You can make it stop at any time.

No.

You and Vella can be like your parents. Die in vain.

Shut up.

Let go.

No.

Don't worry. Everyone else has given up.

I can't.

What are you complaining about then? Be the hero.

I can't do this on my own.

I can't help you. Vella can't help you. No one can.

Please. Someone. Help.

Help yourself.

It's not fair.

Fair? Do you think what's happening to Vella is fair?

No.

Then what's this insufferable self-pity you peddle?

I need to get it out.

Why?

So I can focus.

Focus on what? Spreading your curse?

Can't you say anything of use?

Open your eyes.

He thought of what waited for him on the other side—Vella, safe and happy. Leah, Alex, Edgar. The taste of food, the feel of fresh air in his lungs. Sleep in his own bed. His life and everything that went with it. The good and the bad.

How much of my life I wasted on hate. Hatred of the Wolf. Of people like Alex. Eden. Of myself. None of it mattered. It never had. What a waste.

It felt like he'd lived a lifetime here. He had experienced every emotion, every feeling he could possibly imagine. Now, he felt nothing.

What I wouldn't give to have just one more moment with them. Hell, even to do a day of hard work in the fields. Nothing outside our walls could be better than what I had. Had? No. Have. What I have is what I've always wanted and more. I need nothing else, just more time. And now I have all the time in the world and none of what makes it worth the time.

My life was all wrong.

He laughed. He laughed so hard that if it weren't for the resets, his sides would have ached. When the laughter finally subsided, he crashed back to reality. Panic surged, then gave way to calm, only to return. It was a vicious cycle that soon subsided into an equilibrium he could deal with, giving him a hyperawareness of everything around him.

He opened his eyes and fixed his gaze on Vella.

Then he ran to her, dropped their face masks, and kissed her. Taking a moment, he gazed into her eyes and smiled. She stood there, speechless, her gaze shifting behind him with growing concern.

"Cole, what—?"

With his hand, he gently guided her face to keep her eyes fixed on him.

"My beautiful armor and shield," he whispered.

He reset and clarity returned. He felt light. Nothing could hurt him anymore. On he pressed with his mission.

And soon he found it.

Five hundred and twenty.

Elation was too small a word for what he felt. Tears ran down his face in disbelief when he was able to count past fifteen. The precise actions and instructions were clear. It took some trial and error to repeat it consistently, but he had the fifteen seconds he needed—thanks to Vella.

The long struggle was over.

Only it wasn't. This was only one part of the puzzle.

The next question was: *What to target?* The behemoth seemed to have no visible weaknesses from a distance. The tail? No, a blow there wouldn't kill it. *The heart? Maybe. Its heart must be huge. I can get close enough, eventually, to get a good shot at it.*

The target could wait. First, he needed to sneak up from behind, staying out of sight. Each step had to be precise in timing and placement. One step at a time, literally. He managed to avoid the flailing tail and duck under its legs to get a closer look at its chest. This took several hundred resets just to perfect a period of three seconds.

Now he was standing right under its chest, staring up at its thick, matted fur. Up close, he could see it was too thick to pierce.

Dammit . . . what now—

From the corner of his eye, he spotted its ear, around the middle of its head. An idea formed.

This may be as good as it gets. Through the ear into the brain? What else is there? He took another few resets to look around the body. Nothing better presented itself. *That'll have to do.*

Feeling satisfied in his decision, he planned his next steps. The challenge now was positioning himself to be able to strike with lethal force. Timing was crucial. He had come from behind its hind legs, timing his approach with the moment its head dipped low to lunge at Vella. He couldn't allow her to die; introducing time pressure, every fraction of a second mattered.

Cole had to stay out of harm's way as he weaved and dodged up the Bear's massive body. Achieving this required countless trial and error, careful memorization, and precise, repeated actions. Any deviation meant watching her die. He spoke to Vella in the same steady tone, guiding her through the exact movements, over and over, again and again.

Hundreds upon hundreds of resets. It became a delicate dance with death—one false or careless move, and it would spell the end for both of them. It needed to be the same. Exactly the same.

Each time, he used less energy to repeat the same actions. He streamlined everything to the bare essentials.

Once more, he quelled the urge to force things, fighting every impulse to rush, knowing one false move would doom them. *Patience. Patience.* He repeated the word until it lost meaning, melting into the maelstrom of his mind. He could feel his own heartbeat racing, as if it sat atop his skin.

I don't want to do this anymore. Make it stop. Make it stop. No more. Please. Please.

He slapped himself. Hard. *Focus. You have one goal; there's nothing else until it's done.*

Taking a moment, he focused on his breath, trying to bring himself back. Then, he concentrated on the tips of his fingers, the soles of his feet, and finally his gut, where the feeling of Vella was forever lodged—reminding him of why he was doing this. He used everything at his disposal to keep himself anchored.

He would fade, then bring himself back. Diminish, then return. And on it went.

"I want to go home . . . ," he muttered.

The words triggered a memory that came flooding back, one he'd tried to capture in a drawing countless times but never could. He now came to realize, at last, it was beyond words or lines on a page. A feeling that could never be expressed in a picture.

A couple of years ago, he'd gone home for lunch. Normally, he would've spent the break with Vella, but she wasn't feeling well that day, so he sat alone in the backyard. With no appetite, he just rested, watching the bees drift from flower to flower.

Vella's favorite book, *The Knights of Acidalia*, lay on his lap, a bookmark tucked a third of the way in.

He hadn't expected company—Leah rarely came home during lunch—but then she walked out back and, without a word, handed him a sandwich on a plate.

The warmth of the day wrapped around them as they savored the simple pleasure of each other's company. Every part of his awareness told him to pay attention.

He looked around and noted how surreal everything felt. Nothing felt out of place. Leah seemed content, and he felt her ease.

They never spoke a word the whole time.

And yet, that small moment had stayed with him ever since.

Why that memory? There were grander, more monumental moments, but this one was as small as it got. Now, he understood why. Deep down, he'd always known. It was the feeling. Just the two of them. The person who loved him like a mother and the simple act of love that no one else would do for him.

Unconditional love personified. It was his memory. No one could take it from him.

It told Cole of real love. All he had unknowingly hoped to experience because it wasn't coming from within himself. He wished it wasn't so fleeting, but on reflection, he found it wasn't. It was present every day they were together. Never wavering for a moment. He didn't notice it, didn't see it, even though it was staring him in the face the whole time. A welling of rage at his ignorance made him tremble. All Leah had asked in exchange for her love was that he stay with her until her last day. And he couldn't even honor that one wish.

I miss her so much.

What I wouldn't give to see her again.

I can't let her down now.

The familiar feeling of the fire within returned. This time, it wasn't fueled by rage. Instead, it was ignited by something deeper, something more meaningful, laced with warmth.

He stole one final kiss from Vella before continuing alone in a timeless world.

Progress was slow, but he didn't mind. There were worse things, he knew.

Inch by inch, he forged a path of escape.

Reset after reset.

It went on longer than he could have ever imagined. Each loop brought him a literal step closer to the end. He could see it. Whenever he wavered, he thought of that memory of Leah, and he felt like that same person, free in the past, as if every experience since had been just a dream. The image of them brought it all back, locking him in that small, marvelous, and peaceful window of time.

Five steps away.

Then four.

Three.

Two.

One.

He stood on the final precipice, right under its head. All he had to do was take the final risk—a side step, two hands on the spear, a lunge—and hope it was enough. A second attempt was unlikely. He would need both hands on the weapon, and the orb would be too far out of reach if things went wrong.

He was in a position to launch the attack, standing beneath the creature's mouth. One more step to the side, and he could drive the spear into its brain through the ear. He wasn't sure if he had the strength or the right weapon to deliver a killing blow, but this was his best option. Cutting the throat wasn't viable; the attack needed to be instant and fatal.

The moment had arrived. He'd repeated the loop perfectly a dozen times to make sure he could recreate it on muscle memory alone. Now, on the sixth, he would execute.

He steeled himself as they stepped into their final dance together.

For the last time, they moved as one.

Cole called to Vella the pattern to run. She complied, sprinting wide to the right as he ran to the left, drawing the Bear's attention away from him. He placed the orb in his pocket and gripped the spear with both hands, counting the beats in his head. At seven, he turned and sprinted toward the beast from behind.

Vella cried out as the Bear stalked her along the wall. Its massive form loomed closer with every step; she turned and ran in the opposite direction. The unexpected movement threw it off balance just enough to give her a few precious seconds. She darted between the pillars, using them to keep some separation and avoid the deadly lash of its barbed tail.

Meanwhile, Cole ducked beneath its massive legs, darting around to avoid the tail's dangerous arc. He moved with practiced ease, just as he had countless times before, dancing to the precise beat and rhythm of the creature's movements. Gliding along its body, he stayed just outside its awareness.

As it lowered its head for another attack, Cole was already there, slipping beneath its throat, poised for the final strike.

This was it. No redos. No second chances.

He gripped the makeshift spear as tight as he could.

Stepping to the side, he lowered his body, shifted his weight, and slid his right hand to the base of the handle.

He lined up the shot. And with all his power, he drove the tip of the spear into its ear.

He hit his mark.

All he could do now was hope and pray it was enough. And above all, hope that Vella survived this time.

41

Cole's vision blurred as he stared at the dim blue lights above, their glow flickering like distant stars, fading in and out.

The Bear lay sprawled across the floor in a pool of blood, its colossal body still twitching, even in death. Cole had managed to land a killing blow, but it hadn't been instant. The beast roared and thrashed in agony, blood gushing from its head. Vella managed to narrowly avoid its wild flailing.

Cole wasn't so lucky. He was too close when an inadvertent claw tore across his chest, sending him hurtling across the room. He hit the ground with a sickening thud.

"Cole!" Vella's voice broke through the haze. She knelt beside him, panic gripping her. "You're hurt! Reset! Reset! Where's the orb?"

It took a moment for him to be able to bring her face into focus. "A-are you okay?" he wheezed.

"Where is it?"

"I . . . don't k-know, are . . . you okay?"

"Yes, I'm fine! Now, where is it?"

He tried to laugh, but the blood filling his lungs made him cough in fits. "I did it," he breathed out. "It's finally over."

"Who cares? You're—" She couldn't finish the sentence, her eyes darting over his broken body, blood everywhere. She pressed a trembling hand to one of the sources of flowing blood, but there were too many, the blood too much.

Her hands fumbled over his body, searching for the orb. There was nothing to be found in his shredded clothes.

"Where is it?" she screamed. "What're you doing? Help me!"

Her eyes darted around the floor and the area surrounding her, but the tears blurred her vision. She furiously wiped them away, desperate to see clearly.

"I have to find it. Wait here."

"Please, stop," he whispered. "Just . . . stay."

He reached out and grabbed her arm.

"No! Let go." She broke his grasp with ease as his strength waned.

Getting to her feet was a struggle as she slipped on the blood—Cole's blood, the Bear's blood. Too much blood for her to comprehend. She finally managed to stand, eyes darting as she searched the area in a panic. It was too dark to spot the small black orb, now likely coated in blood. The scattered debris of others sentenced to die here littered the ground, making the search even harder. Blood, both fresh and dried, covered everything.

"No, no, no, no!" Her voice escalated from a mutter to a scream. She tore through the debris, frantically tossing aside anything that wasn't the orb. Her chest heaved with ragged breaths, her mind a swirling storm of panic and fury. She felt overwhelmed by an unbearable feeling that the universe was laughing at her and doing everything it could to conspire against her.

"Vel," Cole called, his voice faint.

She couldn't hear him—or she refused to.

Vella struggled to breathe, her chest heaving, eyes wild as she scanned the vast area. Nothing.

She turned back toward him, tears still streaming unrestrained down her face.

"Where is it?" she wailed, desperation choking her voice. His arm trembled as he held it aloft, hand beckoning her.

"No," she whispered.

Shaking her head, she paused, forcing herself to breathe and think. *I still have time. Calm yourself. Relax. Look around and think. You can do it. This is the most important five minutes of your life.*

A moment's pause steadied her. Her eyes darted around until she glimpsed him holding up one finger: *Stay with me.* And a thumb: *You can't ignore me.*

"Cole, I can't!"

She turned away, pretending not to see the signal. She couldn't deal with this, not now. She had to find the orb.

Once more, she glanced back; he was flashing his finger and thumb over and over to get her attention.

She shook her head violently.

"No! It's not fair; you can't use it now!" she screamed. "Please stop . . . Cole . . ."

Cole lay there, feeling time slipping away from him, the seconds draining out of him. His hand fell to his side, unable to keep the strength to hold it up. From all the time in the world to not enough. Relief to be free of the time loop's trap blunted his pain. Vella was unharmed; that's all he cared about.

Please don't let her find it, he prayed. *If there is a God, please don't let her find it.*

Tears streamed down the side of his face. "N-no more. Please . . . I can't do it anymore," he begged. "I don't want to go back."

Suddenly, Vella's presence filled his fading vision as she was beside him, placing a hand on his chest.

"Thank you," he breathed, his voice barely above a whisper. It was gratitude not directed at her, but for the powers that brought her back.

Seeing her made him long for the chance to say goodbye to Leah, Alex, and Edgar. He would never see them again. The thought was far more agonizing than the relentless pain that peaked every time he moved or breathed.

"Why?" she asked, fighting through tears.

"Stay . . . with me," he pleaded. "Just for . . . a minute. Just . . . one."

"Cole . . . why . . ." She gripped his hand, holding on as if her touch could keep him anchored to the world. "Why won't you let me help you?"

"You can't," he said, each syllable a struggle. "No more. I can't take it. I'm scared . . . scared worse things will happen." He coughed and wheezed, blood staining his lips as he tried to draw breath into his failing lungs.

"If this is the end . . . I want you with me."

"Let me do it," she begged, her voice rising in desperation. "I'll find it and make sure no one has to die."

"No," he said. "You have n-no idea what it took . . . j-just to get here. I-I can't risk you dying."

"I hate you."

He smiled and squeezed her hand. "I watched you die too many times . . . let me die for you once. P-please . . . l-let me go. It's . . . a-all right."

"Why did you do it? You said no being a hero!"

"I . . . m-messed up. I'm no hero," he said between labored breaths. "We were trapped."

"Dammit, Cole . . . you said . . . you said . . . you said you wouldn't leave me."

"I'm sorry, I don't mean to."

She closed her eyes and shook her head, fighting against the reality she didn't want to accept. "No. I have to go. I have to find it. I will find it. I'll be the hero; I'll save you."

He said nothing, fighting through the searing pain as he managed to return a soft smile.

"Cole, stop . . . I'm pregnant! You can't die."

His smile dropped. "You are?"

"Yes. And you have to be here to meet them."

His smile returned. "You're . . . going to be . . . a wonderful mother."

"Don't say that," she pleaded. "Stop it. Don't leave me. I can't do this without you."

But he just smiled, fighting to keep his eyes open. "I'm sorry . . ."

She buried her face in his chest, tears mixing with his blood.

He used the last of his strength to pull her close, embracing her as tightly as he could manage.

"I love you."

"I love you so much."

"I love you more than you could ever know."

"Cole . . . I have to go . . ."

"I know . . . it's all right," he said. "Look a-after Leah for me . . . s-she won't take this well . . . and tell her I love her. Tell them all. I don't think I ever told them . . . h-how dumb is that?"

"They know," she whispered. "We all know."

She pressed her forehead to his, kissed him one last time, and gazed deeply into his eyes before running off.

I did it. She's safe. If this is it, so be it . . . As he told himself this, he suppressed the urge to call out to her for help. Not that he had the strength to.

Part of him begged for her to find it. To be able to live and continue to fight alongside her. Alongside all of them.

Tears streaked down his face. He was fading fast. His life was out of his hands.

This is it . . . please don't be . . . I don't want to . . .

Help me . . . Vella . . .

His mind faded, and so did those thoughts.

The deaths he had experienced through the orb, the final moments of hundreds of people from Eden. Would they still come to pass? He didn't know. Maybe he had changed everything.

But it was out of his hands now.

Then he realized. It might have never been in his control to begin with.

And he thought, *I would have loved to have seen the lives that came before those endings. I wonder what kind of reality they experienced.*

Cole lay there with a faint smile, his eyes drifting shut as he accepted that it might be for the last time. The pain withered as his mind prepared him for the final journey.

Edgar, Alex, Vella . . . I'm sorry. I'm so sorry, Leah.

Mom, Dad . . . did you hear that? I'm a father. Who would have thought . . .

How amazing it is. It . . . all . . . is . . .

The thought of a child of theirs warmed him, filling him with a sense of peace.

He hoped Leah was right. That there was something after this, a place where they could all be together again.

And with his last breath, he believed it.

He was taken to another time and place. The soft light from outside cast a warm glow over the long table where everyone sat. Laughter and conversation filled the air.

He stood at the doorframe, observing the scene. In front of him, his parents were engaged in a lively conversation with Leah. She laughed and passed Amy to Edgar, who sat her on his lap and wrapped her up in a smothering hug. He kissed her on the forehead as she wriggled to break free, drawing a smile from her.

Next to them, a small boy sat between Ellie and Alex. Ellie licked her thumb and wiped food off his cheek, making him recoil and drop the hand-carved wooden wolf he was holding. Alex was quick to reach down and pick it up, putting it back in the little boy's hands.

Across the table, Vella held a little girl on her lap, her hair and eyes distinctly her mother's. The girl giggled, her tiny hands tugging at Vella's sleeve, trying to get her attention.

He took it all in, his face lined with an easy smile.

Outside the window, vast open fields stretched out to the horizon, mountains adorning the distance. A stretch of open space extended kilometers into the distance, further than he had ever imagined possible. The sky had a vast depth, with layers of clouds moving at their own leisurely pace. The sun had a vibrancy he'd never known. The long grass and trees swayed back and forth in a gentle breeze. It all filled him with an elated sense of wonder.

But what he truly relished was the atmosphere in the room. Vella caught his eye as she lifted the little girl, leaning in to whisper something. The girl giggled, waving at Cole.

He waved back, feeling a deep sense of warm contentment.

As everything faded away, he held tight to that warmth, allowing it to guide him into the gentle embrace of the infinite void.

42

> Today was the best day so far. It marks the first day without a
> needless death.
>
> —THE FIRST PEOPLE OF EDEN
> Journal of Morgan #38
> Day 16

Here it was, sitting in her trembling, blood-soaked hands. She squeezed her eyes shut, gritted her teeth, and hoped beyond all reason for a miracle. When she pressed the button, the familiar sharp zap rippled through her. She opened her eyes and found she was in a different spot, telling her nothing. The trail of her desperate search was evident around her.

Panic surged through her, propelling her to Cole's side. Dropping to her knees, she searched his face for any sign of life. Nothing. She squeezed his arm gently, cradling his head as she pressed her ear to his mouth. No breath. No pulse. She held the back of her hand to his cheek, and she felt her insides twist at the lack of warmth.

"No . . ."

She set him down, grabbed the orb, and pressed it again. The result was the same.

"No, no, no!"

Over and over, she pressed it, desperate for it to take her back further than it was capable of. She prayed it would, or that the brain zaps would kill her. Anything to avoid having to face a future without him. When nothing changed, that terrible reality gripped her.

She knew the truth even before she found the orb. It was too late; he was forever lost.

Screams were torn from her throat, violent and guttural. Only when her voice gave out completely did she stop, her throat raw and shredded from the violent strain. A silent, ragged despair enveloped her.

Then rage consumed her.

Vella tore the spear out of the Bear's ear and hacked into its lifeless body. Each strike spilled more blood, and she paused only to wipe it from her face before continuing. She bashed it again and again, until her muscles burned and exhaustion threatened to make her pass out. Finally, she fell back, her flesh drained of all energy, drenched in its blood.

Struggling for air, feeling lightheaded, she cursed the Bear. She cursed Cole, herself, and the entire universe. As the rage ebbed, despair flooded back in and gripped her.

Vella crawled to Cole's lifeless body, cradling him in her arms, her tears mingling with the blood that covered them both.

A mechanical sound made her look up. The door back to Eden had opened, filtering light across the floor of the arena.

She looked between him and the door and shook her head. With the last of her strength, she dragged him out of the nightmare and back into Eden. A heavy trail of blood stained the ground in their wake. The door slid closed as they passed through it.

The stars and moon filled the sky, but they did nothing to ease her emptiness. With painstaking effort, Vella dragged his body to a nearby tree. She sank against it, cradling him in her arms, both of them soaked in blood, as if they had bathed in it.

Pressing him tightly to her chest, she tried to cling to the last traces of his fading warmth. Her knight with impenetrable armor. Her love. The only person who had ever truly been there for her. Her one and only—Cole. Gone.

Tears flowed until there were none left to shed. She clung to him as physical and mental exhaustion blurred her vision and plunged her into deep unconsciousness, offering her a brief mercy.

There were faint sensations of being touched, carried, and of water touching her skin. There were screams and cries, but they seemed distant, like echoes from another world—or perhaps just memories or a dream.

Vella opened her eyes. She squinted as she felt the sunlight ebb and flow across her face through the fluttering of the familiar curtains.

She lay tightly wrapped in a blanket. Her blood-soaked clothes were gone, replaced with fresh ones. For a brief, fleeting moment, she hoped that everything had just been a horrible dream. She would turn over and see Cole lying beside her, just as he had been yesterday. But her body remembered the pain. It hadn't left; it was reemerging, poised to consume her again.

Slowly, she sat up, her body and mind sinking as she heard voices yelling on the other side of the door. She paid no mind. Numbness wrapped around her like a shroud, keeping the dam inside her from breaking.

Her blank gaze drifted around the bed until it landed on one of Cole's shirts lying at the edge.

Hesitating, she reached for it, then brought it up to her nose. His scent filled her senses, and the tears came again, feeling the overpowering waves of agony. She huddled up under the sheets, clutching the shirt to her chest as she quaked with sobs.

A gentle knock at the door startled her. She flinched and curled up tighter. The door creaked open, and someone crept inside. Vella felt the bed shift as they sat down beside her. The person lay down, slipping under the sheets with her, their body shaping around her own, enclosing her in a warm embrace. The person cried in silence, their tears damp against Vella's back.

She tried to hold back her own tears, but her sorrow was too much to bear. When Vella finally felt like she had nothing left, she fell back into a mentally drained state of nonwaking.

Vella woke to a soft kiss on her forehead. The door creaked shut as the person left, leaving her alone once more.

Moonlight filtered into the room, casting a pale glow over everything. She rose from the bed, wrapping herself in a blanket as she moved to the window, running her eyes across the stars.

They mocked her, reminding her of better nights with . . . someone . . . who? She didn't want to remember.

Her head felt heavy, like it belonged to someone else. Her thoughts moved sluggishly, slipping through her fingers before she could hold on to them. She blinked. Once. Twice. *What's going on?*

Her gaze fell to the backyard. Something that hadn't been

there before stood out: a cart with a long wooden box lying on top.

The sight barely registered at first. She stared at it for a long time, not breathing, not blinking, her mind resisting the obvious.

Realization dawned, bringing with it a wave of dread. She gasped and she clutched her mouth, but no tears came, almost as if her body could produce no more. Numbness enveloped her and saturated everything; there was no emotion left to feel. Her hands dropped to her sides, her mouth hanging open as she stared vacantly.

The blanket slipped off her shoulders and fell to the floor. She stepped over it and opened the window. Like a leaf on the wind, she drifted outside, her body carrying her to the box.

She stood over it, her breathing coming in shallow gasps, but she didn't notice. She stared at the lid for what could have been minutes or hours. Then a hand reached out. Was it hers? She couldn't tell. It must have been; there was no one else around. It lifted the lid of the box.

Cole's body lay inside, wrapped in a bloodstained cloth. She longed to see him again. With trembling hands, she lifted the sheet up to see his face. His expression had an effortless ease to it; she could almost swear he was smiling.

She placed the back of her hand to his cheek. Cold. So very cold.

The ache deepened every second that passed and was becoming unbearable. Unable to look anymore, she covered him and closed the lid.

The only thought she could register was, *He doesn't belong here.*

Feeling a resurgence of autonomy in her muscles, but not her mind, she looked around. A shovel rested against the fence; she grabbed it and placed it on top of the box. She walked to the front of the cart, grasped the handle, and dragged it. She strained to pull the cart out of the yard, down the street, and into the woods—back toward the home they'd built together.

The path grew rougher the deeper she went. Roots and thick shrubs snagged the wheels, until the terrain became too difficult to navigate further.

With no other choice, she abandoned the cart and pulled his body from the box. Gritting her teeth, she dragged him the last fifty meters, the shovel resting on top of him. Her muscles, already drained from last night, burned with each agonizing step.

She set him down beneath the oak tree where they had spent so many quiet hours together. After a brief rest, she picked up the shovel. Her eyes scanned the yard before settling on a spot beside the shed, on the opposite side of her garden. With her mind emptied of all else, she began to dig.

Once she started, she didn't stop. Not even when the early-morning rain fell. It soaked her and made the dirt cling to her skin like the blood had the night before. The work was slow and grueling. Her burning muscles begged for relief, and blisters bloomed on her hands, but she didn't rest.

When she finished, she collapsed beside Cole's lifeless body, staring vacantly into the open grave.

In Eden, burials were unheard of—Ghosts always came to take the dead shortly after death. But no Ghost came for him.

As the first light of day broke through the trees, Vella sat motionless. Her fingers drifted to her stomach, trying to feel some connection to him through the life they had created together. She hoped he would one day meet the child and that they could raise them together. Free of Eden. The life they were supposed to have. Not this.

Behind her, leaves rustled. Branches cracked. She didn't turn. She didn't care.

Alex approached and sat beside her, saying nothing. There was nothing to say. Nothing he could say.

After a while, Alex stood up and moved to Cole's lifeless feet. "Come on," he muttered.

Vella clenched her eyes shut, willing herself to move. When she opened them, she stood and took her place at Cole's head. Together, they lifted him and carried him to the grave, lowering him with care to the earth. Alex lifted the sheet for one last look at his friend before covering him again.

Vella stood to one side, shovel in hand; Alex moved to the other. Leah and Edgar, who had been watching from the edge of the tree line, walked over to stand at the foot of the grave.

Vella scooped a mound of dirt into the shovel and brought it over the grave. Her hands trembled as she tried to let go, but her muscles locked, refusing to drop the dirt on him. The shovel grew heavier and heavier. The weight of it grew unbearable, her hands trembling with the strain. Dirt trickled off the edges as she struggled to keep her grip.

Alex came over, placing his hands gently over hers. Then the dirt finally fell.

"It's okay," he whispered. "I'll do it."

Vella froze, her fingers slack as Alex took the shovel from her unresisting hands.

Leah trembled, her arms crossed, tears trickling down her face. She squeezed her eyes shut, unable to watch. Edgar stared at the grave, his eyes vacant and unfocused, his thoughts miles away. His face was pale and hollow, drained of all emotion.

Alex took a patch of loose dirt and moved it over the grave. Before he could drop it, Leah cried out.

"No!" Her scream tore through them, raw and desperate.

She reached a trembling hand. "Stop! Did you check him? He could still be alive! They haven't come to take him. Check him! Alex! Check him!"

Alex shook his head and turned away. He stabbed the ground and hunched over. After a moment, he took a deep breath and continued to shovel dirt over Cole's body.

"Alex! Stop! He's alive!" she continued to scream. "Why is no one listening?"

He cringed, stopping again. "Edgar, please," he choked out.

Edgar seemed to snap out of a daze. He moved to Leah's side, wrapping an arm around her, but she struck his arm away. Edgar grabbed her with both hands, this time refusing to let go despite her frantic struggle.

"He's gone," he whispered. "I'm sorry."

"No . . . he can't be!" she uttered. "Alex?"

He turned toward her and shook his head, unable to meet her gaze.

Finally, it sank in, and she collapsed into Edgar, shaking with grief. He held on, trying to soothe her through her heart-wrenching sobs.

"I promised them . . . I promised them I would keep him safe. I promised . . ."

Alex kept shoveling, trying to finish before he, too, became overwhelmed. He picked up the pace, barely holding on.

Vella saw the whole scene play out as if she were outside her body, floating above and looking down at what was incomprehensible to her mind. For the time being, her mind protected her, numbing the pain and everything around her.

It's a joke, her mind assured her. *They're messing with you. This isn't real.*

Alex finished filling the grave and slumped over. Without a word, he turned and walked away.

Vella thought she saw him break the shovel against a tree. She wasn't sure. She couldn't tell if any of it was real. Was it all her imagination, or was she caught in a vivid dream?

The echo in her mind kept trying to convince her: *This isn't real.*

43

Lyle: I always believed I was bad at soccer as a kid. I was too short, always picked last, and no one would pass me the ball. But I wanted to be good . . . so badly. Eventually, I stopped believing and stopped playing altogether. One day, the orphanage headmaster saw me watching the others play and asked me to meet her in the yard at dawn. She was quite good herself—she played in the weekend leagues. I loved watching her, she always seemed one step ahead of everyone else. Anyway, every morning after that, she practiced with me. She believed in me, and slowly . . . I started to believe in myself. A few months later, I scored my first goal. That's the one I always remember.

Aleister: I didn't think the weekend league's top scorer five years running started out like that.

Lyle: It might have stayed that way if it weren't for someone believing in me. I wanted to be the best I could be. For her. I wanted to repay the favor, make her proud.

Aleister: I'm sure you did.

Lyle: She was the last person I saw. She said I'd lived a life I should be proud of because I never gave up.

Aleister: Do you agree?

Lyle: I tried . . . And she always said that's the important thing.

—"LYLE #8901"

CHILDREN OF THE PEACEFUL PASSAGE
by Aleister #8990

Edgar took it upon himself to look after Vella, who hadn't left the shed since that day.

Three times a day, he brought her food. At first, he would drop it off without lingering, finding her curled up in bed or huddled in the corner. She didn't eat the first day. The second day, she ate one out of three meals.

By the third day, he stayed and sat with her. He would set down the food next to her, then move to the opposite side of the shed, remaining silent. Vella ignored both him and the food, her eyes glazed over, mind gone.

Each day, he stayed a little longer. Five minutes turned to fifteen, and by the fifth day, he sat with her for half an hour, still silent and unmoving. She didn't acknowledge him, but after a few days, she ate with him in the room. A marginal improvement. To Edgar, a win was a win.

Still, there was a long way to go.

He would often watch her put food to her mouth, only to drop it. The purpose of even eating was lost to her. *What's the point? Why eat when what you're really craving can never be satisfied? When it's gone forever? There's nothing more torturous than that,* Edgar thought. *Despair takes hold, and the will dies.* He was all too familiar with the feeling.

What can stop the spiral? How do you no longer feel that craving for what made life worth all that pain?

Accept. Accept that it will never return and appreciate what you had to begin with.

No, but you want it. You crave it. You can't live without it.

And how can you accept what was avoidable? Knowing it wasn't out of your control. The whole time, you could have done something.

If you're lucky, you'd ask yourself what you could have done differently, based on what you knew at the time. Which is nothing. Can you change it? No. That could offer a way out of the trap. But can you accept or believe that? Everything could have been as it should be if you had done something slightly different. Oh, if only.

It's your fault and you know it. But is it really your fault? Someone has to be responsible, right? But you can't blame anyone because you are the one in control. The only thing you could control was your actions.

Could you even control yourself, though? It feels like a distant person, not you. That person in the past, you hate them like it's not you. It's not; it's a worse, more ignorant version of yourself.

For a time, you can't hate that person because they didn't know any better, so you blame the people and experiences that created that flawed person. Anger rises from how it was taken from you. How unfair the world is. You despair over never having been in control.

The cycle repeats and you're back to blaming yourself because blaming external factors cannot satisfy you.

You're stuck changing between blaming internal and external factors.

None of it solves the problem. All it does is keep you trapped.

You just want them back.

Acceptance is not an option.

So how do you actually escape the craving before the soul dies of starvation?

How could he help her with something he could never deal with himself?

He mulled it over while sitting with her.

On the seventh night, Vella finally spoke. Out of irritation or boredom, he wasn't sure; he didn't care.

"How long are you going to keep this up?" she muttered, not looking at him.

Relief washed over Edgar, but he forced himself to remain calm. "As long as it takes."

"For what?"

"For you to come back home with us."

"You might be dead before then," she said, without a hint of humor.

He leaned back against the wall. "So be it. There are worse places to spend my last year."

She remained fixed on the wall like she was speaking to a ghost. "What could possibly be worse?"

He hoped this was the moment he could catch her. "Being alone."

She swallowed, her voice tightening. "Like he left me alone."

"You're not alone," Edgar said. "Leah misses you. Alex misses you. Leah tells me people at work keep asking about you."

She said nothing more, and Edgar knew better than to push her. He sat with her a while longer, but when it grew late, he stood up to leave.

"I put the orb in the box up there," Edgar said, pointing. "I trust you won't use it."

"What's the point? It can't bring him back. It's useless."

Edgar sighed. "I just want to make sure you won't do anything rash. The blue door is gone, and it's causing quite the stir in town. A lot of questions are being asked. No one knows about the orb, Alex assures me. But just in case, make sure to keep it hidden."

As he reached for the door, she spoke up.

"What *is* the point?" she asked.

He pulled his hand back and sat down against the door.

"Without him, I can't see it . . . there's no point in being alive just to be alive."

"For you . . . there are so many reasons," he said. "Your baby, for one."

Her head snapped to him, eyes narrowing. It was the first time she'd actually looked at him in a week, and it was not the look he was hoping to receive.

"How—?"

"I know morning sickness when I see it. It was the same with Leah."

Vella's jaw clenched, her fists curling into the blanket around her. "You were spying on me?"

"Looking out for you," Edgar said. "Don't worry. It will stay between us."

She turned away, shaking her head, anger flashing in her eyes. For Edgar, it was a joy to see the first sign of life she'd shown in days. "I would've ended it by now, if it weren't for . . . ." She glanced down, brushing a hand against her stomach. "Our child. But I'm stuck here, forced to endure every second of my worthless existence. Waiting to spread the curse of this place to them."

"He didn't die so you could stop living."

"He died for nothing."

"It wasn't for nothing."

"I could've saved him. I can't do anything. Do you know what it's like? Always out of your depth. Never being in control, always needing someone else to save you." Her frustration rose with each word. "I had that one chance to save him . . . that was meant to be my moment . . . but I . . . I failed. He died for nothing. What've I ever done for him? For anyone. I feel like I can't even breathe properly, like I'm not in control of that either."

Edgar rose. "I've learned that the moments when we're truly needed to save others aren't when we expect them—or even want them. Most of the time, you don't even realize you're saving someone when it's happening. You did more for him than you'll ever understand. And for me."

"What've I ever done for you?"

He said nothing further and left.

"How is she?" Leah asked.

"She finally spoke."

"Good."

Leah sat curled up in a blanket, her armchair positioned by the front window as she stared at the empty street.

"Do you need anything?" Edgar asked.

She shook her head, not tearing her gaze away from the window.

"You're not going to stay out here all night again?"

She said nothing.

He let out a weary sigh. "Okay . . ." He went to his room, grabbing the blanket and pillow. He dragged the spare armchair next to her.

After getting as comfortable as he could, he watched her wait for something that would never come.

The next morning, after breakfast, Vella sat with a book in her lap—*The Knights of Acidalia*. Edgar noticed the bookmark near the end. She opened it, read for a couple of pages and then flipped it back to the first page, ignoring the last few chapters.

"Why didn't you tell him the real ending?" Edgar asked, gesturing at the book.

Vella lowered the book and glanced at him, eyebrows furrowed.

"I've read it before," he said. "A while ago."

She scowled, remembering. "When I told him the story . . . That was you . . . That noise . . . You were spying on us?"

"I happened to be in the area."

His answer only made her anger more evident.

"Fine . . . I was hanging around outside Cole's place. I wanted to talk to Leah but couldn't work up the nerve . . . How pathetic is that? Then I saw Cole walk out of the house, and he looked troubled. I got worried, so I followed him to make sure he was all right. When I saw he had gone to see you, I thought about leaving. But, against my better judgment, I stuck around."

Vella's expression softened, if only slightly. "Why?"

He took his time, knowing what he wanted to say but unable to do so. He felt himself sinking, reminding himself of things he didn't want to remember. He looked around, seeing a couple of Cole's drawings hung up on the back wall. The one he focused on was one of Vella working in the garden.

"You two have something special," he began.

"Had . . ." she muttered.

"Sorry," he said. "I stuck around because I wanted to feel it again for a few minutes, even if only vicariously, one more time."

Vella rubbed her eye, and he couldn't tell if the gesture was from tears or some irritation.

"I was about to leave. But then I heard you start to tell him your version of the story, so I stayed. I wanted to hear it."

She sniffed and wiped her nose, hiding her face.

"Why did you change it?" he asked.

Her words were short and sharp. "Because the real ending isn't fair. I hate it."

In her version, the boy and girl, Isara and Drystan, defeated the last great chaos beasts together and went on to rule as king and queen, living happily ever after.

In the real ending, Isara was mortally wounded as she delivered the killing blow to the second chaos beast, Ifrit. Drystan stayed by her side, feeling her life slip away. With the queen's death and the barrier fading, he pleaded with the gods to spare Isara, offering himself in her place. His prayers were heard. The powers bestowed upon him by the gods passed to her, along with the last of his life. When she awoke, Drystan was gone, dead by her side. Grief consumed her as she lost what felt like the other half of her, but she had no time to mourn. The great dragon Bahamut descended upon the kingdom. Steeling herself, she rose—now granted Drystan's armor and shield. Alone, she fulfilled the prophecy. The promised knight, strengthened by the sacrifices of Drystan and the queen, slew the dragon and saved the kingdom. Isara became queen, ruling alone, carrying the weight for both of them. She brought peace and prosperity to the kingdom of Acidalia for the rest of her days.

"The end is the best part. I was looking forward to you telling it," Edgar said.

"Why? She's left all alone. How's that a happy ending?"

"It's not. You're seeing it all wrong. I don't blame you—you were misled. It was never a book about knights and monsters. It's about making do with what we are given. Carrying on when what you love the most is taken from you. Trying our best and still giving all we have to offer to others, despite taking all the pain and suffering we could possibly handle. And Isara, despite everything, did that."

She said nothing, eyeing her bookmark still placed at the latter part of the book.

"You deserve to know the truth," he said.

"Know what?"

He took a deep breath. "I should've told you sooner . . . your mother wrote it."

She looked at him, steady and unfazed.

"You knew?" he asked.

"I think I've always known," she said, looking down at the book, then back at him. "How'd you know her?"

He gave her a soft smile. "I was one of the first to read it. She put it on display, but no one touched it for weeks. I noticed how she kept eyeing it, so I decided to try it for her. When I finished, she asked what I thought. I told her it was beautiful. Sad, but beautiful. Bittersweet. But my words didn't seem to sink in," Edgar said. His voice fell soft and low thinking of her. "She was so much like the queen in the story. Her strength was fading every day . . . you were her, Isara, her shining knight."

Something broke in her; tears came unbidden. Her voice cracked as she whispered, "I was supposed to be Drystan, not Isara."

"Most of the time, we don't get a choice," he said. "You might not have slain legendary beasts, but you were Cole's strength. Acts of heroism aren't like the ones in books. The real heroes are the ones who get up every day and try to make a difference. They are the ones who don't give up despite everything. And you don't seem like someone who gives up. After Isara lost her powers and became queen, that's when she truly left her mark. Anyone could've done what she did with those powers. But it was the days and years that followed when she helped her people in the aftermath. That's what really mattered."

Vella stared down at where the bookmark lingered.

"Look at how much you leave unread. It's not exciting or fun to read about, but it's the most important part."

She shook her head, as if trying to shake away his words.

"She wrote that for you," he added. "So you could have the strength she couldn't find."

Vella opened her mouth to speak, but no words could form in her mind. Her focus shifted to the book in her lap. She was fighting a war within, which Edgar could sense as her expression shifted every few seconds.

"She didn't write it for me."

"Did you ever find it strange that there's a page missing after the cover?"

She flipped the book to its cover, opened it, and ran her fingers along the tear in the border. "Could have been anything," she said.

"It wasn't ripped out when I first read it."

She clenched her jaw, afraid to ask him what it said.

"It said, 'Written by Rebecca. For my shining light, Vella.'"

"No." The word came out like a reflex. "Liar. Then why did she rip it out?"

"I swear on Amy, I'm not lying. I can't say for sure why she tore it out . . . I think she was too hard on herself, and she might not have wanted to take any credit for it. I don't know. It feels like she wanted to erase any proof of her existence before she . . . left."

She sat in silence, lost in thought, still feeling for the torn page.

"Can you read it to me? I would like to hear it one more time."

They sat in silence for a time. Then, without a word of confirmation, she flipped it open to the bookmark and read.

What he didn't tell her was what her mother had added after the dedication: *My baby, I'm sorry for the curse of life I have inflicted upon you.*

He stayed with Vella until she finished the story. Then, sometime in the middle of the night, Edgar returned home.

Leah's chair by the window was empty.

He smiled faintly and went to bed.

Lying down alone, he felt something inside him breaking. He hoped and prayed sleep would come and sweep him away before worse things did.

But sleep didn't come. The other things did.

The creaking of the door saved him.

Without a word, Leah slipped into bed, nestling herself in front of him. She grabbed his arm and pulled it around her, shuffling closer.

He held tight to her, needing this as much as she did.

The next day, Edgar sat with Vella in his usual position across the room. He held an effortless smile that persisted too long for Vella's liking.

"I hated it when he smiled like that," Vella muttered.

He overplayed his smile to tempt her. "Like what?"

A hint of a smile ghosted her lips. "Stop."

"Well, at least you haven't forgotten how to smile yourself," he said.

She shook her head. "That damn easy, everything's-gonna-be-fine smile. The annoying smile when there's nothing to actually smile about. It drove me crazy."

He motioned to her ankle. "I noticed your timer," Edgar said. "You've been given ten more years."

She was quick to hide her ankle under the blanket. "As if they thought I hadn't suffered enough. The last thing I want is more time. Those bastards have quite the sense of humor."

"You'll be the first forty-year-old in Eden's history."

"Thirty-nine. At forty, I'll be dead," she corrected, her tone devoid of energy.

"Still, a record, one of a kind."

Vella scoffed, her tone bitter. "Who cares? I can't even bear another minute without him, let alone another twenty years."

Edgar's smile faded. "You need to forgive him . . . and yourself."

She sat silent, retreating further into herself.

"I'm serious. It's not your fault."

She clenched her jaw and gripped the blanket. "I made him do it. He wouldn't have gone in there if it weren't for me. I lied to him. I passed it off as urgency for others when it was selfishness. I didn't want our baby to be born here. He would've stopped me from helping if I'd told him I was pregnant . . . I could have stopped him if I'd told him."

"Or would he have just gone by himself?"

"I could've talked him out of it. I killed him . . ."

"No," Edgar said. "I'm the one who robbed you of your future together. I was selfish. I thought I could let this whole thing go on longer than it should have because, for the first time, I was enjoying my life. I could've stopped it sooner, but I didn't. His death's on me."

Vella's hands trembled, her teeth gritted as tears welled up in her eyes. "I killed him," she managed. "I'm the reason he's dead . . . I couldn't save him."

He'd pressed a thumb into the rawest part of her wound. As the tears fell and didn't stop, her sobs echoed in the small shed. She curled into herself, leaning on the wall, her grief overwhelming her.

"I can't do this," she cried. "How am I supposed to live without him? I can't do it."

Edgar got up and sat beside her, resisting the urge to put an arm around her. "You can do it. You will do it."

But his words had the opposite effect, deepening her pain. "I'm worthless without him. Nothing." She latched onto him out of desperation, burying her face in his shoulder as the tears flowed.

"Don't say that," Edgar whispered. "You mean everything to us. We need you."

She didn't respond; her sobs continued as she pushed her head further into his body.

"I'm sorry," he whispered.

He knew nothing he said would ease her pain. So he stayed. He stayed until all her grief came out.

Vella, utterly exhausted, rested her head on his shoulder. She fell asleep, but it wasn't a peaceful one. As the night wore on, Edgar fell asleep beside her, unwilling to leave her alone.

The following morning, they shared breakfast and lunch in a comfortable silence. Edgar could see small changes in Vella: her posture a little less tight and rigid, her eyes a little less vacant. It was small, important progress.

That evening, after they finished eating, Edgar noticed her still staring at the same small patch of wall, her face still marked with despair but also with a glimmer of life returning.

"I've been asking myself something for a while . . ." he began.

Vella looked at him, but this time, she didn't turn away after a fleeting glance.

"Why did I get a second chance? Out of everyone . . . why me . . . ? Then, one day, I realized why." His stare became unfocused, drifting inward.

"Well?"

He blinked and refocused on her. "I was hoping for a grand purpose. But there isn't one. I got lucky, that's all," Edgar said with deep sadness. "No. No grand plan. No plan for me. Or for any of us."

"You're right about that," Vella muttered under her breath.

"No . . . no grand plan . . ." he mused. Then he cleared his throat and lifted his head. "But I learned what's important. I knew it before, but it made sure to press itself into me. It's people. Cole, you, Alex, Leah, Amy. That's all the purpose I need, anyone needs. We can't exist by ourselves; that's not how it works. We depend on each other; there's very little we can actually do on our own."

He stared at his palm, flexing his fingers, studying the fine workings of his muscles.

"See . . . it's all a matter of beliefs. That is, what you choose to believe. Not what you know but what you believe, deep down. Needing a grand purpose or even the existence of the concept is a belief. Who needs it? All I need is to sit here with you."

She let out a bitter chuckle. "That's why you got a second chance? To sit here and comfort worthless trash like me?"

"I wish you wouldn't talk about yourself that way," Edgar said, a hint of frustration in his voice. "Who knows what great deeds you'll accomplish one day? You could change everything, or you could help someone that does."

"That's insane."

He let out a soft laugh. "Maybe so. You saying that is just a belief, one that can be changed. Beliefs shape everything around us. We're slaves to our beliefs. If we believe that life is meaningless then it's bleak, dreary; if we believe it's worthwhile, then . . ." He glanced around and smiled. "And if you believe you're strong and capable, you can do anything."

"What if I believe you're stupid?"

"Then you wouldn't listen to a word I'm saying. But if you believed I'm smart, wise, flawless, amazing, genius—"

"Enough," she said, shaking her head with a small smile. "You're making me sick."

He returned the smile. "Point is, *I believe* there doesn't need to be anything more than being there for people that might need me. I had no one that needed me before. Now I do and I'll do anything for those people, especially you. So, my second chance gave me something; it did give me a purpose. It might not be defined as a grand one, but it feels grand to me. And by helping those who needed me, I discovered something so amazing I never thought I'd have the chance to experience."

"What's that?"

"I think you know."

She did.

"It can feel like you don't get a choice in what you believe." He paused, smile fading. "There's a difference between what you know and what you actually believe deep down. It's hard to rid those beliefs so deeply ingrained they feel part of your very being. The ones that tell you you're not good enough have roots that have grown too deep. How could you possibly get rid of them? I get it . . . Tell me, do you believe in Cole?"

She nodded.

"What did he think about you?"

"I don't know."

He chuckled. "What would he say about you?"

Her face and posture stiffened; she seemed to withdraw into herself, shaking her head in discomfort.

"You already know but can't believe it. I know. All I ask is that you try."

She said nothing.

"Can you do me a favor?"

She gave a weak nod.

"Believe Cole's death is no one's fault. And if you can't do that and you need to blame someone, blame me. For your sake."

Edgar let out a heavy sigh, as if all his energy had drained from him in that moment. It was as though the past had finally caught up with him, pinning him down, forcing him into submission.

"Can I ask for another favor?"

"What's that?"

"Can I tell you about that night? The night I found the orb."

She hesitated, then gave a small nod.

44

I've never regretted doing or trying anything. It's the things I never did or said that haunt me. It's the moments you know you'll never get a second chance at. That is pure torture. Miss those, and you will never forgive yourself. I could have stopped Laura. I keep replaying our last moments together. The truth was there. She told me everything in one look, and I refused to see it. That's what destroys the soul. You don't realize how little you have been trying until you finally put in the effort. Then it hits on you. You ruined your one small, fragile chance at life. How wrong it's all been. They were right there. You just needed to try a little more for them, to talk to them, to sacrifice for them. But you didn't. Now it's too late and you're all alone.

—THE FIRST PEOPLE OF EDEN
Journal of Morgan #38
Day 1834

The air around Edgar felt thick, heavy, like he existed underwater. Air streamed around him, but his breath came in constricted, shallow, uneven bursts. He saw the air swirling, flowing freely everywhere but through him, as if repelled by his very existence. He felt like an outsider in his own world. His chest remained locked in place, clamped by some invisible force, while his head swam in a fog, disconnected from his body.

Don't go. She doesn't want to see you. She hates you.

The thought hammered into his mind, over and over. A mantra of self-loathing.

He stood frozen at the door, his hand resting on the knob, hoping that something—anything—would stop him. Divine intervention, a freak accident, anything to save him from the weight of his very own existence.

Breathe. You can do this.

With a sharp exhale, Edgar yanked the door open, as if ripping off a bandage. The cool evening air hit him, but it didn't bring the boost of resolve he hoped for. His vision blurred, moisture forming at the corners of his eyes. He brushed them away, refusing to let them fall.

He stepped outside. The reality of his situation gripped him like someone was twisting his insides. Nothing changed. The dread clung to him like a second skin, heavier than before.

Edgar arrived early to the party, hoping a drink would settle his nerves. He'd already had several before leaving the house, so he doubted it would help, but he didn't know what else to do. He sat at a table, alone, watching people file in with bright smiles and laughter. The vibrant sights and sounds grated against him, making the storm inside him rage all the more violently.

What the hell am I doing here? Stupid.

He downed his drink, shot up, and shoved his hands into his pockets to hide the shaking. With his head down, he hurried out, avoiding eye contact with anyone.

He wandered without purpose, his head spinning. Turmoil churned in his mind, thoughts running wild and unchecked. Anger swelled as he desperately willed his mind to stop, but it didn't. Helplessness consumed him, fueling his frustration. The storm inside him grew stronger every second. The more he tried to push his thoughts and feelings away, the more chaos consumed him. His steps quickened, aimless and desperate, his mind begging for help. He felt himself being torn apart from within, with no relief in sight. He needed it to stop.

Finally, his feet brought him to a crimson door.

All rational thought vanished in the face of the despair and dread of his unbearable existence. He couldn't bear the burden anymore—the pain, the torment, the emptiness. It needed to end. One way or another.

With trembling hands, he slammed his hand against the door scanner. He stepped inside, eyes blurred with tears, heart consumed with rage.

"Hey!" Edgar screamed.

The savage growl and the sound of heavy footsteps didn't faze him.

He welcomed it.

The Wolf rounded the corner, monstrous and intimidating. Edgar's gaze darted around until he spotted a spear with a broken handle lying on the ground. He grabbed it, pointing it forward.

He didn't think. He charged, reckless and wild, into the jaws of death.

For the first time in years, he felt alive.

The beast swatted him aside like a bug, sending him crashing into the wall. His body crumpled in the corner, bloodied and broken. Consciousness faded. His bloodied hand stretched out, fingers brushing against something smooth and cold.

With a final burst of fury, he gripped the object, pulling his hand back, attempting to throw it at the beast. Then came an instant surge of nothingness.

His head pulsed. Then, as if waking from a dream, he found himself standing fifty meters outside the door. He looked down at his body—clean, whole. No blood, no broken bones, no holes, no tears. Nothing.

What . . . ?

Edgar stood in a daze for what seemed like an infinite stretch of time, trying to process the impossible. The memory of the Wolf, the blood, the crushing pain.

Did that not happen?

But he knew better. The pain was too sharp, the smells too sickening to imagine, and the sights . . . they would never fade.

Looking down, he finally noticed a black orb sitting in his palm.

He examined the orb closely, gradually piecing together its logic. He tested it several times and returned to the same spot over and over. After further testing, he was able to uncover its secrets, just as Cole would do the next day.

Whatever this thing was, it had given him a second chance. The thought should have filled him with joy, but all he felt was emptiness.

The same question circled in his mind: *Why me? Why am I alive?*

Edgar had been ready to end his life, but now he had been handed a second chance. *Why?* He couldn't find any meaning in it.

His mind, still in turmoil from his near suicide, froze in shock, briefly calming the storm within. In a surge of anger, he threw it as hard as he could against the perimeter wall. It bounced right back, hitting him in the chest. He checked it. Completely undamaged.

Frustrated and with nothing else to do, he walked. Consciously or unconsciously, he found his way back to the party. He looked around, watching the people at the party. They were still laughing, still enjoying themselves.

His eyes fell on Leah. She stood on the stage, with Amy about to present her with a gift.

Edgar watched from afar. His chest tightened. He wanted to be a part of that moment—a real part of it—not just an observer.

Before he knew it, his legs were moving, taking him closer to the stage.

He scooped up Amy in his arms, ignoring the orphanage worker, and strode toward Leah. She froze when she saw him coming; a mix of confusion and panic flashed in her eyes.

Her voice was trembling. "Edgar, what—what are you doing?"

The crowd, unsure of how to react, went quiet.

Ignoring everyone, he pressed Amy into Leah's arms, wrapping both of them in a tight embrace. He disregarded the eyes on him as the crowd watched in stunned silence. All that mattered was what he held in his arms.

"Edgar," she growled.

"I want one moment," he said. "Just one memory of us together. Pretend . . . just for a second that we're a family."

Leah's whole body tensed, but Amy nestled into her arms, resting her small head against her chest. Feeling the warmth of her daughter, Leah glanced down and allowed herself to relax.

"I love you both so much," Edgar whispered.

For a brief moment, the world narrowed to just the three of them. No one else in the universe existed.

But as fast as the moment came, it slipped away.

Edgar stood at the back of the party, watching the events

unfold as they were meant to. Amy stepped forward to give Leah the present, and the two embraced. All without him.

For a long time, he stayed hidden in the shadows, watching, observing the flow of life around him. He felt as if he had already died and no part of him existed in this world anymore.

He tossed the orb up and down, pondering what to do next. After holding Amy in his arms, he felt lighter and more at ease. His thoughts were clearer.

What do I do with this? He took a few more drinks, slipping deeper into delusion and fantasy. *Maybe I could make Leah love me again. Good one, Edgar. No, even if this thing could take me back several years, I'd probably just mess things up again. But if only it could . . . How I wish it could . . . Even if it could . . . Did she ever love me to begin with?*

The orb seemed to mock him. It could fix recent mistakes, but the long-term ones? There was no escape. Just looking at it made him sick. He wanted nothing to do with it. Yet, there was still one thing left he wanted to do.

Edgar approached Leah's table. Luckily for him, Leah sat with only a few others; most had gone to dance, leaving the space around her relatively quiet.

Cole and Vella were there, and Edgar caught Cole's expression. A silent warning flashed across Cole's face: *Don't ruin this night.*

"Hey, Leah," Edgar uttered.

Leah turned, surprised to hear his voice. Cole's stern expression didn't fade, but Leah smiled, her face still warm from the joy of being with Amy earlier.

"Can I talk to you?" he asked. "Alone."

Leah tilted her head, glancing at Cole and Vella, as if to reassure them—especially Cole—that everything was okay.

"Sure," she said.

Together, they moved to the side, finding a quiet corner away from the lights.

"Where've you been?" Leah asked. "I haven't seen you all day."

"You were expecting to see me?" he asked with genuine confusion.

Leah frowned, crossing her arms. "A happy birthday would've been nice," she said with a small huff, though the easy smile remained.

"Sorry," Edgar muttered, his eyes fixed on the ground. "I didn't think . . ."

"What?" she interrupted. "That I wouldn't want to see you?"

Edgar looking up. "Well, yeah."

She jabbed her finger into his forehead. "You always were thick. Get out of your head."

That touch, that familiar gesture—it nearly broke him. He let out a small chuckle, more out of habit than joy. For a moment, he was transported back to a simpler time when Leah was always there to set him straight and push him out of his mind's traps.

"Where have you been hiding anyway?" Leah asked, her tone softening. "You should come see me every now and then."

He could only manage a shrug. There were too many words for him to say.

Leah's eyes softened, her expression shifting from playful to serious. "What's going on?" she asked.

Instead of answering, he shook his head, unable to find the right words. Swallowing hard, he fought to keep the flood of emotions at bay.

"Oh, my dear Edgar . . ." She reached out to place a reassuring hand on his arm. "I'm sorry. I haven't been there for you."

"I'm not your problem," he said.

"You became my problem a long time ago. We're still family, you know. I guess . . . I forgot that." Leah sighed, shaking her head. "Everything's too much. I can barely keep myself together most days. But that's no excuse."

"It's okay," he said. "Really. I'm happy just seeing you now . . . and Amy."

A spark of energy consumed her, her face lit up, and she bounced up and down like she was a teenage girl again. She gave his shoulder a light shove, her eyes widening. "Did you see our girl?"

Edgar couldn't help but smile. "She is something."

"We did that," she exclaimed. "Unbelievable. Isn't it?"

Edgar's smile faltered as he looked away, the words he'd been holding onto bubbling to the surface. He took a deep breath, steadying himself.

"I'm glad I got to talk to you," he said. "Look . . . I want you to know . . . I . . . I love you, Leah. I always have, and I wish you loved me too. That's all I wanted to say."

Leah's eyes welled up, and she opened her mouth to say something. But before she could utter a syllable, he was already back at the fringes of the park. Where he belonged.

Edgar remained in the darkness, watching Leah from afar. The noise of the party buzzed around him, but it felt like a distant hum, not part of his reality. He downed several more drinks, trying to settle the storm still brewing inside him. The alcohol numbed some of the edges, but not enough. It never could.

People filtered out as the night drifted on. Edgar stayed seated, letting the emptiness of the night swallow him whole. He considered talking to Leah again, and this time going a step further. Even in his state, he managed to rid himself of the thought.

He took another drink, his mind still on Leah's confession and how she was struggling. It ate at him. She might not be doing much better than he was, and he wasn't doing anything to help her.

As he sat there in his own silence, Cole and Vella passed by. They shared a quiet laugh in the warm embrace of each other's company. The intimacy between them stung, a sharp reminder of everything he had lost. It felt like a shadow of him and Leah, a echo of something long gone. What they had—what Cole had—could never be returned to him.

He stood up on a whim, his legs moving before his mind caught up. He followed them, keeping to the shadows.

Memories of Cole flooded back—those fiery teenage years, the defiance, the anger. And then, before all that, was that one fateful day. The day Cole's parents were torn apart right in front of him. He remembered Leah struggling to hold him back from running into the carnage. Even now, Edgar wondered how much Leah still fought to keep Cole from self-destructing.

A tinge of resentment burned. Cole had taken so much of Leah's time and energy—time Edgar could've spent with her, time he deserved. But the feeling passed just as quickly as it came. The truth was, without Cole, Leah would still have slipped through his fingers. He knew that. The thing that really made Edgar envious was Cole's fire. The spark of life that burned so brightly inside him was something that Edgar had lost long ago.

And then there was Vella. Cole had love. Edgar only had memories.

He thought back to the countless times Cole spoke fiercely about freeing them all. About being the one to lead them out. Leah and Cole argued about it nonstop. The look Cole had in his eyes burned itself into his memory.

The conviction with which he spoke, the unwavering belief that he could change everything, almost scared Edgar. He meant every word.

It wasn't just his parents; he hated Eden for how they treated Vella, and he wanted to get her out. Edgar could still see that fire flickering in Cole's eyes.

He actually believed it. Does he still? Edgar wondered. He glanced down at the orb in his hand.

I might not be able to use this . . . but maybe he can.

The thought lingered, picking at him, too enticing to ignore. He thought of the creature he'd faced, the monster that had almost killed him. *Impossible.* It was an unstoppable force. But if anyone was crazy enough to try, it was him. Cole could do it— save Leah, save Amy.

He tailed Cole and Vella as they made their way toward Leah's house. He kept his distance, stopping outside the house as they disappeared into the woods. He sat down on the front step, the orb heavy in his hands.

An hour passed, and then the soft crunch of footsteps on gravel pulled him from his thoughts.

"Can I help you?" Cole snapped.

"Cole . . . ," Edgar whispered.

"Leah's still at the party," Cole muttered, rubbing his eyes.

Edgar shook his head, pulling himself up.

"Then what do you want? I'm tired."

After a moment, Edgar's eyes met his. "Do you love her?"

"What're you talking about?"

"Vella."

Cole stiffened. After some hesitation, he responded, "What do you care?"

"Answer the question," Edgar demanded.

Cole looked away, hesitating. Then, with a quiet sigh, he answered, "Yeah. Of course."

"Why?"

"Edgar . . . What . . . ?"

"Humor me."

A smile ghosted across Cole's face. "Because there's no life without her."

Edgar nodded; the answer was enough for him. "Don't let her go. Ever."

Cole swallowed hard.

"How's Leah?" Edgar asked.

"What do you mean?"

"You know what I mean."

Cole took a moment to think. "She's trying. But . . . sometimes . . . I don't know. What's it to you anyway?"

"If I ask it of you, would you save her?"

"What're you talking about?" Cole's confusion deepened at this whole conversation.

"I've got something that can help you," Edgar said. "I'll give it to you if you promise."

Cole's patience was wearing thin. "What thing?"

Edgar held out the orb. "This. It'll let you travel back in time."

Cole chuckled, shaking his head. "You're drunk."

"You won't remember, so it won't matter even if I explain it. So . . . how much do you want to save Leah and Vella?" Edgar asked, his eyes burning into Cole's.

"I'd do anything," Cole said with no hesitation in his voice.

Edgar studied him, searching for something in his eyes. "Are you afraid?"

Cole frowned. "Afraid of what?"

He was met with silence from Edgar.

Cole stared down in thought. "I am . . . but not of pain or death . . ."

"So, do you promise to save them?"

"I don't need to promise anything to you. Of course I will."

Edgar smiled and nodded.

He returned to the time before Cole arrived. He rose from the step and walked toward the street. Cole approached, and they exchanged a few words. Edgar handed him the orb and walked away.

As he wandered by the party, he spotted Leah in the distance. He pretended he wished her a happy birthday and turned away, heading home alone to drink himself to sleep.

45

It's been a week since Laura left us. How does anyone keep going after losing someone so important? I admire the strength of those who can. I have our girls to think about, so I keep going. For them. Why didn't I see it? After giving birth to our second child, Mary, she was never the same. I remember her eyes. She lost something that day. Or maybe it was long before that. I will never know.

—THE FIRST PEOPLE OF EDEN

Journal of Morgan #38

Day 1568

Vella found herself immersed in Edgar's story and in someone else's life. Her own grief, for a moment, seemed distant, even insignificant in comparison. A wave of guilt washed over her.

Her posture softened, her body turning instinctively toward him. He'd left out some of the details about him and Leah, but the weight of what he did reveal resonated with her. She felt something she hadn't quite felt before—someone who was capable of understanding her.

"I wasn't thinking about him. Or you. I used him for my own selfish needs," Edgar admitted. "And I didn't stop things soon enough."

For a moment, Vella stared at him, still processing his experience. When she finally spoke, it wasn't the reaction he was prepared for.

"Why the door? Why the Wolf?" she asked. "Why that way? There were others."

Edgar blinked, thrown off balance. Words expressing her anger or judgment would've made sense, but not this. Not curiosity about the details of his attempted suicide. He fumbled for words. Caught off guard, his mind struggling to connect her reasoning for the question.

Vella filled in the silence as his mind raced. "I never told him, but I almost did it," she confessed. "The day I left the orphanage."

She raised her hand. Staring at the back of it. As though she were back in that moment, one inch from ending it all.

"My hand was right there . . . just a little further, and . . ." Her eyes grew distant, feeling how close it was. "I almost did what you did."

"V-Vella . . . why would you do that?"

As if he never spoke, she pressed on, still caught in that moment long ago. "Then I heard him call my name. He saved me. I have no doubt I would have done it. I wanted nothing more than to be finally rid of it all." She exhaled slowly. "Especially . . . to be rid of myself."

"You don't mean that."

Vella's gaze lifted from her hand and settled on him, piercing him. "Why choose the worst way?" she repeated. "I know why I did. But why did you choose that path?"

"I don't know," he said barely above a whisper. "It happened to be there."

"Was it because you believed it was what you deserved?"

"What I deserved . . . ?"

She nodded, her eyes sharp. "Was it because you couldn't take any more, or did you feel like you deserved to die, not only that but deserved to suffer?"

He could only manage a shrug.

"Well? Which is it?"

She caught him in an invisible bind, freezing his mind. "I couldn't take any more, but did I deserve it? Uh . . ."

His mouth opened, but no words came out. He knew what he wanted to say—*No, of course not*—but it was stopped by what he believed deep down. A block formed in his mind, like a fish trapped in a net, the words unable to pass through. He sat in silence, trying to push it, to force it, but the block held firm. With each second, his distress grew. He couldn't say it. It felt untrue, something he couldn't bring himself to believe.

The only words allowed to pass, which he didn't want to say, were *Yes, of course I deserved to die.*

He glanced at Vella, pleading for help. She sat impassive, resigned, accepting what he could not.

At last, he broke.

Tears welled in his eyes, spilling down his cheeks as the dam wall within him shattered. He finally had someone to share the pain with.

Vella didn't say a word. She moved beside him, curling up against him.

He silently told her everything: *I don't think there is anything I have done right in my whole life. Leah never wanted me around from the start. I can see how she looks at me. How everyone looks at me. I'm a waste of life. I should have died a long time ago.*

She wrapped her arms around his, offering her presence as quiet comfort. Feeling her made him wince, sharpening the ache and driving it deeper.

The only time he actually spoke was to ask a question she couldn't answer: "Why do we think we deserve to die?"

She just held him tighter.

Hours passed without a word uttered. It was a quiet, wondrous comfort, as they silently shared a pain neither could express to anyone else. An unspoken connection that needed no words. Being there together was enough.

"Thank you," he said. The words naturally filled the silence as if they'd been speaking the entire time.

"For what?" she asked.

"I don't know . . . being here, existing. Isn't that enough?"

"Can it ever be?"

"I know it can. Believe me."

"Every day of my life . . . I've felt on edge. Like punishment for my existence is right around the corner. I've always believed all the pain and suffering was deserved. How else could you explain it? It's all my fault. All the awful things that have happened, the way I was treated. Only worthless people get treated like that. And I've only ever been treated like I didn't matter. So what does that tell you? If I've been treated like I'm nothing, then maybe that's what I am. I feel like I was never meant to exist. Like every breath is unearned. Only Cole made me feel like I was worth something. Like it was okay to enjoy the simple things, to just be myself. And now he's gone . . ."

"I know how you feel. But every second you're here brings joy to everyone around you. I hope you can see that. Can you do me a favor?"

She said nothing.

"I want you to blindly believe that your being here is enough. Don't question it. If you need a reason, it's because I said so."

"I'll try."

Edgar softly exhaled and smiled. "I don't think I have ever felt anything like this."

"Like what?"

"To have someone actually understand me. Like, really understand what it's like. All my life, it's felt like there's this barrier between me and the rest of the world. Like I'm not really part of it, never have been. Most of the time, I feel like I can't engage with it at all. It pushes me away, like I'm not meant to exist in it naturally. Sometimes, I get these fleeting feelings . . . like maybe I do have the right to exist. But then it fades, and I realize I just forgot I was looking through glass, through the window into a world I don't belong to. But with you . . . it's always felt like we're on the same side of the glass."

"It's a nice view from here."

"It is, isn't it?"

Vella exhaled slowly, shifting into a more comfortable position.

"Do you remember what you said to me when you and Cole visited me that first night?"

"No."

"I told you I wished I would have died in there and you scolded me for saying that. Then you told me, 'We're glad you're alive.' You said that. Why? You didn't know me."

She hesitated and muttered, "You were getting on my nerves. That's all."

"I'm sorry you never heard that yourself. I'm very glad you are still with us."

"Shut up," she whispered.

"But it was more than that. You're a kind, caring person."

"I'm not . . ."

"Just take my word for it."

"You've got it all wrong. When we first came to talk to you about the orb, it wasn't me who was worried about you. It was Cole. He wanted to keep an eye on you. I wasn't thinking about trying to help you like I should have."

"Cole . . . really . . . ?" Edgar smiled at the thought. "I was supposed to be the one looking out for him," he muttered. Then louder to Vella, he asked, "And when he asked you about keeping an eye on me. What did you say?"

"I was unsure at first, but I knew he was right, of course. So I agreed."

"See."

"See what?"

"You could've said no but you didn't."

"So? Any normal person would have agreed. I'm not a monster."

"Yes, you're right . . . you're not. By saying yes, by telling me you were glad I was alive, you saved me. Those words and actions meant everything. Sometimes you don't realize you're saving someone in the moment. Just like Cole saved you without him even knowing it."

"I get what you're saying. But . . ."

"I'm sure there were countless times you saved Cole without realizing it. Even if it was just sitting with him, sharing a conversation, or as simple as asking how his day was."

She didn't respond.

"I realized something since I got my second chance."

"What's that?"

"Those small acts are the most heroic things anyone could do. In the end, all anyone truly wants is to feel like they're not alone."

She shifted and rested her head on his shoulder.

"Vella."

"Yeah."

"I hope Amy grows up to be like you."

She said nothing.

"Vella."

"Yeah."

"You don't deserve to die."

"What about you?"

"If you believe it, I will. Deal?"

"Deal."

They remained huddled together in silence a while longer. When Edgar lifted his head, he found Vella's gaze fixed on one of Cole's drawings.

"Tell me something about Cole."

"What do you mean?"

"Anything. Tell me your favorite memory of him. What made you fall in love with him?"

She stared down, thinking about him. Her eyes came to life, and a smile formed. A real one.

Without a word, she stood and rummaged through a nearby shelf and pulled out a small tin box. Inside that, she took out a small, crumpled piece of cream-colored paper. It was worn and crinkled from years of being handled.

She sat back down, running her fingers over the faded surface. Then she began.

"During class, on my eleventh birthday . . . the teacher announced it was my birthday to the class. Like they did for everyone. I remember it was right before lunch when the teacher told them. They would say something like, 'make sure you wish them a happy birthday.' No one would say it. They just looked back at me, laughing.

"I tried to hide my face in a book. I didn't want anyone to know; I wanted to stay out of sight. Only bad things happened when I got attention. I was hoping everyone would ignore me and forget about it as soon as possible. I didn't want them to have another reminder that I existed. Better to remain invisible so they couldn't target me.

"But Cole . . . he turned around and smiled for a split second. It wasn't like the other looks I got. It was like he knew something I didn't, and I wasn't sure what to make of it. Part of me thought maybe he was hiding his laughter behind that smile.

But his eyes weren't like the others'. The ones that looked down on me . . . like they thought they were better than me. Like I was nothing.

"Luckily, the bell rang, and I ran out of class and back to my room. Then . . . I noticed the book I was reading . . . it was placed differently from how I'd left it. At first, I was scared. I didn't want to open it.

"I always used these torn pieces of paper as bookmarks. But it was gone, and something was inside, where the paper should have been. I was afraid. I thought it would be another note or drawing they had done to make fun of me. I didn't want to open it, so I just stared at it.

"Anyway, I thought I would have to do it sooner or later. So, I opened it. And when I did . . . There it was. Sitting inside. An actual bookmark. A real one. This one.

"It was beautiful. There were hand-drawn flowers all over it, tied with a bit of red string at the end. And right in the middle of the flowers on the backside, in careful writing, was my name.

"That's when it all made sense. His look. His smile in class. He knew it was my birthday before it was even announced. No one else knew; even I'd forgotten. I knew it was sometime that week, but it didn't matter to me. But it mattered to him."

She turned the worn bookmark over in her hands, tracing the faded flowers with her fingers.

"I remember staring at it for so long. No one had ever done anything like that for me before. It wasn't the present."

Edgar reached out, and Vella handed it to him.

"No. It wasn't that . . . it was that he remembered. He cared enough to do something. I hadn't known that feeling before. But in that moment, I actually felt it: someone saw me. Like, truly saw me. For the first time in my life. That's when I knew . . . there would never be anyone else but him."

Edgar asked for another story, and without missing a beat, Vella recounted another.

She told him about when another boy in the orphanage was giving her a hard time. In retaliation, Cole had filled the boy's bed and pillow with dirt. By the end of the story, she was laughing; so was Edgar.

Then she told him about how they used to sneak around at night. Stealing flowers from around people's homes so she could create her own garden. Explaining how they narrowly avoided getting caught several times.

She laughed harder as she recalled one birthday when Cole tried to bake her a cake all by himself. It was a disaster. But they ate it anyway, and both ended up sick for days.

Two stories became three, then four, and soon she couldn't stop. Each one brought more life to her eyes. By the time she finished the sixth story, Edgar felt she had transformed back into the person he had known and loved before Cole's passing. Her laughter came easily. Her smile felt natural, like breathing. It was effortless again.

Soon, she shifted to her bed, lying down and staring at the ceiling, still telling stories about Cole. As time passed, her fatigue became more visible. She yawned and stretched, her eyes growing heavier with each word.

By the time she finished her eighth story, sleep had claimed her, the warmth of Cole's memories carrying her away.

Edgar sat for a little longer, watching her gentle smile and the lines of grief softening on her face. He draped a blanket over her and smiled. He was grateful for this, her first moment of peace since losing the irreplaceable.

He lingered, watching her a while longer, feeling that it had all been worth it for this one moment.

"I'm sorry. I hope you can forgive me," he whispered.

46

How should I end my life? Fight? I cannot. Call me a coward if you must. I would not blame you for thinking it. What strength, or foolishness, would it take to attempt it, knowing full well what lies beyond the doors? I keep considering it because it may be possible. Who knows, I may get lucky. For our children, I would like to try. But I cannot.

—THE FIRST PEOPLE OF EDEN
Journal of Morgan #38
Day 1943

The blue door vanished, leaving only a seamless stretch of wall behind, as though it had never existed at all. Not even a mark or blemish to say the door stood there. Above the green door, one of the two red lights had turned green. They had confirmation at last.

Excitement permeated Eden once the word got out, which was quicker than Alex had anticipated. It was only two days before the life transition specialist, Riley, discovered the missing door and word spread from there. For over a week now, in hushed conversations, people debated the same questions: Did someone really kill the Bear? Could this mean freedom was within reach? If someone could deal with the Wolf in the red door, would the green door finally open? They could only hope. But with all the enthusiasm came an undercurrent of anxiety.

The status quo had been disturbed. Change was something none of them were accustomed to. Nothing like this had ever happened in Eden's four-hundred-year history. Was this actually a sign of something worse in store for them? Were their jailers up to something? No one could answer for sure.

The mayor, inundated with questions, leaned on Alex to quell the growing unrest. Alex had already spoken with Owen, explaining as much as he could about what happened. He told Owen about Cole and Vella, and how they had slain the Bear under special circumstances. But when pressed about what exactly "special circumstances" meant, Alex feigned ignorance.

Not wanting to lose credibility by mentioning the absurd notion of a time-travelling orb.

"People are going to want to know if this is our way out of here," Owen had said, his voice tinged with a mix of hope and skepticism.

"I don't know," Alex had replied, trying to keep his tone measured. "Cole lost his life in the process. It's still dangerous to even attempt. We don't know if the method can be repeated."

Owen nodded, his excitement tempered. "We can't get people's hopes up, then. Who knows what some might do? Are you sure you don't want me to handle this?"

"I can do it," Alex insisted. "I was close to them, so I can take any unexpected questions that might come up."

"All right. I trust you." Owen stared out the window, a hopeful smile forming. "It's hard not to get excited, though. To think I might not have to die in a couple of years . . ."

"I wouldn't hold on to hope," Alex said, not wanting to dampen Owen's spirits but knowing it was necessary. False hope could be dangerous.

"Yes . . . yes, you're right." His smile faded. "One can dream, though. I'm sorry about your friend."

Alex lowered his gaze, marveling at the monumental effort it must have taken to do what he did.

Was it worth it, Cole?

Now, as the town gathered for an emergency meeting, Alex stood to the side of the stage, his eyes fixed on the floorboards and his stomach churning. The hall buzzed with restless energy, the crowd tense and anxious for answers.

Owen turned to him, wide-eyed. "Good luck," he said, giving Alex a clap on the back.

Alex stirred, glancing up, took a breath, and pulled his shoulders back.

Owen stepped onto the stage to quiet the crowd. The clamor of the throng died down to low-level murmurs.

Alex looked around to see Ellie sitting in the front row. She directed a smile at him, and he forced a smile back at her. He wished Leah, Vella, and Edgar were there. Having any of them might've helped, but he knew that was never going to happen.

Owen introduced him and he stepped to the middle of the stage. The weight of hundreds of expectant eyes bore down on him. He cleared his throat, looking out at the hopeful expressions on many of the people in the crowd.

"As you all know, there has been a change to the doors," he began, his voice steady despite an invisible hand gripping his chest. "Two of our citizens entered the blue door and defeated what we commonly refer to as the Bear."

Whispers spread in the crowd. Alex pressed on.

"One of them . . . didn't make it. However, one was able to survive."

"Was it eight-seven-four-nine?" someone shouted. "We heard they got an extra ten years!"

More chatter spread through the crowd, building in intensity. Alex put up a hand and raised his voice to regain control.

"Yes, it was eight-seven-four-nine. Her name is Vella. She survived a great ordeal and received an extra ten years. I don't know exactly why. I can only assume it's some kind of reward. She paid a terrible price for it. I ask that you give her space. She's been through a lot and needs time to grieve."

"How did she do it?" another voice called out.

Alex paused, carefully choosing his words. "It was under very special circumstances," he said. "It's my understanding it was Cole, the deceased, who killed the Bear. And he gave his life to do it."

"Cole?" A voice from the front row exclaimed in disbelief as more talk spread among the crowd.

"Yes, Cole," Alex confirmed. "I'm sure some of you knew him growing up. What he did was as brave as it was reckless. I don't believe what he did can be repeated, so I want to caution anyone considering trying the same. You *will* die. I cannot emphasize that enough."

"There must be a way, though. Or did he get lucky?"

"That's what we're looking into, and we want to make sure no one takes matters into their own hands in the meantime," Alex said.

Someone yelled from the back and finally aired the one question Alex didn't want to hear: "Are we going to be free?"

Before he could answer, a man near the front, his face lined with desperation, called out, "My wife has a week left. Will she live?" The woman beside him grabbed his arm, trying to stop him.

"Please, I don't want to give false hope. Nothing has changed in our situation. I only want to inform you and urge you not to do anything drastic."

But his words did little to calm the crowd. Voices rose again, louder and more intense this time.

"If it can be done once, it can be done again!"

"What are you hiding?"

"How did they do it?"

"Enough!" Alex's shout tore from his throat, his voice cracking under the strain. "It was a miracle they succeeded. We can't kill the Wolf. We're not even close. We'll never be free!"

The hall fell into a stunned silence, his words echoing in the stillness. In that moment, Alex glanced down at two empty seats in front.

He pictured Bernard and Kathy, the couple he had helped through their final stages. They had passed away almost a month ago, leaving together as they had planned. He saw them now as he had last seen them: Bernard reading a book to Kathy in the park. They looked content, their expressions light and effortless. In that moment, it felt as if he were looking at ghosts who had already passed on. Eden seemed to have faded away, leaving only the small, precious time they'd shared together. He imagined those same peaceful expressions now, looking up at him from those empty seats.

Regret filled him. Regret that they had been robbed of the time they deserved. Regret that they couldn't have their happy ending.

No. They did have it. With each other. The ending didn't matter. It was the journey that did. And theirs had been a good one. And for a moment, he wondered, *Did Cole enjoy the journey? I hope so. No. I know he did.*

His words echoed in his mind: *We'll never be free!*

But Bernard and Kathy were free. Freer than any of them could ever hope to be.

"I'm sorry," he said, his voice softer now. "I didn't mean it like that. One day, we may be free. But I can't promise anything right now. Cole . . . my friend . . . sacrificed himself and I don't believe it was in vain. I urge everyone to exercise patience. Even if some of us don't have time for patience."

He glanced at the woman who only had a week left, then at Ellie, worry etched across her face.

"I'm sorry," he said.

Without waiting for any more questions, Alex turned and walked off the stage.

"Coward!" an anonymous voice called out among the stillness.

Alex froze halfway off the stage, rage flaring up quickly and insidiously. He turned and glared at the person who'd called out, fists clenched at his sides.

He wanted to yell, *Go ahead, you do it, then! Go die! Be my guest!*

But when he looked at the person, lost in a sea of faces, he noticed the anger in their eyes. But underlying that anger, he saw fear. Glancing around at the others nearby, he saw that same fear mirrored on every face. His fury dissipated, replaced by a deep, aching sorrow.

Owen was quick to act. He placed a reassuring hand on Alex's shoulder before stepping forward to address the crowd. Alex took a deep breath to collect himself and walked out the back door.

Once outside, he collapsed onto a nearby bench and stared up at the sky, hoping for an answer. Much like those sleepless nights staring at the ceiling, no divine intervention came.

"What am I supposed to do now, Cole? Damn you," he muttered under his breath. "I can't do what you did . . ."

He squeezed his eyes shut and tried to focus. Cole's words flashed into his head; he opened his eyes and whispered, "We don't give up."

He turned, hearing the back door close; Ellie emerged and sat beside him. "I'm sorry," she said.

"I'm the last person you should be sorry for," Alex said, his expression vacant.

"Why keep torturing yourself? I can't stand seeing you like this. You don't talk or eat; I don't know if you ever sleep; it feels like you're not here."

"*I* wasn't there, Ellie. I should've been, but I wasn't. I should've known he was up to something."

"You couldn't have known."

"I can see it so clearly now. The days leading up to it . . . and I let it happen."

She brushed up next to him, trying to bring him back to the present moment. "Promise me you won't try what he did."

"Even if it means you get to live? What if everyone gets to live? No more people have to die, Ellie."

"Even then."

"I can't do it."

Her tone remained calm and even. "Yes, you can."

"I haven't told you everything," he said. "There's a good chance we can do it."

"I don't care."

"Why not?" Frustration built in his voice as he clenched his fists, the whites of his knuckles spreading as his grip tightened.

She wrapped both hands around his fist. "It doesn't matter."

"Of course it does. I can't just give up on you," he whispered.

"You can."

"Ellie . . . I feel this fire. I can't ignore it. It tells me I can and should do more. It tells me not to give up."

"That's just fear talking. Nothing more."

"It's part of it, but I know there's more."

"It's all fear. Listen to it, really listen, and you'll see it for what it is. Trust me."

He retracted his hand, stood up, paced away, and turned to her.

"So what if it is?"

"It's stopping you from thinking clearly."

Alex struggled to find the right words, unable to say anything.

The silence fueled his frustration, tightening in his chest. Shaking his head, he turned his back on her.

"You want things to be different; I get it. But these are circumstances beyond your control, and you suffer by struggling against them. I see it, and it hurts me just as much as it hurts you."

"And you? Want nothing to change?"

"I don't wish for a single thing to be different."

"I can't do it anymore," he said, turning back to face her. "I can't sit around and do nothing!"

"That's all you need to do. Sit with me," she said. "You can't save me. That's perfectly fine. I don't want you to. I just need you."

He pushed down a lump in his throat, vision blurring.

"I need time to think," he said.

Fleeing as soon as the words left his lips.

47

Every day feels harder than the last. I don't have much strength to do these entries anymore. My final task is to help our girls adjust to life without me. There is no one I can give them to, so I've started getting them ready for the orphanage. I get the feeling no matter how much I prepare them, it won't be enough. What cruelty to inflict on such young children. I hope they can forgive us . . . They look so much like her.

—THE FIRST PEOPLE OF EDEN

Journal of Morgan #38

Day 1621

After leaving Vella to her untroubled sleep, Edgar returned home to find Leah slumped at the dining room table. A bottle of all-too-familiar clear liquid sat in front of her, already a quarter empty. A glass in her hand.

Pulling out a chair, he faced her and took her hand, prying the glass from her fingers. After finishing the drink, he set it down.

"She'll be back very soon."

She could only manage a soft nod. Her face was pale and expressionless, drained of all life, a stark contrast to the life that was returning to Vella, now faded from her. The light in her eyes grew dimmer day by day.

Eyes fixed on the table, her head swayed from side to side. Her hand thoughtlessly reached for the bottle.

Edgar placed a hand over hers to stop her; she ripped it away from him, glaring.

"Please stop," he said.

She took a drink and slammed it back on the table. "What're you gonna do? *Nothing!*"

He snatched the bottle, took it to the sink, and poured it all out.

As the last of the clear liquid swirled down the sink, he winced at the sharp sound of glass shattering at his feet. Gripping the edge of the sink, he took a deep breath, the motion making the pain swell where the glass had hit his back.

"Do you think you're the only one who cared about Cole?" he asked.

"Leave."

"No."

"I hate you . . . I don't want you around. What're you even doing here?"

He squeezed his eyes shut, feeling his chest close in on itself. With great effort, he pushed himself off the sink, dragged a chair over next to hers, and sank into it beside her.

"I understand how you feel . . . losing Cole . . . it felt like I lost Amy . . . like we lost a son."

She hunched over, her head in her hands, hair covering her face. "What do you know? He's dead 'cause of *you*."

"I know."

She groaned in frustration. "I hate you."

"I know."

"Stop saying that!" She jerked up and hit him in the chest. Again, and again.

"Why won't you leave me? Why won't you do anything?"

"I love you."

"Shut up!" she screamed, continuing to throw punches. "Leave me!"

"I can't."

He caught her hand as her punches weakened. Pulling her closer, she collapsed against him. He wrapped his arms around her, holding her close.

"I deserve to be alone," she said through sobs.

"No, you don't," he said.

"Shut up . . ." she muttered.

"Come on. Let's go to bed."

He helped her up, steadying her as she stumbled to her bed. After tucking her in, he turned to leave, but she stopped him.

"Stay, please."

He knelt on the floor beside her, holding her hand.

She closed her eyes as tears fell down her cheeks and whispered, "I didn't mean it, I didn't mean any of it . . . I'm sorry."

"I know."

"Please stay with me. Please. I don't want to be alone . . . lie down."

She turned and shuffled along so he could fit in. He sank in behind her, wrapping an arm around her.

"It felt like we had our own family," she whispered.

"It was nice."

"We can't lose her too."

"We won't; she's strong. Stronger than us."

"I know."

He felt her fading into sleep.

"I love you," she whispered.

"I know."

When he felt her drift into unconsciousness, Edgar eased himself out of bed, despite every instinct telling him not to.

He lingered at the door, his eyes fixed on her peaceful expression. He let his mind drift and indulge in the unreal, longing for a long life that stretched the feeling of this moment forever.

A life with her was his reality.

He pictured Amy sleeping peacefully in the other room. An hour ago, he'd read her a bedtime story, tucked her in, and kissed her goodnight. Tomorrow, he would wake up to Amy jumping on their bed, sandwiching herself between them. They'd eat breakfast together and spend the day as a family. At the park, Amy would play with kids her age while he and Leah sat together, enjoying each other's company. Much like the past fifteen years had been. No troubles, no arguments, no heartache. Nothing could disturb them. A life that stretched out, simple and endless. Perfect.

He blinked, and it was gone. *If only.*

"I'm sorry," he whispered.

With a heavy heart, he stepped away and left her.

Edgar found himself wandering the perimeter of Eden, stalling for time.

Even after all these years . . . I'm still an ignorant fool . . .

Cole and Vella had changed everything, forcing events to unfold faster than they were supposed to. All his plans had gone up in smoke. They had caught him off guard as he'd become content going with the flow. He cursed himself for growing complacent and underestimating them. There were supposed to be several months before they would feel pressured to take any drastic action. When he saw the signs, he would act. Now it was too late. He'd promised to protect them, and he had failed. He had failed Leah. He had failed Vella. Most of all, he had failed Cole.

The cool night air did little to calm the storm raging inside him. His thoughts above the storm were oddly unclouded. There were emotions rolling within him with no possible outlet. All he could do was walk.

The sound of rustling leaves awakened him. Edgar stopped and looked around. He realized he was near the clearing where they had spent so many mornings and afternoons together. Bathed in the unfiltered moonlight, a solitary figure stood, staring up at and through the artificial ceiling that held them captive.

Alex jerked his head, startled by the footsteps.

Edgar walked toward him and sat down on a fallen tree trunk at the clearing's edge. "Didn't mean to scare you."

"It's fine," Alex said. "How's Vella?"

Edgar shrugged. "Getting better."

"I'll come by tomorrow if you think she'd be up for it."

"I think she would like that. How are you?"

"I'll be okay," Alex said, though his voice held no conviction. "This place . . . it feels empty without him. He was the glue that kept us together."

"We're still together," Edgar said. Though he lacked the emotion to back up the statement.

"If by together, you mean together in Eden, then you're right." Alex took a moment; the silence stirred him. "It's weird. I don't know how to feel. Restlessness is the only constant."

"Sounds like you need to lie down," Edgar suggested.

"It doesn't feel possible," Alex muttered, staring at his

fingertips. "Can't you feel it? We're so close, Edgar. One step away from freedom. Cole showed us it was possible. He gave us hope." Alex let out a long, weary sigh. "At the same time, the price we paid doesn't feel like it was worth it."

Edgar studied him, his expression unreadable. "The Bear isn't on the same level as the Wolf. We're not as close as you think."

"You know what I mean," Alex said. "It's possible."

"Sure," Edgar said, his tone flat.

"When I first saw the Bear, I almost gave up completely."

"Why didn't you?"

"That would mean giving up on Ellie."

"You should have."

Alex stared stunned, like he'd been struck. "What?"

"You should've given up. All of you should have. But you didn't. I should have known then . . ."

"We had hope; you gave us that hope. We had too much to fight for to give up. There's nothing I wouldn't do to have more time with Ellie."

"You already have that time. Why aren't you with her now?"

Alex took a moment, turning and stepping away, confused by Edgar's demeanor. He turned back to Edgar. "I don't get it. What're you talking about?"

"Do you even know what you have?" Edgar repeated. "Why aren't you with her now?"

"I needed time to think."

"Is that right?"

"Yeah."

This time, Edgar was insistent in his tone. "Go home."

Alex shook his head, frustration mounting. "What are you doing, Edgar?"

"Trying to clear your head."

"Cole's death isn't on you," Alex said, his voice rising. "Do you think you could have stopped him? Stopped us? Did you even know Cole?"

"I should've known better," Edgar said, returning to a placid tone.

"Why are you so against this? We're so close."

"It's a curse."

"The orb?"

Edgar sighed, standing up to face him. "You all think it's some gift from the heavens, our way out of here. But have you thought about what happens after? Do you *really* think they'll let us go?"

"I-I don't . . . know. Maybe."

"No one promised us freedom if we killed those monstrosities."

"Course not, but it's implied."

"But you don't know that for sure."

"I don't . . ." Alex squeezed his eyes shut. "Edgar, what are you doing?"

"Here's a question. If they actually let us go, do you think it'll be better out there?"

Alex found himself pushed further and further into a corner by Edgar. "At least we'll get to choose."

"You don't get it. We're their property, and until they're done with us, we won't be free. We don't get to choose." He gestured toward the artificial sky above them. "Can you imagine the resources it takes to build a place like this and keep it running for over four hundred years? It's not just what they have, it's that they're choosing to spend it on us. Think about that. They're not going to just let us go. We must mean something to them. There are a few questions I've had on my mind, and I'm sure you've thought about them too. Why haven't they stopped us? Why haven't they taken the orb? The reason: they want us to have it. Why? I can't think of a single good reason."

"There could be a million reasons," Alex insisted. "Maybe they don't know about the orb."

"When I was ten, I took a knife, locked myself in my room, and hid under a blanket. I moved the point toward my implant on my ankle. It didn't even touch my skin, and they hit me with five minutes of the most intense pain you could imagine. They knew about that, but you think they don't know about the orb? Nothing gets past them. If anything happens, it's because they allow it."

Edgar moved closer, his voice low but fierce. "You're not thinking, Alex. Wake up. Let's say you do manage to kill the Wolf—then what? They're going to be our friends and let us walk out of here? You can't seriously think killing those monsters is the real reason we're here. No. There's much more we don't know. Can't possibly know. Whatever it is, those monsters are just the start of it. A test? A sick game? Maybe it's not, maybe it's a distraction and means nothing and we're wasting our time. Are you prepared to open that box and find out? Will you take responsibility for everyone's lives? And when everything gets so much worse than you could ever imagine? What then? What's the plan?"

"I-I—" Alex stammered.

Edgar stood firm, staring him down. "Look at your ankle. Remember all the people who've died here. Now think about the benevolence you believe awaits us on the other side. We're vastly outmatched; we are at their mercy. There is no escape. Did you think of any of that? Or are you only thinking of yourself? Is this what Ellie wants or is it what you want? It's what you want, Alex. Look past your own selfishness and think of everyone else."

Edgar inched closer to Alex, who averted his gaze, his jaw tightening as he struggled to keep his composure. "Look at me, Alex. You're being a child. A naïve little child. And you want to run this place? Be responsible for everyone? Go home to Ellie and appreciate what you have while you have it. Do you even understand how lucky you are?"

"I can't give up," he muttered.

"Yes, you can. Go home. Now."

"What about Leah and Amy?" Alex asked, desperation creeping into his voice.

"Leah doesn't want anyone risking their lives for her. She wants Cole back. Can you give her that?"

Alex shook his head. "No . . . but A-Amy?"

"She'll have a good life here."

"You can't be serious."

Edgar grabbed Alex by the front of his shirt and pulled him

to within an inch of his face, his fist clenched by his side.

"Alex. What part of this are you not getting? Think about everything we know about this place. You have no idea what you're doing. Connect the dots. This doesn't end well under any scenario. And you know it. Enjoy your small, insignificant life. Go home. Be with Ellie. You have no idea how good you have it. Go!"

Edgar threw him away, and Alex stumbled back.

"What—" Alex stammered, but the rest of the words died in his throat.

"Go!"

After a moment, Alex glanced at Edgar, who returned nothing but contempt. Alex turned and ambled away. He paused several times to look back before finally leaving Edgar's sight.

Edgar smiled, finally free of the last hurdle. Exhaustion engulfed him. He slumped over, the weight of the world pressing down on his shoulders.

"I'm sorry," Edgar whispered. "This is my task to finish. Mine alone. I'll kill it . . ."

He walked to the center of the clearing and lay down, feeling the cool grass and dirt against his skin. He took a deep breath, letting the tension drain from his body, and smiled. The meaningless lights above stared back at him, and he laughed. Like he was truly happy.

"It's time."

48

I have not passed away yet, but I would like to leave an entry of my own. My mother was a strong person, my iron wall. She made me feel like I could be anything, do anything. The day she died, it felt like those doors shut, and my future was decided for me. Once, she told me about a dream she had: she was walking down a dirt road in a world beyond Eden wall of light shone before her, and from within it, a hand reached out. She reached toward it, feeling the warmth. But she pulled back. Not ready to go. She said that when her time comes, that hand will be waiting to take her to a better place, where she will be waiting for me. I hold to that, knowing that however bad things may get, I have something to look forward to.

—"MY ENTRY"

CHILDREN OF THE PEACEFUL PASSAGE

by Aleister #8990

By now, a knock at the door would have woken Vella. Edgar would have stepped in with breakfast. Not today. Only the shed's creaking kept her company.

Relief washed over her as the morning quiet settled in. Yet she felt conflicted. She missed his presence. A crushing loneliness loomed on the horizon, which he usually kept at bay. She lingered in bed for hours, savoring the silence. Still, a longing for company ate at her. To relieve some of it, she thumbed through Cole's sketchbooks. After a short time, she put them aside as looking through them deepened her longing for more.

Hunger forced her out of bed. She unpacked the extra food Edgar had left behind and ate a banana while stretching her stiff legs.

Today, for some reason, didn't feel quite as bleak as the others had. Thoughts of going outside and doing something with her day crossed her mind.

She was getting dressed when a sudden, hurried knock startled her.

"Vella," a familiar voice called out, one she couldn't ignore.

She cracked the door open. Leah stood there, tapping her arm restlessly.

"Vella, is Edgar inside?"

She shook her head, unable to look at her.

"When did you last see him?" Leah pressed.

"Last night," she murmured.

"What time?"

"Don't know . . . don't think it was too late."

"Where is he?" Leah muttered to herself.

"Have you checked his place?"

"Not yet. I'll do that." Leah moved to leave but stopped. "How are you?"

Vella could only manage a weak shrug.

Leah studied her face, noticing the scars of grief that Cole's death had left on her. Without warning, she stepped closer, pried the door open, and pulled Vella into a fierce embrace.

"Please come back," Leah pleaded. "At least come home for dinner tonight. Please."

Feeling her warmth reminded her of Cole's final words: *Look after Leah for me. She won't take this well.*

In that moment, it dawned on her: Who was looking out for the one who looked out for everyone else? Vella noticed how her face looked hollow, drained of energy, with dark circles lining her eyes and the skin around them dry and worn.

Leah had every reason to be furious with her and Edgar, blaming them for Cole's death and holed up in her room like she was. But she wasn't. Why? It made no sense. Instead, Leah was here, running around, searching for him.

"I will," Vella said. And she forced a smile with her mouth, though her eyes remained heavy and filled with despair.

Leah returned a similar smile and turned to leave.

"Wait," Vella called out. "Why aren't you mad at Edgar?"

Leah paused, then turned back, her expression softening. "I was . . . he told me everything. I took it all out on him. He never tried to defend himself. I could see he already blamed himself enough. He loved Cole and wanted to protect him. Vella, I can't hate him more than he already hates himself." Fury flickered in

Leah's eyes. "I'm tired of arguing. I don't want to lose anyone else. We're family. We're all we have."

Family, Vella thought. She had never needed to use that term or apply it to herself. Yet, in his final weeks, Edgar had discovered it, just as she had. She had felt it without ever saying the word.

And deep down, she knew Leah was right. They were as close as any family could be. They argued and fought, but they never wavered when it came to supporting each other.

Guilt welled up in Vella. She hadn't been there for Leah like Cole had asked. Leah had lost just as much as she had, yet here she was, still putting herself out there for others.

"I'm sorry," Vella blurted out. "I made him do it. He's dead because of me. You should hate me. It's all my fault!"

Leah rushed to her, holding her. "It's not your fault. Never say those words or even think them."

"Why don't you hate me?" Vella sobbed.

Leah pulled back, meeting Vella's tear-filled eyes. "I can't blame anyone else because I'm the one responsible. I promised his parents I'd protect him. I failed. That was my one job in life, and I couldn't do it."

Vella stood in stunned silence.

Leah wiped her eyes, steadying her voice. "We all think we could've done more. Blame, blame, blame. It's useless. It gets us nowhere. We don't live long enough to waste time being mad at anyone or anything. We have to love what we have while we still have it, while we still have time. At least, that's what I try to tell myself." Her voice faded as she spoke the words. "I used to tell Cole that wishing for things to be different is useless. It's the same with blame. You can't change the past. We have to make do. And not let the past destroy us. Be around for those still here."

She lifted Vella's chin, forcing her to meet her gaze. "I need someone to believe that. Can you do that for me?"

Vella attempted to nod, unsure if she actually meant it. "I wish I were as strong as you."

"Strong? Me? Strong people don't do what I've done . . . what

I've done to Edgar . . . no, Vella, you're the strong one. Not many could endure what you have and keep going. That's something to be proud of. I'm proud of you, and so was Cole," Leah said, offering a small, sad smile. "You're strong."

"I'm not . . ."

"All you need to do is remember that I think you are. And that Cole and Edgar did too. Believe in us, if nothing else."

Leah sensed the resistance still present. "Strong people aren't strong because of who they are. They are strong because of their actions despite who they are. Despite what they have gone through," she said. "Some people have all the natural gifts in the world, but they can still be weak. Weak people don't try. You try."

Leah left it at that, stepping back. "I'll see you tonight for dinner. All right?"

"Okay," Vella whispered.

Leah leaned in, pressing a gentle kiss on Vella's forehead.

As Leah began to pull away, Vella remembered Cole's other last words. "Leah . . . the last thing Cole said was to tell you . . . he wanted you to know he loved you."

Leah froze for a moment, then turned, glanced at Vella, and then her eyes drifted past Vella as they lost focus.

"Leah?"

It was as if a switch flipped; she looked at Vella with a smile she didn't seem to want. "Not even an apology, huh?" Without another word, she walked away.

Vella watched her disappear out of sight and winced.

Cole wanted me to be there for her, and I haven't. I will now, Vella told herself.

Leah's words kept echoing in her mind, but she felt them being rejected: *You try.*

And she thought, *nowhere near hard enough. Not anymore, though.*

For the first time in over a week, Vella looked around at the world outside. Grass and other plants overran her garden, and some of the flowers were wilting. It was a small thing, but something she could attend to. She went into the shed to grab her gardening tools, but as she reached for her gloves, she froze.

Her eyes landed on the corner where Edgar had sat the night before.

A folded piece of paper sat in his place. A sickening sensation welled up in her gut as she stared at it.

"He wouldn't . . ." she muttered.

Her gaze crept to the box where Edgar had put the orb. Dread kept her feet frozen in place, not wanting to confirm her worst fears. Every second she remained there, immobile, her chest tightened further.

She willed herself to move, stepping within reach of the box. Her vision blurred, and she grew lightheaded as her breathing had halted altogether. With trembling hands, she reached up and gripped the box, wishing against all hope that she was wrong. She lowered it and stared inside.

It was gone.

"Can't be . . . no . . . no, no, no."

Something inside gripped her and set her off, forcing her into action. She flipped the box upside down, dumping the contents on the ground. She dropped to her knees, tearing through the scattered clothes. Nothing.

Panic seized her. She scoured every corner of the shed, overturning every box, clearing out every cupboard and shelf, and checking every possible hiding place. But it was nowhere to be found.

She kicked the wall, doubled over, pulling her shirt over her mouth and screamed.

He wouldn't. He can't! He took it for safekeeping. Right? RIGHT?

She glanced over at the folded piece of paper in the corner; it taunted her with its implications.

No!

Without a second thought, she bolted out of the shed. She ran as fast as she could without stopping until she reached the doors.

Her heart pounded as her eyes darted around. Both remaining doors were still there, with no green lights to say anyone was inside. She looked up at the board showing everyone's numbers and countdowns.

What was his number? Eight-five-nine, something. What is it? What is it!

She remembered staring at the numbers as they'd sat in the clearing one day. Unlike the others, he didn't bother to hide his death timer. She couldn't help but watch as it ticked down with less than a year remaining. It was hypnotizing, seeing someone's life run down to nothing. She tried to recall the numbers above it as the ticking clock stole all her attention.

Finally, it clicked: *Eight-five-nine-eight! That's it.*

She scanned the board for Edgar's number. She checked once, twice, and a third time.

Can't be . . .

A numbing ring saturated her surroundings.

It's not there . . . he's . . . gone . . .

She stood there, in a state of shock, her body paralyzed. Breathing became nonexistent, the ringing growing louder, drowning out everything else. It swelled until it was deafening, until she could hear nothing but the silent scream of her mind. It pleaded for this not to be real.

The ticking of numbers was all she could stare at.

Maybe I'm not seeing it right.

They slowed and quickened without her control. Her vision blurred as they warped into meaningless symbols.

She had no idea how long she had stood there until a cry of anguish behind her wrenched her back to reality.

There was no need to turn around.

She already knew who it was.

There was only one person it could be.

49

It can feel like most of life is an uphill battle you can't win. We struggle day in and day out just to keep our head above the sinking sand, trying not to succumb to anxiety and regret. Then, out of nowhere, little moments appear that make it all feel worth it. And those moments? They only come from other people. Specific people. In the end, it's those people that make the struggle feel worth it but what happens when they are no longer there? How can it still be worth it?

—THE FIRST PEOPLE OF EDEN
Journal of Morgan #38
Day 1700

"One step at a time . . . one . . . step . . . at . . . a . . . time . . ." Vella mumbled.

Late afternoon settled over another day Vella desperately wanted to forget.

She made her way through the woods to see Leah for dinner, as promised. Though she doubted there would be any food. Nor any conversation, smiles, or laughter, but she knew her presence alone might offer Leah some comfort.

She slumped, her hands dangling at her sides as she dragged her feet. It felt as though her body was moving on its own, without her. Every emotion had drained from her, leaving her to trudge through the world in a haze with no end in sight. All she wanted was to turn back and hide, but she couldn't; she had to press on for Cole and Edgar.

Approaching the end of the woods, Vella could hear Leah long before she could see her. It wasn't a cry or a wail, but a scream—raw, angry, and full of frustration. Emotions long held in, bottled up for far too long, were now unleashed, forcing everyone to feel her pain. The sounds forced Vella out of her haze, making her quicken her pace.

When she reached the street, she saw people standing in front of their houses, silent and stunned.

Leah stumbled across the roof, a half-empty bottle dangling

from her hand. Her glassy eyes stared into the void as she screamed curses. Vella waved off the onlookers, sending them back inside, telling them she would take care of the situation.

Leah glared off into the distance, oblivious to the world around her.

Vella rushed to the house, climbed onto the roof, and joined her. She approached with slow, careful steps. "Leah, it's a little unstable up here."

"So what?" Leah retorted, her tone mocking. "That's what they'd say. Why shouldn't I do whatever I want as well? Who cares?"

Vella closed the distance, doing her best not to startle her. When she got close enough, Vella caught her off guard, wrapping her arms around Leah's chest from behind. Leah stiffened, holding her arms out with the bottle in one hand.

"Get off me," Leah muttered, trying to squirm free. Vella wouldn't budge, making her agitation grow. "Get off! Leave me alone!"

Vella tightened her hold, refusing to let go. "I care," she whispered.

Leah kept trying to push her off. She flicked her hips, losing her balance. But Vella held them steady.

"I'm not going anywhere," Vella grunted.

Leah's struggle subsided as Vella pulled her closer.

After a minute, her resistance faded. Leah's eyes dulled, looking down and around her like she was waking from a dream. The rage subsided, soothed by her anchor. She finally brought her arms down and hugged Vella back.

"My dear girl, I'm sorry. I didn't mean to scare you."

"I'm so sorry," Vella whispered, still gripping her as if her life depended on it.

Vella slowly released her and sat down on the roof, catching her breath. Leah followed, dropping down beside her.

They sat in silence, looking out at the houses and trees that faded into the walls and skybox above.

Leah took a long swig from the bottle and offered it to Vella, who shook her head.

"I'm sorry," Vella repeated.

Leah glanced at her, then stared back into the abyss. "What could I have done, Vella?" she asked. "Where did I go wrong? Did I not do enough? Did I do too much?"

Her questions grew sharper with each word. "Tell me, Vella. Did I hold on too tightly? Not tight enough?" Leah asked, almost pleading.

"It's not about what you did," Vella said. "It's just . . . how they were."

"People are who they are because of the people around them. That includes me."

"They were lucky to have you in their lives. I'm fortunate to have you."

Leah took another drink. "Lucky to have me . . . what a joke," she muttered. "Here's some advice, Vella—stay away from me. For your own good."

"I'm not leaving you."

Leah didn't respond. Moments later, she shook her head and said, "Nothing matters. It's all for nothing."

"Everything matters."

"Cut the shit, please. I don't need anyone to patronize me."

Vella refused to get drawn into her harsh words. "Edgar told me he felt lucky to have you in his life." She didn't know if he had actually said this to her, but she knew it to be true regardless.

Leah shook her head. "Lucky to have me? Here's something you don't know. I treated Edgar like he wasn't even a person. I pushed him around. I took him for granted; I abused his loyalty and love. You have no idea the things I did to him. You know, there was a time he didn't leave his bed for three days, wouldn't eat, wouldn't move. One of his many episodes. And what did I do? Yell at him, abuse him. I made him feel worse. I made him feel alone. I wasn't there for him. That's what he had to deal with, and I couldn't accept it. What kind of monster does that to someone? His last few years were hell, and where was I? He's never been well, and I knew that . . . I've always known."

"That's not why he did what he did. He did what he thought

was best for us," Vella said. "You did your best."

"My best," Leah scoffed. "My best? My best . . . no. If that was my best, then that should tell you how much of a monster I really am. I failed them all. Cole's parents, Cole, Edgar, you, Amy . . . my life was a waste."

"You know it wasn't. You didn't fail me or any of us. What was it you told me about blame? It's useless, you said."

Leah shook her head.

"Why don't you hold yourself to the same standards you hold others to?" Vella asked.

"I expect better. I should've done better."

"Why? How are you any different?"

"I know what you're trying to do. Don't bother."

"Well? How are you different? Do you think you're that much better than everyone else? Are you not human like the rest of us?" Vella pressed.

"Vella . . ." Leah's tone softened but it also carried a heavy warning.

"How are you to blame after everything you've given to me, to them, to everyone? What have you kept for yourself? And you think you're somehow to blame?"

"Vella, stop," Leah whispered.

"I'm sorry," Vella said. "I'm sorry we haven't been there for you."

Leah's voice faded. "No. I'm . . ."

"I'm sorry you've had to suffer alone for so long. But I'm here for you. I'm here for you now and always."

Vella leaned on her shoulder, and it was as if a valve had been released—Leah's barrier crumbled. She tried to hold it back, but it was too late; the tears streamed unrestrained. The bottle slipped from her grasp, rolling into the gutter. She collapsed into herself, crying an uncaring, ugly cry. The anguish she had been hiding was out now, and there was no stopping it.

She fell into Vella's lap, and Vella held her, not saying a word, just being there for her, as Leah's tears soaked through her clothes. When one wave of tears seemed to end, another began—waves of sobs, screams, wails, and moments of calm.

Vella sat with her through it all, watching the sun sink below the horizon as the orange sky faded into darkness.

When Leah's tears finally subsided, she lay on Vella's lap, too drained to move. They stared up at the night sky, both wishing for a world that was different but knowing that it would never be. Things were as they were—nothing more, nothing less. That reality still felt too much to accept.

Leah found her strength. She sat up, shifted behind Vella, and wrapped her arms around her, holding her close to her chest.

"I'm sorry," she whispered.

"You have nothing to be sorry for."

They sat in silence, the weight of their shared grief pressing down on them.

After a while, Leah broke the silence. "I want to hold my baby," she whispered. "I should've raised her myself and left her with Cole. I thought I was doing the right thing, but I regret it. I'll never get another chance to raise her. I want to see her, hear her, hold her, smell her. I want to wring the neck of my younger self for doing that to us."

"You did what you thought was right for Amy," Vella said.

Leah swallowed hard. "I robbed Edgar of his only joy in life. I cut him off from even visiting her. Why would anyone do something so heartless?"

"You had good reasons. It was very selfless of you. I think that girl did her best with the experiences and information she had, don't you?"

"She tried," Leah mumbled. After a pause, she added, "Ignore me, it's just the ramblings of a hypocrite. I'm glad Amy will have you." She leaned in closer to Vella's ear and whispered, "I'm glad I have you."

Vella felt a lump in her throat as she recalled the note Edgar left behind. When she returned home, she stared at it for hours, too afraid to open it. But anxiety became too much to bear, and in a snap decision, she tore it open.

It simply read: *Be there for them.*

Her eyes lingered on those four words. Rage flooded through her, sudden and intense.

She screamed, cursing Edgar for leaving, for not being there for them. For her.

In a burst of fury, she balled up the note and hurled it against the wall. Then, consumed by rage, she tore through the shed, throwing and smashing everything within reach until the place was completely destroyed.

For a long while, she sat there in silence, curled up as the light faded outside. It reminded her that she still had to see Leah for dinner. She still had a duty to fulfill. Despair or not, she had an unspoken promise to keep to all of them.

It was her turn to be there for them.

In the note, there had been a smaller folded-up piece of paper with Leah's name on it. Vella felt for it in her pocket, pulled it out, and placed it in Leah's hand.

"He wanted you to have this."

Leah stared at the slip of paper, seeing the imprint of words on the other side.

"What does it say?" Leah asked.

"It's only for you to know."

Leah pushed herself back, took a deep breath, and opened the note.

She stared at the paper for several minutes, while Vella waited in silence. All of a sudden, she scrunched it up and threw it off the roof as far as she could manage. A moment later, Vella felt Leah's head rest against her back. Then she wrapped her arms around her and squeezed tight, so tight that Vella had trouble breathing. The hug was almost too intense, bordering on aggressive.

"Leah . . ." Vella wheezed.

She released her grip. "Sorry," she said through gritted teeth.

"He loved you a lot."

"That's the part I can't stand."

Leah embraced Vella a lot more gently this time, resting her head next to Vella's.

They sat in silence for a time. Their quiet reflection ended with the sound of footsteps approaching from the street.

Alex appeared and, without a word, climbed onto the roof to

huddle beside Leah. His eyes landed on the bottle in the gutter. He grabbed it, took a long drink, and gasped as it burned its way down his throat.

"Dammit, Edgar," he spat. "Sorry, Leah."

"I suppose it's your turn to get yourself killed," she replied.

"Maybe." He sighed. "No. There's nothing that we can do now. It would be suicide." Alex let out a bitter laugh. "I can't believe he actually convinced me to give up and then he goes and does that . . ."

"He didn't want anyone else to risk their lives," Vella said. "He was trying to protect us."

"Was that his plan all along?"

"I think so. We caught him by surprise. He must have felt he had to act now or risk another one of us dying."

"I hate to say it, but he was right. I might've taken matters into my own hands."

"Stupid," Leah muttered.

"Ellie means that much to me. So do you. I'm sorry."

"And how would Ellie have felt if you died?"

"You sound like him."

"I'm not angry. I'm just happy you're still here."

"I wish they both were." Alex sighed. "I wonder if he got close to killing it . . ."

"There is no doubt in my mind," Vella said. "He had too much to fight for."

Alex wiped the corner of his eyes. "To the two biggest fools I knew," he said, raising the bottle and taking a drink.

He passed it to Leah, who said, "To the two biggest morons I knew." She took a sip and then handed it to Vella.

She accepted it but stopped before drinking. "I can't. I'm pregnant," she said in a low voice.

Leah looked at her in shock as Alex did the same.

"They won't ever know each other," Vella said, her voice heavy with pain.

Leah kissed her and squeezed her tighter. "That's wonderful. Truly."

"Did he know?" Alex asked, staring into the distance.

"I told him just before he . . ." She swallowed hard. "I hid it from him. If he knew, he would've stopped me from helping. I didn't want our child to grow up in this place . . . so I pushed him into action before I couldn't help anymore."

"If you had told him, he would've gone alone," Alex said. "No . . . no matter what we said or did. He was just . . . he was too much for this place to contain."

Vella swirled the last of the liquid in the bottle before pouring it out. She watched as it trickled into the gutter.

"To the two kindest souls I knew."

They sat together, staring into the night, not wanting to leave each other's company.

"What are we supposed to do now?" Alex asked.

"We take it one day at a time, one step at a time," Vella said. "That's what Edgar would say."

"That's what I used to tell him," Leah said. "And it's what Rose used to tell me."

"Here's the plan," Vella said. "We try to make it through today. Then the next one. Then the one after that."

Leah,

If you're reading this, then I failed.

I'm sorry it had to come to this.

Thank you for these past few weeks. It was a small glimpse of a good life that could have been. I was happy.

I'm sorry I let you down. I tried. We all did. I suppose we all wish we could change things, but maybe none of it was ever in our control to begin with.

I find peace knowing that Amy will have Vella. She really is the best of us. I hope you can find some joy in your remaining days. You deserve it.

That night we were fifteen. You know the one. You found me alone in the woods with the bottle of wine you stole. We stayed up all night drinking and talking, and you sat in my arms as we watched the sun come up. There's nothing I've ever hated more than that sunrise. It ruined everything. I wish that night lasted forever. You left that moment when it ended. I never did.

If I leave with anything, it's that feeling. Because of that, I have nothing to fear.

I love you.

Forever yours,
Edgar

50

I remember when I was eleven. We had to do a three-person act, reenacting a scene from a script for a class play, to see who would get what part. Instead of learning our lines, we went off and played ball games instead. When it came time to perform, me and James had no idea what to do. Luckily or unluckily, Cameron "saved us" by improvising a routine where he played the Wolf and we his two helpless victims. The Wolf, Cameron, would set up a joke, and if we didn't get the punchline, he would eat us. It was hilarious to us and the class. God, I remember when we finished. The laughter died down, and we stood in silence, terrified of the teacher's reaction. She gave away no sign of emotion the whole time. Then, Vella just smiled and said, "Guess this punchline and I'll ignore you not completing the assignment." It went: "What has three heads, six arms and legs, and is writing and staring in the new play?"

—"AVERY #8895"

CHILDREN OF THE PEACEFUL PASSAGE

by Aleister #8990

The sky filled with fading stars marked that the first light of dawn was only hours away. Vella walked through the motionless streets of Eden. She moved slowly, deliberately, soaking in every detail. She stopped to observe each home she passed, every tree, garden bed, and flower.

A full week had passed since they'd mourned Edgar's death. They were still grappling with how to begin their new lives without both Cole and Edgar. Everywhere she looked there was some reminder of them. A tulip sparked a memory of Cole, while a soccer ball lying in a front yard triggered one of Edgar. That wasn't what she was out for. Not for the past but for the future.

In Vella's bid for some understanding of what to do next, she walked.

This wasn't a restless, sleepless walk. She had chosen this.

She was searching for something—what, she wasn't sure—but she was determined to find it nonetheless.

As she passed a fenced-off playground to her left, her chest tightened instinctively. She took an involuntary step back. After a deep breath, she pressed on. The playground soon gave way to buildings. She slowed, her steps faltering as she recognized the buildings.

Familiar demons from her past, built of well-worn brick and aged wood. She stopped and stared at one of those buildings where she had spent much of her life. This was the first time she'd seen the orphanage since the day she ran away.

Her breathing felt ragged and uncontrollable. Her mind was screaming at her. She wanted nothing more than to escape.

Run! it demanded.

But she didn't move or look away.

Instead, Vella took a shaky step back and lowered herself onto a nearby bench, with her eyes fixed on the orphanage. Her hands trembled; she clenched them together in her lap to keep them steady. All those bad memories, all those painful moments, came rushing back. They tore and ripped at her, trying to break her completely.

Still, she was determined not to relent. Every time she felt her gaze instinctively slip away, she took a few deep breaths and forced her eyes back up. Even as tears welled in the corners of her eyes, she kept her gaze fixed ahead, brushing them away without blinking.

She could feel Cole with her, giving her strength, telling her to stay and not look away. No matter what.

With a shaky breath, she wiped her eyes again, determined to persist until every memory played out. No matter how much it hurt.

Much like when she faced Ivy with Cole by her side, she worked her way through it step by step. There was only one way she would leave this place, and that would be on her terms. Not until she could stare down all the pain, the grief, and suffering without flinching.

Her breathing evened out as the memories continued to play out in her mind. In all the endless hours of torment she had faced alone, there was someone new in them. That child was no longer alone. She was there to comfort that child and show them a way out of the darkness.

As the first light of dawn crept across the sky, it all became clear to her. The orphanage that had caused her so much pain and suffering wasn't the answer she wanted when she began her long walk. But she knew it was *the answer.*

The battle wasn't over, but she had worked through as much as she could for today. It would take time to conquer her demons, and she was ready for the fight.

With renewed resolve, she rose, smiled, and walked away.

At the same time, Alex stood at the head of Cole's grave. He had just finished digging a shallow, rectangular hole. Bending down, he strained to lift a rough sandstone slab and fit it into place. Once it was in, he twisted and straightened it. Then, using the loose dirt around him, he filled the extra space and packed it down to keep the slab steady.

Satisfied, he stepped back to the foot of the grave, his gaze fixed on it.

Not long after, Vella approached, her footsteps soft on the leaves. She stood next to him and took note of the slab and the two names engraved on it.

"It's perfect," she said.

Alex shifted closer, resting a hand on her shoulder. "I've been thinking," he began, his voice low.

Vella's gaze turned wary. "You're not considering going in to find it, are you?"

"The thought has crossed my mind. We have a way out, just sitting there," he said, his voice tinged with frustration. He sighed, shaking his head. "But no. We'd be throwing our lives away."

"Good," she murmured.

"The last time I saw Edgar . . . he said it was a curse." He paused. "Do you think the orb is a curse?"

Her jaw tightened as she thought. "I'm not sure."

"That night, Edgar told me it might lead to disaster if we were successful. I'm starting to think he was right. They're not just going to let us go, are they? And what if it does make everything worse?"

"Maybe it will," Vella said, voice somber. "Maybe it's all pointless, but that's not going to stop us. That didn't stop Edgar from trying. There's only one way to find out, right?"

"Right," Alex said. "But we won't be the ones to do that."

"No. But someday, someone will."

"I hope for their sake Edgar is wrong," Alex muttered.

They stood in silence. Their minds drifting through the past, tangled in "what-ifs" and "if onlys." Vella was the first to pull herself back and instead contemplated what lay ahead.

"I promise I'll be there for your child," she said.

"I know."

"He wanted you to know that he loved you."

"I know."

After a pause, Vella continued, her tone more tentative. "There's something I want to ask you about."

Alex sat at the table, staring at the breakfast Ellie prepared for him: eggs on toast with a side of fresh fruit. His gaze lingered on the plate, then crept up to Ellie's face. He didn't speak. He just watched her as if searching for something in her expression, but there was nothing he needed to find. Ellie, noticing him staring, slowed her chewing and looked back at him.

"You all right?"

"Uh-huh."

Ellie raised an eyebrow and pointed at his plate. "Eat."

"I am."

They ate in silence.

They left the house together.

They ate lunch together.

He wanted more of this, but he was happy if this was all there was.

If this was the last day, he would accept that.

They sat in the middle of the park together.

"What do you want to do tonight?" she asked.

"Whatever you want."

"Are you okay?"

"Never better."

"Alex. Spit it out."

"You were right."

"Oh?"

"I haven't been present. But not anymore. I want to spend every second with you. Here."

"Good."

"Good? Is that it?"

"I knew you would come around."

"I had people I loved . . . and I acted the same way. I came around like I knew you would. When you have exhausted all other options, all you have left is acceptance. So, you do just that. Accept. Or . . ."

"Or what?"

"Suffer."

"Easier said than done."

"Yes. It's unbelievably difficult."

"Who was it for you?"

"It wasn't just one person."

"I'm sorry."

"Don't be. Everyone has their turn eventually."

"Ellie."

"What?"

"Why do you want nothing to be different?"

"It's not a matter of want. It's choosing not to play a game you can't win. One that only leads to suffering."

"How do you choose not to play?"

"Listen carefully and pay fierce attention. Channel all your regrets, anger, and fears into what's around you, here and now."

Work felt oddly muted without Vella's presence, even though the hum of lively chatter surrounded Leah. Vella had moved back in with her, but she hadn't returned to work yet. Leah sat at her workstation, unsure why she was there herself. Anything to distract herself was better than being alone with her thoughts.

Her hands moved mechanically, crafting shoes on autopilot,

but her mind was elsewhere. *What's she going to do now? It'll take her a long time to adjust without Cole. I can't push her too hard.*

She refocused on her work; the repetitive motion of her task gave her a brief break from thinking.

All of a sudden, her hands froze mid-task without her realizing it. Her thoughts surged, turning dark. She stared with a vacant expression at the floor. The familiar feeling of hopelessness took her over.

Cole . . . Edgar . . . Dammit . . . She bit her bottom lip as a familiar voice played on autopilot. *They're dead because of you. You failed them. Monster. It should have been you instead. Look at what you did.*

She could feel it building, the storm of emotions threatening to break her. Leah's breathing quickened, and she set her tools aside, trying to push it all down.

Not now, Leah. Not here. But it was too late.

She stood and fled, leaving everything behind without a word. The moment she got home, she slammed her bedroom door shut and let the tears fall.

When Vella returned from a walk, she prepared a simple lunch and brought it to Leah. They sat together on the bed, eating in silence, the comfort of each other's presence more than enough.

After clearing the dishes, Vella came back with a small stack of papers in hand.

"I think he'd want you to have these," she said, passing them to Leah.

Leah took the papers and flipped through them, feeling the lump in her throat build. Each page was the same picture, the moment Cole had tried to capture many times—the memory of them sitting in the backyard together. Leah noticed how the sketches had evolved, each one more detailed and refined than the last. She picked out the one she liked best and stared at it.

"Why this scene of us? If it's something that happened, I don't remember it."

Vella shrugged. "It was important to him. That's all that matters."

"I miss him so much," Leah whispered. Her eyes lingered on the drawing. "It's beautiful."

She soaked in every detail of Cole's familiar lines and shading.

"I remember earlier versions of this. They weren't as nice as this one," Leah said, wiping her eyes. "Did you find any more of his work?"

"I think I found all of them."

"Did you throw out the . . . bad ones?"

"No. He must have done that himself. The ones left . . . they're amazing. I'll show you later."

Leah let out a deep breath. "Good . . . Very good . . . It was the only way he knew how to express himself . . . he bottled up too much, refusing to let anyone help. I'm glad he found his peace before the end."

Vella placed the papers aside and settled against Leah.

"I talked to Alex today," Vella said.

"What about?"

"I've given it some thought . . . . I want to work at the orphanage."

Leah looked at her, surprised. "The orphanage?"

"Yeah."

"Even after . . . all you went through . . ."

"Because of what I went through," Vella said. "I don't want anyone else to suffer the way I did."

Leah smiled and nodded. "That's wonderful. I'm proud of you. He would be proud of you."

Vella swallowed and cleared her throat. "Alex said it wouldn't be an issue to start in a small role, then maybe move into teaching and other areas."

Leah pulled her into a tight embrace, tears welling. "And here I was, worried about you. Of course, you'll be fine."

"I can keep an eye on Amy for you too."

"You don't need—"

"I want to," she said. "I'll take her in as soon as I can. I'll tell her all about her amazing mother and father."

Leah turned away, wiping her eyes. "Thank you," she said. "Dammit, I'm tired of crying. I'm not some little girl."

"It's all right. It's just us."

Leah sighed, rubbing her eyes. "I'm supposed to be the strong one. I'm supposed to help others."

"You're not supposed to do anything. You've had to hide it for too long. You're allowed to let it out; it doesn't make you weak or a little girl. It makes you human . . . it means you're alive."

Leah tightened her embrace and kissed her. "I know. But I've always prided myself on being the one people could rely on. And yet, I feel like I'm relying on you to keep me going."

"Why can't we rely on each other?"

Leah hesitated before nodding. "I . . . I can live with that."

"I had a wonderful role model to learn from. I'll keep throwing your own advice back at you until you take it."

Leah smiled, a little more at ease. Vella added, "These days should be for you. What do you want to do?"

"I don't know."

"It's not too late to start thinking about enjoying yourself. Do the things you've always wanted to."

"I don't need much more than I already have."

"Even . . . maybe . . . just, you know, have some fun. There's Harry from work; he always seems to have an eye on you. He's not too bad. There's a bit of an age gap, but that doesn't seem to bother him."

"Vella!"

She shrugged. "I'm just saying."

They both burst into laughter.

"I'm well past my prime anyway," Leah said.

"Not to Harry."

"Stop it," Leah said through laughter. "You're so bad."

The laughter faded, leaving behind a comfortable silence.

"No, Vella . . . I can't."

"I know. I'm just messing around . . . he chews with his mouth open anyway."

They shared a light chuckle. "God, I hate that."

Leah's eyes drifted to the window, her smile slipping away, eyes growing distant.

She drew in a breath and released it slowly, deliberately through her nose. "I can't help but think of these wasted years. I had it all . . . I could've had unconditional love every day with Edgar and Amy, but instead, I chose nothing and will leave with nothing. Truth is . . . I never deserved it."

"No one's deserving of love."

"You are."

"No, that's not what I mean. We trick ourselves into thinking we aren't deserving of things that are freely available. The truth is no one needs to be deserving of love. It's everywhere. The only thing we need is to have the strength to accept it."

"I . . . couldn't. It was all given to me, and I didn't even see it. Everything I ever needed and wanted, and now it's gone."

"You may not have got what you wanted but you were able to give Cole all he ever wanted. None of your love went to waste. It's all right there in the drawing."

"And where is he now?"

"Where we all end up . . . doesn't mean it was a waste."

Leah wiped her eyes. "Please don't ever leave me," she whispered.

"Never."

The light from outside faded as they stayed in bed.

"Are you sure you're ready to get back out there and start working?" Leah asked.

Vella nodded. "Yeah. I'm ready." After a pause, she added, "Edgar was there for me, morning, noon, and night. He never spoke; he just sat there. It helped. Having someone around. He taught me that sometimes, just being there can make all the difference. So I decided that, no matter how small, I'll do something to help . . . for those still around."

We were right about you, Leah thought.

"I'm done with hiding away. That's not what Cole would have wanted . . . or Edgar," Vella said.

"You make me feel like I did something right," Leah said.

Vella fidgeted with loose strands of hair. "There's something I wanted to ask you."

"What's that?"

"I know its early, but I have decided on a name for our child."

Leah looked at her, curious. "Oh?"

"Edgar if it's a boy, and Leah if it's a girl—with your permission, of course."

Leah could feel her throat constricting. She was about to flat out refuse, but she stopped herself. "You can do whatever you like, but . . . are you sure you want to?"

"This place could always use a Leah."

Leah shook her head. "That—" She paused, straightened up, and cleared her throat, struggling to find the words. "I would be honored . . . so would he."

Leah ran a gentle hand over Vella's stomach.

"Well," Leah said. "With your new job, we should cut your hair. I have an idea for something that will look great on you."

Without a second thought, Vella responded.

"No. I like it the way it is," she said, sweeping her bangs to the other side, away from her droopy eyelid.

51

Today comes my turn. When it's yours I hope it's an end not chosen for you by others.

—THE FIRST PEOPLE OF EDEN
Journal of Morgan #38
Day 1945

Vella woke to a familiar, beautiful Eden morning, like every other day. Sliding her feet off the bed, she stretched as she sat up.

She pulled an old, worn note from the drawer of her bedside table and unfolded it. With a smile, she took in the final reminder of the simple value she needed to bring to life. To honor the one who had written her the note, she worked every day with the same care and dedication he had once shown her.

After folding the note and slipping it into her pocket, Vella caught her reflection in the mirror across the room. The same face from twenty years ago stared back at her, though now thoroughly worn in by time and holding a few more lines. The extra definition didn't bother her; each wrinkle was proof that she'd lived. Content with what she saw, she grabbed a ribbon from the table and tied her hair back into a simple ponytail.

She did her morning stretches, repeating the same routine they had followed every dawn in the clearing. Her gaze glided across the room, where children's drawings covered the walls, scattered like wildflowers in a meadow. Bright splashes of color bloomed everywhere—crayon suns, handprints, stick-figure families, and fantastical creatures. They filled every inch, a chaotic patchwork of imagination, as if the room itself had been painted by countless tiny hands.

Two of her favorites sat framed on her bedside table. One from Amy, given to Edgar, and another from her little Leah, only five years old at the time. She glanced at them, her smile deepening.

A section of the wall interrupted the explosion of color,

reserved for Cole's sketches. At the center was a drawing of him and Leah sitting in the backyard, soaking in a rare moment of peace. A favorite of hers hung beside it—a picture of her and Cole by the shed. She knelt in the garden, planting some orchids, while he sat off to the side, dozing in the sun. Originally, the sketch had only shown her. A small lone figure among the sea of flowers and trees. She asked Leah to add him in later, as she felt the girl in the drawing seemed lonely. She had inherited enough of her father's talent to make the inclusion seamless. Blending him into the scene as if he had always been there.

Finishing her stretches, she turned to the window, where Eden's beauty never failed to bring a smile to her face. The sun was beginning to rise, its light creeping into the room. Vella opened the window, savoring the feel of the morning breeze on her skin. From her second-floor vantage, Eden stretched out before her, tranquil and awash in the morning light.

She rubbed her left eye, aware that the years hadn't been kind to her vision. The sagging of her eyelid led to issues with distortion and blurriness that had worsened over the years. It was manageable, but frustrating nonetheless. Today, though, was a good day. She wiped away some of the cold from her eye and felt thankful she could experience the view with clarity. One last time.

The creak at the bedroom door broke her reverie.

"You're up already? I was hoping to surprise you."

A girl of nineteen stepped into the room, balancing a tray piled with food. A fresh pot of tea teetered on the edge, threatening to spill over.

"What's all this?"

"I made all your favorite breakfast foods."

"It smells wonderful. Thank you, Leah," Vella said. She sat down and patted the bed beside her. "I'm not finishing that alone. Come, sit."

Leah set the tray down and climbed onto the bed, facing her.

"It looks amazing. Thank you."

As Vella picked at the food, Leah sat in silence, her eyes never leaving her mother's face. She seemed to be memorizing every detail, absorbing the moment as if trying to make it last forever.

"Are you just gonna stare at me, or are you going to eat?"

"Sorry," Leah said. She picked up a slice of roasted tomato and ate it. Her face seemed to darken with each chew.

"Hey," Vella said in a low voice.

"No, it's okay. I'm okay," Leah said, forcing a smile that didn't quite reach her eyes.

A voice at the door interrupted them.

"Leah! Dammit . . . I knew we should have planned this together," said a girl of twenty-five standing in the doorway. She stepped in carrying a large wooden box, steam billowing from its seams.

"Amy! Don't tell me," Leah said.

"I spent an hour making all this. I woke up so early," Amy groaned.

Vella chuckled. "Thank you, Amy. I'm the luckiest woman in Eden. Come, sit. We can have a feast."

They made room on the bed, and Amy opened the box, releasing a cloud of mist that billowed over them.

"Mine's better. It doesn't give you third-degree burns," Leah said, swatting away the steam.

"They both look amazing. Thank you, Amy," Vella said.

"As if, Leah. Try the eggs and the breakfast smoothie I made," Amy urged.

Leah picked out some of the eggs, and her face contorted into an exaggerated grimace.

"Yeah, right. It's delicious, and you know it," Amy said.

"It's poison, Mum. Don't eat it," Leah said, holding the face.

Amy scraped a bit of blackened toast with her fingernail. "Look at that toast you made; it's all burnt."

Vella laughed at their petty squabble. It reminded her of when they were little girls fighting for her attention.

"Girls, enough," Vella said. "I'm going to try everything. It all looks delicious. Thank you, both of you."

"Anything for you," Amy said.

"Today's your day," Leah said. "Name it and it's yours."

"I got all I need," Vella said.

They ate, talked, and laughed together. But as the minutes passed, Vella sensed their moods shifting. The chatter quieted, and the air grew heavy with the sorrow they were trying to push away.

Vella finished off some toast and brushed off her hands. "Hey, come on. The day's still young. No getting sad yet."

"Sorry," Amy and Leah said in almost unison.

"I know it's tough, but we have today. That's what matters. Be with me now."

They nodded faintly, their inner turmoil written all over their faces.

"Aunty Vella!" a chorus of voices shouted from the doorway. Six children, ages five to ten, crowded the entrance. A boy of nineteen stood behind them. Two of the girls carried trays of fruit, toast, and tea.

"We made you breakfast," one of the girls declared. Their collective joy wilted when they saw Leah and Amy already sitting on the bed.

"I should've known," the boy of nineteen said, shaking his head, grinning.

"Ha! Too slow, Simon," Leah gloated.

Vella waved them in. "Thank you, everyone. I have way too much food here; I need help eating it."

They squeezed onto the bed, Vella in the middle, flanked on all sides. Simon hovered at the edge. Vella smiled, noticing that he bore all the trademark features of his parents—tall and fair-haired like Alex, with the soft eyes and slender face of Ellie.

"That means you too, Simon," Vella insisted.

Leah made room next to her, and Simon joined them, perched on the bed's edge.

"We're going to miss you," a six-year-old boy said, his voice small and sad.

Vella's chest ached as she glanced around at the children's faces. "I'm sorry, I have to go away for a while. I'll miss you too, but you have Amy, Leah, and Simon to look after you."

"But we want you," another girl blurted out, her eyes welling with tears.

"I wouldn't want to be stuck with Leah either," Simon said, nudging her.

Leah gave him a light shove, a smile breaking through. "They like me a lot more than you," she retorted.

Vella observed them, savoring the moment. Pride swelled in her chest, tightening with emotion.

What did I do to deserve this? she wondered.

A little girl chimed in, breaking the light, playful scene. "When will you be back?"

Vella's whole body tensed. Everyone froze, caught in the threat of being overwhelmed by grief. Not a whisper of a breath could be heard.

Vella ran a hand through her hair and embraced her. "We'll be together again, one day soon."

"Promise?"

"I promise."

Leah was quick to brush her eye. Then, before it all got too much for them she cleared her throat and declared, "Mom, I think everyone would like to hear a story."

A chorus of affirmation surrounded her, clamoring for one of her stories.

"All right, all right, what would you like to hear?"

"The Knights of Acidalia," Amy said.

"Haven't you heard it enough?"

"Impossible."

So she told them the story her mother had written. Sharing it one last time. Simon, Amy, and Leah had heard it many times, but they still enjoyed hearing it come from her. They finished off the food as they listened, leaving nothing behind. As the last bites disappeared and the story ended, she noticed their grip on their emotions slipping. Conversation grew quieter and faces dropped.

Amy caught this and announced, "Come on, everyone out, let Aunty Vella get dressed."

Vella gave each of them a hug, and they exchanged "I love yous." The children clung to Vella, writhing and shouting in protest as they were pried away. Leah, Amy, and Simon shepherded them out, leaving Vella alone.

She took a deep breath, letting the bittersweet moment sink in before she rose to wash and dress.

Before leaving, one of Cole's drawings caught her eye. It was of her as Isara. The knight from her mother's book, clad in impenetrable armor, with a shield, a bow of light, and the radiant sword. She stood defiantly, sword held high. But she was no longer that knight. Like Isara, her power left her—lost over the years. Vella's power came in a different form; the people around her—Cole, Edgar, Leah, and Alex. They passed away one after another, leaving her behind. Still, she carried on for them.

Edgar's words played in her mind: *After Isara lost her powers and became queen, that's when she truly left her mark. Anyone could've done what she did with those powers. But it was the days and years that followed when she helped her people in the aftermath. That's what really mattered.*

And she thought, *I hope I did enough.*

Unlike Isara, there was no grand victory. No freedom. No slaying of great beasts. Only the quiet duty of living on and making things better for those who would come long after she faded away.

Leah sat on a bench in the hallway, her fingers tapping on the wood restlessly. The moment Vella emerged, she shot up and approached her with a drawing in hand.

"Can I keep this one?" she asked.

It was a top-down view of Cole, Vella, Leah, Alex, and Edgar sprawled out in the clearing. Vella's head rested on Cole's chest as they looked up at the sky. Edgar and Leah were lying on their backs, head to toe, asleep. Alex sat leaning against a log, staring out into the distance, with Ellie on his shoulder.

Vella's gaze lingered on the drawing. The day he captured had been one filled with unspoken dread. Yet seeing how peaceful they all looked now filled her with a bittersweet warmth. And a deep ache, longing for one more day with them.

"Of course, you can keep all of them."

Leah took another look at it. "Dad had incredible talent."

Vella stared at it, attempting to hold a smile.

"I know . . . But you're not far off."

"I wish." Leah put the picture back in Vella's room and ran back out.

"Come on, let's go for a walk," Leah said, slipping her arm through Vella's, guiding her forward.

Vella raised an eyebrow. "What're you up to?"

"Nothing."

"Sure you aren't. Where did everyone else go?"

"Don't worry about that. Let's go see Dad."

Vella nodded, a soft smile forming.

"That sounds nice."

Before heading to their destination, Vella requested a stop at the memorial. The early morning ensured they were alone, allowing them to walk in peace.

At the memorial, the morning sun glinted off the engraved names. Vella's eyes traced the list of those born around the same time as her, Cole and Alex among them. Each name bore the years of birth and death. Her name stood alone without the latter. At least for one more day.

They continued on, beginning the walk through the display of handprints of the past. They stopped where Vella's clay handprint was embedded in the wall. She placed her hand over it, whispering to the little girl that made it. *I have one hell of a story to tell you. Hang in there. It'll all turn out all right.*

They moved on and soon came to Amy's.

When Vella started working at the orphanage full-time, she made it a priority to spend as much time with Amy as she could. She even moved into the orphanage with baby Leah to be closer to her, and before long, she became a mother figure to Amy. True to her word, Vella shared everything she could about Amy's parents over the years—mostly the good parts. As Amy grew older, she decided she wanted to work at the orphanage too. Inspired by her hero, Vella.

She began by helping with the younger children. Then, bit by bit, she took on more responsibility, soon becoming Vella's second in command. Just as Vella had been like a mother to Amy, Simon, and Leah, Amy became an older sister to Simon and Leah. And like an older sister, she was fierce in her protection of them. In those moments, Vella could see flashes of Amy's mother, ready to dispense divine judgment on anyone who so much as looked at them the wrong way. Under Vella's guidance, Amy had grown to embody the best parts of both Leah and Edgar. But she couldn't escape her parents, and that meant she couldn't escape their struggles either. Vella saw it early on and helped her learn to express those feelings and seek help when she needed it.

Simon and Leah's handprints came a little further down.

Growing up, Simon had been easy to keep track of since he was the same age as Leah. Simon was raised by Alex until his father passed away when he was eight. After that, he moved into the orphanage, where Vella could look after him. Vella shared as much as she could with him about his parents. He inherited their calm temperament, which made him easy to work with. He was more reserved than Leah, but a thoughtful communicator all the same. Still, there was a layer of determination and fire that lay beneath the surface, ready to come out when needed.

Leah, on the other hand, was very much her parents' child. She had their competitive nature and brashness. She was vibrant and intense, with a natural energy like Vella and combative like Cole. Leah, too, wanted to follow in her mother's footsteps. When she was old enough, she started working at the orphanage. Determined in her ultimate goal to take over from Amy and carry on the legacy that her mother had built.

Vella had poured all her time and love into them, and it showed. They cared for her dearly and were almost fanatical in their protectiveness of her. A surge of pride ran through her thinking of the compassionate, outstanding adults they had become. It gave her a boost of energy she was in desperate need of.

Throughout their stroll, Vella noticed the names of those she had watched grow up at the orphanage. The children she helped raise. She paused at each, plucking a memory of them from her mind, one by one. There were almost too many for her to keep track of.

The names moved from those who had passed away to adults, then to teenagers, and finally to children still trying to find their place in the world.

All those lives she touched, and that had touched her, filled her with a bittersweet ache of pride and sorrow.

She held back tears. *Not yet*, she pleaded.

Leah crept closer to her. "Don't worry, it's just us," she whispered.

Vella allowed herself to let go, tears slipping down her cheeks as she surrendered to the flood of emotions. Allowing whatever needed to fall, to fall. She'd hoped to find the strength to make it through most of the day without breaking. But in truth, she knew that would never happen. She just didn't think it would be this early.

Who was I fooling?

When they finished at the memorial, they took a slow walk through the heart of Eden. People stopped them along the way, greeting Vella warmly. Many heartfelt final conversations and goodbyes were exchanged, some knowingly, others unknowingly. Almost everyone in Eden knew her, whether from growing up in the orphanage or from taking her classes. She'd become an important matriarchal figure. One that many turned to for support and guidance over the last twenty years.

They reached the edge of a familiar street. They stopped in front of a home that used to hold her greatest treasures—Cole, Leah, Edgar, and the little family they had built. The house was gone, demolished and rebuilt. Its time had come and gone as all things did, but in her mind's eye, she could still see it as it once was, filled with warmth and love. The memories played out like scenes from an old, beloved film.

A young boy and girl were ushered out of the new house by a woman, who called out when she saw Vella. A moment later, she ran over and embraced her.

"I can't believe it's your last day," the woman said. "I'm going to miss you so much."

"I'm going to miss you too, Megan."

Megan was Ivy's daughter. Ivy, once Vella's childhood tormentor, had become a friend. Toward the end of Ivy's life, she had apologized and they had reconciled. The end of one's existence does many things to the mind; regrets blare, refusing to be ignored, something Vella had become painfully aware of as people passed away while she remained. Though Vella had forgiven her, Ivy refused to accept it and carried the weight of her regret and guilt to the end.

"I'd better see you again today," Megan said.

She gave one final squeeze before letting go.

"You will," Vella assured her.

"We'll be back at the orphanage soon," Leah added. "I'm just taking her for a walk."

The rest of their walk through Eden had followed the same pattern—hugs and kisses, goodbyes, and many whispered words of gratitude.

When they reached the edge of the woods, the rest of their walk was peaceful. It allowed Vella to gather some strength back that she knew she would need to get through the day.

Her former home was unrecognizable from how it had been twenty years ago. A towering tree now reached for the sky where the shed once stood. Vella planted it herself a decade earlier. Its branches swayed gently in the breeze.

It was surrounded by a vibrant garden of flowers that bloomed in a riot of colors. Off to the side, the gentle mound of Cole's grave rose from the earth.

Vella and Cole's wooden swords stood planted beside the headstone, their once-sturdy frames now worn and rotting. Over the years, additional names had been carved into the sandstone slab. Leah and Alex now rested alongside Cole and Edgar.

Stepping closer, Vella knelt down, pulling away the encroaching weeds and tall grass that had begun to obscure the names. She took a small knife from her pocket. Then she etched her name with the others.

She smiled and whispered, "It's finally my time. I'll be joining you soon."

Vella rose and walked back to her daughter's side, where they stood together at the foot of the grave.

Even after all these years, Vella's heartache had never left. The scar had never fully healed. And as the years passed, the ache only seemed to grow worse.

Those fateful five minutes still haunted her. Her missed opportunity to save Cole always came flooding back. She thought that if she had only searched the area where she eventually found the orb—gone this way instead of that, done this instead of that—he might still be there with her. Weeks would pass without the thought crossing her mind. Then there were days when it tortured her every excruciating waking second.

She only had months of what she wanted a lifetime of. In the context of her life, it was a brief flash. Being alone remained the only constant and being alone only felt worse now. She knew what she was missing.

All those lonely mornings, waking up to stare at a blank wall, did nothing to help. She'd even considered taking down his drawings, to avoid the constant reminder of what she was missing. During those times, when the pain of her life felt inescapable, only the children of her loved ones could offer the spark she needed to carry on.

Her throat and eyes burned as memories of him flooded back. Luckily for her, Leah saved her.

"I wish we could bury you here with him," Leah murmured.

Vella blinked, and chuckled. "Why?"

"You belong here with him . . . and me."

"I'll always be with you." She turned to face her daughter. "You carry the best parts of your father and me. That's how I know you'll be fine. Though I hope you didn't inherit too much of our impulsiveness."

A smile broke through Leah's heavy expression, a mischievous glint in her eye. "I hope I got all of it."

They wanted to laugh, but nothing came. Leah could only tighten her grip on her mother's hand.

"Promise you'll find it and come back to us," Leah whispered.

Vella put an arm around her. "I promise I'll try."

"Is it really in there?"

"It is."

Vella's thoughts wandered to Alex's last day. She'd stood beside him at the crimson door, feeling the weight of his dread as he prepared to face certain death. Before he entered, she assured him she would look after Simon like he was her own child. It was an assurance he didn't need. He already knew.

Few had dared to enter since rumors of the time-traveling orb had spread, none successful so far. The horrors waiting beyond the door were too great a burden for most, but Alex stood resolute, conviction steadying his trembling hands. Even knowing the odds, even with no clear chance of victory, he stood firm. Ready.

Alex had lived a full and meaningful life. He had become mayor at the young age of twenty-three and dedicated the rest of his years to serving the people of Eden. His leadership left an indelible mark on the community. Recognizing the struggles many faced, he established a new branch of administration: social services. He tasked them with identifying and supporting those most at risk of self-harm. The team reached out to those who had become isolated, helping them navigate the grief and trauma that often followed the loss of a friend or loved one. They sought not only to prevent people from slipping into despair but also to help bring them out of it, offering tools to cope, heal, and reconnect with the community. What started with two dedicated individuals grew into a team of five. Together, they drastically reduced suicide rates, fostering a closer and more compassionate community. Despite these successes, each loss that slipped through their net weighed on Alex. He took each one personally, driving him to improve the system.

When Ellie passed away, grief threatened to overwhelm him. But Vella stood by him, offering comfort and support. Simon, with his mother's bright smile and spirit, became a beacon of hope for Alex, reminding him of all the reasons to keep fighting. Years after Alex's passing, Simon continued his father's legacy by joining social services at just fourteen.

Like his father, he dedicated himself to the well-being of Eden's citizens.

Vella remembered embracing Alex one final time. They'd held each other close as the magnitude of the moment dawned on them.

"What a good life it was," he had said.

"You made a real difference," she'd assured him.

Alex was far from the picture of strength, breaking down several times in his final moments. He almost backed out many times, and Vella reassured him that he didn't have to go through with it. But he pressed on anyway, aware of what awaited him.

The last thing she heard him say was, "I have to try. If we don't, who will?"

When the door opened, she remembered him staring up at the sky, as if hoping for something to happen. When nothing did, he dropped his head and stepped inside.

She stood alone and took it all in. It wasn't heroic; it wasn't pretty, but she watched anyway, ensuring she was there for him. It was the least she could do, making sure he wasn't alone at the end.

As Vella and Leah approached the orphanage, a large crowd of children and adults awaited them. Amy stood at the head of the group, her eyes brimming with excitement. The children waved and cheered when they saw Vella.

"So, this is what you were distracting me from?" Vella asked.

"I don't know what you're talking about. Come on," Leah said with a sly grin.

Amy joined Vella's side. "What's going on?" Vella asked.

She shared the same sly expression as Leah. "We prepared a special surprise."

It was then that Vella noticed an object covered in cloth hanging above the front door of the orphanage.

Amy stepped forward, clearing her throat to gather everyone's attention.

"On behalf of everyone at the orphanage and all the citizens of Eden," she began, her voice steady but wavering with emotion. "Vella, we want to thank you for your immeasurable contribution over the past twenty years, including your seventeen years as head of the orphanage. You made this place what it is today. Without you, many of us wouldn't be who we are."

Vella felt the lump in her throat building. She tried to push it down, to maintain her composure, but the emotion was overwhelming.

Hold on, she told herself, *not yet*.

Amy continued, "Your impact goes beyond anything that can be measured in numbers or years. You've shaped lives. You gave us more than a place to live. You gave us a home. You gave us family. There wasn't a time I can recall when you turned anyone away or refused to help. In fact, you seemed to seek out as many people as possible, making it your mission to talk to everyone you saw, almost as if you were trying to break your record from the day before. Honestly, it was a little terrifying because if she caught sight of you, she would talk to you whether you wanted her to or not. You could run, but you couldn't hide."

She paused as laughter rose from the crowd.

"But it was amazing, really. You always tried to find anyone in need because you recognize that when someone doesn't want to talk, that's often when they need to the most. That's what I love about you. You understand people."

Amy took a moment to clear her throat and shift her tone.

"I cannot replace you. No one can. But I promise I will do my best to follow in your footsteps and keep this place as beautiful as you left it. All I can hope for is to make even half the impact you've had on so many lives."

Vella wiped away the tears forming in her eyes. Amy's voice softened as she met Vella's gaze. "We all love you with all our hearts, like you do us. It would be our honor to dedicate the orphanage in your name."

With that, she gave the signal and a rope was pulled. The cloth fell away, revealing a plaque.

It read: *Vella's Home for the Children of Eden.*

Vella's hands moved to her mouth, her face twisting with the effort to hold back tears. She turned her head, eyes fluttering, but it was no use. The tears spilled over. Amy was beside her in an instant, pulling her into a comforting embrace.

"Dammit, Amy," Vella whispered, her voice thick with emotion. "What've you done?"

Amy held her tighter. "This way, you'll always be with us."

Vella pulled back. "It's too much . . . thank you."

She turned to Leah, pulling her into a hug as well, spreading her appreciation. The children, unable to contain their excitement, called out her name. Vella laughed through her tears as dozens of small arms swarmed her, with each child eager to give her a hug.

Minutes passed in a blur of hugs, smiles, and whispered words of gratitude. Vella did her best to acknowledge everyone. Her composure slipping further with each embrace. It was too much.

It was going to be a much harder day than she'd anticipated.

In Vella's final weeks, things didn't go as she had hoped. The joy and celebration of life she wanted were overshadowed by many difficult days. Amy was with her on one such day and asked how her mother dealt with it. Vella lied, telling her that her mother, Leah, had been unwavering and strong until the very end.

The truth was that Leah's end was a painful, agonizing, drawn-out ordeal. Vella did what she could, but her newborn, Leah, demanded most of her attention. Looking after both was a full-time job that drained her physically and emotionally.

The decline started with two months left. During dinner one night, Leah stopped eating, her spoon slipping from her grasp, food spilling everywhere. She broke into tears, begging for help.

That marked the beginning of a difficult stretch for all of them. Leah lost the strength to manage her lingering grief and ability to deal with her impending death.

Work became a struggle; she managed to go only a few days a week, and soon, even leaving the house was too much. The headstrong, vibrant woman Vella knew faded to a shadow of her former self.

Alex was there daily, trying to help alleviate the burden on Vella. He offered to bring Amy to visit, but Leah refused. "She can't remember me like this," she had said.

Despite the tough times, Leah had her stable days. On those rare, precious days, Vella would take her and the baby out to bask in the sunshine, wasting the day away together. Those were the days Vella held on to, the ones she remembered with fondness.

Her last two weeks were excruciating for all of them. She had constant manic episodes, making her even more difficult to manage. Alex was over at the house almost the whole time, working with her to help prepare her for the end.

Vella resigned herself to the belief that there were no more days left of the Leah she had once known and loved. Then, with three days left, Leah had an unexpectedly good day. A burst of clarity and resolve that seemed to come from nowhere. Leah decided that would be the day, while she could still find beauty in the world around her.

Vella and Alex assisted her to the Peaceful Passage, where they helped guide her through the transition themselves. For Vella, there were few moments in life as painful as that. She wasn't sure if even Cole's death had been as heartbreaking as that.

Vella had once promised she would never leave Leah, and she meant it. She stayed by Leah's side, gripping her hand and holding her gaze until Leah's eyes closed for the final time. It wasn't heroic; it wasn't pretty, but they were there for her. It was the least they could do for her, making sure she wasn't alone at the end.

It was late afternoon when Vella decided it was time. She'd finished her final goodbyes and tied up all loose ends. Emotionally drained, her body felt weighed down, struggling to stay upright. Her eyes were bloodshot, her eyelids swollen, and the skin around them was dry and dark from too many tears.

Only Simon, Amy, and Leah followed Vella to the red door. They were the only ones she had told about the path she'd chosen, while everyone else believed she would be taking the Peaceful Passage as her way out.

Vella sat facing the doors while the other three stood back, giving her space. They endured the painful wait in silence. For the three of them, time felt like it was flying by and dragging endlessly all at once.

Then, out of nowhere, Vella straightened up and looked around. They saw her shaking and they thought they heard a muffled laugh. But just as soon as it started, it stopped.

She jumped up and turned around, grinning. "You know what? I need to warm up. I'm going for a short run."

They exchanged confused looks and before they could say anything, Vella took off at a brisk pace. She disappeared for a couple of minutes before returning, still smiling. This time, she came back with what looked like a spade in her hand. She threw it to the side and stretched.

"Okay, I'm ready," she declared.

"What's that?" Amy asked, pointing at the spade.

"That's what your father used to kill the Bear."

They glanced at each other with wide eyes. "With that?"

"Uh-huh."

Leah picked up the spade-turned-spear, examining it in her hands. The wood had weathered and worn, its surface rough with years of neglect. But the tip gleamed, looking recently sharpened. She gripped the handle, wondering how her father had killed such a monster with just this. She knew the story well, but some part of her still found it hard to believe.

Her eyes traced down the handle where a red stain caught her eye. It lay between the base and the handle. A sick, twisting feeling built up in her stomach.

Vella gently took it from her hands. "Don't worry, that's not his blood."

Leah looked up, her face pale. She gave a weak nod and went back to stand with the others. Vella went to place it next to the door and went back to face them.

Her eyes drifted past them, and she smiled.

Leah turned her head. "What are you looking at?"

Vella's eyes shifted back to Leah. "Nothing."

"Mom . . . are you sure about this?" Leah asked.

Vella glanced across them, her gaze steady. "I have to try," she said.

"No, you don't!" Leah said.

Amy stepped forward, her voice trembling. "Don't go. Take the painless way. Please."

Vella shook her head, a sad smile playing on her lips. "There is no such thing . . . and I can't, Amy. It's not who I am. They never gave up, so I don't. Ever."

"You'll never find it," Amy implored.

Vella's smile widened, a bit of mischief slipping into her voice. "Who says I already haven't?"

"This is not a joke," Amy snapped. "I don't doubt it's in there but . . . I can't watch you . . ." Amy stopped, unable to say the words.

"It's okay," Vella said. "You don't have to."

"I can't either," Leah said, teary-eyed.

"I will," Simon said. This was the first thing he'd said, and he made sure to meet her eye when he said it.

Vella smiled with warmth in her eyes. "It's up to you to decide what to do with your lives."

She shifted her attention to include all of them. "I know it's hard," she began, her voice gentle but firm. "I want you to think of one memory to remember me by. It doesn't need to be anything special or important, just something that makes you smile. Hold it close. When it all gets too much, use it. I have one with each of your parents, and in all of them we never even spoke a word."

A series of images flashed through Vella's mind. Watching Leah and Simon play in the park with Alex by her side. Sitting with Edgar in the shed. Lying in bed with Leah. Sitting on the park bench with Cole after he helped with Ivy. And, finally, all of them together in the clearing.

Simon nodded and swallowed against the lump in his throat. "The time when—"

"Don't tell me or anyone else," Vella said. "Keep it for

yourself. It's yours."

He nodded.

She looked across at them, and a smile formed, and she exhaled a soft laugh.

"What part of this is funny to you?" Amy snapped.

Leah attempted to hold her hand, but she ripped it away.

"No, it's not funny," Vella agreed, her tone calm and even.

"You're acting like this is a joke," Amy said, her voice shaking with anger.

"It's not," Vella said. "Far from it."

She walked over to Amy and pulled her into a tight hug. Amy collapsed against her, sobbing.

"I'm just so happy with how you three turned out."

"Don't go," Amy pleaded, her voice muffled against Vella's shoulder.

"I know it's hard, but I have to," Vella whispered.

Vella took care setting Amy back on her feet and motioned for Leah to hold her. Then she turned to Simon, who couldn't meet her gaze. Watching the woman who'd raised him leave forever was something he couldn't bear. She held out her arms, and he fell into her embrace, tears slipping down his cheeks.

"I'm going to miss you so much," he choked out. "I love you."

"*I* love you," Vella murmured, kissing him on the forehead. "Look after them for me."

When he regained his composure, she pulled him a step to the side and leaned in close and whispered something in his ear.

He pulled back, staring, face frozen. She held a faint smile and squinted her eyes at him, tilting her head.

Simon flicked a quick glance at Leah, then shifted his gaze around, unable to meet Vella's eyes for long.

She leaned in again and whispered more words to him.

He hesitated, mouth tight and nodded. "I'll look after her regardless. I promise."

"I know you will."

Leah's voice cut through. "Mom, what are you talking about?"

Vella gave Simon a knowing smile. "Nothing."

"Goddammit, Mom—" Leah cut herself off, looking away.

Vella held his gaze, feeling the struggle in his eyes to let her go.

"If you don't find it, I will, and I'll get them all out of here. I swear," he said, gritting his teeth.

Vella smiled. "I know you will."

She wiped away his tears with her thumb. "Cole used to speak of a fire burning within. I don't know if he ever realized it was anger disguised as fear. That's all it is. When you feel that, remember that and don't lose your head. It can be used, but don't let it use you."

Simon nodded, trying to regain his composure.

"Look at you. They would be so proud of you. I'm so proud of you."

Simon clung to her for one last reminder.

When she moved back to Amy, the young woman leaped into her arms, holding on as if her grip could keep her from leaving. Vella took the opportunity to slip a note into Amy's pocket— the one her father had written for her all those years ago.

"I don't know what I'll do without you," Amy whispered through her tears.

"You do," Vella assured her. "And when you don't, you have these two. I'm glad the orphanage and Eden are in such capable hands."

Vella pulled back to study her face; Leah and Edgar stared back at her.

I hope they're proud of me, Vella thought.

"I love you," Vella said.

"I love you more," Amy said, pulling her in again. She was able to let go after much effort, overcoming heavy internal resistance.

Leah was last. She wrapped her arms around Vella and gripped her shirt, pulling her close.

"I can't breathe," Vella exhaled with a chuckle.

She loosened her grip but kept a firm hold on her mother. "I can't do it without you."

"You can do it. If it ever feels like too much, just remember—"

"One day, one step at a time," Leah cut in.

Vella smiled with pride. "Exactly. You have people who need you. Be there for them," Vella said in a stern tone. Then, leaning in closer, she whispered, "When I'm gone, go see your father."

"What—?"

"Just do it. For me."

"Okay . . ."

"There's something important I need to tell you . . . if you ever come across the orb, be careful. Your father told me it made him see things . . . He never said what, only that I couldn't know. Whatever it was, it was bad. I think he used it too much, so use it sparingly."

Leah nodded.

Vella pulled back, gazing into her daughter's pain-filled eyes. "We're so proud of you."

"I love you," Leah said, breaking further with every syllable.

"My beautiful girl, I love you."

Amy and Simon joined in, creating a suffocating group hug. Vella let out an exaggerated cry. "You're going to kill me yourselves!"

"We can live with that," Amy said.

They clung to her, wishing in desperation that they could make the moment last forever.

Slowly, they released her, and Vella took a step toward the door, glancing back at them. She grasped the spear in one hand and with the other placed it on the scanner.

With one final, determined breath, she faced the darkness, confident and unshaken. That was what she would let them see.

She stepped inside and turned to face them, her eyes unfocused.

Silently, she prayed her courage would hold out a little longer, as the urge to call out rose suddenly and viciously. In a desperate bid to remain quiet, she bit her lip and gripped her arm with all the force she could muster. The pain had to be great enough to drown out her mind's pleas for help.

The door slid closed, and she watched her legacy, her purpose, the only reason she'd ever needed to keep going, fade from her sight forever. Blood began to drip from her mouth and arm.

When they were finally out of sight, she doubled over, grabbing her mouth until the door sealed completely. She finally let the scream escape when it could no longer be heard.

A familiar growl rippled through her. Instinctively, she tightened her hands around the spear, reminded of what had been taken from her in this place. Then she mustered all her rage and turned to face it.

For the last time, Amy, Simon, and Leah saw her face as she looked up at the screen, offering a bittersweet smile and a wave. Vella only hoped they couldn't get a clear view of her face.

They stood together and took it all in. It wasn't heroic; it wasn't pretty, but they watched anyway, ensuring they were there for her. It was the least they could do, making sure she wasn't alone at the end.

But she wasn't alone. She never had been.

We're free to go anywhere we want among the stars.
Where do you want to go?

Why would I want to go anywhere?

My thoughts exactly.
Come on. Dance with me.
Just you, me, and the music.

There is no music.

Can't you hear it? It's all around us. Always has been. Listen.

Acknowledgments

I'd like to thank Peggy Bartlett, Izzy Grace, Nikki B, Danny Raye, and Alyx R. for their time and care as beta readers. Your feedback on early drafts helped shape the final version of this story and made it the best it could be.

Sean and Emma, thank you for your valuable feedback.

A big thank you to my editor, Eliza Dee. Your guidance was invaluable. You helped bring everything together.

To my greatest inspirations, Frank and Beverley Herbert: in their honor, I named my cat after my favorite literary character, Leto, my little god emperor of the universe and ever-supportive tiny terror.

Richelle, this wouldn't exist without you. Thank you for everything.

And to you. Thank you for taking the time to read this book. I hope you enjoyed it as much as I enjoyed writing it. If this story resonated with you or brought something personal to mind, I'd love to hear from you. Sharing stories is one of the most powerful ways we connect. Feel free to reach out and share yours. You can contact me at dovigi.m@gmail.com. And if you'd like to leave an online review or recommend this book to a friend, it would mean a great deal, as it helps others find this story.

Always remember: you're not alone.